LIBRARIES

This book is to be returned on or before the date below.
It may be borrowed for a further period if not in demand.

A NOTE THAT BREAKS
THE SILENCE

A NOTE
THAT BREAKS
THE SILENCE

The Story of Peire Carcasse
and Little Beast

ADAM JOHN MUNTHE

THE BODLEY HEAD
LONDON SYDNEY
TORONTO

ACKNOWLEDGEMENTS

To Gina Natali, who very carefully but at
break-neck speed typed the M.S.; to Liliane de
Rothschild, whose gifts as a researcher produced
several valuable surprises; to Peter R. who took
the trouble to offer valid criticisms; to Partho G.
who knew what I was writing about; to my neighbour François R. a painter from Languedoc,
whose own efforts put spurs to mine; to Euan C.;
and last, and most of all, to my wife who suffered
and cherished me for the months this book took
to write—my hearty thanks.

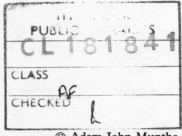
© Adam John Munthe 1977
ISBN 0 370 30035 1
Printed in Great Britain for
The Bodley Head Ltd
9 Bow Street, London WC2E 7AL
by Cox & Wyman, Fakenham
set in Monotype Plantin 113
First published 1977

For Nelly,
in Memory of Peter

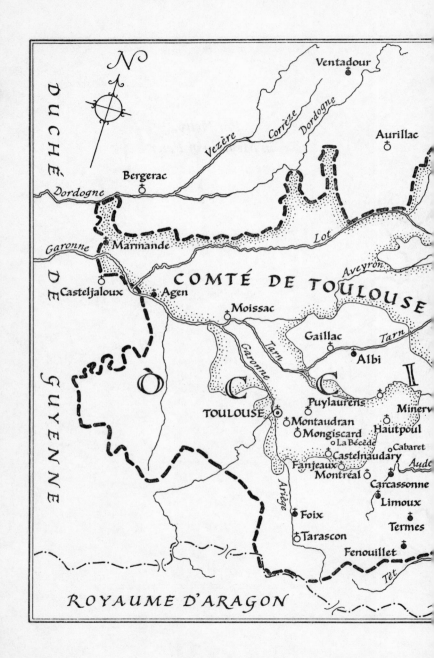

N

DUCHÉ

Ventadour

Vezère   Corrèze   Dordogne

Aurillac

Bergerac

Dordogne

Garonne   Marmande

DE

Lot

COMTÉ DE TOULOUSE

Aveyron

Casteljaloux

Agen

Moissac

Gaillac   Tarn

Albi

GUYENNE

Tarn

Garonne

Puylaurens

Minerv

TOULOUSE

Montaudran

Hautpoul

Mongiscard

Cabaret

La Bécède

Castelnaudary

Fanjeaux

Aude

Montréal

Carcassonne

Ariège

Limoux

Foix

Termes

Tarascon

Fenouillet

Têt

ROYAUME D'ARAGON

Vienne

Loire

Isère

Grenoble

Allier

Valence

Marvejols

Rhône

E

I

N

Uzès

Avignon

A

Durance

Hérault

Montpellier

Arles

Aix

Aiguemortes

Gazanac

MARSEILLE

Beziers

Toulon

pestang

Agde

Narbonne

Perpignan

MER MÉDITERRANÉE

EDGAR HOLLOWAY

0   50   100 MILES

0   50   100 KILOMETRES

I

Peire Carcasse, it's the Little Beast now who takes up his pen to write of you. Little Beast! The name still clings to me as yours has done to you. 'If there's anything of truth in me, if there's anything to understand, you'll find it in the songs,' you used to tell me. But now, Master, this knock-kneed juggler of yours must write of you, because his heart says so, because of a woman's promise, but above all because of the men who tried to obliterate your having been.

How strange that it should be All Saints' Day again—no, not strange, for your terrible God surely ordains such things; that God who reduced his troubadour, yes, his, despite what the priests and Catholics say, to a candle flame, and who brought this old mountebank to a cloister. He's full of fear. He's not much used to words. Where shall he start his search for you? Tell him that, at least, with a jog to his elbow.

'Start with yourself old friend,' I can hear you mutter; but it's easier said than done. The hump tucked between my shoulder-blades still squeezes down, and those pink-faced loons here tell me that I shan't walk again, but it's not my legs I need, saving your presence. My hand shakes, and the pen between my fingers splutters wide, far wide of the mark. If it were balls of fire I had to juggle, or my blue and golden spheres . . .

Forgive me, Master . . . Do you remember? Do you remember it was early autumn when we met? Like now. And the vines of Carcassonne fluttered red and gold across the hills. And it wasn't just chance, was it, when you picked me up after the buffet I'd taken? 'Beware of the Devil,' you laughed, pushing those scented gallants from us, 'and treat him with respect!' And you kissed me, saying that you kissed pestilence, deformity and death, and my first thought was to hate you, and that the urchin was right when he said you'd been spawned by Lucifer. But there was also a part of me that believed you. I cowered back, silent in the midst of your

9

carolling. The laughter was wild in my ears. Peire, I hear you still...

My trade of tricks had carried me from peak to peak, from low-land castle to cragged fortress, from the wilderness, from the Devil's wind who'd push and kick me down the high Corbières, from sleet and spite and barren friendlessness, from false laughter through untidy loneliness, to what? To another hostel attic, to another crowded bench against a tavern wall where my hopes and sly movements were mostly to avoid the laughter. I would hold a slice of bread in one hand, and a fistful of olives in the other, and my eyes would skitter about the crowd, leaning towards the joke, the jest which would single out the scapegoat for their evening's enter-tainment. Famished, I forgot to eat, my jaw muscles contracted, eyes blinking in slow surprise, and I'd forget to laugh. A juggler or a mountebank, he lives on laughter. When the laughter leaves him, an audience grows cruel. They squeeze the remaining sap from him, with thirsty tongues laid out to catch the tears.

The tavern door would still be open, the attic window wide on the night. A sergeant-at-arms, a drunken minstrel, a lazy whore rolling off her catch for the night, would throw me a coin across the straw. 'Little Beast,' they'd grumble, 'take your hump and your sack off somewhere else. Ill-luck and the evil eye are poor bed-fellows for the likes of us!' I'd catch up my bundle of gewgaws, my ropes and coloured balls, sling the old viol on my back, and slip out.

I walked a little sideways, like a crab, to balance better the hump, my feet, puffed up and somewhat red with the blisters, in my long over-patched leather shoes. I walked so much I forgot my hump, my feet—I forgot everything—and that was bad. So when I caught myself disappearing like that into thin air, I'd have to remember my reasons, and I'd repeat the old chit-chat: 'Where do you go?' say I.

'I walk my feet to Hell.'

'And why to Hell?' say I.

'Because truth stands at the gates of Hell.'

'What for?' say I.

'Don't you know, imbecile, of him who questions every man there?'

'Indeed I don't,' say I, 'enlighten me.'

'If a man tells the truth, he is allowed in, if not he will be hanged. Now tell me where you go?'

'To be hanged,' say I.

'I don't believe you.'

'Then hang me for the lie,' say I.

'But then the lie turns into truth.'

'That's truth,' say I . . . but Little Beast was tired, the game was too old, and there were no real reasons any more for the walking, laughing, joking, journeying. I was weary of knocking on postern gates with my hand stretched out. 'The fool is here,' I'd shout, 'with his bottomless bag of tricks, with his viol, his multi-coloured balls, with enough rope to hang himself for your amusement!' They'd let me in, and lead me through the antechambers. The great hunting dogs stretched and yawned, growling softly in the firelight. We nodded in recognition to each other. I'd beg my bowl of soup in the kitchens, a slice of dark bread, a kind word. I'd remember to laugh, and then on into the great hall. 'A poor fool my liege lady, a mountebank, a monkey of little worth, to pass an hour my lord.'

'What do you do, wretch?'

I caught their faces briefly in the candlelight, in the bright flames cast from the stone fireplace; painted grimaces, soft voices cooing and chuckling far from me, but reflecting deep into my heart. My good hand on a cold stone pillar would wander on its own. The sculpted plinths released their carvings to my hand's touch. A face, an eye, a gargoyle's head. 'I juggle, sing and dance, my lord, after my fashion.'

'Then to it little animal, let's see you twitch!' Their laughter echoed in my head. Before the fire, with the smell of the dogs to keep me sane, I danced and played.

'I'm tired,' I'd say, 'I'm human after all. I'm tired of walking, of hunger, of the thin soup in the castle kitchens. I'm tired of the cold and the loneliness, and the olives in my claw which never reach my mouth. I'm weary of the Devil's wind, and the sour straw pallets in the sculleries of a hundred castles, of the walking.' But it was only in my dreams that I spoke like this, only to myself, as I approached that abyss into which one ambles so carelessly. That was before the Dark Angel raised his claw, and brought you, Peire, and I together.

Today it's cold, Peire. There's a mist rising off the water, and a haze upon the land. A horseman moves over the horizon, black as night against the day. The last cigales creak in the meadows. The soil hardens fast. Winter's threadbare blanket is half thrown across my view, as it was before. But the oranges are ripening, red and green upon the trees I know, and the vines tangle, disembowelled across the fields. There's the smell of man and dung, and rain high in the sky—oh, my heart's still not in this strange pen-pushing, Peire, though I'm trying, I'm trying to remember on my own . . .

We met that night in Carcassonne, with an autumn moon hanging low and lazy on the citadel's tower. It was hardly cold, but as I threaded my way up towards the cité, I shivered with the fever. The wind, that rattling Devil's wind, was in my bones still, and aching in my ears. I'd half-determined to risk the night in a ditch—cowardice, it was—but tavern laughter was more laughter than could be borne. The evening before a group of tipsy ruffians had tossed me on to the table. To make me dance the better, they'd poked torches at my feet.

But then on the bridge I stopped, for the lights, reflecting on the water like leaping fish, were gay and magical. I stared for a space up at the massive buttressed walls. 'Hail again, Carcassonne, the Little Beast is back and he wishes you well,' I said. I started murmuring one of my old rhymes. I caught the attention of some peasant children. In a moment they were about me, staring gravely up into my face, as though waiting for a small mystery to be revealed to them. 'Are you a jongleur?' one of them asked. 'Don't be stupid,' said another, 'can't you see his viol?' I grinned gently at them so they'd not be frightened.

'Why are you talking to yourself? Only old people and madmen talk to themselves. Why do you have a hump?'

'Shsh!' whispered a little girl of eight or nine summers who had flaming red hair. 'You must pretend not to notice.'

'I was born like that,' I told them, 'and perhaps I sing and talk to myself just because I'm mad!'

'There's a real madman up in the cité,' said the red-haired girl with a giggle of awe. 'He sings terrible songs, which Mamma says we mustn't listen to or we'll be burnt as heretics when we're grown up! And his eyebrows grow together, black and bristly!'

A little boy piped up, 'The Curé of St Nazaire's says he was sp. . . sp. . .'

'Spawned?' I encouraged.

'Spunned by the Devil. What's in your sack?'

'Magic spinning balls.' I pulled the sack off my shoulders, and took out my juggling balls. Their eyes glistened. They had no fear of me and I forgot the fever, standing there on the bridge tossing the transparent spheres higher and higher into the reddening sky. A voice cried out, 'Away, home with you all.' I saw farther up the hill a woman waving a fist at me. The children ran. 'You should go and juggle with the mad minstrel,' shouted the girl, 'he wouldn't mind your being like you are. He's a great fool!' Their feet faded into the shadows, and I nodded to myself hearing the woman scolding them.

It was dusk as I entered Carcassonne through the Dame's Gate. The sentinels were busy, cock feathers swaying dizzily in their caps as they rattled to attention for the Papal Legate's retinue, who pranced towards the gates. Through peasants, tinkers and a group of Jewish merchants, they rode carelessly enough; amongst the rowdy children, the plump shopkeepers and their puffing apprentices laden with bales of silk or a rich fur mantle on its way to some burgher's wife. I watched them surge past, listening to the women protesting noisily at their roughness, and I crept in. Beyond, the town was silent. Who shall this great fool be, I whispered to myself. How shall I know him? I looked about me. Houses, towers, the citadel and keep above me floated in a moving sky. I smelt old clay, new mortar calked, moss, wind and water in the gutters, stiff sheets drying, rosemary and thyme upon a window-sill. A burst of laughter echoed down the town. 'Follow the laughter,' I cried silently, clenching teeth to stop the shivering, and the town stood still once more.

I climbed the twisting lanes towards the growing bustle of raised voices. A large crowd seethed in the square beneath the keep. There were vendors hawking their sweetmeats, and the oils, unguents and spices so dear to the women; there were two swarthy tumblers dressed in bright patches prancing on their hands, tambourines, drums rattled, a squeaking viol echoed from a balcony. There was a gipsy with a lumbering brown bear, whose manacled front paws beat the air, and the merrymakers. And then there was the smell, the sight of a roasting pig, of hams, of singed spices, marjoram, basilico and rue—of food! My belly groaned most musically, my throat itched for the light wine's taste. It was indeed a feast for all the Saints, and for the villains too. Why not?

'Good masters,' I called, approaching a group of young boisterers whom I recognized from the taverns, 'who can tell me where to find a most great and wide-renowned fool? A prince of fools.' For a moment my interruption startled them, and then one shouted, 'It's the Little Beast!'

'Come closer,' shouted another, 'so that we can admire this seeker after fools!'

I edged apprehensively towards them. 'Indeed,' I thought, 'I am not mad. What desperation is this which sends me chasing madmen?'

'A nest of devil-worshippers has sent you spying on us saintly folk,' laughed one. 'Tremble, Little Beast! Tremble before the righteous.'

'I'm trembling alright, your lordships; there's a huge monster in my belly—he's called starvation—and the way he rattles would make a house tremble! And as for the other, even a heretical mountebank might be looking for a master in devilry, might he not? It's only the best scallywags who make a living these days!'

'Be wary what you say,' one wag let loose, 'or we'll throw you over the walls as would be fitting on this Saints' Day. Quick now, vanish!' A swaggering fellow with a mean mouth gave me a push, and, caught off balance, I tumbled down, clinging to my sack. They burst into laughter and then, as suddenly, were silent. Behind me I felt hands beneath my elbows.

'You treat the Devil with much disregard, my friends.'

I was picked up and dusted down. I craned my head.

'No! Don't turn around,' I heard. 'Your wicked face might send me running all the way to church.' The others began to chuckle.

'We must make amends for our ill manners. Here, Devil, let me kiss you!' With my feet off the ground, I discovered myself in a bear's hug.

'I kiss you,' he cried, 'and, to be on the safe side, your sisters, pestilence, deformity and death. You carry them for all of us.'

He set me down, laughed shortly without joy or pleasure, and strode away. Their mirth shook loud in their wake.

'Stop!' I hollered. 'I pray you, stop. What is his name?'

'The Dame's bastard,' came an answer, 'Peire Carcasse, a Prince of fools!'

Dame Carcasse, protectress of the city, whose legendary stone face gleamed humorous and cruel from her plinth over the St Martin Gate.

I came to myself a little dazed, as a window opened above my head. A pale white oval framed in a mass of dark red curls peeped out. Her eyes looked sleepy and mocking. Her mouth curled in a smile.

'So, the Little Beast looks for Peire Carcasse too. And what does he expect to find?' I gaped at her. 'Someone like himself?' Her voice tinkled like a wineglass tapped with a knife.

'Well, no, damoselle.' I stopped and curled a finger round my ear to think better. I've always done that. If I can separate the sounds of words in my head, I manage sometimes to get a hold on my brain and shake a piece of sense out. 'No, good lady, I don't expect to find anybody or anything I know about. Maybe something I don't know about. Maybe a person who can recognize the fits in him, who's got knowledge of his madness and can show me a mouthful of sanity.'

'So what sends you looking for Peire Carcasse who knows nothing?'

'A girl with bare black feet and red hair who told me he was a great fool and would like my dancing and juggling the way she did.'

'Little Beast is lonely—is that it?'

'Perhaps it's that,' I muttered.

'And you have hopes that this great buffoon will recognize you?'

'And feel the kinship,' I said to myself, 'in the differences between us, and share the fear of it!'

'Perhaps you'll be lucky,' she said softly. 'He's back with his tail between his legs. The Sieur de Roquemartine gave him a fine thrashing for his blasphemous lays beneath a certain lady's window. And he thinks to be a knightly troubadour!' A malicious giggle slipped over the window-sill like a little frog. 'That's why he left us, decked out like a bantam cock in his slashed silk jerkin and fine scarlet hose. Blasphemy in his heart, and bleeding words upon his stutterer's lips.' She clapped her hands, and made to close the casement. 'You'll find him in the tavern by the citadel.'

15

The window shut with a snap, and a broken yellow daisy head fell at my feet.

Picking up the daisy, I stumbled up the town; my knees chattering to each other, my stomach tight and round. Smoke rose over the chimneys casting shadows on the moon, and drifting higher into the blue. 'And then what do I want with this famous fool?' I muttered to myself. 'Food I want, a bed, a soft real bed, not straw but a bed with a slice of stuffed mattress, and why not? Rough soft sheets like the washerwoman mends at Puivert for the damoselles. And then what, imbecile?' I shouted. 'You'll be needing a woman next, with sturdy thighs, who won't mind your hump in the dark, who'll warm you up with a hug to her easy billowed body; and a kiss or two, a lick; a woman who'll let you tuck your cold hand in her armpit to cozen you, to pleasure you. Ah, Little Beast,' said I, 'cease your whining. A man dreams to escape his misery, and you should not laugh at dreams!'

The lights pricked out about me. I saw the snoring citizens in my mind, with their gods, carved and cobwebbed, perched on their mantelpieces; their heirlooms of holiness. 'And then, why had he kissed me? For laughter? To exorcise a ghost? Was there bravery in that? Was there, Little Beast?'

The watchman tolled his bronze bell for the strokes of midnight, and the church clock chimed in behind. The hum of the bells quivered in my ears. I hesitated outside the tavern. I picked out a lute, a gentle viol, my ear caught the jangling threads of a guitar and I tried to separate the lowering conversations that hissed and bubbled through the open door. A man was singing as if veiled by the voices, the smoke and the laughter. I pushed my nose in and sidled up against the wall so that I wouldn't have to watch behind me if the need arose. Serving wenches swayed past carrying tumblers and flagons of dry red wine. He was singing with the others grouped around him, one foot upon the bench, and the lute across his knee. I could see his head, a swarthy face, and his nose carving a heavy broken arch down between the thick overlapping eyebrows, and his gaze which was directed at something on the other side of the table. Those around him laughed and snickered now and then. I curled a hand round my ear, the sounds separated in my head, until all I heard was that low rough voice, a mocking gentleness which cleaved deep into me, and a melody that drifted back and forth like the sea tide. The words I remember—defiant and painful—they do not escape me. He sang of myth breaking, and of a struggle towards meeting the faces of his destiny . . .

> Like a dragon scorched by fire,
> Like a Unicorn unsworn,
> Like the lark calls night a liar,
> Like a moonbeam halfway torn,
> Like a note that breaks the silence,
> Like an echo still unborn,
> I'm listening for your coming
> Through the blind eye of the storm . . .

Yes, it was like that. He seemed to be crying a challenge out, from within his bile and bitterness, to a secret bird of paradise,

> Like a pilgrim dreams his longing,
> Like a marksman sees his goal,
> Like the wise man sees the mountain
> Which the Fool climbs to his soul . . .

I moved forward through the throng. Wasn't it a challenge? Hadn't I heard a song like this once? Sung by a coward with a crystal of glory in his heart, and a butcher's knife pressed to his brain; sung by a desperate coward more pitiable than a thousand brave men, and weaker than a pestilent whore; sung by a hunchback in his prime, clinging to his soul on a buttered pole before an audience of princes, peacocks, and philosophers, who were wise enough to laugh at him! Oh, yes, I'd heard a song like that before. Hah! Was it possible I still hadn't learned? No, said I, and I cuffed my ear sharply for listening to such lies. My feet took me on.

People separated, the students stepped back under the blackened beams, and I tugged at his doublet, fierce and fearful.

'Peire Carcasse?' His arm flung up to push me off, but he caught sight of me in time.

'It's the little devil again,' he guffawed. 'Come join our hymn to beauty.'

'No,' said I softly. 'The Devil sits on your brain not mine.'

'Ha! Don't speak too fast, my pretty, or I'll take a saw to both our brains. What do you want from me? Come, speak up, or else we'll make you partner to this lovesick bear!'

I saw for the first time the object of his serenade. The beast, with its claws cut to the quick, was seated at the table, tongue lolling through its teeth. Its head weaved back and forth. His owner cowered hard by, laden most comically with the animal's chains. I stared into the troubadour's glittering, half-drunken eyes, the smile left his face, and with its going came a silence.

'Sieur Carcasse, are you a rich man?'

He stared down at me and, pulling some silver pieces from his pouch, let them drop to the floor.

'So, the hunchback's a m-man after all!' The stutter took my first fears away.

'And your father's a rich dealer in furs and skins, is it not so?' I asked, stepping carefully over the coins. 'And you cut a fine figure in silk hose, doublet and boots, with an ostrich feather in your cap to be sure.'

'I'm my own man, and misfortune,' he muttered. 'What questions are these, hunchback?'

'And the girls,' I persisted tremulously and recklessly. 'The damoselles flutter eyes and hearts when you lift your voice and lute?'

'From here and throughout the four corners of Terre d'Oc,' he shouted.

'A noble lady or two into the bargain has fallen for that ruffian's brow, those lips, that dangerous voice.'

About me breaths were caught. A wooden tankard broke on the stone flagons.

'What of that?' he said. For a brief instant he and I stood alone, caught like shadows on a wall and condemned to watch each other, moving but always apart, until darkness drowned us.

'You'll be needing a man to pull up your britches after the thrashings, and to carry your lute and cloak when your back's bleeding from a husband's cuts; someone who knows the land, the secrets of flight and travel, someone to beat your temper out upon when the lady escapes, when the hare flees. Here I am.'

With a quick folding movement he sat down. The lute was leant beside him. Behind him in the swooping torchlight I saw the bear's tongue flop over its teeth, and its glassy panicked eyes. The man's head was bent down, and his hands covered his ears. I liked him for that. So he too had to pick out a voice, and make a choice amongst the noises in his head. He looked at me.

'Who sent you? What courage gives you tongue to frighten me with this knowledge and recognition?' He took a step forward, coming close to me. I felt his breath as he leaned down. 'Stop your staring,' he hissed. 'How do you know me, to risk such foolery? Who sent you?'

But I wasn't frightened. His body smelt of wax and the leather jerkin and fresh sweat.

'The Devil crouching on your brow, Messer. I recognized him when he called out to me in the square.'

Snatching his lute, he brushed through the crowd. Collecting up the silver pieces from the floor, I followed him into the street.

'Let me be,' he cried, quickening his pace. 'I have nothing to give you!'

I ran behind him, my bag jumping and rattling on my shoulder. Then all at once I couldn't go on. I tried to touch his elbow.

'Messer, your silver,' I cried, overreached myself and fell. 'Sieur Carcasse, saving your presence but I wanted to ask you . . .'

His figure retreated before me. 'I wanted to ask you if you can live with your loneliness.'

He halted.

'It was just a child, a little red-haired girl; she said that you'd understand.'

He turned and retraced his footsteps. His lips moved as though he wanted to question me. I wondered if the stutter would return.

The skin on his face had melted away under the moonlight; I saw the sharp cheekbones jutting out from beneath his eyes and running in hard, painful lines to his ears. He helped me to my feet, and reached for my sack. I grabbed it from him, fearful for a second.

'It's all I have,' I mumbled.

He smiled. 'How do they call you?' he asked.

'Little Beast, and I'm hungry.'

'Well, Little Beast, on your feet.' He showed no surprise. I saw him looking steadily at me. 'So you want to accompany me to the Devil. D-d-did he really s-s-send you?' The low harsh voice stuttered now.

'It was a joke,' I said reluctantly. 'But I can serve you. I'll play my viol, and dance and juggle. I'm quick to learn a song. I'm strong, the hump withal. And my belly, Sieur, cries out, if it please you!'

19

He laughed. 'Your l-l-looks belie you, Little Beast, as my silken doublet belies my poverty. Come!'

The night was cold, and the sky full of stars as we stumbled down through the town. Beyond the walls overlooking the river, cold steam was rising off the waters and edging in pale swathes across the fields and vineyards. He paused in the square where he'd picked me up.

'Confess,' he said, 'that the Devil, or the Legate's spies or our liege lord's police sent you to watch me, eh?'

'No one sent me. Beggars have no masters, for poverty serves no man.'

'Do you know the tale of the Prince and the Beggar?'

'No,' I told him, 'but my belly knows a sorry tale.'

'A little more patience with your belly, friend! And as we trot, I'll tell you the tale of a beggar. A p-p-prince took a beggar, on a tour of his kingdom. Perhaps the prince was our Raimon. He showed him his treasures, coffers of gold, silver, precious stones. He showed him the philosophers he'd collected with their different notions of faith and knowledge. He showed him poets, architects, and doctors arguing over the right way to cure a man of love and death. And then he pointed out to the beggar a map of his travels which covered the known world. He pulled out books of the laws he'd invented, and last of all he showed him his private diary, wherein lay his innermost thoughts about God and gods he'd followed, and the deep truths he'd elicited from life. And at the end he asked the beggar, 'What impressed you most of all?' And the beggar answered: 'That mother earth is capable of supporting such a weight of dung.'

He was silent.

I'd listened, agape, at this multitude of words.

'But dung's good for the earth, Sieur Carcasse, is it not?'

'But the smell for him who lives on it is evilness itself.' He laughed, and then speaking very softly said, 'I have a few silver pieces in my pocket, earned or stolen it's their presence which gives value. I have silk on my back, and people cock an ear to my songs and my rages. You come to laugh at me, and at this plague which I am. It's the same. And the Devil ordains that we recognize each other, is it possible?'

Two young men rolled out of one of the houses. They were

20

disputing their poetic or musical gifts. Catching sight of Peire Carcasse, one of them pulled a guitar off his back. Glancing derisively at him, he began to sing, until others fell out of the rattling red-lit brothel to hear . . .

> Oh Peire Carcasse what fate
> Has moulded you a snake,
> With leaping fangs to rake
> Your mortal changing skins?
>
> Cry hold to God on high,
> Take heed the holy cry,
> And torture not this lie
> Of love, which the Devil bids you sing!

'Who doesn't know the Sessions of the poet Hariri?' said the Sieur Carcasse. 'Even such a sorry plagiarist as him, searching for his own blunted fangs!' He watched me, ignoring the singer, and then, as if releasing a source of energy by catapult, seized me by the arm. I believed for an instant that I would be crushed beneath the furious pressure. 'Come,' he said, 'we'll feed you, or at least my father's larder shall take the nub off your hunger.' He still grasped my hand as though afraid I'd lose him. 'Did you hear their s-song?' he stuttered. 'You've found me out too quickly, Little Beast. Shall I now have to hide from the Devil's crooked minion too?' He shook his head from side to side; it made me recollect the bear in the tavern. 'Aie, aie!' he cried out. 'Our worthy Prince Raimon has a fine dunghill indeed on which to dance his measures, and we'll dance too! Perhaps a jig, my friend, just you and I, with the warm ants running up our nostrils for company, and white worms glistening from our lips to remind us of mortality.'

I listened to him, my white ugly face poking out of my clothes. There was cruelty in him, a little good cowardice. In me there was a deep, deep breath of stillness. I listened, and I could hear the stillness within, moving softly like a swelling wave.

'Yes, for faith, Sieur Carcasse,' I whispered, and then for no reason repeated at the top of my voice. 'For faith! So long as my feet will carry me, and the rock between my shoulder-blades doesn't ache too much, and my belly's not yawning, I'll dance along behind you!'

But there was an ounce of fear trickling through my entrails.

'Throw down your sack!' he shouted, and, grasping my arms, he began to whirl me round. My temples throbbed. I heard the raucous cries of the drunks and whores, and his bitter laughter beating closer to me. 'Dance!' he urged. 'Dance for the wise men, and the clowns and beggars who've forgotten how to dance.' Faster and faster we swung until tavern, streets, lights, stars swum dizzily before my eyes.

'No more, I can't. No more,' I whispered. 'Pray hold, good master.'

You took me home that first night, and we crept into your father's house. The floorboards still creaked for all our efforts, and the house smelled of colic, cured hides, yellow candle grease, and ink. We passed through the shop where the furs hung like a thousand small corpses from their miniature gibbets. You stole a half-devoured ham from the larder, some black bread, and you set me down in your father's chair saying with a grin that he'd skin me like one of his pelts if he saw me sitting there. You cast some olives on my plate, and I grasped a handful in my cold right hand. Out of habit my mouth opened, for a second my hand stayed motionless, and then I broke my fast—on that feast of all the Saints—and ate till my ribs would stretch no more. You watched, brows knit in that strange angry fashion of yours, oblivious to the beams over our heads which seemed to shake with the ogre's rhythmic snores. We slept. You'd taken rough white sheets from your mother's oaken chest, and made my bed with your own hands, like a woman. And you laughed when I insisted on keeping my sack of tricks for a pillow.

'It's my habit,' I pleaded.

'It's a dishonour to my mother's linen chest,' you said, 'but take your ragged bundle.'

I was awoken by his shaking me.

'Beast! Little Beast, awake, the sun is up an hour ago. Are you so fast accustomed to soft living?'

I blinked and stared at him slowly.

'Sieur Carcasse? I thought I was in paradise. There were hundreds of birds singing, and I was warm—not a hungry thought in me—and it seemed that someone came and lifted the hump off my shoulders with wondrous ease, and that I could run and dance as well as any man.' I touched the place between my shoulder-blades to make sure, but it had been returned to me.

'How is it that this pale twisted cripple has found me out?' He spoke to himself, staring up into the light. I was about to speak but with a swift motion of his head he flung his gaze upon me.

'I too have had a dream.' The knuckles of his hands turned white against each other.

'You saw the Devil,' I cried, 'dressed in bright scarlet, and he had a thousand purple lashes across his back. He was cutting out the heart of a gallowsbird with a pair of steel pincers. You saw the Devil, Messer, it's the saint in you!' And I chuckled.

He grasped my face in one hand and shook me.

'Don't laugh at me! What made you say the Devil, wretch?'

I watched his unslept face, and a sudden misery rising in it, that I could not abide.

'No one. But you're quivering all over, Sieur, and I know. When a man stares and trembles like that, he's either seen God or the Old Villain, and saving your presence the Devil was the more likely, if it please you.'

'You're right, you miserable hobgoblin.' Releasing me, he jumped to his feet with a laugh and a shrug. His gestures convinced neither him nor me. I was awake, so now I could stare at him, listening carefully, and learning how to separate the noises he threw into my head.

'I saw the Devil dressed in a scarlet robe.' He spoke urgently and comically, like a soothsayer. 'He had a black skull-cap on his head to hide his horns, and black shoes with long pointed toes. He stood with our Prince Raimon, on the right-hand panel of a holy triptych. On the left panel stood Lucifer's sister whispering into the Pope's ear. Her face, though veiled in silk, released her eyes to fasten on to mine. I threw up my hand in terror to hide the beauty which seemed to burn through my face. Her hands were clasped upon her abdomen which stretched wonderfully warm and soft beneath the glowing stuff she wore. The centre panel was full of a raw tempest, but high up in one corner there flew a bird, gashed with a dozen wounds, and she brought light. All the figures stood on a mountain of steaming dung. Running beneath their feet were men, crawling like ants, and they toiled feverishly in the fields and vineyards, in the forests. And I saw Carcassonne

23

on that mighty dunghill. White doves flew around her battlements, and for every white dove there hovered a raven close as a shadow to its prey. There, too, I saw messengers and tale-bearers who screamed their songs to the four winds. Little Beast,' he rushed on, as I stared at this holy picture, 'I then caught sight of you. You stood before me with your great sack slung between hump and bone. The smell of cord and hemp was strong in my nostrils, and I awaited you fearfully. "Who is this man?" I asked myself. "Why does he bear his sack towards me? How does he recognize the vipers in my brain?" You frightened me. Then your hands reappeared. In your left hand was a dove, like one of those that fly over Carcassonne, and in your other hand was a raven, who pecked your fingers until the blood oozed, though you smiled your white smile. You cast the birds in the air but, instead of flying to the roof, with a clatter of wings they burst into my head. I cried out. My fists flew up to beat them away.' He paused, and then he made a grimace. 'I stared at you, at myself, believing that my head would burst with the madness of it,' he continued, 'and not knowing how to escape.'

'But the real strangeness, Messer,' I said eagerly, 'was that you felt some odd affection for the man you were. Forgive me, Master, but I've seen a little of your hatred. You must learn to care for the broken pieces, not just hate them, saving your presence.'

He looked with surprise at me.

'Not only that, Little Beast; the strangeness was also in knowing that I was bound suddenly to relinquish that gilded picture I'd been staring at so long. There was my life to hunt, a task to accomplish, even if I have to wrestle with your demons.'

'I have no nightmares hidden with my toys, Messer,' I told him. 'I have a pair of new britches for a small boy who'll never wear them. Those that I have . . . those nightmares that I have, walk beside me, or sit curled between my shoulder-blades.'

I was silent, full of a moment's hatred for having spoken, and I lowered my gaze, now sitting on my clumsy hands to stop them weaving fruitlessly.

'Forgive me,' he said.

I glanced up at him. It must have been a trick of light. He seemed to gaze through me. I felt as transparent as one of my glass balls thrown against the sun—as if I were catching a reflection of his hurt, and eagerness.

24

'Messer Peire,' I said, 'you dream mighty dreams, but mine are all little ones. I think I was born on that magic dunghill of yours, too, but my parents were not there to teach me how to look after dreams and legends.'

He stopped pacing about the room, raised his head and appeared to shake off some misgiving.

'Tell me, Little Beast,' he said slowly. 'Tell me carefully who you are. Companions on the road should know each other, not so?'

'I remember a woman weeping, and gazing at me through her fingers,' I told him. 'I remember her crying, and her red eyes, and her thick, scored hands. Perhaps that was my mother. When I had reached fourteen summers or thereabouts, it was my father's younger brother and his wife who took me off the streets. They were travelling mountebanks. He was a pink, friendly man whose round, surprised eyes feasted on his wife. She was hardly older than I, a pretty creature with a straight, proud back and pointed elbows. She had lovely delicate hands. She often told me that they mustn't be sullied by dirty work. I agreed. She was the most beautiful thing I'd ever known. They had a son too.' I stopped.

He looked at me.

'My uncle had a cart which served as home for us as well as carrying the bits of painted scenery, the props, instruments, and costumes we stitched together on the road.'

'And their son?' he chided me.

'Their son called me by my name. Never "Little Beast". He was the only one. When I unslung my viol and sang, or when I was juggling, or miming a devil come to bear Amor (that was Fiametta, his mother) down to pleasure the Dark One, he was always beside me. We were mummers and mimers travelling from village to village, and his mother often left him alone. His greatest joy was to watch me toss the coloured balls. I did it for him. He said that if I tried hard the balls would fly in the air without my touching them, just so long as I watched them and told them to go on spinning. Sometimes I believed him, and ceased to feel the spheres passing through my hands.'

'What is your name?' he asked me gently.

For a moment I was silent.

'Little Beast,' I said, shaking my head. 'I live with no other

25

name.' I caught sight of my face in the polished metal mirror on the wall by the barred casement. My eyes were too far apart for such a narrow rocky head, and their expression was mournful. I tried a grin, watching my eyebrows fly up under the shock of black hair. It's as if my eyebrows and mouth are worked by the same puppet string.

'Shall I go on, Messer Peire?'

'Speak what your mind bids you.'

'After our performances, his mother took to slipping off with the crowd, especially when we were in towns. She was such a gay, laughing lady. My uncle always pretended not to notice, so I'd put Bernard to bed in the back of the cart. "Where's Mama?" he'd ask me. "Back soon," I'd whisper. "Do you think she'll bring me the yellow britches?" She'd often promised him a good pair of hose. "Yes," I'd say, "perhaps this time." But she was too young to need to remember such things. She vanished more often, before the show too, so that we had to wait for her. I'd tell Fiametta that she was hurting her husband and that he loved her and was worrying for her. Sometimes I said that even when I meant that she was hurting me, and she'd tell me not to stare at her "out of whirlpool eyes". I don't think she'd ever seen a whirlpool. "Why doesn't he tell me himself if he worries for me?" she asked, tossing her dark ringlets about her face, but I couldn't explain that he didn't know how to tell her or perhaps that he didn't dare. One day she returned late for the afternoon show, and left again shortly afterwards. We were on the outskirts of Toulouse. She kissed my uncle gaily saying that she was tired of her rags and wanted some fine brocade for a dress. She also told him what a fine boy he had, that it was more that he deserved. Fiametta had torn one of the wings of her costume for Amor. I spent the afternoon sewing the tinsel back. We let down the side of the cart, and rigged up our stage. The scenery had been newly painted, the torches were lit and our performance would be less tattered than usual, I thought. I remember laying out her dress in pieces so that she could hasten into it. We waited, the peasants, serfs, and children became restless. Little Bernard whispered to me behind the curtain that he was sure she'd bring him the britches. He stared into my eyes with the tortured willing of a five-year old. "Say it's true!" he hissed, "say she will!" He forced the tears back and I nodded. We began the show with my

26

entrance, breathing fire, and miming the Devil's arrival into this world. First he whispers in the ear of a little child—that was Bernard—who in his innocence tries to box his nose. Then he searches out the lover and describes all the soft beds of Hell where infinite pleasure and satiety welcome him. My uncle played a comic part rolling his eyes and throwing his huge belly out before him as if he would squash me, but his longing for Amor overcomes the temptation, and he girds on sword and buckler to do battle for his lady with the forces of darkness. Still Fiametta had not come. We improvised. I juggled with my transparent spheres. Bernard stood close and pulled my tunic with the question in his eyes. The audience sensed that they had been cheated and began to whistle.'

'That night I rocked Bernard to sleep in my arms. My uncle would not speak to me. I told the boy that he would have his britches the next day. He looked at me and said in his high clear voice, "Tell Mama when she comes back that I don't really need the britches," and he turned his head away and shut his eyes. But she never came back. The next morning Bernard had disappeared. My uncle hanged himself from the crossbar of the village well just before the afternoon show, so there were no more performances.'

I was silent, and Peire, my Master, did not speak either. The room was cool and all my words and talking had dissolved into the air.

'Little Beast,' he said finally, 'you took the leap.'

'More of a hop and a jump, Sieur Carcasse,' I grinned, 'and even that nearly brought me over the precipice, saving your presence!'

'But we go to leap into that abyss,' he said gently, 'to burn the bark off what we call our souls.'

I shivered and glanced at him. 'And if those tongue-thumping servants of God are anything to go by, Messer, we'll jump clean out of our skins from sheer terror, and find ourselves shivering in Paradise. I'm not smart, mind you, but I'm not in a hurry either, and I don't trust anyone who bids me jump before I've seen them hop off first.'

'You're right, Little Beast, we'll go warily, I promise you. And I'll hop off first, if we run out of alternatives, but we'll dance through the furnace in each other's arms if need be, won't we?'

27

A thunderclap of laughter echoed in the chamber, and he caught me to him, throwing long arms about me that squeezed a choking grin from my lop-sided white face. As suddenly, he released me. His brows contracted, the heavy nose sprung out from his face. Lowering his head, he plunged deep into himself. 'Little Beast, you have had courage,' he murmured after a moment.

'Not courage, Messer, but fear!'

'The difference is small, imbecile! You have lived under the law of the Little Beast, who was a reality. I've not even been true to the carcass, who was a mockery of reality.' He stared at me.

'Saving your presence, Sieur, I'm not used to talking.'

'And I'm too used to it. But you told me a true life, and you have made its terrors and its pity mine. Little Beast, who knows, perhaps you'll help me to come to grips with the Carcasse, with the abyss, with the Devil and my faithlessness.'

'What do you mean, Messer?' I asked him, trembling a little with foreboding. He didn't answer, and my gaze strayed to the window. Outside I could hear the acrobats driving in their poles and stakes, shouting and joking with each other as they tested the ropes and canvas flaps for their evening performance. Today was a holiday, and they would make a tidy wage. It crossed my mind that wages henceforth for me, for us, would be untidy and dependent on the nobility's whim, rather than mother church's pleasure in public holidays. A gay figure in blue and red danced up close to the casement. He was whistling and muttering a dangerous tune . . .

> The Vatican recipe fiddlededee,
> Let this a good lesson be fiddlededee,
> Murther and war
> Burn Sin to the raw,
> A drop of incense then bake,
> Sure the Pope cooks for God's sake . . .

My Master sat down heavily, and then rose, striding once or twice around the chamber. He turned on his heel and faced me.

'Little Beast, it's now my turn to be confessed. You have given me an example.'

'Yes, indeed, Sieur Peire. I'll run for a priest.' I coughed and made hastily for the door, filled with relief that I could escape, but uncertain as to what man would risk confessing this fugitive from order and law and the rituals of our age.

'Where are you running to, monster?' he roared. 'It's you who'll play at priest for me.'

My heart sank, with my rooted heels, to the floor.

'There's no need, Sieur! There's no need to be putting cudgels to your brain. There's time enough to burst your lees before some holy man.'

'What is it, wretch? What's on your mind? F-f-food, I'll wager. Eat then, go fill that yawning belly. There's food and wine in the kitchens. But you'll confess me willy-nilly. Our game's a dangerous one, and I need an honest man; a man who's suffered for himself, for the love and the pity in him, not a scoundrel who flays himself towards piety and a god of misery, hatred and abstinence!' The sweat was pulsing down his forehead, and a blue vein jumped across his left temple. 'A simple sage—no priest—once told me that the body of a man was born from holy darkness and sanctity. We need not abstinence and fasting and self-flagellation to return to God, but life, which lays its own burden of terror and pain on our shoulders.' His voice just as suddenly grew calm. 'Little Beast, your b-burden you carry for all men to s-see, and few perhaps bother to look. You gave me the chance to stare at you willingly, now help me face my own load.'

'My Master should not,' I muttered firmly, 'speak gently to the Little Beast. Or he'll wither overnight.' I shook my head violently, slapping one cheek with my bad hand sharply to come back to myself.

'Go eat!' he told me touching my shoulder. I glanced at him, but he was calm and the anger had slipped away.

I hopped through the house, smacking my lips I'm sorry to say. There was ham, and wine, white bread, sour cream, oil and olives in a majolica bowl on the dresser. As I reached towards the ham, a shrill voice bade me leave off on pain of a public whipping. I jumped round to see a small man clad in long furs, furiously rubbing his red, chapped hands together, as though he were washing them.

'And who or what the devil are you, scoundrel?' he shot at me.

I fell to the floor. 'Saving your worship, I'm a guest of Messer Peire's,' I started, on one knee. 'That's to say . . . I mean . . .'

29

Peire interrupted me. 'Gracious father, this man's a tramp. Off your knees tramp!' He looked at his father straight in the eyes as I climbed off the floor, with a mixture of attention and coldness. 'Don't you recognize the Little Beast, father? It seems all Carcassonne knew him besides myself until a few hours ago. He's here to rid you of a son.'

Peire's father glared from one to the other. His chest rose and fell as if with careful breaths he might prevent himself from floating to the ceiling with fury.

'You, you thieves and scoundrels. Yes, the both of you. That good-for-nothing son of mine, rightly called Carcasse! Why must I endure the tales of your misdeeds, your rioting, your whoring, your blasphemy against the true church? Why did God curse me with such a monster?' He washed his hands more strenuously and was silent. He stalked towards his son with blazing, blood-veined eyes. 'You have arms and legs. You have a head on your shoulders. You're strong, strong and full of secrets and hostile silence like your mother.' His voice was bitter. 'But you lie to me, you steal my reputation and my goods to throw at a whore's feet, at a heretic's laughter, at a hunchback's mouth. You gallop off on your father's Arab mare, you use his gold, you ride away, you hide from him with childish dreams of minstrelsy and chivalry above your station, which you dishonour!' He shouted, 'Which you dishonour as you dishonour your father!'

Peire restrained himself. He said nothing but watched his father as though he would empty the other's coffer of indignation and anger.

'But you're still my son, whether your mother disdains and hates me or no. The son of a Christian merchant of furs, who pays his dues to church and state. You will never escape that!' He said this with a spite and hatred that I couldn't understand. I stepped back from them. 'And now you come with your boundless insolence and this crippled mountebank, to tell me that he relieves me of a son. Yes, leave, leave!' He turned suddenly away exhausted.

'Your opinion of me is too high, still too high father,' Peire said softly and clearly. 'This last time I go from you not to make amends, nor with hope to do so, but so that we shall both be free from the need of mutual torture.'

'Why will you not work with me?' The father's head dropped

to his chest. The red hands, like spiders tangled in their own web, struggled with each other.

'Because, for all your longing and determination I was not taught to be a merchant of furs.'

His voice was a whisper.

'You bring evil and deformity into my house, and then you fly around our country, your loins work at siring bastards, your ditties and songs work at creating anarchy and at destroying the security of a Christian life—for those who bother to listen,' he added.

'Perhaps our country needs new and angry blood, father. The unmixed, unfused b-blood of bastards.' Peire was stumbling for his words, stumbling for a truth to tell his sire. '. . . to wield together the dissolute, the envious, the soft and yielding, the angry, and the pampered slaves of tolerance. Perhaps we need a race of bastards to breathe new fire and live longing—not the perfumed lovesick kind—into our sleep-walking princes and un-sexed courtiers.'

Peire's father hastened on, attempting to block out his son's words with the insistence and eagerness of his own. 'Peire,' he called out, 'work with your father. It shall be yours, all yours. Work with me,' he hissed, 'it's easier than dreaming.'

My Master seemed to retreat from his father. He shook his head and I watched him drawing farther and deeper into himself.

'I can't,' he said. His words were hardly audible. They stared at each other for a moment, like animals of different species.

'But what good are you to me?' the older man shouted. 'Tell me that!' Without waiting for an answer he turned and left the room.

'He goes to church to beg mercy for his soul, good prices for his skins, and peace of his son,' murmured Peire without bitter-ness.

'And your lady mother?' I asked.

'My mother's not a Christian,' he answered. 'Eat, and then attend me.' He loped out of the room silently, his arms crossed over his chest, and the great head sunk between his wide angular shoulders.

I was ashamed of my appetite, but the growling companion gnawing my stomach flesh was too old a colleague for me to resist his cries when there was food at hand. And the fat never grew on

31

my bones. I sucked the fresh olives dipped in oil, and carved some lean slices from the ham, trying to eat slowly—yes, I admit it—so as to be able to eat the more. My hunger ebbed away, and I thought of Peire Carcasse, this new Master for me, the fever and the fire in him, and of where his need and temper might take us. He offered me the spirit and the anguish of a quest. It sounds a poor fairy-tale to speak of it, but on my own I'd only strength to live, and that but nakedly. The seeds of heaven and hell were sown deep in him, the wind carried off those that shook to the surface of his mind, and implanted them in others, in me too now. Shaking a few drops of wine on my tongue, I ran to find him. He was in the shop, perched on the counter, half-hidden among the skins.

'Bring me water, I'm thirsty,' he called to me. He drank, set the pewter tankard down in the stillness and cocked his ear. The house was silent except for the rhythmic tipple of a spinning wheel upstairs. The acrobats had departed to break their fast, the town was at church or still asleep. Nothing moved around us, even the skins hung stiff and cold. The tall frame slipped from its perch, and he was beside me.

'Little Beast,' he said, 'unwrap your hands.' He spoke so softly that I could hardly hear him, but his voice was firm and without the stammer. His eyes glittered. I saw he was trembling.

'I don't understand, Messer.'

'You are going to confess me. Come put those paws on my head!' He turned slightly away from me, and fell to his knees, facing the early sunlight that streamed in through the window. I looked at him, aware of my heart pumping and thumping in my chest, and I drew closer to him.

'Sieur Carcasse, you've really gone off your head. I'm a hunchback; not a priest, but a juggler. Not that a priest would take kindly to this notion of yours I'm thinking.'

'You're a man,' he cried out in a low voice, 'and the only difference between us is that I can see the rock between your shoulder-blades!'

'No, Messer, that's not it,' but I placed my hands on his head. Perhaps I was mad too. I shook my head in disbelief.

'Say this after me as I speak it!' he ordered me.

I nodded stupidly down at him.

'Peire Carcasse, vagabond, f-full of f-fear and pity,' he began to stutter brokenly. I followed his words as best I could. 'Devoured by emptiness and longing—beggar and proud churl, seeker after moonbeams, echoes, and like disorders of the soul and body, open now your heart, spit out the misery, the selfishness, the discontent and hatred, make your confession faithfully before your fellow man . . .'

I stared down at your black wiry head, glad that you could not see me, Master, and listened to each trembling nerve in your body as it found an echo in mine, and repeated your words aloud. The sun fell upon your face, upon my hands. Your voice lost its stutter, became steady.

'My life has been a constant evasion,' you began again. 'As a sullen child I hid behind my mother's door, listening to my sick half-brother's screams, and her rocking him, until a board creaked, and she'd cry angrily, "Child, why do you spy upon me? Run and play in the yard with the other children." But I could not play, so I wept, snuffled my dirty tears, and would slip away into the streets, awed and heavy with her dark beauty, her tongue, her strangeness, and her disdain for us. As a beardless youth I stood in the shop staring sightless at the dusty strips of sunlight, until my father's cries of "Work, boy!" and "Money, boy!" and "Don't you want respect from your fellow citizens, boy?" drove me into the streets so that I would not pounce upon his thin, chicken's neck, and beat at his chapped, soapy hands with my fists. "You're still my son!" he'd squeal after me. "And one of these days I'll beat the secrets out of both you and your mother!" But I have no secrets, I'd whisper to the paving-stones. As a growing ragamuffin I crept to the tavern and the brothel, to forget my mother, my father, my sick, holy half-brother, and to learn the secrets of grown men. I listened to the tavern songs, I watched the brawls, the tavern whores, with their scarlet mouths, pinched noses, floating water-pale breasts tumbling from their bodices. I watched their diseased gallants, wishing likewise to be plagued and wizened, until their broken-puppet violence, their vomit, their whorish strength and cruelty sickened me, and I fled once more.

'I stole my father's Arab mare—it was the single thing he never forgot—his money, clothes, took my lute and staggered into the world. There was a man who helped me. For close on seven years I wandered: to Castile, to Aragon, Leon, Rome, to the olive

33

slopes and vineyards of Tuscany, once even to the land of the Danes, the cup-bearers and slayers of love-drunk minstrels. I parrot-learned the Diwan of Ibn Quzman, and resolved to build my life and songs on his simplicity in verse. Those thrown aside, I ran to the disciples of Ali Ibn Hazm, mystic poet, and holy man of Cordoba. Faith, they told me, like the peacock, will not sit in an unworthy place. Seek it as you will, they said, it will flee you if you are unworthy. But it was I who fled faith, mounted on Beni-Alfonso's own dove-grey palfrey, until courteous Navarre relieved me of both gold and gift. I've listened and then stopped up my ears to the Muezzin's call to prayer from the towers of Toledo and Saragossa and to the mingling Christian bells; neither eased my heart, for I cared not a jot for myself, nor life nor death. And thus I earned a name. Carcasse! "There is no man inside that skin," they'd say, "only the Devil's wind puffing it up. It's an empty carcass." I would beat their heads a little till the blood ran, then send them on their way with broken bones. I'd cry, "Then neither man nor beast, nor god, nor devil, dare lay a finger on me, for I'm like the pitcher, emptied dry before my neighbour's lips have drunk." I learned to laugh, as the young pedants in their turn, the jongleurs, whores and mountebanks learned to cringe before me. We were bound by hatred, and they travelled behind me like vultures waiting on a death. Back in my native land I rode from castle to palace. Noble knights with white hands, eager squires, the slender damoselles, their noble ladies, quivered first with laughter and then with apprehension at my songs. But they often let me be, telling me that life and love and the Pope were all safely in their places, that Joi d'Amour would reign for ever in our land, that I was a little crazed. They sought to soothe me with their eyes, their lips. I bedded chatelaines, I hurt them for their husbands' sakes. I sang their praises, their pale merits with mockery, hypocrisy in my voice and mind, and they were pleased and soothed in their turn, thinking for fame and druery.* "Oh, Little Beast," he cried, "this was Peire Carcasse!"'

'Your voice is hoarse,' I whispered. 'Cease awhile.' Your shoulders rose and fell in shudders. I pitied you. Yes, the pity rose like a sickness through me and laughter trickled from my mouth—dead leaves of laughter.

'That's not all,' you said. 'Hear me out.'

* See Glossary on p. 240.

34

'Master, I don't know how to. Forgive me. Be seated at least. Not on your knees before me.'

'The Lord Trencavel took me up and brought me to Raimon's court. For a week I was a curiosity, for a month a misfit and a monster, until the fury struck me, and I sang of their wives and leaky maidens, of their spiritual father bursting with his own stopped-up manure, of their courtly games, and of the fate which overtakes men without blood and bile and which chokes them finally to an impotent destruction. I even told them of my own emptiness, and begged their judgement and *their* rule of faith.' He smiled. 'It was then they saw their strength. I met the Lady Azelais—Aniara as I called her for the trobar clus—or they sent her to me. She came to Raimon's court at thrice-walled Toulouse. A slip of a girl who never laughed, and when Raimon had ceased to be amused, and I was thrown in prison, it was she who came to release me. The keys in her hands seemed to weigh her slight frame to the earth. Ha! Keys of heaven and hell. And her magic seemed to offer me a clue to joy. Yes, yes, Little Beast, two and two make four or even eight loaves of bread to a hungry man. I sang once more beneath their oyster vaults when dusk was come, and the steaming boars' heads were laid ready for the banqueting, and the tinkle of goblets, chased crystal, women's voices, and the lutes were heard before the rumbling of a wide fire. I sang again, cursing my cracked voice, of this woman, and without my knowing it, the mockery was gone from my voice, I was naked but no longer empty. I sang of a rock out to sea against which the waves, like mortal men, lap and flow. A rock whose silhouette against the sky is like a beacon, or a landmark for a salt-lipped, sea-crusted vagabond. I sang of how men approached her with their arms outstretched, to kiss that holy spark of land, tendering their arms and lips to her green sides, to the soft firmness of her body, as if she was their only salvation. They heard my song in silence. There was a pause I recollect when I unslung my lute and stumbled from the gallery. "Peire Carcasse!" someone shouted. I turned. "What is amiss? Has your head turned soft at last?" In the gale of laughter I sought out Aniara's gaze, and found her mouth shaking and her eyes sharing the jest with Raimon. The lute crumpled on the stone flagons, and with all the strength in my chest I howled at them like a wolf, again and again until my throat was empty. No, Little Beast, I didn't stop my songs.

35

Aniara was my lady now. And all d'Oc and Provence will hear of her.' His voice dipped and was silent.

The sun was high over the town. I heard a door open and close without. My finger stroked his head unconsciously, feeling the sweat and the heat on him and that his bones had relaxed.

'This last night, Little Beast, I could not sleep. I was on the ramparts. It seemed to me that an echo reached me out of the darkness. I stared over the valleys, straining my eyes in the dark, and I heard another voice then, calling to me angrily, secretly . . .

> Leave the pilgrims to their prayers,
> Your townsfolk to their cares.
> Leave shepherds to their sheep,
> The pedants deep asleep.
> Leave Hope, the Pope behind,
> Your road's another kind.
> To weep a little, then to die?
> You think that's all—You LIE!

I listened to the wind. I thought of you, our meeting, Little Beast, that you would hear me.' He stopped abruptly, and was on his feet in a flash. 'You'll go with me?' He turned on me fiercely, seizing my arms and staring at me.

'I'm no good with words, Messer. My schooling is best forgotten, and my brain isn't very extensive either. But my heart's in it, Sieur Carcasse, and my feet.' I coughed. 'If it please you, when shall we be leaving?'

He glanced at me. His features were calm, and the young lines soft in the skin. He lifted his hands to his face. I found myself murmuring an old verse under my breath unconsciously.

'Aloud! Speak up!' he cried. 'What do you say?'

'A scrap of verse, Messer, no more.' I remembered the door opening, and creaking on its hinges. 'Was that your father back from Mass? Perhaps we should be leaving already?'

My anxiety amused him. 'No, be patient, he shall not harm you, and we must bid him farewell. Tell me, what do you really have in that sack of yours?'

'Just the tricks of my trade, Sieur. Just my tricks and gewgaws.'

He moved, staring at me curiously. 'I believe you are an omen. Perhaps you do carry my fate in your hands. Well met then, fate! It was fitting that you should confess me. Come!' he said softly.

I hurried after him into the hall, tying up my sack and throwing it on my shoulders.

'Leave it here,' he said.

I pleaded with him.

'Leave it here.'

Dropping it carefully by the door, I followed him up the polished stairs, and then ran back to regain my sack. He said nothing, the blue vein on his temple sprang up and subsided, a smile touched his lips. Above us a woman was singing in a low voice, muffled by the closed doors, and the hangings.

'You shall not speak until she bids you,' Peire muttered. 'My lady mother is a fiery law unto herself. She devoured her husband long ago, and looks even on her son with dangerous hooded eyes.' He grimaced. 'Be wary, and silent!'

The room we stepped into was deeply shaded though the sun had long since thrown its rays at the casements. There was a scent of musk, ambergris and lotus oils. The voice sang on magically in Arabic, accompanied by the rubbing shuttle slipping through a loom. Peire bade me wait. I nodded, my eyes starting out of my head. I was in a mosque, no, rather an Emir's palace in Muslim lands. The rich brocaded hangings on the wall were woven by Berber women, even I could see that, and the oriental rugs on the floor were not made by Christian fingers, nor Muslims, but by far easterners. There were silk cushions scattered everywhere, except at the far end of the room which seemed bare and austere. There stood her loom, beside it a narrow, low bed with a rough blue patched cloth thrown over it, and the wooden floor was bare. Two tiny pointed slippers lay, toes towards me, beneath the bed. The singing stopped.

'Who is there?' she demanded curtly without turning.

'Your son.'

'I have a son who's a whoremonger, drunkard, and brawler. Do you speak of him?'

'No, mother.'

'I have a son who's a coward, who flies his fate, who weeps woman's tears and who seeks refuge in self-pity. Do you speak of him?'

'No, mother.'

'I have a son, daily growing in loneliness and pity. A son who

37

loves himself but little, yet looks for the spirit of wisdom both within and without himself. It cannot be him for he should have already departed on his true journey.'

'It is him,' Peire called out. 'I've come to bid farewell.'

She rose, hands clasped loosely over her abdomen and, as she turned, black hair mingled with threads of silver tumbled down from the back of her neck in glossy heavy ringlets. Her face was veiled, but from beneath a jutting brow I could see deep-hollowed eyes, her son's eyes, turn their gaze first on my Master and then on myself. I quailed before her stare, slow and piercing and melting it was, melting my eyes to reach the heart's truth. I bowed my head.

'Pardon, gentle mother, this is to be my road companion. He's known as Little Beast. He refuses to give another name.'

'As you, I believe, are known as Carcasse,' she said, still looking on me, 'having refused to answer to a worthier name.'

'He's a juggler who was on the road to Hell's gates to challenge the Devil to a game of truth!' He grinned. 'But his stomach was too empty to carry him farther on his own!'

She made a small obeisance and put a hand to her forehead, her lips and then to her heart. I shook in her presence, at her beauty, but I remembered to keep my mouth shut. Her greeting I mimicked solemnly. She was small and wondrously formed. Peire was different in her presence. His words were gentle, and careful, as though the two of them performed a ritual together, like a stately dance. I hardly knew him. But then, muttered a voice within me, what will you ever learn of him? I glanced shyly at this mother and son. He, wiry and vital in movement, but in repose tortured and massive. He was not a big man, excepting his head which reared out of his shoulders like that of an ox. And beside him, his mother, who stood to within a finger of his eye; she, who moved like a willow in the wind, and motionless, seemed to quiver with strength and perception.

'At last, my son!' she cried fiercely. 'At last you leave our wretched caravan of souls, and strike into the desert. Pray God you find your Master, and yourself.' She looked at me again. 'Oh yes, he's run away a thousand times I know. And now no more. One day it will be for you to tell his tale,' she suddenly pointed at me. Feeling her eyes sink into me, I trembled with a great fear and a drifting heart. 'A sorry tale, perhaps. The tale of a thief or

38

a murderer, who knows?' She gazed at her son. 'But this man will speak true for he rarely uses words.'

'How do you know, Madam?' My mouth opened involuntarily.

'Is it the truth?'

'Yes, Ma'am, but . . .'

'Maybe you'll only have to whisper the tale to the Devil!' Her eyes sparkled. 'No more than that. Peire!' she called. 'Leave me with your jongleur now, and don't weary yourself to know our conversations. He'll doubtless bring them back to you as delicately as he would porcelain!' She kissed her son on the forehead, and pushed him towards the door. He left reluctantly. I stood before her wondering what she desired from me. She beckoned me to the cushions.

'I want to look at this man to whom my son has opened himself,' she said, smiling, and then to herself, 'the Little Beast!' but I felt she spoke the words as you would call to mind the name of a country or a strange plant, without intention of cruelty.

A young serving girl slipped into the chamber and busied herself with plumping the cushions, and opened one of the windows. I sat with Peire's mother a long while. She returned to her loom, occasionally breaking off from her work to tell me something of her son.

'He has my Arab Jewish blood in his veins, mingled with the Christian, and the two course through his veins like fire and water.'

'He spoke to his father of siring a race of bastards,' I muttered.

She nodded. 'He has both shame and honour of his mother, who was sold for rare pelts though already joined to another man.' Her dark, hooded eyes caught mine and lingered over my features. 'Your face is a travelled one, though you can't be much older than my son. A white, still, uncracked face, but lived behind. How did he find you?' she asked.

'I found him, Madam. I wasn't fit to go on alone, and he was afflicted with a disease that I recognized. He acknowledged me too, and, Madam, I trusted him.'

She was silent for some minutes, the shuttle sped in silence, making a gentle, rhythmic click and the loom jogged now and then on the floor. She asked me about my trade, and even pointed to my patched hemp sack, but though I offered she would not permit me to show her my juggling balls and tricks. At last she

39

rose, I smelt her bitter perfume, seeking to hold her image in my brain. Without embarrassment she took my cold hand between hers and tried to straighten out the fingers. Her touch was cool and reassuring, it seemed to soothe the twisted muscles. She beckoned to the girl, asked me to come once more with her son before we departed, and with the same obeisance as before took leave of me.

We slept one more night in that house. The following morning I heard Peire and his father speaking in the shop.

'Good fur merchant, we leave this day. I've come to kiss your hand, beg pity, and bid farewell.' My Master's voice was properly filial, clean of mockery and touched with regret. I waited, holding my breath.

'But you'll be back again, scoundrel, I doubt it not, to plague me with your lies. That is if they don't hang you first.' The old man was blustering and spoke heedlessly, as though he dared not moot his sadnesses. For a moment I understood him, this anxious, lacking, skin-dealer; with his careful bills of sale, and the shipments to be thought of, lost or late, and the pages tripping in for their masters' goods, heedless of payment, and the silver growing in his coffers which did not warm his soul, and mother church who cursed and excommunicated such merchants for usury, painting images of them all in Hell.

'Then leave!' I heard. 'What keeps you? A honeyed word to speed you from your mother? I have no family, no wife, no son, to share my hearth and law!'

'F-father!' Peire called.

'Father be damned, I have no blessing for you.' He shuffled away. My Master appeared.

'Your mother asks to see us before leaving,' I told him.

He nodded curtly.

We mounted the stairs once more, knocked, and were bidden to enter. She came to greet us, bowed to me, and opened her arms to her son. I can't describe her face. Her eyes smouldered slowly. Her lips were parted as she kissed her son, and I could see a drop of sweat glistening on her upper lip against the faint down. She drew away from him, saying that she had had a clear vision of us that night.

'In my mind,' she began, 'I saw your sack, Little Beast, emptied on the floor. I saw a broken doll with angel's wings.'

40

'Madam, please don't go on. Why should you see such things. I'm only a mountebank.'

'I saw a hangman's noose,' she continued, ignoring me. 'Seven blue and golden balls, an eighth painted black. I saw a cat jump out with scarlet eyes, who was devouring a verse of song. I saw a red rose blooming whose thorns pricked my heart. I saw a silver star whose tips melted into light when you, Peire, reached out to touch them.' She stopped as suddenly as she had begun. 'The cat, the rose, the star.'

'What does it mean?' my Master asked.

'Remember, and perhaps one day you'll learn,' she said, shaking her head. Completing her sentence in a low, guttural voice, she raised the veil from her face. I heard Peire's gasp.

She kissed her son thrice, and then touched my forehead with her palm.

'Love him well,' she murmured. 'And bravely!'

Victuals were packed, our baggage prepared, and we departed from Carcassonne. Turning out of the gates, my Master, who had not spoken since we had left his mother, turned to me.

'Little Beast, yesterday morning you muttered a verse under your breath, and were shy to tell me of it.'

For a space I was silent, before repeating the old words . . .

Cease man to mourn, to weep, to wail—sip up the sun;
We dance along Death's icy rim, but is the dance less fun?

The Sieur Carcasse smiled, and then burst into laughter.

2

'One day it will be for you to tell his tale,' she'd said. But I'm
just a juggler, a mountebank. I don't open my mouth unless I
have to. Oh God in Heaven, help me unroll my tongue, knit up
my words, and turn these black devils that wriggle from my pen
into truth. Else how shall I write of him who left me behind
when the furies struck? I know he fought long and hard against
you, your church, your priests, even against his own soul. Yes I
know you'll throw that in my face. Quite right too, but he had to
find himself, didn't he? How else could he go about the business?
All he had was his lute, and his voice, and that tortured brain of
his. He could only follow his heart, and I'd stumble behind him,
because he needed someone. There was no one else, God. There
was no other way. I wish there had been. For a scrawny hunchback who likes his stomach full, and a warm bed with a friendly
female rump awaiting him—saving your presence Lord—it
wasn't always skittles and fun. Frozen, beaten, starving one
moment, the next admired and courted, dressed in velvet and
damask only to have the tunics and robes dragged off our backs,
because that terrible mouth of his would open up again, and the
little dizzy notes would tumble out in the dining halls, and into
the ears of courtiers, who offended easily and were afraid to be
warned of their coming downfall. Aie! That's natural, I agree.
Who cares to be told that they smile and simper, all unawares,
to death? But such people, perhaps they die laughing. I'd know,
just as soon as the first notes escaped him, what our fate would be:
whether I'd be curled up cosily by the banqueting hall fire and
him tucked in some perfumed chamber, or whether the both
of us would be thrown into the snow. That sort of life has no
regularity. I used to be a creature of habit. It was nearly alright
to starve, if you knew you were starving the next day too. But
I'm talking about my stomach again, Lord. It's a bad sign. How
can I talk about Peire? He always talked in riddles. That wasn't
too bad. Sometimes I even understood. But the man was in the
songs. Look at this for example. Does it make sense to you?

I am Carcasse who reaps the wind,
Who hunts Love's hare
His soul unskinned.
I am Carcasse who lives his dream,
Who swims sans care
Against the stream . . .

And then sometimes I think I do understand, Peire! But when I understand you, you frighten me. I see your eyes in my mind, even though the rest of you grows indistinct; those great swollen, burning eyes beneath the scowling brow, and they seem to say to me, 'Go on, Little Beast! Go on until you burn, and then, even then, go on until you're just a flaming particle, until there is nothing left of you except the white-hot flame projecting you towards eternity.'

It's strange, even when we first set out from Carcassonne on that late autumn morning, I knew one day you'd leave me behind. Even then, as we passed through the blood-red vines, almost despoiled of their fruit, and stumbled by the shorn fields, seeing a stray poppy or two, purpled and dazed in the leftover sun, even then when my heart was a thousand times lighter than it had ever been, I knew that I could only keep up with you for a certain time. And time's never enough.

We stopped that day to break our midday fast in the woods by Azille, where we came across a travelling tinker, and his mate, a journeyman. They joined us, even shared their wine-flasks with us, and we got to talking. Peire was in a mood to set the moon a-dancing. He pulled me to my feet, and, springing into the air, let out a bellow to herald our steps. And we danced like madmen with the tinker batting away at his tin kettles to keep the time. Rolling in the grass with laughter, they said that they knew another lunatic like him, who danced and bellowed as well as any angry bear.

'Who's that?' Peire asked.

'Oh, a great strong fellow, puffed up with Pride's bellows. A jongleur. We met him once in Béziers. He could lift a man up in the seat of his hand, play the lute with his teeth, and singing all the time,' they said. 'We've seen him at it with our own eyes!' I stared at Peire's muscled chest. He was not tall, and his frame was more wiry than broad.

43

'And what's this fine fellow's name?' my Master asked.

'Peire Carcasse. Two metres tall he is!'

Peire burst into laughter, and slapped their shoulders. 'Facts are the idlest of superstitions,' he said. 'Peire Carcasse can lift two men up with one hand. He told me so himself!'

Tinker and journeyman stared dubiously at him.

'Can you do it?' they asked.

'Not me, but then who said I was Peire Carcasse? Did you, or you? Did I?'

Facts, facts, facts. What's a fact? Something that stays where it is, and doesn't run away. Let's see. Raimon is Lord of Toulouse. Raimon d'Avinho holds sway over this, that and the other. But be careful! Is he lord, for instance, shivering in his slippers when an embassy from France tramps through his courts, or when the northern barons prance into his realm, dour and disdainful of our pretty ways and painted faces, grim in their business-like mail and hauberk, and trailing retinues of real soldiers? Is he lord, or is it a whispering lady who commands his ear? And when Alphonso lumbered through the land a short time back, with his mercenaries and gallow-glasses, who was lord? Tell me that! And the Pope, what would he say on this question? You set a word down, and it blinks and winks back at you, for all the world like a well-trapped fact, until you turn your back for a second. And Peire, who used to ask me sometimes to tie us together with a rope at night in case he lost himself before dawn. HE wasn't even sure if he was a fact. Perhaps he mocked me. Still, it makes me wary now when I'm trying to think straight.

And how many years have passed since then! Peire Carcasse has left me, he's gone for good, but I'm still here, like a lop-sided cabbage that the farmer forgot to pull up, because the effort wasn't worth the meal. Old and cracked now, hairless, toothless. I sit here with the quill in my trembling fingers. The paper is already smudged, and one of those pink-faced imbeciles, kindly imbeciles I'll agree, will be up shortly with my broth and a prayer, and that usual concentrated astonishment of theirs, that an old mountebank like me has been begging parchment and quill. But even so, as I remember our departure that day, I feel like jumping up, pulling my tatters about me, grabbing a stick and making off once more. Who knows, I might even bump into his

44

ghost, and he might tell me where Peire's gone, and point me out the right road. Oh Peire Carcasse, maybe after all a little of your flame has entered me, so on fool! Hurry on before the farmer comes to plough you back into the dark earth.

Our roads parted after a while. The tinker and his mate were bound for Béziers.

'And us, Messer? Where are we aimed for?'

Peire stopped and eyed me. There was white road dust in his black hair, and on his fur-lined cloak and boots.

'Us, Little Beast? Why, we're bound for Gazanac.' He spoke lightly, but there was a thick vein bouncing across his forehead, from eyebrow to scalp-line, and I was learning how it presaged trouble.

'But why thither?' I bit my tongue.

His brows creased. 'You'll know soon enough.'

We tramped on, and with time and a warm sun on our backs, his tongue loosened. He asked me how I'd known where to look for him in Carcassonne.

'A girl with red hair, Messer, and a face like a wild flower. She lives in the square by St Nazaire, where you first picked me up. She seemed to know you. A spiteful, unhappy creature I'm thinking. She told me that you'd come back from Puivert after a thrashing.'

'And so I had,' he answered with amusement. 'It was Na Louva who told you where to find me. She must have sixteen winters behind her by now. She's young but she's daily waxing! Waxing to marriage or the cloister, as surely as the Devil knows his own. And her father wags behind, quick to anger, and slow to his own blind pedantry. Last summer I was serenading her mother, a plump cosy soul who deserves more than that stick of a husband, his pretensions to courtly behaviour, and his chests stuffed with yards of parchment declaring his pedigree. And that little vixen leant out of her window whispering my name. I mistook the whelp for the dam, and cast her a rose. "Noble Sieur Carcasse," she says, in her high childish voice, "you drag my mother's honour through the gutter. One day I shall watch you cry out with pain, and your hurt will only make me laugh." "And what has unleashed this fury on poor Carcasse?" I cried, but all my answer was the rose thrown back in my face, torn and unpetalled.'

45

'The married ones are always less trouble, Sieur. That's a fact!'

'If facts are so easily determined, Little Beast, I'm grateful to you!'

I glanced at him, and clamped my lips together.

The shadows started to lengthen, and the afternoon sun was reddening the flat-topped pines.

'Shall we not stop for victuals, Messer, and to rest? My legs aren't tired,' I continued hurriedly, 'but Carcassonne lies far behind us now.'

'A way farther,' he told me gently. 'We've yet an hour's day-light to speed our steps, and then you'll rest. Look yonder. Perhaps those priests will give you a ride on the crupper. You can scarcely weigh much, and so long as your bones aren't so sharp that they tear the prelate's saddle-cloth you can hardly constitute an impediment, unless they are ashamed to bear a scarecrow!'

'My uncle and his wife used to say the same,' I said. 'Even in a new jerkin I looked like a scarecrow they'd tell me, "so better leave him like he is, no use in wasting money".' I grinned, out of breath, and pulled my sack higher up my back.

'Good day, servants of God,' Peire called out to the men in black. 'Can you give a lift to this poor cripple?'

The two reined in their mules, and twisted round with alarm.

'Don't trouble them,' I whispered, 'my feet are really quite fresh. I could walk a hundred leagues, and then you never know with priests. They might excommunicate us on the spot, or have us shipped back to the "Mure" prison, Sieur!' I tugged his coat. 'You know what they think about jugglers? They think twice as unpleasantly about troubadours, and you have the lute on your back.'

'I know, my friend, and that's the charm of it.'

'Approach no closer,' ordered the senior of the two, wagging a crucifix at us as though he intended it for a battle-axe. 'State your business, and be off.'

He was a solid, over-ripe tomato of a priest, with a thatch of bristling grey hair, and the mule's back swung like a bent bridge between his thighs. His companion, a fresh-faced novice, stared anxiously at my Master.

'A lift for my companion to the next village, your honour, is all

I crave. He's lighter than a bag of bones. I'll toss him up behind your altar-boy.'

'No such thing, scoundrel!' The crucifix waggled more hotly. 'How dare you challenge our passage.'

'We dared, knowing servants of God to be also servants of the needy among men.'

'Beware the dignity of the Church, and her authority,' he cried, 'if you fear the path to Hell. A free ride you want! And then you'll be needing the mule as well, no doubt. And then God knows what.'

'We shan't need your mules, your cassocks, gentlemen, nor your sacks of hard-won gold, and yes, we make the best time we can to Hell's gates. Do you refuse to give charity in God's name?'

'And you, unholy wretch, with that instrument of Satan stretched across your back, do you mock his servants so lightly?'

'Servants, holy father? Shall I sing a canticle, a psalm in praise of Mother Church? Would that unbend a proud heart? Priest!' he cried, seizing the bridle and quite ignoring the crucifix with which the patriarch was threatening him, 'I think you put both God and your vocation to shame!'

'Unhand my mount, thieves, mountebanks, murderers!'

The novice turned white, and attempted feebly to disengage Peire's arm from the bridle.

'Father,' he whispered sibilantly, 'the cripple would not trouble me, and he seems an honest fellow. I could even walk a short space, the exercise . . .'

He wasn't allowed to finish before his superior, sweating mightily, berated him soundly, and bid him set spurs to his mount.

'Ha!' roared Peire between laughter and rage. 'It seems we must help you to save your own souls before the Almighty.' Grasping the fat priest about his waist, he heaved him from the saddle, and set him on the road, where that unworthy creature gobbled silently betwixt apoplexy and terror.

'It's the Abbot of Fontfroide,' muttered the novice desperately. 'You can't do that to the Abbot. He'll have you stretched out like them.' His eyes rose to the cartwheel suspended ten feet in the air, on which was roped the bloody remains of some criminal, hung to dry in the sun. The coincidence turned my blood.

'My brains will burst with all this brewing,' I cried to my Master. 'Allow us to leave. They don't know you, and we might escape with our lives if you don't speak anymore.'

He came to his senses. 'Enough games. It's true. On your mounts, gentlemen. I expected no better from you.'

The novice dismounted to push the other back on to his perch.

'But wait, tell me this. How then, do you fish for souls? What is the bait you use? You shall not leave before you answer.'

The proud Abbot, once more in the saddle, was attempting to contain himself, and was bitterly aware of his recent loss of dignity. I watched him biting his lips, with my cloak over my nose in the hope that he wouldn't remember me.

'Accursed child of Satan, Mother Church has many tools with which to fish, amongst them are the sword, the net, the lightning, and the stake.'

'A fair collection of hooks,' said Peire in a low voice.

'Our hooks are sharp, and few escape the confessional. Perhaps you won't be an exception. Your face I shan't forget.' With that he put spurs to his steed, and his acolyte, with a shocked, pitiful glance at us, galloped after him.

'Sieur Carcasse, why did you do it?' I mumbled. 'Saving your presence, I'm likely to be in a permanent state of terror for weeks.'

'Stop your lamentations, you're no such coward,' he clipped out coldly, and then to himself, 'Is this, is this all we have, and those poor fanatical Cathari?'

We proceeded in silence close to the banks of the Aude.

'Know this,' he suddenly spoke. 'Such men as we have seen look out upon the world as through a keyhole. They blink, and think to see the rising sun, but all they see is their eye reflected in a particle of light. They watch a bud begin to blossom, a leaf unfold, turn green, then red, then gold, and say they've seen the world. They blink again, and jostle for the spot in turns. "Look there!" they say. "That's truth, that bud of ours. We've watched it!" And then a stranger knocks on their door, and all they see is that he blocks the keyhole, doubtless with his cod-piece. "Away, a traitor, cur, blasphemer! He steals our light!" "It's the door which stops the light," you tell them, "be brave and open it." But they've forgotten how to. "This vagabond who stops our sun-light," they whine, "a heretic who dares to question our under-

48

standing of the universe!" But it's they who are the vagabonds, vagabonds self-locked within their chosen cells. They are poor curs, sad hypocrites, snails crawling in their hoods across a four-walled world.' He turned to me and with a slow, wide shrug of his shoulders he threw his hands out. His voice shrank away until it became hardly audible. 'Who knows, perhaps one day a rich man will become a holy wanderer, will take a cripple on his back and change men's sins for love; a man who's had his fill of authority and power; a man who needs no gold to keep the church's coffers rattling. And then . . . and then there won't be need of swords and nets and curses when we fish for souls.' He stopped. 'But now, my friend, you and I must set to fishing for ourselves.'

'And get the Devil to explain himself a little better as far as priests are concerned.'

'You have it, Little Beast.' He grinned.

'But we'll try to avoid finishing up as carrion food for the crows, roped to a cartwheel above the ground, won't we?' I suggested timidly.

'Are you afraid?'

'No, Messer, not afraid, but terrified now and again when I forget myself.' I looked humbly at the ground.

'And so am I,' he said. He touched my shoulder with his hand. 'Remember that you carry a load for both of us, kind scarecrow though you are.'

'Just so long as we keep away from the clerical vultures,' I muttered to myself. 'Usually I can smell them. They perfume their lips with sulphur so that a man can't smell their rot.'

We reached the tavern late. There was a party of jugglers and mummers, some of whom I knew from before. People also like myself. We spoke and reminisced. Peire had cast his eyes on one of the serving wenches, a tall girl with a nut-brown bosom shaking when she laughed, and black come-hither eyes. He started to sing . . .

> No castle locked on rocky height,
> No vines, no flocks have I,
> But my eyrie stands within Hell's sight,
> And men, they fear my cry.

She rolled her eyes a little at him, bustling close. I wished it had been me, tall and straight, on whom she cast her wise, eager glance. Aie! What a rump! what a plump friendly armful she was. Peire caught my desperate face and refused to take me seriously.

'A lecher? Is it possible?'

I nodded my head enthusiastically at him. 'Yes, yes!'

'Your turn will come, don't fear. The widows and married ones are best, is it not so?'

Heads turned to listen.

'But when shall it be my turn? Don't laugh at me, Master.' I couldn't keep the plaintiveness out of my voice, nor the envy. 'Not that many a stray dwarf lady hasn't longed for my charms!'

I attempted a chuckle, but it was too late. A wag took up the strain. 'A bedmate for the hunchback!' he shouted. 'What offers have we?'

'Don't let them laugh,' I pleaded to myself, stupidly. I should have known better.

'There's a well-humped ox in the stable, soft and sweet-smelling, I'll wager!'

A chorus of laughter greeted this sally, and someone else responded, 'Our taverner's old dam. She's so bent up it would be a charity to unroll her. That's if she wouldn't crack.'

Lamplight caught the eyes of an old crone, seated in the fire-place. 'He He!' she cackled, her eyes darting about fearfully.

I shrank into my corner, staring at Peire, but he was already on his feet. A bench fell to the floor behind him.

'Who mocks my friend?' His voice was a breath, as if it were only his lips that formed the words. The tables for a moment were silent. The serving wench, casting a glance and a sigh of resignation at Peire, slipped into the scullery.

'Why surely it was I,' drawled out the fellow who had first spoken. 'If it's you who calls this runt your friend.'

I hadn't time to reach him, but I caught sight of the blue vein throbbing across his temple, before chaos broke loose. Benches were pushed back surreptitiously, sleeves rolled up. It was a brave fellow who answered my Master. A hefty giant, a sergeant-at-arms by his dress, his hands and shoulders, and he launched a stool through the air, before grabbing a heavy iron poker from the fireplace. Peire unsheathed his sword, and to my astonishment he then cast it, hilt first into my lap, and taking the scabbard leapt across the table towards his adversary. I wondered little for the outcome. Peire was a head smaller, and I'd never seen him fighting, but he went into the struggle careless if every bone in his body were broken, and looking for relief. He had unfair advantages.

'For Carcasse and the Devil!' he cried lustily.

The other swayed before the onslaught. The scabbard was a hindrance. He hurled it across the room and stretched his hands out like claws. The poker landed square enough a couple of times on his pate, and the blood ran, though I cried out for him to save himself.

'That's it, my bonny, I love your clouts. Let loose your strokes!' he called to the other with the laughter breaking out of him. 'Here's my other cheek.'

He turned and, as his assailant raised his weapon to deal him another buffet, Peire caught his neck in both hands, and wrenched the fellow towards him. I believe he wanted to squeeze the juice and the brains from his opponent. The latter lost his balance, and my Master despatched him with a terrible cuff headlong into the wall. For a second he stood in the centre of the room, shuddering the air into his lungs with people jostling and pushing him. There was a roar, and the sergeant-at-arms reappeared holding a sword. Peire glanced at him with a look amounting to weary affection, stretched out his hand lazily as I tossed him his weapon, and then stood, blade stroking the floor, staring at nothing. His inaction was short-lived, and the ill-matched half of this odd dance lay unarmed between my Master's feet within moments.

'And now, my chickens, you, plump turtle-dove,' he said in the wench's direction, 'bring us your best red wine.' His shoulders heaved, the sweat and blood mingled on his face. 'Little Beast, what an excuse he gave us, is it not so?' Turning about towards the revellers and onlookers he cried, 'My friends, you should not laugh. We owe the Little Beast here, much. In his sack he carries the troubles of the world, fire, pestilence and war. On his shoulders, there between the bones, he carries our pain, our mortal fear of ugliness, but in his heart—you haven't poked your snouts in there, have you, my chickens? In his heart there flutters a raven and a dove, and the dove is joi d'amour. But you, you're all so filled with beauty and refinement that you fail to notice it beneath a hunchback's load.'

'And the raven, worthy minstrel?' someone called out slyly.

'Don't press too hotly. You'll hear the beating of the raven's wings. Little Beast will let him loose all in good time.'

The tumult subsided, people smirked and giggled at Peire's poetic touches. I didn't care for his words at all. Scurrying to pick up his sheath, I hurried back to my place beside him. His words made me shiver more than all the laughter, and yet I also felt pride flickering within me. I was used to mockery, I had lived on it, and I was used to the disgust and loathing which men inflict on the twisted and deformed of their race. Their race? It's as if the tall and straight-limbed have made us outcasts. Are we descended from a breed of ghouls or dwarfs? Sometimes I have thought so. Sometimes in the darkness I've wept on it, and on that loneliness. I admit my weakness. It's strange to live with other men's belief that such as I have been pitched on earth by error. Peire, my Master, was giving back to me something I'd forgotten about. It's said that no one loves another like himself. Why then does he live off other men's opinion of him, rather than his own? And the answer is from fear. It seemed less foolish now, to hope that I could lose that fear. He said that I carried pestilence in my old sack of gewgaws, and that's not possible, but he was also saying that we, him, the Little Beast, and all men, share life and fear and feeling together. It made me feel like a man again, like a human creature.

I stared at him while the red liquid cascaded from his lips. I stared at the scarred throat's convulsive movements, and tried to understand things, tossing my slow thoughts about the barn that was my head.

'A great draughty barn,' I muttered angrily, 'with half the timbers loose.'

'Are you so far gone that you talk to yourself now?'

'No, I've always done it, though it's none . . .' I looked up hastily. 'I mean not always, and Messer, saving . . .' I blundered into rueful silence.

The dark-eyed girl came up beside us. 'Shall you have another flask?' She eyed Peire with her bosom dancing a melody of its own. 'I thought he'd kill you,' she murmured with over-friendly concern.

'Shameless creature,' I growled, to no one in particular.

'Rather a bed, my beauty,' he answered, cupping a cunning hand beneath her rump. 'We have a long stroll tomorrow.' His hands slid round those wide cheeks, as if he were determining the shape of a private mystery. I turned my head away, whistling a slip of a tune, though I heard the slap.

'A man earns the wage he deserves,' I said nonchalantly.

Peire grinned at us both as though we were agents to his vice.

'Your Master's uncourteous, and no gentleman,' she hissed, throwing the last word at me from between white teeth. She bent towards him heatedly pushing a lock of black hair out of her eyes with a strong glistening wrist.

He laughed, and caught her arm between his fingers. 'My dove, you should not feign your anger and neither your pleasure.'

She glanced at him, and then pushed him off with the strength of a wrestler. 'I'll show you your chamber,' she curtsied to us, angry, seductive and eager for the pleasure she sought.

There was only the attic for us. She pointed out her door as we climbed the stairs.

'I'll scream if anyone comes near me this night,' she lisped . . . like an actress, like a woman.

I crept under the sheepskin, and pushed my sack into place beneath my head. Peire didn't move.

'Sieur Peire,' I whispered, 'what did you mean with that dove you were talking about? And in Carcassonne too, do you remember, you dreamt of the dove and a raven? There are always white doves flying over the walls of Carcassonne, aren't there? People feed them because of the superstition that the citadel can't fall while they stay.'

He was silent.

'Saving your pleasure, I didn't understand what you were up to, making folk think I've got evil tucked in my sack. They might take it amiss, and choose to whack the daylights out of me as being a bad omen. But on the other hand,' I mused, 'perhaps they might leave me alone. Was that it, Messer Peire?'

'Listen to me,' he broke the stillness. 'Listen. We travel like two gaudy scarecrows, is it not so?'

'To make a living, Master.'

53

'No, Little Beast. People believe that what they do, they do for a necessity! For glory, gold, for hunger's sake—and they deceive themselves. The poorest serf in d'Oc, like the prince for whom he toils, labours from a choice that's been made at his birth, and which he's accepted, however hatefully. He labours in a mould. If he breaks his chains in sullen misery and rage, kills the bailiff, and becomes an outlaw, it's the same. Men follow the instinct of their first choice wherever it leads them, bravely, with cowardice, it matters little. We travel not to eat, not to sing, nor dance, though we're called minstrels, as the bondsman or the serf are named for what they're knotted to. We travel not to bed a warm wench, but chasing, as all men do, the roots of our hunger. In every creature there's a genius buried deep, bidding him to his fate, to break out of the mould cast for him. We too are rising to the bait. The mould is hot and all-embracing but it shrinks. We hunger the more. You bury your face in a fistful of bread and olives,' he smiled, 'or in the secrets of your sack, your trade; I bury my head between a woman's breasts, but the hunger's there again in heart and stomach when we wake. Each moment of satiety only recalls more vividly the surrounding starvation. And so we seek to break out of our mould. We shall either shatter into a thousand fragments, or surpass ourselves.'

My Master spoke slowly and hesitantly. I listened with my hand curled about my ear for his meaning and intention.

'Forgive me,' he muttered, 'if I fog your brains, but you, Little Beast, are my looking-glass.'

'Joi d'amour has little to do with either Devil or a maid, I'm thinking, and the dove sits with her shadow the raven, on Carcassonne's towers, as much as in men's heads and hearts.'

'That's it indeed. Look at our fair land. A country ruled by corrupted, pampered, shadows. The dove they've chased from their souls, and replaced with a mechanical whore imported from the land of opium dreamers. To her they make their libations, seeking ever more exotic pleasures as their senses thicken and lose feeling. Our knights and courtiers,' he continued more urgently, 'our princes, prelates, once hardy, learned and vital, now play at government, like petty merchants bartering their wares, before their colleagues realize the trickery. They play at chivalry at a thousand pretty lists where wit and doggerel have more strength than their arms. They play at Epicurus—Beauty is a woman

54

melted out of wax and dreams; Love is a debate in honeyed images, waged in a Court of Love; Desire is a beast which needs to be flayed rampant by self-torture and literary humility; and Life, oh Life, Little Beast, is the number of maidenheads you've cracked! Yes, we need a race of bastards to turn the ravens back; ravens, northern barons, jealous Popes and priestlings.

'And yes, you're right, I wish us to grow into a mystery for those we travel among. If men quail at your sack and its secrets as I've done; if women and courtiers shiver at my songs, my folly, or my wretchedness, we grow to the dignity of madmen. In this age of ours, when Mother Church preys on men's reason with fantasies of Hell, and the Prince creates his own, more prettily, the madman has a rôle to play, and the authority of his solitude.'

This was another Carcasse whose calmness and determination I hardly recognized.

'Do you hear me?' he said. 'And understand that when we met, it was this which you helped me to see?'

'I hear you,' I whispered, 'but such things have never echoed in my pate, saving your presence.' I stopped, trying to think how to say it. 'But we'll still sing, Messer, won't we, and try and avoid getting thrown into prison, and you won't get too angry with yourself, because then there wouldn't be anything left to give? And you'll tell me perhaps about the real joi d'amour, and how I might set about winkling it out, so as to be able to get a hold on it?'

'We'll sing and dance, and you'll learn one day to juggle your spheres in the sky without even touching them, Little Beast. That's what scarecrows are good for, not so?'

I awoke with the sun, and to the sound of cocks crowing in the courtyard. The clouds were running high, pink and grey in a shepherd's sky, and the wind was cold, carrying a nip of frost from the mountains. In the stable below me I could hear men harnessing their beasts, and beyond the dipping village I saw the olive trees glistening to one side of the road, and the red lines of vine to the other. Peire's bed was empty, and a grin tickled my white face.

'I hope you've lulled those devils for a space, my lady,' I said to the floorboards.

Gathering up our possessions, I crept downstairs. The chamber door was open. The girl had gone, but my Master was sitting on the window-ledge with the lute in his hands. A pale muscled hand glided over the strings carelessly, and the notes dropped like spray through the dusty sunlight. He growled a scrap of song. The boards creaked, and he spun round.

'Out!' he shouted, 'leave me a moment's silence after this night of prattling.' But then he saw it was me. He glared. 'Is this the way the soul awakens? To the braying of its own foolishness, and the false sighs of an over-ploughed wench? Let's be off!' He clambered from the window and seized his sword and cloak.

'But, Master, you asked for it,' I ventured.

'It doesn't make me any the less of an imbecile, does it?' We tumbled downstairs, and he cast two pieces of silver on the table. 'Messer, some food?' I coughed apologetically.

'Go take our needs,' he replied, 'we've paid for them generously.'

Once on the road he told me that we'd be in Gazanac within two days. 'We go to sing a ditty for our Belle Dame sans Merci,' he muttered with a sarcastic shrug. 'If the Devil hasn't drained her to the lees before me.'

We travelled in earnest for there was a cold wind on our backs, snow in the air, and the promise of warmth and cheer somewhere before us. I had my breath again, my aches had dried up, and pushing sideways, I tumbled briskly along beside my Master. He, casting an eye at me from time to time, strode on, now whistling, now humming, now throwing a line or two of a song into the teeth of the wind. I was getting used to the dozen masters I served wrapped in my Peire Carcasse. My long shoes, his boots, were soon painted with mud and fine flakes of snow. Today he'd tossed a blue velvet cap on his head, the jewelled pin glittered over his eye, and the material hung full and slack at the back.

'Ridiculous! Treating good clothes like that in this weather,' I muttered, but, perhaps fortunately, he didn't hear me.

That night we halted in a hamlet close to Béziers. With the dawn we had already passed the town, lying far beneath us in the haze. Later we were rattling along in a farm cart whose owners had patiently pulled up for us. An old couple, she with the skin wrinkled into a hundred strange crevices over the bones, and a white thatch of hair flying in the wind; he with the transparent flesh stretched tight across his face like the hide on a drum. Tied to their cart was a young milking cow.

'Two sons murdered, fighting Aragon,' cackled the old woman, 'and our daughter dead in childbirth this last month. What shall we do? There's nothing left. No strength to weed the crop, to pull the vines, so we go to beg alms and a roof from the Lord Trencavel. The times are soft, but not for us, eh, my handsome gentlemen?'

She let loose another chuckle, but her husband never opened his mouth. The reins shook in his paws, as he flicked their old nag on to greater efforts. He only stared ahead, his lips compressed, his jaw thick and heavy like an outcrop of rock.

'How do you live on half a hectare of land? Tell me that!' The woman's voice quavered as she turned to glare at us. 'How do you live when you share half your crop out to the great Lord Trencavel? When you give your sons to him and they don't come back? They're better dead, you say. He! He! How do you live when his lusty squires pull down their hose to plough your daughter to the bung? Tell me that, eh?' She spat bitterly, and was still. 'Badly,' she whispered, 'badly, and the winter frost will kill you in your burnt-down hut, if you haven't gone and broke your brains out. Hee, hee!'

Her cackle slid into the air above our heads. I stared at my Master. Bitterness pulled his mouth into a thin arc, and his eyes stared out, hollow and bloody, along the road behind us. I kept my tongue, and gnawed a piece of black bread to keep my stomach from making conversation either. The blue vein was throbbing on his temples.

'Don't look too deep inside you, Messer,' I pleaded silently. 'It's no good to be hating the bits and pieces. The hating makes the good things rotten as well.'

As if he'd caught my words, he jerked about and told me that we would continue on foot. He thanked them, I bade them good day, and hopped off too.

'Messer, they could have brought us to the gates of Gazanac,' I protested.

'I know it, and we walk,' was all his answer.

'A plague take the moral and the righteous,' I muttered. 'Not that we're examples of either.'

The sun was rolling drunkenly along the skyline. Venus had

57

poked a bright finger nail through the sky, and was twinkling faintly. We were passing a ruined church, and Peire threw himself into the long grass.

'A few moments' grace, and a mouthful of bread,' he called.

I knelt beside him, and opened my sack. A flurry of bats skittered over our heads. I ducked sheepishly, full of the old superstitions. 'The Devil's pushed his cloven foot within these walls,' I mumbled, 'and he's left behind the ghosts of a few sinners and charlatan priests to keep an eye on his precincts.'

Peire turned to me with a word on his lips. I was attending it when a noise startled us. Someone was laughing.

'Let's leave this place,' I said hurriedly. 'We're late,' I added. Peire looked round.

'Yes, Master, you're right. I'm frightened again.'

He put a finger to his mouth, and we awaited possibilities, but it was only a poor idiot who tipped and wobbled towards us timidly. He had a long stick in his hand, and cast his feet before him like broken sticks. Noises and half words broke from his mouth, and it was clear he wanted to accompany us to Gazanac. He gazed at us out of two black holes in his skull.

'Nettles, brambles, roses on my tongue, the young buck's dung, a sprig of heather and the thistle's thumb,' he lilted in a high quavering sing-song voice.

'Another troubadour,' Peire said gently, and then: 'We pass the same road, join us if you will.'

We reached Gazanac in darkness. The castellan at the gate allowed the three of us to pass because he recognized Peire. The idiot had not left us. I'd listened cautiously to the movement of his broken limbs behind us, and to his heedless chattering. I couldn't understand why my Master took such pains to listen to him, and make reply. Perhaps he was afraid of the idiot.

The porter had told us that supper was long since begun. I cursed my groaning stomach and our travelling companion into the bargain, and felt ashamed. Peire bade me inform the steward of our arrival, and to find our quarters. Then with a curt nod to me, he strode across the courtyard, and into the shadows. The other had also vanished into the gloom, so I set off to find the kitchens, with a scent of venison in my nostrils, and my spirits rising.

'Stay, jongleur!' cried a sing-song voice. 'Don't you cast a gaze at heaven before filling your belly?'

I sighed and shivered. He hadn't done with me still. He emerged from between two saddled horses who neighed and pawed the ground as he passed them. Approaching me he laid a moth-like hand on my shoulder.

'There, up there! You see, that's Boötes, the lodestar of great travellers and brave wanderers, such as you and I. Heigh, ho!' The stars were like white stitches in the sky's dark cloak. 'But an empty belly makes you blind, eh? And Luna up there.' He beckoned me closer. 'It's certainly a country, shshsh!' He glanced about. 'There may even be somebody living there. A king or a great duke like Raimon, with a treasury full of precious stones, and eastern pearls, and gold coins with Arabic inscriptions, which he stole. Ha! And weapons tempered in Damascus and Toledo, which he pulls up when he needs 'em in baskets, and silk cloth, Cordoba leather, and carpets from the Orient. Spices, too, and one thousand pigs' heads roasted to a turn, for hungry fellows like us. Look. Look harder!'

I opened my eyes again, listening against my will.

'It's said there are fields and meadows on the moon, sown with golden grass, and silver seeds. Can you see?' His hand fastened itself into my arm. 'Don't you long to pay the moon a visit?'

For a moment his eagerness and mad sincerity touched me; he danced away giggling his mocking laugh. The torchlight cast monstrous shadows about him which leapt and twisted like him. I heaved a sigh. The breath of the wind, the fragrance of the cold night, the dusty winter perfume of the stars, Hell's devils! That sort of thing was all right for an idiot or the plump shopkeeper who poked his nose out of his window once a fortnight! But for the scarecrow, the fox, the rat who spends his life shivering under those stars, it's a different matter. Still, I thought, life must be a cosy affair for the Lord of the Moon. If he'd just drop a bucket full of silver and the odd emerald back to earth, I'd vouch to catch it. I hurried up the kitchen steps.

A half-hour later, watered and fed, I stole into the great hall behind the steward. At the south end seated behind a stone table some four metres long, sat the Lord Gazanhat, to his right the Lord Trencavel, Count of Béziers and Carcassonne, and to his left in a position of honour sat a shaved pate whom I thought to recognize. There were a number of other knights, esquires, and pages alongside, and two further tables, at right-angles to the first, hosted the ladies and damoselles. Supper had been finished, but the goblets were still on the table, together with heavy dishes of nuts, spiced fruit, and sweetmeats. The men were talking boisterously. Now and again a word would bring forth a sally of laughter, or an abrupt gesture which stirred the candle flames. The women whispered and giggled, casting warm glances at their richly caparisoned stallions, who, in their turn, licked red lips, and winked back slyly. Skirts of silk taffeta, of velvet, of satin, rustled beneath snow-white bodices of silk-camlet, like thin breezes. In the dancing light, cloth-of-gold crispings, silver needlework, and gold knots twisted with fine Indian pearls, flashed and sparkled. I glanced at the monk, and pondered ruefully on his cosy garment, lined showily with Calabrian sable, so it looked. Oh, I was an expert on warm clothes!

'That would suit me a treat when the frost falls,' I said to myself. 'No more chattering with cold, no frozen calves, nor chills tickling my hump!'

Above me, there were already minstrels playing in the high gallery. The mewling viols vibrated with clear high voices singing a plaintive Murabba.

'Wait here,' the steward told me. 'Do you have your tricks?'

I pointed at my sack.

'Are you alone?' he asked.

'No,' I was proud of this moment. 'No, I come as juggler to Peire Carcasse.'

I stiffened up as straight as my hump would permit and looked straight into his eyes. The steward, a bandy-legged fellow with a plague scar on his right cheek, eyed me with faint amusement.

'So the mad troubadour has taken a helpmate,' he chuckled, not unkindly. 'Rather you than me. You wait here until their lordships call you.'

Taking a stool I slid as close as I could to the huge fireplace. The great logs burned evenly, an occasional spark exploding in a branch of beech or pine. There was a bowl of nuts in the corner, and for a moment, as I cracked them, tossing the kernels into my mouth and throwing the shells into the blaze, I thought of this person, this fellow they called Little Beast, Peire Carcasse's juggler, and of his state in life. I closed my eyes, and leant my head against the warm stone behind me.

My hump ceased to ache, my bones were tired, but easy in their sockets. There passed through my mind again an image of the little boy who'd been my uncle's son, of his curly head, of the sweet childish smell of his hair and soft skin, of his round lips forming the name Adam—the only human creature who'd ever used my name. I thought then of the cold years which had passed, my livelihood scratched unevenly across the length and breadth of d'Oc and Provence, from Foix and Fenouillet to Béziers, from Toulouse's bazaars in the rue de la Pourpointerie, to the seats of ancient learning at Narbonne and Montpellier. I remembered many a peasant hauling out his oxen at daybreak, as I trudged my road, with a torn blanket thrown over his shoulders. He'd be driving the beast to field, to yoke them to the plough, with a great field for his day's work, and only a snivelling boy, hoarse with cold and shouting, to hold the ox's head; and many a tenant farmer filling the bins that didn't belong to him, with the hay he'd sweated to save, watering cattle, carrying out the dung; and the labour of it, for he was not free. I remembered myself, mixing chalk taken from the earth, with flour, which the women would use for making something akin to bread. It made you vomit blood and gave you the colic, but it was like food. A thousand lean faces that had not had the strength to drag themselves around swam before my eyes, and the pits we'd dug once beneath Queribus, into which we'd dragged the dying quickly, so that the wolves would not get them first. I remembered the plague when it had briefly swept over the Pyrenees, pushing its way through the hamlets, sweeping villages clean, and the people fleeing from the buildings, the sick bundled into church for a belated miracle, and contaminating those who came to pray.

And I also remembered the patience which a sufferer has; and then the dull, dour obstinacy of these men who wrested freedom from their masters, hand over hand, until the patch of vine, the bullock, and the ox were theirs, and they could sell their wine in the towns, to the bonhommes, the well-to-dos. I thought of the laughter of these people on a feast day, when tumblers balanced cart-wheels on their hands and shoulders, when two blind men, armed with wooden swords would set upon each other, belabouring thin air; when the pirouette dancers came, circling slowly to the twanging of a viol, or when a little hunchback joined them with a red wigged beard, belching Greek fire from his mouth like the Devil, and pulling out a chair on which he'd turn strange tricks and acrobatics. And there slipped across my mind the castles I had passed, the abbeys where fat priests slobbered in their cups, the fortresses where the straying good men, the Cathari, would try humbly to preach a holy gospel and a one great God for all men and living things, who shared his bounty even with the poor, yes even with the poor they said, and gave faith in return for love. I thought of the wise men teaching science and philosophy at Montpellier, whom I'd seen once with my own eyes at the University, the followers of Aben-Ezra, and the Arab Jews from Cordoba and Seville who preached a mystic dream through the marvellous Sufi poetry.

And then at last my wandering thought touched on the vagabonds, the poets and wastrels whose songs echoed through the land. What did they say? That things aren't equal? That justice and the Pope, and whichever prince they'd taken a grudge to, had grown cock-eyed and foul? It takes a genius to see that, I thought to myself! How wonderful these strutting humans are, in their pride and wisdom; how sure the poet, the philosopher, the prince, and poetaster is, each of the baubles he carries himself, each of his own truth! How blinded are they to their neighbour's version of the tale! And how ridiculous we must seem, seen from the sky! And does it matter? I mumbled to myself. No one has my remembrance of little Bernard. No one else is juggler to my Master Peire. Me? I'm an old caterpillar, I suddenly realized with a chuckle. The earth's over my head, not the sky, and then just when it seems that I'll be crushed by the weight of it, along comes a man who wiggles his finger enough to loosen the earth, and I start crawling away as fast as I can to the surface. It's hard work with all that weight to carry, and remembering to move my legs properly, but who knows? Once I'm up into the light, maybe I'll become a butterfly!

3

Someone shook my shoulder.

'Hey, jongleur, wake up! Stop dreaming. You've been called up to the Lord Gazanhat. Mind your manners, eh?'

I climbed to my feet.

'Tell me something,' said the steward a little sheepishly. 'Is it true that Peire Carcasse can't be hurt by a priest, because he made a pact with the Devil as a child?' He coughed, and his eyes jumped around to make sure no one could overhear his superstition.

'All things considered, it's very possible,' I nodded wisely. 'Very possible!' My words had a weighty seriousness to them I felt. Approaching the great table, I glanced timidly at the throng of lords and ladies. How soft and sweet-smelling, how delicate they seemed! There was a fragility about them which amazed me. With their murmured words in strange languages, and their billowing voices which fluttered about me like exotic birds' wings, they appeared hardly real. How precious and noble they must be, I thought. It's people like these who have made our land the envy of the world.

There was a lady who particularly fascinated me. She sat to the right of the lord of the castle, with a little court of women about her. She spoke little, but the others were plying her with furtive questions, pulling her yellow damask sleeve, and hanging on the words that slipped from her lips. She was looking up towards the minstrels' gallery with glittering eyes, and a half smile touching the corners of her mouth. In the candlelight the wide sweep of her forehead was like a plain of alabaster. Her nose, a little heavy and semitic, curved down towards a full red mouth. It was a head that reminded me of a Greek mask I'd once seen in Montpellier—strong, daunting, and with a prophetic sadness in the tilt of the mouth, the shape of the eyes, the heavy harsh cheekbones. A confusion of black hair, wavy and rich with lights, leapt out from beneath the head-dress she wore. She turned her head, and I saw her profile. For a moment she was different. The mouth looked harder, the cheek-bones more pointed. She seemed suddenly like one of those sybils crept off the pages of some illuminated manuscript, whose eye could damn a man to an infinite hunger. Surely the candlelight was betraying me?

I wrenched my gaze away, and fell, clumsily as always, to one knee before Lord Gazanhat, and his chief guests at the high table whose roistering now quietened.

'What have we here!' exclaimed a precious, overhearty voice. 'A human bodkin, or I'm the Pope disguised. By God and St Christopher, it wearies me to drop my eyes on yet another hunchback. The sight's as bad as a damoselle who admires her own plump thighs too much to spread them, or a skinflint lord who mangles his serfs so as to squeeze a better yield. By St Marcel, this hunchback's worse to look on than a fat whore's shrivelled nether lips!'

The monk was in boisterous mood. I bit my lips, feeling the blood pulsing to my head, not daring to look at him. 'It was a joke,' I said to myself. 'He's on duty like me, to amuse their lordships, or they'll kick him back to Montaudran, to squabble in the cloisters with his eunuch brothers.' A voice broke in.

'Come, fellow, you're a jongleur are you not?'

'Yes, Sieur,' I murmured. 'Little Beast I'm called if it please your worship. Shall I conjure out my tricks?' The false smile slid over my face, the hypocrite was back in business . . . 'The Devil's fire, an act of miraculous acrobatics on the seat of a chair, my gold and silver balls are ready, and the rope . . .' I giggled fatuously.

Where was Peire, why had he not made an appearance?

'Are you not come with Peire Carcasse?' A lean, hardy nobleman leant forward, staring into me as if he'd read my thoughts.

'It is so, my lord.'

'And where is that paragon of virtue?' tittered my lord Gazanhat, flicking his hands dry from the silver rose bowl into which he'd dipped them. 'Shall we not have the pleasure of his folly?' He smirked at me, with raised eyebrows, watching me wipe the drops of water, still smelling faintly of roses, from my face.

'Even roses cannot sweeten the hunchback,' I grimaced.

The monk set to laughing heartily. 'What no master all of a

sudden?' His mottled nose twitched with mirth and the eyes protruded from pinched, yet over-fat cheeks, fixing me with malice rather than charity. A spy's face, a betrayer's face, I thought to myself suddenly. And then behind me the minstrels grew silent, a high voice died on a half-note, and the silence was greater. There was a crackling lute chord wrenched from the poor instrument's guts, a falsetto chuckle. Speech blurred at the tables, and a hundred heads turned, some with misgiving, some expectantly, towards the gallery. I knew it was him. There was laughter, and the sound of indrawn breaths. My eyes dragged upwards. Yes, my Master stood there. A mockery of grace. His face was pasted with rouge, and white powder, his lips daubed with red paint. He was dressed in a red silk gown, the white bodice was loose, and his naked chest burst from the seams. His voice was a high-pitched mimic . . .

> Gentle lords and ladies fair,
> In this Court of Love beware,
> Speak to little beasts with care
> Or Peire Carcasse will call your dare!

I began to dread what would follow, wondering if it would be possible to steal the monk's fur cloak at least, for when we'd be thrown out into the cold. I looked about for a place of retreat; the hall seemed vast, and the shadows were far away. Even the servants had slid in to watch, whispering at the doors in twos and threes. My eyes fell on the lady with the dark curls. Her nostrils flared slightly; the head jerked imperceptibly. Not entirely made of ice and witchery, I thought to myself with a grin. A bright flush was spreading over her features; it touched her ears, crept over her throat, rose lightly upon her bosom. Her smile, and her proudness had gone. In their place was anticipation, and an emotion, half disdainful, half afeared. She knew my Master. Now I understood! It must be the Lady Azelais, whom my Master called Aniara. This was the lady who had pricked Count Raimon's defences, who played shuttlecock with my Master, and many others doubtless. Glee sprang up in me, and I hugged the shiver of fear tight in my arms, for my Master's tongue, for the watchful silence in the great hall. The burning logs were rash to contradict the stillness with their crackling flames. The lute strings whispered sibilantly, and then Peire sang with his true voice. I thanked God and the Devil for that, at least. He would not dishonour the music . . .

> Now hear! I have a tale to tell
> For monks and lords, ladies as well;
> A tale of Paradise and Hell,
> This last, where all of us shall dwell.

'Easy does it, Messer. Don't go too far.' I cupped my ear nervously. 'Our bellies have been filled, we'll sleep warm and cosy, we've the easy life for a few days, if only you don't press too angrily upon them!'

> Now hear!
> I speak of Lady Love, who taxes youth,
> Who pulls the heart like an unlanced tooth,
> Who flares the embers in a man forsooth,
> Who sells false hopes disguised in Truth.
> Now hear my tear!

> Now hear!
> How love was true once on a time
> And love was loving in her prime,
> But grew a sting, a scorpion's spine
> Which I'd hack off if t'were no crime.
> So hear, my dear!

The scent was warming. The singer was vibrant and unleashed. 'Don't let him curse the monk,' I thought, 'or Lord Gazanhat, or . . .' The mask above me curled, showing its teeth, and his eyes danced over the guests . . .

> Now hear!
> Since love has learnt the evil guile
> To separate Truth from a smile,
> Like wax from honey, bliss from bile,
> It's time we put Dame Love on trial.
> So hear me clear!

'. . . or Aniara! Just this first time let him pass over her, and then tomorrow if we're thrown out, I'll make sure I'm stuffed full to the gorge. Will you make the bargain, good Master?' The melody whispered down to me, its gentleness and sweetness belied the words . . .

> Now hear!
> This Dame of Love I now condemn
> For unarmed murder of a thousand men,
> For chaining man to a perchance when
> She'll play the mare in his stallion's pen.
> You hear, Aniare?

I shrugged my shoulders.

> Her limbs shall wither 'ere the heat
> Of honest passion comes to greet
> Her falsity, her ageing meat.
> So shall she die
> Unsung, unmourned,
> Uncovered in her lie!

There was uproar. Lord Gazanhat was on his feet, perplexed and sweating fiercely. She had turned away, like a bird who tucks its head beneath a wing to hide from the light. Peire's last chords still echoed up to the high scalloped vaults. Ladies and damoselles clucked and stared, not knowing whether to be appalled or in tears, the knights and courtiers grew wroth and noisy with complaint.

'By God and the angels, that was too close to the bone!' cried the host. He glanced at his guests with a frown. 'No chivalry, eh noble brothers? The rapscallion shall pay for this discourtesy.' He glanced about him nervously, and it was clear he knew not what to do.

'What else do you expect from the Carcasse!' chided the lean-rimmed courtier with the short-cropped, iron-grey hair and humorous eyes.

'He lives close to the bone, and adds variety to our diet. And then we can celebrate the salvation of our damoselles and chatelaines! But look at his clothes, and pinked-up features! The fellow's joined the fairer sex!'

Lord Gazanhat blustered more gently of the dishonour to his court, voices were raised in favour of banishment and retribution, but they mingled now with the women's jibes at Peire's disguise.

A handle had been found to ridicule him, so the tension subsided. I caught the man's eyes who had turned aside the danger. He looked at me opaquely, but I thought to see briefly understanding, relief, and a warning flicker, before he turned his eyes to the gallery again.

I stared up at my Master. He'd taken no part in the debate. Now with eyes for no one but Aniara he ripped the bodice off his chest, using it to wipe the paint from his face. She ignored his gaze, and with much self control inclined her head this way and that, as she resumed conversation with the girls about her. I noticed that the colour was still high on her cheekbones, high and bright, and that the soft neck swelled and sank a little tremulously.

'Mad Peire Carcasse, I'm thinking you made mention in your ditty of a certain lady, disguised with a trobar clus. Who now could that be, who inspires such cruel treatment?' Gazanhat laughed shortly; he seemed unsure of how to turn his mood, and yet unable to release the bait.

It was the monk who riposted. 'Our minstrel is not to be taken over-earnestly as usual.' He mimicked a deep sigh. 'Poor soul, without mind or sense. Oh for a subtle lay, an erudite sirventes, an exercise in intellect, in studied craftsmanship, in magic trobar clus, from a Cercamon, or a Daniel! Something to awaken the brain, not to trample on it.'

'Shave-pated fool,' retorted Peire, 'your brain mistakes itself for a soul, and yet no one expects to find such a commodity in a monk!'

The monk's little eyes glittered. 'I shall die from the boredom of such melodrama.' He heaved a vast yawn, and cast his head in his hands, as though in despair. 'This man's salvation is my purgatory!'

'But you, namesake, poor Peire de Vic,' chuckled my Master, 'you wedded to a temperate life, to chastity and poverty. How could you not be unsexed? You love mankind, not us, not Tom, Dick, Harry. Not so? You plough in holy traces, and your furrows run not in our fertile soil, but from this stinking world to the next; or rather shall we say from d'Oc to Popish Rome. Your mind is on eternity, not love, and also on the price it costs a traitor to win a bull to paradise, selling off his countrymen as heretics!'

68

'Plague take you, Carcasse!' shouted the monk, nettled by the stinging laughter which saluted this remark. 'I've succoured more outlaws from the Church than you've set eyes upon.'

'Because it suited you to curry favour with the Lords of Terre d'Oc?' asked my Master in a low voice.

'And I've carried my skirts higher, left more wool on the hedges, and ploughed deeper than a hundred troubadours with their lily-limp members playing at exercise. And you should know, fool, that a priest's frock is better bait than the sugary ditties such as you unloose!'

'Sir priest, you talk too much.'

Gazanhat and the Lord Trencavel showed signs that they agreed.

The shave-pate flushed. 'Come down then, and I'll wring your neck if you can't keep pace with my drinking. By Corpus Christi you've made me a thirst that would overflow St Benedict's boot. Come down and risk that hapless neck of yours with this good juice, or by the rump of an untickled nun I'll come and get you!'

'You godless bag of bones, I'll drink with you,' Peire spoke wearily, 'though of all those to amuse, you amuse me least!'

'Off with your woman's clothes, Carcasse. By Christ these boasters and sorry liers on women make me fart.' He turned to his companions, winking and grimacing. 'Sieur Blacatz, have you lost your humour so soon? Does our speech offend you?'

'It lacks the edge of a Marcabru,' replied the thin-lipped one who had stared at me. 'It lacks the courtesy of one accustomed to the presence of damoselles, but then you're from a cloistered species.' The lips wrinkled faintly. 'But why do you curse like a whore-master, sturdy Abbot of Montaudran?'

The monk was ill at ease, and recognized the laughter cutting against his lurching wit. Tongue slipped across his lips. 'Just a little colour that I picked up from my studies in Ciceronian rhetoric,' he laughed. 'Tinsel to adorn a plain man's prose.'

'Indeed, Sieur Blacatz,' called out Peire gaily, descending from the gallery, 'I think we shall be deafened by these Ciceronian farts, and will soon have to hide underground, for safety from the popish odours that assail our land!'

'My poor Carcasse, it's true! We serve our times but passively, and play into fate's hand.'

His eyebrows rose humorously, and as he spoke the harsh lines on either side of his nose creased more deeply, more cynically. His voice, directed at Peire, was dry, penetrating, but deep for a man of his light build. He looked brittle, cunning, but not cruel. I thought he had affection for my Master. I thought also that he had the restraint and patience of real curiosity, to study both his friends and enemies attentively.

My Master caught sight of me and, unslinging his lute from his shoulder, came over to clap me on the back.

'So Little Beast, we're warm, we're fed, are we not? And we've sung a little for our supper.'

'But it was a near thing,' I whispered to him. 'I could have wished for more peaceful chords, if it please you,' I grinned weakly. 'Shall I string my viol?'

'Why not? Go join the minstrels, and take my place. They'll breathe more easily!'

He turned away, his eyes lingered briefly on Aniara, who plucked courage up, and held his gaze, though the colour faded from her face.

'She changes temperature as fast as sunshine on an autumn day,' I chuckled, and hopped across the flagstones.

He made her a small obeisance, and then continued round the table. Making a deep reverence to the Lords Trencavel and Gazanhat, and placing a hand on his heart, he begged indulgence.

'A dispensation is all I ask, my lords. The moment caught me, like a dry log on a fire, and I burst in flames. A note of discord sometimes makes the merriment more keen. Is it not so? I hope at least the damoselles will forgive an ardent heart, and even the good Abbot?'

'What! And abandon a religious debate once started? Not for all the churls and fools in Christendom would I keep my peace; it would be a failure in my invested duty, even if I'm forced to pit my wits against this most infected and profane of savages.'

'Let's keep our arguments less loud and thunderous, or else we'll be turned out of favour with the damoselles,' smiled Trencavel smoothly.

'You spoke of wind, sir minstrel,' gobbled the monk. 'A wind from Rome wasn't it? Well the sinners shall indeed be deafened by this wind: deafened and blinded by its roar. The wicked shall sink into their own excrement, Carcasse, but the virtuous and godly shall be uplifted, and borne to heaven on this mighty blast!'

'In whose excrement do you wallow, sweet Peire?' My Master's knuckles gleamed pale on the chair-head behind Blacatz. 'No doubt you sit and fill that swollen belly, and sit and squat between your sister's lust and treachery, so as to get a better look at virtue; in case this mighty blast gets a hold of your skirts and blows you to the next world before you've prayed Amen to dirty life!'

'Don't go too far,' muttered the other. 'A chain of ears carry your remarks to Rome.'

Peire's voice rose above his adversary's. 'It's you who feed on the excrement of our world, on human tragedy, on weakness, sin, on frailty, sipping and cherishing each wretched morsel, until your jaded palates know no other remedy for living than death. You're like the pet monkey in my liege lady's chamber, like all false preachers, who live like parasites on men's souls. You guard not your domain like the dog. You disdain to haul the plough as does the ox, you don't clothe our backs like the sheep, nor feed us like the cow, nor lighten our burden as does the horse or mule. After defiling your monastic cage, you escape into the world, full of lies, tricks, and cunning. At first you're amusing, for we stare into your spiteful features, and see our own reflected there. We watch your antics, listen to your endless chattering, and fancy that we hear a mimicry of human hearts and craft. But it is not that. Your kind have not the concentration to maintain a thing once started. You live off the eagerness, simplicity, and faith of others. One day surely, when the land grows weary of you, you'll try to steal our souls, and sell them, out of viciousness and hatred, to a foreigner who strokes your perfumed fur and tells you, "Good little monkey, afterwards you'll have the entrails!"''

I watched him from above, sawing I don't know what music from the viol. Gazanhat, dabbing a kerchief about his wet face, seemed on the point of tears. He teetered to his feet.

'Our guest, the Abbot of Montaudran, will, I hope, forgive us this, um, coarse interruption. Just a boisterous mistake, ha, ha!' He choked and faltered. 'But we do him grave discourtesy. We have much to be grateful for. Our brave Abbot has the ear of the Papal Legate, you know. We have his blessing here at our

Court of Love, and on our activities. We live, may I remind you, in the fold of Mother Church, in the fold! We live in peace, with power and wealth, no writs and bulls of condemnation to disturb our serenity . . .'

'Fail not to add, my lord,' broke in Peire with a laugh, 'that the world swoons in admiration for our learned parts, and courts our favour in the art of love and life, and luxury. The which must therefore be more carefully protected. By all means let's forget that Raimon went to Italy on his knees, for fear of destitution and excommunication.'

Gazanhat's cheeks sagged and puckered with rage. Wetting his lips nervously, he glanced about him for support. 'It shall not be said that we were party to d'Oc's fall from Papal grace for cause of loud-mouthed minstrels and vagabonds. Remember that, Peire Carcasse, and stick to your ditties!'

A glance passed between Peire and Blacatz. The chattering ceased. Benches creaked, plates tinkled, and my viol whined on.

'If we have not already fallen from this precious state of grace,' murmured the Sieur Blacatz.

The Abbot of Montaudran rose from his chair. One white hand supported his balance, palm stretched on the table. The old raillery and gluttonous malice had left him. There was no foolishness in him now. His face looked bigger, wide and loose with ugliness, because I saw it from above. It was filled with a kind of exaltation which transformed his features. The muddy pouches under his eyes had relaxed, and his expression of fatigued satiety was now replaced with one of energy and brutality. You judged him ill before, I noted ruefully.

'The Lord Gazanhat is right,' he declared briskly. 'Of course we won't misunderstand the jests that have passed amongst us.' Then he paused. 'But we certainly won't forget these jests,' there was an inflection on the word, 'nor their origins . . . It's rash to vilify the Church, Peire Carcasse—very rash—and dangerous . . . You called me, in jest, I noted, a monkey. I call you, more courteously, a very vulnerable sinner. Perhaps even a future martyr, Peire Carcasse. A martyr for the Church, of course. Dear friends, it's wise—isn't it—to remember just how much authority the Church has. Some call it power. Rash word "power",' he shrugged, 'but occasionally appropriate. And power must be protected against abuse. For the good of men naturally!' He beamed good-naturedly about him. 'The Church has power to guard her own, power to save sinners, even those sinners who show no inclination to be saved.' The Abbot snickered, 'Perhaps you'll want to ask why Mother Church finds it necessary to maintain so much . . . authority? Surely Peire Carcasse has an answer?' The small eyes narrowed at my Master.

But Peire did not speak for a moment. Weariness seemed suddenly to have touched him. And then slowly and painstakingly he spoke. 'You wield power to hold and to destroy, because the having of it is habit-forming and becomes a disease. "You hold the truth," you'll say, "and men are too frail to endure it without direction and leadership. Freedom from your orthodoxy, dogma, freedom from a tyrant is unthinkable," you'll say, "because man rots and falls apart in liberty. His puppet strings are broken. He cannot wag alone." But you wield power in the end to substitute God's kingdom with your own, tossing tit-bits of land, gold, and immortal dust in the eyes of the princes and barons who help maintain your equilibrium.'

Lord Gazanhat jumped to his feet. 'Stop your filthy talking,' he shouted. 'Don't you understand that your rebelliousness threatens us all?'

Peire roused himself with an effort, but before he could open his mouth, a woman's voice broke out clearly. 'Speak on Sieur Carcasse. Will you be cowed by such words?' Her tones were light and mocking. Peire glanced at the Sieur Blacatz, and then sought my eyes in the gallery.

'It's the Church you seek to immortalize, not God,' he said gently.

The monk, not at all put out, tucked his hands up the copious sleeves of his habit, and eased his feet. 'Even a liar and damned heretic can know something of the truth, it appears.' His voice had taken on a dreamy quality. There was something monstrous, and predatory about him. 'But let us, dear friends, be sure of this!' Iron assurance gripped his words. 'Power is peace. Power is also the destruction of any individual who stands apart. Power is the eternal guardian of the faithful.' He looked thoughtfully about him.

The guests shifted restlessly, their eyes moving surreptitiously from the monk, to Peire, to the Sieur Blacatz, occasionally pausing to alight, with a flicker of disdainful reproach, on the perspiring features of their host.

'Power means one law of redemption, one justice, one road to salvation, one road to hell and torture. The Christian one, my friends. Power is confusion harnessed to the plough of God—in other words the Church—confusion trained to walk along the furrows where the seeds of faith are sown. Confusion, like "legion", is Man.' The little eyes flickered with amusement.

'I was in Sahagun,' said Peire, over the heads of the guests, 'in Spain, shortly after the monks of Cluny had installed themselves. They were very busy, and their vision of power was most elevating. They were even so meticulous as to issue decrees forbidding the inhabitants to bake their bread elsewhere than in the convent's ovens on pain of imprisonment. They prohibited the gathering of fuel until they had enough themselves, and they took all there was. They prohibited the selling of wine until the monks had sold theirs. No meat, no vegetables, no cloth, no footwear could be bought until the needs of the monastery had been fully met. The convent lands were the richest and the most fertile in the area, the villagers were left the marshes, and the rocks. When they had devoured the last remnants of their pride, these people worked for nothing beneath the shave-pates' whips. And they starved. If it interests you there are a hundred other similar cases, a thousand.'

'It interests me hardly at all,' murmured the monk softly.

Peire's great head, with the vein throbbing across the temples, was thrown up. He waited for the other to face him. His black wiry hair, combed and glinting now, fell about his face like unruly shadows. The swinging firelight touched him fitfully to catch an expression of burning distaste, or once, as his glance passed Aniara and swept over the courtiers, a shudder of strange fearfulness.

'And you dare admit it,' muttered Peire. 'God, how this country must suffer!' He straightened. 'But the Abbot has surely his justifications! The meek shall inherit the earth, or is it that only the poor shall inherit the kingdom of Heaven? And these monks of Cluny did but offer a better chance of salvation to the people over whom they came to wield authority. Indeed I'm slow. That must certainly be the answer.'

'Yes, Peire Carcasse,' responded the monk sibilantly, 'there is a piece of truth there. The Church, when one thinks on it, almost invented suffering. I mean in the collective sense of the word. Suffering for salvation that is!' The words slipped out like a schoolmaster's lecture. 'It's an interesting point.'

'Your thoughts, your words, monk, reflect nothing but the chasm into which your own soul flies; they offer little towards salvation!'

'A brave cockerel, this Carcasse, no?' The Abbot cast a glance about him. For a moment they stared at each other. The shave-pate's eyes dropped. Peire laughed harshly.

'But the world is changing, and the power of your kind is withering, even as you deploy the forces that could destroy us. Those forces, those Iron Men whom you believe to fight for Christendom, fight to supersede you. The world is changing Peire de Vic, and the forces of despotism, jealousy and in-humanity will grasp the power which was yours . . . because we— we men of Occitanie—*compromise* with violence instead of fight-ing it. Our tragedy is that there are not enough men left to wage war against this new order of violence. There are too few who see this coming change. There are too few who would grasp this change and direct it . . . and our people will wallow in fear, in horror, through a long night of chaos . . .'

'Speak up minstrel, your voice grows faint,' cried his adversary. 'And afterwards . . . who will be left from this chaos?'

Peire ignored him, and turned to the whole company. 'My lords, most gentle ladies,' he frowned at them, 'I appeal to you now with my uncouth laughter and tears; I appeal to your secret energy, to that part of your spirit which seeks to surpass itself . . . Let *us* be the ones to grasp the change and to direct it. Let us be the ones to sow the seeds for a new revolution in Occitanie. Let us be brave, and hardy enough, to relinquish tranquility and to say to ourselves, "We, men of Terre d'Oc, shall forget self-pity, we shall forget old grudges, we shall build a new dream on the rights of man; rights to both spiritual and temporal food and freedom." The battle is truly thrust upon us, my lords. We fight, or die like slaves.'

'There'll be many dead men left in the chaos,' sniggered the monk.

'There'll be men left in search of their souls, priest. They will be legion. There'll be men left, holy men, whose wisdom is only

75

understood through God's anguish for mortals. We shall count them on the fingers of one hand. And they will heed those in anguish. All Occitanie will suffer because of you, and suffer destroying you and everything you have once stood for. We shall suffer long after your breed has left the earth, hollow in our loneliness and independence . . . until we learn to live again, with our solitude, before God, the Devil and our fellow-men.'

He turned away, the great shoulders sagged. I was unnerved to see my Master so naked suddenly, and shivering.

'My species, Peire Carcasse, which is the Church, which is Christianity, will most certainly survive. You may not, on the other hand!'

'What a childish threat,' muttered Peire, with a grimace.

'You say that men will suffer. It will be because of beasts like you. But yes, minstrel, you're right. Men will suffer!' The abbot chuckled faintly. 'But now I'm afraid they'll suffer mostly because the Faith requires their suffering.' The monk was still cool in his speech, but the anger was flaming up in him, and mottling his cheeks. 'And we'll have martyrs, no doubt. Yes, we'll still need martyrs, but they'll be anonymous. They won't exist except as cyphers, testifying to the Church's authority. Otherwise they won't exist at all, my worthy friends. Very sad. And in the future these martyrs will always be more faceless. The reason's very simple.' He smiled gently about him. 'The Church conditions our times, and history in the making always needs justifications. Where else to turn than to the Church? So it's us, I mean Rome and the Faithful, who ink in the footnotes and wipe out the extraneous matter across History's pages.'

His sly ominous threats now held the hall in thrall. Many a knight cast his eyes down to his plate, shifting uneasily. Even Gazanhat looked grey about the eyes. Blacatz was shaking his head almost imperceptibly at my Master. I trembled for him, for he was branded now.

'So let's not be rash,' spat the shave-pate, 'let's not be overbold. Suffering is for the chosen few. It's terribly hard for ordinary mortals; even unnecessary! There are no heroes in the teeth of pain, eh? And certainly no heroes outside the Faith. Let's not be rash when we make our little protests. Unnecessary little protests, that quickly come to grief, I assure you. It would be such a pity, when a perfectly acceptable bending of the knee can turn the possibility of misery into those joys that we, for example, experience here, and in all corners of Terre d'Oc, unstained by heresy.' He coughed once, twice, winding down the curtains to his performance. 'I'm sure you'll forgive my discursive mood, understanding the charitable spirit . . .' his voice drifted away. 'A man can be saved in so many ways.'

I noticed that he wouldn't look Peire in the face any more. That worried me more than all the rest. He smiled his old bemused grin, half subservient, half mocking once more, and sat down again, nodding and twitching at the ladies and damoselles, as though he'd never left off admiring them.

My Master, after staring at him for a long moment, shook his head in shock and comprehension, and took his seat next to Blacatz.

'Thank you Peire de Vic for your words of reassurance,' said the Sieur Blacatz silkily. 'How truly you speak when you say that our fate lies in God's hands—you did mention that, did you not? And the Pope's of course. This Pope who does proxy as estate agent for the Almighty. Shall we quibble if the Church gives us a stool in Paradise in exchange for our lands on earth? I mean, if crowns are bartered with fiefdoms, independence and freedom, for safe passage to eternity, shall we poke our avaricious snouts into argument with the Church? Shall we quibble, Peire de Vic? And when Grace takes on the pleasing proportions of a properly nourished gentleman in Holy Orders, who contemplates us with compassion, surely I'll be grateful, and humbly lay me down to worship him, made as he is, in the image of the Pope, nay . . . even in God's image perhaps?' He sighed deeply, and shrugged. 'I for one will not quibble. Instead I'll pawn my birthright, poor thing that it is, for peace of mind, and fear of excommunication. We're humans after all. Poor weak creatures. Don't you agree Lord Trencavel, Lord Gazanhat?'

The first of these looked confused, as though he was longing to join the debate, but knew not how to insert his wheel. The second looked comically glum. Trencavel opened his mouth.

'But shall we not . . .' he started.

'But we cannot expect mere knights and courtiers,' continued Blacatz smoothly, 'to seize fate by the throat. Besides it would be sacrilege to seize the Pope's throat, wouldn't it, abbot? Almost worse than a quibble. Let's rather draw comfort, as the worthy

77

monk bids us, from the attention with which Holy Church protects our more immortal parts. That is indeed relief, and a vast improvement, is it not, on . . . protest!'

Peire de Vic listened to the conversation more with his eyes and gaping mouth, than with his ears. He sat, as still and concentrated as a heaving toad, and with a similar unconcern.

'Good neighbours,' broke in Lord Trencavel, 'but you talk heedlessly! You misjudge our times, this age of excellence, this newborn century! Do we not stand on the threshold of a glorious renaissance? Are we not labouring to give heaven-guided birth to the wonders in science and art which our civilization creates? Every day, we step farther and closer to an understanding of our universe, to grasping the meaning of the stars, the causes of sickness, the inspiration of man-made beauty in all its forms. What have we to fear from hostile strangers?'

'How rightly, how truly, he speaks,' murmured the monk.

'Our realms in Terre d'Oc and Provence have a hundred thousand brave knights to defend their borders . . .'

'Whose lances, forgive the interruption my lord, are cork-tipped that the ladies do not swoon at murder in the lists.' Peire spoke jestingly but Blacatz stared at him with warning.

'But our land,' continued Trencavel with youthful gravity, 'remains the mirror into which our neighbouring peers look for reassurance, and a kind of immortality. We are rather an inspiration to be followed!'

'Indeed, indeed,' said Peire de Vic, patting his hands together in genteel agreement.

'Or a glass to be shattered,' cried my Master losing restraint, 'for such reality reflected in a man's eyes hurts to the quick! Or a lesson to be mastered; a pearl, cold with ill-use, to be snatched and warmed again.'

From my perch in the minstrels' gallery, I watched. The viol hung silent by my side. I thought of the peasants we had travelled with. 'Or a dream to be buried,' I said to myself, not angrily (I had no status to be angry) but in wonderment. 'Ask your peasants who die for you!'

'Enough! Enough now, my good lords! We forget our better selves, and our fair companions. Let's not stir up useless bitterness,' pleaded Lord Gazanhat, 'when so much beauty sits about us unattended!'

Trencavel smiled, the argument was dropped, lost and past. He threw a pouch to Peire, my Master. 'Even wicked minstrels and vagabonds must live,' he said, casting a sly grin at the priest, and trying, I felt, to look older than his years. He was hardly bearded, the fair hair sprouted patchily on his chin, but a strong open nobleman he was, with lusty features, and a spark of poetry written on his forehead and in the wide eyes.

My Master bowed, gave thanks respectfully I was glad to see, and then asked if he might do his whim with the gift. Trencavel nodded, and to my horror, Peire emptied out the half in glittering gold on the table. The pouch he threw in a great arc up to the gallery where I nearly broke my viol in catching it.

'My share of gold,' he said laughing, 'in order that I may escape the sin of greed and avarice, shall go to God!' Scooping up the coins in his hands he showered them upon the Abbot. 'And for the upkeep of my soul.'

The coins spun and trickled on the table. The monk flicked them one by one into his palm. He turned away and the Sieur Blacatz led him amongst the ladies. But I'd seen the expression with which Peire de Vic received my Master's gift. I hoped never to be too close to such hatred, in a man.

'Small assistance he'll render us in Heaven,' I grumbled bitterly. 'And certainly not worth losing a little comfort on this earth for!'

The minstrels had begun to tune up. I chorded my instrument once more, as the boy started to sing Bernard de Ventadorn's famous pastoral . . .

Joi ai de lui, e joi de la flor; I joy in the song, I joy in the flower,
Joi ai de me, e de midons major; I joy in myself, but in my lady more.

From time to time I looked down. The ladies and damoselles had crossed the floor, raising their swirling skirts from the dust. They sat about the great fireplace. Sometimes their whispering and tattling swelled, and I caught a word or a phrase. The violent language, the threats which had passed between priest and minstrel, had been forgotten. They did not mean anything. There was no danger. If there was it was infinitely far away. There was no danger to them.

'He's ugly,' whispered one, 'and he stutters.'

'Not always. Never when he sings.'

'What a temper,' lilted another voice. 'Does he pretend his insults like everyone else.'

'No, but when he sings what does it matter! It's like a waterfall which chokes you as you stand beneath it.'

'Would that he sang for me,' giggled another voice.

'You'd be known and praised throughout Terre d'Oc perhaps, but who knows when his sting would turn on you!'

'Why is it that he only sings for Aniara now. It's hardly fair when there are so many of us yearning for a little glory!' A tinkle of laughter greeted this.

The knights and courtiers began to mingle with their fairer companions. Peire was joking noisily with Blacatz. Lord Gazan-hat had left the table and was approaching Aniara, looking hot, worried and swollen, like an overgrown pumpkin. Was she his lady wife?

Now and again the fire threw out a spark, blazed, crackled noisily when the wind heaved down the chimney to be greeted by a squeal. Two yawning wolf-hounds sprawled on the flag-stones, toasting their eyeballs before the blaze. We played on, with a scent of musk and heavy perfume drifting to our nostrils, the voices murmuring gently below, as if, with the hour, thoughts changed, turned to the pleasures of a kiss, a tremulous caress, a lover's lullaby, the secret pleasures of the bedchamber. Velvet and taffeta, leather doublet and silk bodice brushed, touched, and the sexes reunited before sleep called them to their nightly stations. Little Beast watched with large eyes, a little loneliness, a wink of envy in his heart.

4

We spent many days, weeks at Gazanac. My Master seemed often in high spirits, and would play the unexpected fool to the courtiers' sallies. Peire de Vic had fallen back into his boisterous, heavy-humoured mood, and there were no references to that first bitter evening. The abbot, I noticed, watched the Sieur Blacatz with attention and respect, wary of the other's gaze, and obsequious in his presence. I was lulled to carelessness on a solid stomach, soft clean straw at night, a warm blanket, and the look of affection that Peire cast on me when he thought my mind was elsewhere.

I'd struck up an acquaintance with one of the scullery wenches. Like so many others, she was nervous and cat-curious about my sack. People are odd creatures. If I were a woodman carrying firewood, or a tinker with his pots and pans rattling merrily in a bag on his shoulders, no one would pay me a second glance. But my patched and darned old sack rattles in a hundred secret ways, and my wares are never emptied on the floor as some do, but picked out and brought into the light like mysteries. Indeed, a mummer or a juggler must know the art of bringing a person's longing to life; if he can magnetise an audience into fascination at the secret held in an empty fist, he's worth something! A madman is invented in other people's minds, like my Master said, and if he *knows* his madness, such people give him the power to work miracles out of air. Agnes, my scullery maid, would sometimes watch me for hours, entranced at the way one juggling sphere would vanish after another, only to reappear from my sleeve or out of my hump as though called up by the Devil. Her friendliness too was unassumed, and her gaiety infectious when the black monkey—it was Peire's expression—crept on to my shoulder, and nothing else could lift the mood; though I would have wished her eyes to follow suit more closely!

Even the lunatic we'd picked up in the ruined church, and brought to Gazanac, seemed more content, and less prone to raging prophecies. I once danced with him in the stable to

humour the creature, though his twisted limbs and my lop-
sided gait managed only a sorry measure to the tunes he screeched
in my ears. Sometimes he'd crumple up in a corner and juggle
with my spinning balls as well as a professional. But he never
relinquished that crazy laugh. I grew accustomed to him, to his
moments of silence when he'd look slowly upon me, on Agnes
if she was there, to the occasional smile that would light up his
face, to his hands that wriggled like mice or butterflies. He had
a strange trick. At those times when his face cleared, and his
eyes focused out of the blurred, lost country where he lived,
there came a moment when he seemed to understand the world
about him. This wrought a terrible change. His hands would fly
to his cheeks, scratching and scratching at the skin, into the
hollow eyes, at his cracked mouth; he'd fling his head this way
and that, covering his eyes, and moaning the while. There'd be a
pause, the hands would creep down from his features, releasing
them once more to public scrutiny, and the loose mouth, the
blurred, sightless eyes mocked us from a face disoccupied, like
a house without lights at night. The horror of his life struck me
deeply. The pity in me ebbed and rose, but more often it was
fear that tugged me when I watched him.

Then one day he was gone. Agnes said that he'd slipped past
the castellan at dusk, tripping and shaking, with his staff to hold
him upright, and muttering in his sing-song madness that Peire
Carcasse had not done with him.

'Not by any means, it seems! Not only shall we meet in dreams,
he he!'

Such was his parting gift, directed at the porter. The foolish,
senseless rimes were for me the more sinister because his wits
still permitted him to versify.

After that first night, my Master's songs were gentle, full of
guile and courtesy. He sang many of the traditional azajal, culled
and altered from the wonderful Diwan of Ibn Quzman, writing
in the speech of ordinary mortals, in our Romance idiom. But
Peire rarely sang his own songs now. He too had become watchful. Sometimes he would ask me to sing a sirventes that he'd
reshaped, an attack on the uncouth French clerks and barons, or
on indelicate husbands who refuse faithful druery to their
lemans, and who likewise scream and snarl when their wives

take a belami after their own hearts; but the fire and honesty were not in him. I felt it keenly. And ribaldry, coarse speech, even the dry lust of a Marcabru or Arnaud Daniel was foreign to his true singing. It hurt me to play for him, though such ditties were well-worn and acceptable enough to those who clapped our performances, and tittered like senile old men before a naked whore . . .

> Three 'scape me naked down the corridor,
> A fourth I plough her on the wing,
> A fifth pants waiting at the door,
> My shaft her whorishness doth sting,
> Upon her back,
> Limbs slack,
> She satiates my lack
> 'Till passion's lost her spring!

The good moments were when he and the Sieur Blacatz would exchange a 'Tenson' on the reality of Love or Courtly Measure. They both knew how to prick each other's wit, like soap bubbles bursting in the eye, so that the words stung sharp and true. It was good to see him then. I was proud of his poetry. My viol sang with his lute strings. When the harsh voice leapt high, or tried to mute its wild rough edge, and I saw that even the Lady Azelais' head was turned up to the gallery, it made me glad to be jongleur to such a music-maker.

On that particular afternoon, a heavy snowstorm had forced the huntsmen to call off the chase. The wide horns piped a mournful retreat, the boar hounds bayed and fretted as they were brought once more to the leash, their lean backs bobbing and threshing across the white fields. Lord Gazanhat was in bad temper. He'd been wanting to show off his black hound Dragonard to the young Master of Béziers and Carcassonne. But Lord Trencavel had other interests which craved his attention more; among them was a lithe, blithe, innocent-eyed girl called Staphanie, of the house of Guillaume de Montpellier. She looked to me (when I watched her fluttering a pretty mouth and long lashes in the mirrors at table), she looked to me bored with her well-preserved virginity. So the Lord Trencavel had not gone to the chase. The noblemen and knights were quickly served by their varlets and, after changing to softer clothes, had dispersed, many moving towards the women's quarters.

The ladies and damoselles had taken their siestas and, as was the custom, the minstrels had then been invited to play their best pieces. The concerts and dances were usually of a higher quality when we played in their chambers. Voices were muted, and attention paid us, so that each strove to do his utmost. The lutes quivered, voices rang high and light. There was a young boy who pleased the ladies with his fluting treble voice, and the men, or some of them, with his girlish flushed cheeks and coy glances. Belatedly the chatelaine came in. She'd thrown a shawl about her shoulders, and wore a pale grey linen robe with wide sleeves, which sank to the ground like the folds on a marble statue. Her eyes were slow, and still heavy with sleep, and her features for a moment were vulnerable to the men's bold glances. Softly, with a lilting voice that I hadn't heard before, she asked the Sieur Blacatz for a 'Tenson'.

'With whom shall I perform?' he asked Aniara.

She smiled lightly at him. Her hands separated and rose, as though to say 'Should I know the answer to such a question?'

Their 'Tenson' quickly developed into a contest to see who could create the quickest response, properly riming and maintaining to the melody. Sieur Blacatz had a smooth low voice, and it framed well with Peire's that was rougher and more urgent. My Master started shyly: he always told me that he could sing to one woman about love, but not to a dozen at the same time. I think that was part of his gift, for each woman or girl who listened to him felt that it was to her that he directed his words. This time he even stuttered at the beginning, but I was aware that he had something to say, and had already listened to his mind in private so as to clear his thoughts. He rebuked the Courts of Love for turning joy and mystery into a clever art. Today the art of Love, he said, looks more for definition and information than to possess the truth, truth not only in the soul but also in the body . . .

> Blacatz, to you I leave the waiting,
> Let 'Measure' be your baiting,
> Desire seeks joyous mating,
> To the target speeds my dart.

And Blacatz replied with a sly grin . . .

> Carcasse! You trample Love with hasting,
> Your leman's not for wasting,
> And Passion grows with fasting,
> It's Hunger feeds the heart . . .

So they continued to the chuckles and sighs of the company. The damoselles wished to hear Peire; they wished to be frightened and caressed with that breaking voice of his, and to have those devil's eyes upon them, if only for a moment. They'd skip up to him with their languishing eyes and wrists aflutter.

'It's as if they were screwing their courage to its seat so as to stare the dragon eye to eye better,' I chuckled to my Master.

I'd catch him squinting at them with misgiving. 'Little Beast,' he'd murmur, 'what do they want with me, with this scarecrow? Can't they see that I'm a renegade to their "art" of Love: that I hate their peace and harmony. Don't they see that I'd destroy their well-being? These creatures have the reality of shadows playing on a wall at sunset.'

'But poetry and music too, Master—they're made by all of us.'

'If that's true, then why can't they see the emptiness in me, and its deadliness?' He fixed me with his luminous, furious eyes.

I opened my mouth, and he watched me with interest, until the curtain suddenly fell across his expression, while I stumbled out my friendly words.

'Pity be damned! Damned, Little Beast. Are we such cowards that we shall not face their music too?' He grimaced wryly.

I hung my head.

Others took up their instruments. Flutes tinkled, viols and cymbals clashed gently. Later there came a lull in the music. Knights and ladies drew together seeking a window-seat or a corner-bench, where over the dice or a chess game they could murmur their privacies. Lord Trencavel was seated next to the ripe Staphanie in one of the window casements, and had made hostage of her hand.

'A lady's belami should never be of higher estate than she! Brave knights and damoselles would take her for a courtesan.'

She blushed and giggled, fending him off to little purpose, and rolling her eyes comically at Aniara. I watched him biting his lips, a flush of irritation crept over his young cheeks. Baulked of immediate access to the maid's citadel, he sought another entrance.

The Lady of Gazanac, sleep gone from her eyes, had taken up a corner of the great embroidery which her women were executing under her orders. I'd heard that it was for the monastery where her nephew had recently taken his vows. It was to go behind the altar. Though she worked little on it herself, it was clear that she took great interest in its progress, and had much taste, choosing the colours, and designing additions round the great star and the mythical beasts and figures already drawn on the rough weave. From those parts which she allowed others to see, it seemed to tell a kind of fairy-tale in pictures. The work had been in progress since before our arrival, and advanced slowly, but its beauty was such that all the damoselles and ladies paused to admire her art. Even Blacatz, his words for once unfeigned and generous, had stooped to render his hommage. The gold threads picked out here and there with vivid greens and reds on the cornflower-blue background—it was her favourite colour—were so harmonious that no Bird of Paradise's feathers could have been more rich or magical.

Now she was pricking out the form of a Unicorn, symbol of solitude and mystery, with neat, flying fingers. She worked with deep concentration, as though she put all her heart into the labour. Only occasionally would she look up round the room, her eyes alighting on Staphanie with a twinkle of amusement, or once, more uncertainly, on the Little Beast. Although there were girls about her, she had, like the unicorn she laboured upon, a stillness and a spirit of solitude which enveloped her—that seemed to guard her from the throng.

'No beauty lasts much,' I thought to myself, 'except if there's a flash of it hidden in your heart. That's when you're lucky. Perhaps she's trying to put what's in her heart on to the work. Perhaps that's what makes it beautiful.' My brain lumbered slowly. 'But beauty or joy, it's a bit like chasing fireflies: hard to catch and harder still to keep alight once captured.'

A slip of a girl detached herself from the group around our chatelaine and bobbed up to me.

'My lady craves a word with you,' she simpered.

I started. 'With the Little Beast?'

She nodded at me reassuringly. 'You have magic in your fingers, she says.'

'Your mistress is too generous with praise, but the music is fairly honoured.' I hesitated, feeling Peire's eyes on me.

'Are you frightened of my lady?' She stared curiously into my lop-sided face.

'Frightened?' I grinned shortly.

My Master's gaze fell away. His hands were shaking. 'Frightened? Is it possible?'

She was seated on a carpet-covered chest.

'My lady wished to see me?' I bowed. 'Not my Master?'

Her eyes were dark and deep-set. She looked me straight in the face. Her head was tilted upwards, the chin firm and forward. 'You play well—do you talk as prettily of chivalry?' And then half-aloud I heard her add: 'As does your Master?'

I remained silent, and she pointed me to a stool close by her. The embroidery was put away, and I watched one white hand playing with the fine gold chains that hung around her neck. The damoselles sitting about her chattered and giggled amongst each other. She clapped her palms. 'My sisters, let's sing a song to distract our minstrel from his sombre mood. And remember,' her voice relaxed, 'you sing for a real musician!'

Their voices hummed softly in descant. She watched him for a moment, her hands steadied, and intertwined on the small knees. The knuckles were pale, and she wore no rings which was unusual.

'You know how to play to his voice,' she said, 'you give it back what he tries to destroy—the fear and pity.'

I kept my eyes down, because I was nervous of her expression, but her voice was hard, and the words came out like pebbles, thrown into the sea at regular intervals. She glanced at her maids to make sure they couldn't overhear us.

'Do you know of me?' she asked abruptly.

'Yes, Ma'am.'

'And what do you know?'

I wondered what she wanted from me. Praise? Peace? Knowledge of my Master? I listened, for a moment, feeling the expectancy in her, but more clearly the cool discipline she kept upon herself. Her arrogance towards her beauty made me uneasy and fearful. Even the Little Beast looked on his reflection in the

87

mirror with friendliness; hate and pity sometimes too, but mostly with friendliness now. She appeared to despise her beauty, and by doing so, to overrule it. Thus she had authority over men, I thought, but surely you can't be a dictator over territory you don't recognize?

'You know of my embroidery at least. That you may praise if you like!' She glanced at me with haughty amusement. 'But what else?'

'I think I know, saving your presence, that your beautiful embroidery unveils a mystery which your heart perhaps doesn't care to disclose.'

'Is this a riddle?' Her laughter was slow and supercilious.

'The work, to a humble musician, is full of grace and desire.'

'How can that be, jongleur?'

I felt the slight she put on me; her marking of the social distinction between a chatelaine and a lowly, itinerant jongleur, who dared discern her feelings.

'It lacks the careless hauteur of its creator!' I said shortly. 'Though it is perhaps for such things that you are so much admired by men.'

'You must continue with your revelations,' she said softly.

'I believe, my lady, that sometimes the mystery of great beauty is increased when a man is unable to penetrate it.'

'Is that *your* thought revealed?'

'No, my lady,' I stumbled, 'no, it's my . . .'

She interposed swiftly. 'Tell me more. Don't blush! Your looks require pallor to be seen at their most haunting!'

She looked so gravely at me. Her eyes passed slowly, painstakingly over my face, as though she wanted to remember it. For the life of me I couldn't tell any more if she was jeering at my rusty features, reminding me of the vanities of human looks, or rebuking me in kind, for talking about her from hearsay. Her glance moved from me and ran down the long chamber. She blinked, and for a second I imagined that I saw a gleam of hurt twist and then die behind the lid. She'd been looking at Sieur Blacatz and my Master.

'Go on!'

'It's said that both the humble and the greatest seek a smile from you . . .'

'Any man can be cheated with a smile. Is it not so?'

'. . . but that you have a preference for princes.'

'So base? Am I taken for a courtesan who seeks the highest bid?' She chided me, seeming to enjoy the game.

'Hasn't the Pope put his personal seal of approval on a courtesan, only recently?' I stared at my hands mournfully.

Her eyebrows lifted quizzically. 'Courtesans sell their bodies, others sell their souls to the Prince of Darkness, others still to God.'

'Come! Be bold,' I heard. 'What else do these men say?'

'That they serve you for love! But that you are hard, that you give out the same light as a splinter of ice touched by the sun; that you send men even to the Prince of Darkness,' I smiled, 'looking for light strong enough to kindle warmth in you.'

'Look at me!'

I found her eyes. We stared with a bond of surprise and hatred, violently and transiently into each other.

'Love is for Death!'

The four words forced their way from between her white teeth. Full lips were parted, quivered, then tightened into thin curving lines. The colour flew out of her cheeks.

'Love is for happiness say the cuckolds, the lying priests, the hypocrites and callow farm-boys, the thieving gallants sniffing into a damoselle's bed for a wager or cheap relief. They lie! They lie! Love is for unhappiness and Death. I want to live. I don't believe in this God of Church and Pope and priest. I hate him, and with him I hate this knowledge that my soul bears. My soul! We talk about this precious soul. I'd kill my soul; yes, perhaps you could destroy me with those words . . .'

I shook my head, amazed by her.

'. . . I'd kill my soul, for it knows no truth, nothing except the horror of Death. Kill that desire and I live! To live, be honoured through Occitanie, Provence and our world, to rule over men perhaps, to live without pain, without this inner dying . . .'

She ceased, heaved a silent breath. With thumb and middle finger I could have spanned her neck, and even, like one trained to the art, have smoothed the trembling skin as with a swan's.

'You hate yourself very much, my lady,' I whispered in awe.

'Who told you such things of me? From whom do you *know* what you have said?'

Her voice was tight, but light and gay once more. Was it

really a game? Her smile, as quick as her anger, passed over the girls around her, sparkling.

'It was my Master, Peire Carcasse. We've been talking of him since the beginning.'

'No, Little Beast,' she said. 'Not only him.'

The damoselles sweet descant drew to its close.

She'd used my name like a lullaby, and I watched her with wonder. I understood something more of my Master, and could not hate her for his sake.

The season of Candlemas and Christmas was upon us. The day before, Lord Trencavel had loosed his young falcon for the hunt. Its eyelids had only recently been unsewn after its training programme, so the bird's flight was at first shaky and tortured. It had caught the silver stoat well enough, but had then flown off with its prey into an oak. This had afforded much satisfaction to the Lord Gazanhat. After one varlet had broken his arm falling from the tree, and after much whistling, the bird of prey had returned to his master's gauntlet. The stoat's pelt had been expertly skinned by my Master—he was not for nothing the son of a fur merchant—and then presented to pretty Staphanie on Lord Trencavel's behalf as a parting gift.

Today our chatelain had finally shown his hound Dragonard to advantage. There was snow in the air and on the ground. Six good-sized boars lay in their bloody traces on the trampled dirt. Their entrails, still steaming, had been thrown to the tangle of snarling hounds, who fought and squabbled for the prize between the horses' legs. Horses neighing, men shouting, knights laughing, ladies crying—the noise in the courtyard was enough to drive a madman into sanity.

I hurried over to where my Master and Sieur Blacatz were hurling insults at each other as they tumbled off their sweating mounts. I was late for I'd been with Agnes, my lazy-eyed scullery maid. She'd called me her magician of dreams, her juggling knight with a wry grin, and had touched my eyes with fingers wet from tears. She'd touched me gently, without bravery, saying that even scullery maids could have honour and pitié. It had made me smile—my ghostly white smile she called it—and I'd kissed the red ugly fingertips thinking that they were still beautiful, wondering why the cooks liked to mock her and humiliate her. She was strong and well-made. It was only her eyes that were crooked.

'Little Beast, your cheeks are flushed,' cried Peire. 'What amorous mischief have you been about?'

A wide grin settled between my ears and, doubtless, I blushed still better.

'Did you have good hunting?' I looked at Sieur Blacatz. 'And was my Master chasing the boars or the hounds this time?'

'Both I suspect,' Sieur Blacatz smiled his thin smile, 'but he had a keeper to hold him to the proper scent!'

Peire cast his friend a strange cold glance. 'The man's a pedant for facts. Think, Little Beast, when we'd be discussing something profound such as which side of a maid to sleep on, he'd pull me off my horse to admire pig-tracks in the snow.' He spoke jestingly but without fun.

'This boorish Master of yours, who can't even judge a stag's points to precision, rode the whole afternoon in silence, if the truth be told.' Blacatz's eyes had tightened; he looked pointedly at Peire and then myself, before throwing a leg over the saddle, and leaping nimbly to the ground. Peire followed suit, pulling bridle and saddle off his beast. He never allowed the varlets to do the work.

I glanced at him stealthily. Since I'd spoken to Aniara he'd been sombre and restless. His unease showed itself in many ways: in his courtesies to me, in his silences, in his sudden fits of activity when he'd leap on his horse and thunder out through the gates; in his absences from the dining hall and the minstrels' gallery; in his empty bed and chamber when, unable to sleep, I'd tiptoe up to look. He'd spoken of leaving, only to hesitate until the decision had left him.

But they'd met. They had met and mouthed politenesses in public to each other. She too now kept more frequently to her apartments.

Lord Gazanhat was in hearty mood. He'd been presented with the tusks as was fitting, and was bawling to those within earshot how his faithful Dragonard, all alone, and against the pack, had caught the right scent, had bayed twice, nose high in the air, and had then aimed unerringly for the thicket where the great sow lay.

'I was the only one to follow at first,' he said, the great round face still sweating from his exertions. 'Pity young Trencavel couldn't be here.' The wet mouth puckered with deep regret. 'He'd have really seen a well-trained animal.'

He caught sight of his lady wife and hailed her across the courtyard. She waited until he had approached her. The two came forward, he full of his achievement, she silent and casting him a veiled insolent glance from time to time. But he would not see it. Now and then he squeezed her arm so that she would start. He tried hard to impress her with his courage and skill, and seemed prepared to stand on his head to get her to turn hers towards him. She did not break away from his grasp, but walked independently as though her right arm no longer belonged to her. I would never have dared to hold a woman like that, even a scullery wench. It's strange how a man becomes jailer to his love, and then doesn't notice when it's flown away.

'Sieur Blacatz,' she spoke. 'It seems my lord had all the luck and that the skill was his too!' Her head was slightly turned to one side and she ignored my Master. 'What glory comes to me then—the wife of such a hunter!' The smile hovered on her lips, beckoning to flattery and yet rebuking it.

'Glory indeed,' murmured Blacatz very softly, 'but then how little need you have for such additions, my lady, when nature has bestowed so bounteously on you. Should we be greedy when we have too much already?'

Her gaze hardened a fraction, and swung inadvertently on Peire. He bowed, and turned to go, but Blacatz caught his arm with a vice-like rapidity.

For a moment they were both caught there on the red snow, like hostages or trophies in no-man's-land. She, deadly pale, her features carved as smooth and bold as a statue. Her grey woollen dress with its wide long sleeves eddied in the wind. About her throat and shoulders she'd thrown a blue shawl, and her hair was uncovered, swept up into wings from a pale centre parting and held with a silver brooch. My Master also wore grey. I can't forget the look he threw about him. He seemed at once full of light and agony. The skin flushed beneath its swarthiness. He stooped, appeared to be listening to echoes of a conversation that had nothing to do with those near him, and as he shook his head I had the impression that the flame and the sap rose in him until the sparks would break out of his eyes. With a hardly perceptible movement he shook his arm free. The jaw tightened, his brow darkened, but he sought no longer to depart. Thin sunlight touched the four of them and then withdrew. Peire's gaze rested on me but his mind was elsewhere. He turned to Blacatz, and the pain in his eyes made even that man step back unconsciously.

'So my friend,' his voice was halting and rough like a whisper of snow, 'we take the leap.'

Aniara glanced at him. Her eyes held no laughter, no pride, no mockery. Gazanhat shifted stupidly and amiably from one foot to the other. They waited for Peire.

'My lord,' he said gently, 'shall you not allow a poor troubadour a few moments of grace?'

'How's that, good Carcasse?'

'To take my lady on a journey.'

Aniara shivered, moving closer to her husband. Her lips opened as though to refuse, but no sound issued. Peire grinned.

'A short journey, a leisurely movement through your gardens, my lord. No more than that. To renew inspiration for the songs I try to entertain you with!'

'By the saints, you had me fooled,' Gazanhat burst out laughing. 'Hush wife! If our minstrel's golden songs are not to suffer we must hasten to his aid, eh?'

Blacatz nodded to himself, running his nails lightly up and down his cheek as he stared coolly at Aniara. The colour rose to her cheeks. She flashed a look at her husband which seemed to call him a fool and a coward. I saw the words form, and then with a brief movement she disengaged herself from him, her arms fell to her sides, and she and my Master raised their heads to the devils in each other's eyes.

'Come, my lady, let's not tarry our encounter, or inspiration will seek fresh waters in which to slake her thirst.'

He took her arm. They left. I saw her biting her lips. Was it so as not to cry out at the pain of his hold, or to contain her tongue? I knew not, but made to follow.

'Hold, jongleur!' I turned.

'Where do you hurry to?'

'To keep an eye on . . . I mean to see that he's all . . .' I stopped, fixed beneath the curious, half-friendly, half-cruel regard.

'Your Master is a grown man, with some knowledge of the gentler sex, I think.'

93

Blacatz turned carelessly to Gazanhat. 'Yes, well,' the latter coughed into a thick fist, 'I have affairs to attend to. You know Trencavel is making an embassy to Rome? Until tonight. My lady is in safe hands to be sure, ha!' He looked uncertainly at Blacatz, and lumbered off, lifting his heels neatly, as if he were practising a dance step. 'Safe hands!'

'So Little Beast, do you care to keep me company for a space?'

'No my lord, that is . . .' I looked across the courtyard uncomfortably, to the door through which Peire and Aniara had vanished.

'You worry for your Master, Little Beast?' Blacatz stood with his legs apart, slapping a stick against the black and green striped hose. His fur mantle was thrown back over his shoulders. A wisp of the iron-grey hair escaped from the loose velvet cap sitting high over his temples.

'Yes, my lord.'

The grey eyes with myriad little wrinkles of laughter and cunning about them forced me to return his gaze. The thin mouth curled slowly at the edges. He had that solitary, emaciated look of a real priest, if it hadn't been for the razor-sharp jawline, and those hooded fierce eyes. I stood irresolutely.

'How well do you know him?'

'I know who's his worst enemy, my lord.'

The grey eyes glinted. 'And shall that enemy be vanquished?'

'Not unless he burns himself to ashes, Sieur Blacatz. My Master has too many devils in him. Then sometimes I think God tucked an angel into his brain to even things up, and the clatter they make will be enough to waken Mister Death, before even an appointment's been made, saving your honour's presence.'

'But now, is he not himself? Since your first night here I think my friend Peire Carcasse has confined his ravings to song, and to flights of mild insanity on his lute's strings.'

'Yes, your lordship, I was thinking the same, but then a full belly, and your Master's smile on you to boot, lulls a hungry man to carelessness. Sieur Blacatz did not see his expression just now perhaps?' I spoke unwillingly, aware that this nobleman was forcing me to talk of Peire, and yet feeling that he would not hurt my Master. My hump ached with the change in the weather. I straightened my shoulders, wondering into which garden they'd passed.

Blacatz let loose a chuckle. 'You care for him, and have honest eyes in that ill-forged skull of yours. But a patient sometimes needs the freedom of his nurse.'

'Yes, I care for him.' I stared into his face, but there was no threat, nor sarcasm there.

'You know, Little Beast, that your master is no vagabond.'

I waited.

'A vagabond runs before each change of breeze. Peire chases God and Death with uncommon vigour, and some singleness of spirit.'

'Unlike our chatelaine who runs away.'

'Why do you say that?' he shot out.

I came hastily to myself. I hesitated a moment. 'She says that Death masquerades behind a lover's face, and that passion is a mortal wound.'

'Perhaps she's right.' The thin lips curled. 'It's said, the flame once leapt from the wick dissolves forever into darkness.'

'He said to me once, Sieur Blacatz—perhaps he spoke to the Devil—but he said to me that he loved the darkness for it was filled with stars.'

'A pretty speech, Little Beast. Do you understand it? No matter! But there are a growing number who would shut his eyes with hot pokers, so that he could not see the stars, nor comment on them.'

'What can that mean?' I stared blankly at him.

'Misfortune, I suspect.'

The dangerous smile touched his lips. I dropped my head before the piercing steady glance. Rarely had I met a man whose mask so covered the working of his mind.

'I don't understand. Forgive me. Is my Master in danger? What has he done?'

'Consider the following, Little Beast.'

He began to stroll in the direction of the postern gate. Tucking my hands in my armpits to warm them, I hurried to keep up.

'Your Master disapproves of priests. Why not, you say? He unleashes his tongue against the languid and the fripperous of my species. A small risk?' He tapped his chest with a long index finger. 'And yet they have power to destroy. His songs grow hoarse with anger for us gentle knights who languish from one tourney to the next, from one bedchamber to another. I speak the truth?'

I nodded dumbly.

'He loves not the fawning slave nor yet the lord. He seems to have affection for the bastard sired by the first upon the latter . . . hardly surprising in a half-breed such as he. But I mean no disrespect! A strange mixture of opposites, your Master, which, Little Beast,' he stopped and swivelled round, 'which an even stranger assortment of individuals now looks askance on.'

'Sieur Blacatz,' I stuttered, 'he's done nothing wrong unless it be to bring attention to the waste and misery of people's lot. It's the waste that drives him to fury. And then he hurts himself more than anyone else, I . . .'

'The Papal Legate has proposed his name for investigation. Count Raimon desires, I believe, to castrate him, at the first opportunity, for his own future peace of mind. The Cistercians bandy his name about as a gentleman in need of Catholic correction. Even the Cathari bishops, and Principals among the "Good Men", have mooted his dispatch to Rome, there to face interrogation for his blasphemies, or possibly the stake. They do it more to protect themselves than out of spite, but still . . .'

'Is it conceivable that Peire Carcasse is known by all these famous gentlemen? Why, my lord? Why?'

Blacatz shook his head slowly, and moved on. 'Your master is not a genius. Does that surprise you, Little Beast? He has neither the temper nor the restraint to create poetry of the order of Bernard de Ventadorn or Arnaud Daniel. But he is something almost rarer. How can I say it? He has the makings and the trappings of Everyman. He speaks to the tavern-keeper, the shepherd or the village whore as intimately as he does to Raimon of Toulouse.'

'A hundred troubadours, raised from humble origins have done the same.'

'But none that I know of have kept the common touch. For your Master it's as though he made a pact with his future. A pact which keeps him true to life, or to that version which he's living. But he's no better for it.'

Blacatz stared sardonically into the distance. 'I've known him since his father first sold me a winter mantle. Later that whining money-grubbing burgher brought him to me in despair. It was I, for my sins, who taught him his first songs, who constructed his first sirventes, and then sent him to learn his art in Moorish Castile, in Aragon and Leon. He has not told you that I think.' The eyebrows lifted. 'Peire has learnt to leapfrog over men's backs; but they are men who aren't amused to have their caste so rudely handled!'

'It does not give him happiness,' I muttered.

'Why should it?'

I was silent.

'Oh, there's doubtless wisdom and beauty in his songs. Perhaps too much for many ears. But the times grow bitter. A man who steps so noisily on princely feet, who awakens awkward memories with his fast-flung words, with his own wounds bared in public, ends by infecting others with his disenchantment. Infection spreads. An antidote is discovered. And Everyman, like the plague, is burnt to cinders.' He shrugged his shoulders. 'Though I envy him occasionally. What was that he used to say? You plough the waves, Blacatz, up and down in the world like a cork on the water. I reap the wind, which is the voice of Occitanie. Peire,' he murmured to himself, 'you're a clumsy prophet!'

'He can't change his songs,' I said angrily, 'that's all the clarity there is in him.'

'Not quite, Little Beast! Peire Carcasse speaks like a free man; like a man disdainful of the world that feeds him. He should be more wary of the elements that condition his existence. Truth is a luxury for those powerful enough to dictate it. Taken in large doses by a solitary man, it can prove fatal.'

'By the Devil, Sieur Blacatz, you'd think that freedom was a plague that murdered men!'

'Our Terre d'Oc, our fair Provence, begin to live on borrowed moments. Don't you see that as you travel?'

He paused, and glanced at me as if to cast his words more suitably, like a fisherman judging the river's curling ripples.

'Blacatz,' he continued, 'is but a cracked husk. Do you understand? His thoughts murmur like an evil winter breeze and are forgotten when the spring and the sunshine return. He speaks not, jongleur, therefore the memory of his words is nothing. Do you follow?'

The thin smile tested me briefly and I understood.

'Freedom,' he continued lightly, 'is the dream of those in tithe, those yoked beneath a foreign plough, but we, for want of novelty, of new sensation, play games with freedom. Our serfs and peasants are discovering a democratic urge. They talk of wages, property, security from the ravages of a careless aristocracy. Our knights and nobles retire, exhausted with this growing fashion, within their castle walls. They talk of Love. Our priests deny the scriptures, and out-lust lechery. Our church bells ring no more on Catholic decree. These "Good Men" prance along our social rim, barefoot and chaste, to herald in a new age. And your Master cries out for Everyman! The world is changing. Let's build a new land, he sings, but let's build it ourselves. He means I suppose that there always exist men willing to liberate their neighbours from tyranny. So let's have a new age! Philippe Auguste sits in Paris with a hundred thousand disciplined murderers waiting to liberate our peoples; and there are others—many others. This Pope in Rome is asking mildly who'll rid him of these heretics. He says—so it's rumoured—that there is a great reward. What, jongleur, might be this reward?'

'They'd take away our land?'

'You have a fantastical imagination, Little Beast. Don't let it chase you into trouble.'

Blacatz looked at me disdainfully. His eyes shut momentarily, the forehead smoothed. He seemed to be gazing serenely into space.

'Go run and save your Master,' he murmured sarcastically. Wheeling about, he strode towards the keep.

I hopped crab-like to the postern-gate. It was folly to be abroad in this weather. The sun had gone, and a cool, biting wind was already hurrying the light-fallen snow to cover the dark blood that stained the courtyard. For a moment I had a fierce longing to be back in some little hamlet, juggling my sticks and balls for an audience of children; listening to their merriment, watching their dirty faces. Bernard's face surfaced in my mind. It struck me that he might be dead, and I imagined him still, and stiff beneath the earth, wishing that his features would not rot away into nothing, and that I might look on him as he'd been. But even children grow up to die, I thought.

Was it true what the Sieur Blacatz had said? Were my Master's songs a plague upon the land? Was he in danger from some old man's curse? It's always old men who invent war and death, but it's only the young ones who die . . .

The gate was open and I slipped through. Their footsteps were clear in the snow. At one place they'd halted. Peire's cap lay on the ground. Rose trees stood like wraiths bending to the wind. The garden was empty. I leant out to stroke the dark rose trees, wondering what I was doing there. I didn't feel the wind anymore. Sometimes when you're alone, maybe waiting to meet a person, and it's still and quiet, your imagination really does jump free of you. I could almost see them there on the steps of the deserted bower. She stood with one arm stretched round the trunk of a bare fig tree. My Master had his back to her, and with her free hand she was reaching to touch his shoulder, leaning a little towards him. One strand of dark hair had fallen straight down from the white centre parting and curled close to her mouth. He straightened up and turned slowly about. His fingers brushed the dangling curl away over a tiny ear, and she then raised heavy eyelids, like a waking child's . . . she was no child though, and I was a hopeful imbecile. I stooped to pick up his cap. And the rose trees were only rose trees, I thought, dusting the snow from the velvet border. It was then I heard her laughter.

I looked up, my hand springing automatically to curl itself about my ear, not to listen, I said to myself, but to understand. That's another lie, Little Beast, I told myself sharply. But I hopped close to the wall, to avoid detection.

'So you'd frighten me with your songs?'

'If I could, Aniara.'

'You talk so much of love, Peire Carcasse, but your love burns like hatred.' Her voice was low. 'You suffocate me. I've sought for a gentler friend. Prince Raimon has protected me. Through him I've found favour, and a measure of true courtly friendship. Let me be in peace!' she whispered.

'"Courtly" means nothing! Love is not peace nor harmony,' my Master spoke softly, 'however much you may desire it, or will it, Aniara. There's no peace for you. You accepted my service once. You shall have it until one of us is destroyed.'

'I release you from service.'

'It's too late,' he stuttered furiously, 'you d-deceive yourself with a false hope. Peace has no meaning in either of us.'

99

Her voice was strong and clear. 'I believe your death would give me peace, Sieur Peire.'

'Not if it was offered as a gift to you,' he murmured. 'My poor liege lady. Our goals lie always beyond our fingertips. Men were born hungry. Women too! We advance, not through guarding the pretence of happiness, but through struggling with the wretchedness and suffering that lie in us. Aniara!' he pleaded. 'Do you remember the legend of a youth called Jacob, who became Israel? How all night he wrestled in agony with the terrible stranger who was bent on killing him. And at dawn the stranger tried to leave, but Jacob held him tight, saying I will not let you go unless you bless me! The destroyer blessed him and promised him fulfilment of his struggle.'

'No doubt that's why you seek a blessing from the Devil. An acknowledgement of your servitude. Oh, beware to swell old wounds! Your future weeps down upon you from the edge of a precipice. My dreams shall not be blood-stained by your hands. Let me go, Lord Gazanhat will surely be concerned.'

'I don't keep you, my lady.'

'I've made you suffer. It's the truth. You've made much suffering for me, but now it's past, Sieur Peire. The loneliness of it is only an echo. I'm no longer a prisoner of that hurt.' Her voice rose.

'So what have we two left, to sanctify with a blessing?'

There was a pause, as though they stared at each other.

'Turn your eyes away from me,' she cried abruptly, and then: 'Release me from this love! I do not lie when I tell you that our time has gone. Time has gone when I could have been your leman. Believe it!'

Above me there was a flutter of wings. It was a wild falcon circling over the tower. He beat upwards against the wind, and then hovered for a moment in the white sky. I wondered what prey he was seeking, and I shivered, mindful again of the cold, and the snow-laden wind. Stamping my feet, I marked the window, and slipped inside. I clambered up the spiral stairs.

They were in the chamber where the looms were kept, and where the seamstresses worked in the mornings. I slid down on to the stone step, with Peire's cap in my hand. If someone passed couldn't I warn them? Gazanhat had not given up his lady to

Peire for kindness, had he? And his fear of my Master boded little good.

I could hear the rustle of her gown, Peire's footsteps. I could almost see her long fingers interlacing, her knuckles twisting in agitation, and the vein throbbing wild over his angry eyes.

'You rebelled from your service.' She spoke more calmly. 'With your songs you threw my name and honour into the public pit, to be chewed and savoured by any scandal-monger! You've lost all rights to me.'

'I gave you a name,' he said bitterly. 'Count Raimon took away your honour.'

She stopped moving. I heard her gasp. 'It was you, Carcasse, who laughed at my vow of purity.'

'I laughed not at the vow, but at your subterfuge. Your purity was only terror in the face of hurt, and the implacable movement of your own soul. Your loins are drying fast, Aniara. The sap sinks in you, the paint begins to run from round those proud eyes. Don't you feel the weight of pity and honesty on your shoulders, even now? You do, Aniara!'

'No, no! Stop, you poor wretch. Enough of your words. Enough of this childish torture you do to me. You can't bludgeon me to weakness!'

Her voice had changed; it rang out clearly, as though there was joy in her, and she was glad to stand against him, and fight him. 'If your life, your songs once pleased me, if I once saw wonder in you, that was another life. Now, my life is mine. My world blooms gently. And so it shall. Raimon is my guarantee. I need no vagabond's stench between my sheets! You shall not torment me!'

'Afraid, Aniara?' His words came reluctantly.

There was silence, and then she drew a shudder of breath. 'Peire Carcasse, most tortured of men, yes, I am afraid.'

'I'm glad,' he said.

'Why do you follow me?' she broke out. 'Everyday I see your eyes upon me, staring, staring. Why do you hunt me down? Since you left Raimon's court, I've learnt to live without fury, without needing too much, without the anguish that your driving, mad spirit set alight. The flame's gone out. The ashes are cold. I've crept off the rack you stretched me on. There's no reason left to persecute me!'

'You try to forget your fate. I am your fate, Aniara. As much as Raimon and the others are. More even. And I remind you of it, as you remind me of mine.'

'Your arrogance is deadly and consummate. You threaten me?'

'You threaten yourself. Your heart threatens you.'

'Stop it!' she cried, and her self-control seeped away.

'What is it that threatens you? What is the ache, Aniara? Won't you bathe the pain in daylight?'

I heard her indrawn breath. And then there were footsteps above me. I twisted hastily, raising my knuckles to the door. It wasn't shut, and swung silently ajar. I stood up as one of the varlets came running down. He glanced at me but didn't stop. Peire had her wrist caught in his hand. His other hand had slid under the heavy hair at the nape of her neck. She was staring wretchedly at him.

'Speak the pain,' he whispered.

She intoned the words, her lips barely moving. 'That love is horror, fear, loneliness and dying . . . since the beginning . . . I saw the men who looked on me at court. They wooed me. Because my father bade me (for his honour!), I took a lover. When he had had his fill of me, when he'd stripped my clothes off, and had hurt me enough, he found other girls to break. And I was left with the knowledge of this carnal dying . . . I grew cold, and beautiful they said, hating the word "joi d'amour" . . . Years passed, though I was still barely a woman. Peire Carcasse came. He frightened me because he asked nothing. I loved him at Raimon's court. But Peire Carcasse was too dangerous to love. When I touched him I knew that I touched an enemy of their love . . . but I knew as well, that what he offered me was a love still more hurtful and lonely. This Carcasse was beaten, imprisoned, derided and scorned . . . but Aniara surely had the right to live? Without the dread, and the fear, and the inhumanity of that love . . . I took a husband, banishing the other, so that I might live . . . and there was Raimon, whose lust was gentle . . . but the horror still comes . . .' She still stared at Peire, with a wonderful courage, I believe even scorn for him, that he'd forced such weakness out of her.

'Then destroy that word "Love",' he said viciously. 'Destroy it!' Her hands rose as though to defend her eyes. She sunk away beneath his hands.

'Aniara!' he cried out in desperation, 'you must destroy, you must murder the Word, if you want your peace and harmony, your courtoisie, measure, and all the rest!'

The pale, strong face in its frame of lustrous hair turned away as though she'd been slapped, and then sank into her hands. A vein in her neck throbbed once, twice, thrice.

He released her. His back was to her, and all the fury had left him. 'Accept the murderess in you, my liege lady,' he said softly, entreatingly.

'You're mad,' she whispered. 'It's true that you're mad.'

'Accept that you want to destroy the possibility of wanting, or loving. Accept it, but for love of the spirit in you—not out of hatred, my lady, so that you'll murder fear and weakness—all the weaknesses that sift into you like a foreign poison. And then the Word will cease to exist for you. It will *be* in you!'

Words broke from her mouth. 'I don't need your dreams of Hell and immortality. I don't need you. My life is mine!' She laughed in his face. 'The scars have healed. They'll heal now on their own!' She snatched a mouthful of air into her lungs. 'It's you who murder love. It's you who have no pity or proportion. You, Peire Carcasse of the Devil's blood . . . And it's you who'll die a forgotten clown, and your agony will be knowing that no one hears you at the end.' She paused. 'Who are you, Peire Carcasse? Aniara will grasp eternity in men's praise. Her beauty will last in the songs of a dozen troubadours, even in your songs . . . but you, who are you? What do you do in a woman's chamber? Tell me so that I may burst with mirth, when a stray idiot minstrel sings of you by mistake.' A smile twisted her lips at odds with the glistening tears which trailed on her cheeks. 'Who are you?' she cried again. 'What are you?'

He didn't move except to turn his head towards the window looking out to the hills and the dull grey sky.

'I am a stutterer,' he began, separating the syllables carefully.

'You're a fool and a vagabond,' she murmured coldly, her eyes wide with cruelty. She saw him flinch a little.

'I'm a fool and a vagabond . . . and a coward,' he said clearly, turning back towards her. 'My path takes me out across the world we've learnt to know a little.'

'In search of lost innocence, your legitimacy, and revenge on more contented mortals,' she smiled.

'In search . . .' he wavered. 'In search of my love. I was blind-folded, often beggared of my purpose . . .'

'By drunken fits of rage, by vanity, and arrogance,' she stopped suddenly with a hand on her mouth. 'What am I saying? No, no! Stop this.'

He laughed very softly at her.

'By friendly gifts of luxury, ease, forgetfulness, by the world's gifts to a man.'

His face had now come into the light. He was looking past her, and spoke with a careful, gentle coolness.

'I've sought heart's relief more often than heart's desire,' he murmured. 'I've loved what I had, more often than that which I believed in. I've trusted fact more than faith.'

'Go away,' she cried. 'Go away from me! I did wrong to ask you.'

'But I shall reach my true goal,' he spoke proudly. 'I'm sure of it now. My liege lady will be there for there's nothing left to raise up between us. She'll be there. It will be when the dross has been worn off our shoulders, like the moss and lichen is worn from a rock—by sand and sun and wind and water. We'll be ready!'

She gazed up at him in amazement, not answering any more, nor seeking to prevent him speaking.

'We'll be allowed to recognize each other then. I'll recognize my mistress's true spirit—the true God and the true Devil will be one in her. And she'll recognize me.' His rough, insistent voice trembled.

'No, Peire Carcasse, no! No more.'

'Our coming together will be the fruit of our journeys. Its reward. Our coming together will take us through the places of death and beyond.'

Aniara drew herself erect, and began to speak painstakingly, as though to a foreigner. 'No more of this love of yours. You see Sieur Peire, it's only pain. You see that!' Her eyes glistened in their deep sockets. 'Only pain unto death.' She backed away from him, then stopped. Like a sleep-walker, holding out her hands before her face, as though to hide a nightmare, or to touch the darkness, she moved towards him.

'In that final consummation,' he spoke unsteadily, 'we shall leap from longing to pure flame . . .'

He was almost empty, and fumbling. He put out a spread-eagled hand towards hers. Their fingers touched, and then their palms came together. They looked, in that moment, as if they'd given life to each other.

There was nothing else. Only their two hands together, the stillness, the love and hatred meeting, and touching, like the two sides of a prayer.

I stumbled down the stairs.

'Is that love?' I blurted out.

For three days I didn't lay eyes on my Master. And then afterwards but rarely.

He'd vanish through the main gates at dawn with the shepherds, and return mud-spattered, drenched with sweat and rain only at night, to sing his lays, sirventes and sonnets at supper in the great hall. On these occasions he sang distantly, as though he was not there, but had left his ghost behind to play for him. However merrily I caught the notes, running the sets without missing a beat, the urgency and affection in him was lacking. It was not that he was downcast or loitering secretly with his wretchedness, no, not that at all. He was thoughtful, silent, and absent from me. Fifes fifed, the harpers harped, many jongleurs coming in for Christmas thronged to hear him, and to accompany the two of us, but it was not the same. I questioned him once timidly, as to how his day had passed, but he just looked at me with a grin, tossing into my hands a bag of silver.

'We'll be gone soon, Little Beast,' he said. 'But look here, now you too have a patron! And wipe the anguish off that skinny face of yours, or people might mistake you for a martyr resurrected from the worms!'

I learnt from Jean d'Acre—one of the tenant labourers—that he'd been spending many hours with the shepherds and peasants. He'd take bread and wine and victuals from the kitchens, and share his meals with them in their hovels, listening to their bawdy tales, their woes, and then, as they grew less shy of him, to the stories they told of their masters and their hard-earned lives. Perhaps it did him good, I thought, to be with real folk.

It was Christmas Eve. As usual I was up sharp and early, gnawing my cold hand to get the blood moving in it, and watching the window uneasily for my Master's departure.

I heard his step ring on the stones, and then he came into

view below me wrapped in his old woollen mantle. I couldn't abide it that he'd be wandering on his own again. Without realizing it, I called his name. He looked up.

'Messer Peire, let me go with you,' I cried.

He stood motionless for a second, with his head down, and then called softly: 'Come, then!'

Once in the fields beneath the snowline he seemed to know where the flocks were grazing. We passed from one to another. The sheep were skinny, and the flesh hung loose on them, because there was not enough fodder. The shepherds too. They accepted Peire's victuals with surly grunts, and the rough tones of those too shy or hungry to be grateful with words.

I was ready to drop by mid-morning, but Peire told me that we were now going down to the valley.

He knew the people's mood, and would never speak too much. He asked now and then how a child was, whether a mother had lived through childbirth, whether a cobbler still had the fever. People answered him with familiarity, now asking if he would be singing at Jaufrey's that evening, or telling him slyly that the priest had got Grazide's sister into a maternal quandary, or that Gazanhat had demanded more corn than was customary for the castle bins. We also heard that there was a fugitive hiding up at Jaufrey's shack.

'Maybe you'd better not go, eh, Sieur Minstrel, so as you don't know what you shouldn't . . .'

We walked through dirty alleyways where there were many poor. Half-naked children rolled in the dirt, women were washing, or cooking a few turnips in the middle of the street, men squatted in the doorways throwing dice. It reminded me of this and that, of my mother maybe, of a little boy like myself.

Our store of provisions was about exhausted. Dusk was falling, and Peire was awaited.

'Shall we go back?'

He shook his head. 'These people enjoy my singing,' he said, 'and I play better for them.'

Once again we struck away from the village, and moved steadily up the valley to the edge of the great forest. Once or twice I fancied that I heard uneven footsteps behind me, but when I turned it was quiet, and nothing moved. My Master strode before me. He had no lute with him. I wondered how he meant to play, but I didn't disturb him. Sometimes a voice would come up from the valley like a wisp of smoke, and be joined by others. I heard a church bell tolling for Nones, and then all three bells began a reverberating chant. If the Pope wanted to stop the bells, he doesn't know much about his flock. The woman's voice came again through the clear air . . .

> I sing of a Maiden,
> A matchless one,
> King of all Kings
> She chose for her son . . .

It was Christmas Eve.

Smoke was rising from the hut. Lights shone within. There must have been half a dozen souls there. Jaufrey's family. A big-boned woman was laughing with her head thrown back, and brown neck shaking. She had a goblin on her lap who grinned back at her.

'Sieur Peire came after all, and he wasn't afraid? Jaufrey said he wouldn't dare!' The woman smiled without malice.

I bristled for my Master. 'Of course he dares!'

There was laughter. Jaufrey glared at Peire with a mixture of sullenness, irritation, and affection in his deeply scored features. The woman stretched out a hand to touch Peire's arm. It was a strange gesture.

We sat close to the fire, trying to turn away from the smoke.

'Wood's stolen from his lordship's forest,' said Jaufrey defiantly. 'Seeing as it's Christmas.'

'I'd never have done such a thing,' my Master said solemnly.

Jaufrey stared back, and then his shaggy, weathered face creased with a real greeting. 'We're glad you came.'

The rushes strewn on the ground smelt clean, and faintly bitter. The two eldest children stared at Peire not daring to come close, but crouching by their mother. Their knees, shiny and scratched, peered up at us like faces. The only other person there, was a gaunt old man, with a wiry thatch of white hair and a horse-like, stubborn head. He had a blanket thrown over his rags, and sat, face in his hands, staring into the fire. I remembered him. It was the fellow who'd given us a lift with his wife, coming up to Gazanac. There was a battered harp in the corner away from the fire, I noticed.

'Is this your fugitive?' my Master asked.

There was no response from the old labourer.

Jaufrey nodded. 'Says he stole food from the castle kitchens. Then he killed a stag in the lord's forests. Had to feed the wife, he said.'

Peire looked at him in silence.

'But she died anyway,' said the woman.

The embers puffed and spat softly in the grate.

'Didn't Lord Trencavel give you restitution?' Peire asked.

The old peasant turned his gaze slowly. 'Didn't see him. Wasn't allowed to.' He was fingering a small cross that hung from his neck. 'No one'd listen. Broth, vegetables. Marie was dying. All she needed was a drop of warmth in her belly.' He spoke clearly in a deep voice.

'The keepers caught him while he was gutting the stag. But he escaped.'

Jaufrey shrugged. 'Can't keep him here. Too dangerous for me. He took an arrow in the arm. Needs attending. I need my job.'

'I'll talk to Gazanhat.'

'May it serve him better than when I spoke to the head huntsman.'

'Don't speak to no one for me,' said the culprit. 'Don't have anything left to lose now, have I, or to fear?'

There was a knock on the door. We started. Jaufrey glanced fearfully at my Master. He nodded, and took the old harp on his knees, strumming it gently. The woman went to the door. I heard a cackle that sent shivers down my spine.

'Christmas time and all's fine. Be wise, O men, and cheerfully know, a little torment here below!'

It was the idiot we'd known at Gazanac who hobbled in. He stopped on the threshold, staring from one to the other, until his eyes alighted on me. He wobbled closer.

'Little Beast be wise and know, agony on earth below, shrink from your pleasures often, then deathly pangs shall soften, when you suffer bitter pain, consider well your heavenly gain! He, He!'

I glanced at my Master, but he just smiled. The others were not alarmed. They knew him. They'd been expecting him.

'Did you follow us here?' I accused him.

'Did I, didn't I, but why?' He collapsed like a broken chair on the rushes, perfectly at home. 'That's the criminal,' he pointed fiercely at the old fellow, 'and you're nearly dead!'

'I'm nearly dead?'

The man nodded slowly back. 'Which is bad. When I'm dead it'll be good.' His gaze reverted to the fire.

There was soup, a good soup with bits of chicken floating in it, and some husks of bread. Peire brought out of his pouch the last strips of cold venison. The children and the idiot took most of it. It was the idiot who fed the old man, piece by piece.

The children crept towards my Master. The girl, first looking to her mother for assent, asked Peire to sing.

He did, in a low voice. Wonder, helplessness, and more gentleness than I'd known before, was in his singing. He sang many songs, some his, some of others, but all tenderly.

The crazed poet sat close to the old man on the floor. Now and then he would pat the other's knee, or tap the lantern jaw with a light fist. 'Heigh ho, it's Christmas time, and all's fine,' he'd whisper nodding away so furiously that his companion, in a dazed way, would follow suit. Their heads tipped and wallowed almost in time to the music.

The door opened many times. People crept in, some with a log for the fire, others with a drop of wine, others with nothing. The door was left open, and the smoke drifted away. It was warm. A girl sang, or now a couple of shy boys, and my Master would then take up the harp once more to play for them. The hours turned; it was day and the vigil was done.

Peire stretched wearily. The children had been put to sleep. Jaufrey's wife had fallen off, after kissing Peire's hand. Her husband slept too. The fugitive's angular head had fallen on to his chest.

We stood up to leave. My Master sought to put a hand on the old fellow's arm, but the idiot put a finger to his lips, warning us off.

'I'll do all I can.'

'Leave him alone, he's only bones!' A titter reached into the dark. 'Next Christmas day in earth he'll lay!' The voice softened, and we both waited, though for what I wasn't sure.

He stuck four fingers in front of our faces. 'Live,' he ticked the first one off, 'Learn, Love, Lose!' said the lunatic, before glancing back to watch his charge. 'Any way round it'll do . . .'

'Love!' I said to myself as we walked home.

Peire spoke to Lord Gazanhat, begging pardon for the man as a Christmas clemency. The guests were amused that he should interest himself in such a ridiculous case. He was warned not to meddle in matters of local justice. The man was caught. I heard that the idiot gave him away. He was thrown into a dungeon. Sometimes you could hear his cries. Pain or hunger, it was hard to tell. An example had to be made, said Lord Gazanhat, on his way to chapel for Vespers. He was to be drawn and quartered in the courtyard on New Year's Day.

'That's a kind of love too,' I thought.

My Master persisted at every opportunity to confront Lord Gazanhat with the cruelty of such justice. The Lady Azelais was present on one occasion. For a moment it seemed that she might say something to her husband. She looked worn and deathly tired. Work on her tapestry had gone forward prodigiously. She was hardly ever at table, preferring to take her meals with her damoselles and her tiring women. Sometimes we'd catch a glimpse of her walking in the little garden, where I'd first overheard them. She walked alone, with one attendant some way behind her, for hours at a time. Her husband never disturbed her. It was said that the tapestry was the most beautiful ever created in Occitanie. It was also said that no such work could ever hang in a monastery.

She'd looked at Peire, and then at her husband from deep-set eyes, under which the dark circles bore witness to her sleeplessness.

'If you seek justice, give him back his family,' my Master had said. 'If it's mercy you look for, release him.'

Aniara watched him, her fingers interlacing, and finally he felt her eyes.

'My lady,' he said, turning to her. 'Help me.'

Her gaze broke, and she turned to the other.

'The man's lost his wife and children. Is it a necessary cruelty to treat him thus?'

Gazanhat paused. 'You both talk as if my treatment of this wretch was singular,' he blurted. 'There are a thousand others like him who receive worse!'

'Worse?' Peire flung out.

'To be blinded or unsexed is worse, is it not?'

The prisoner's feeble shouts continued a day or two. Gazanhat had become obdurate.

It was the day before New Year's Eve. The dungeon keys were kept in the porter's house inside the door. Before dawn I sneaked to find them. We slipped down the spiral stairs beneath the keep. Peire in a cold fury was raking doors open, and throwing back bolts, as if he hoped to be caught in the act. He called out at the first and second cells. There was no answer. At the last, silence greeted us too. We unlocked the heavy door. The dripping wet, the stench of human dirt struck into our faces. By degrees our eyes grew accustomed to the dark for the only light came through the door we'd entered.

He lay in the centre of the cell on his side, so that his feet almost touched the back of his head, like a bow stretched beyond endurance. His wrists were manacled behind him. The lower part of his face had been nibbled by rats.

'How did he die?'

'There's a haft, Messer, through his back.'

He'd stabbed himself a number of times. There was much blood. It must have been a slow way to leave the world.

'No!' cried my Master. 'No!'

He knelt down to close the corpse's eyes.

'Yes,' I said under my breath. 'He died for love perhaps?'

We saddled, packed our chattels, beat on the gate, and, with the porter cursing us to hell-fire as I threw him his keys, rode out.

'Where do we go?' I asked.

'To borrow light from Lucifer,' he shouted.

'What for, Master?' I trembled.

'To make a funeral pyre for Love and Occitanie,' he hurled out in fury.

5

We'd been riding all day. Now it was pitch dark again. Clouds covered the sky, and a damp wind slapped our faces in gusts. I turned my nose to the west, and smelt rain in the air, but it took us four or five leagues' riding to reach the gathering storm. Sometimes I took the bridle of my Master's mare to guide her through the rocks.

We passed close to the sea just before dawn came, and I let the horses have their heads, as we followed the shore line. The beasts had determined on their direction, if we had not.

Now and again I could hear dogs barking from the outskirts of a village, and once, a sliver of moon rose above the far rim of the sea to our left, cracked like an old cheese, and full of affliction.

My Master didn't speak unless we paused, and then only to urge his horse on again. Tears leapt from his eye-sockets, but his mouth was set in a grim line.

He was beginning another journey. A journey that began deep in his brain and that stretched winding and tortuously to his heart. I hoped there was a path that joined the two, and pulled my jerkin tighter round my back.

'Little Beast,' said I, 'admit that you've been forgetting your appointments lately. You've been dreaming of scullery wenches, and soft white bread, and aromatic wines, and sweet luxury. You've been dreaming lately of dancing into Paradise, clutching the skirts of a nun or a virgin lady, and of juggling one more time on the threshold of Heaven with your hump instead of skittles. And admit that you were secretly avoiding old Beelzebub—tiptoeing in the shadows round the blaze, eh?

'Well my friend, cast an eye on your Master there, and see if you still forget. Can you see the Devil perched behind him? By the Rood, he's got a hump just like you! Can you make out your Master's white knuckles gripping the reins? And if you squint beneath those wild black locks, won't you get a glimpse of bloodshot eyes, and a gaping mouth? Does he carry your devils too?

Will you let him? But why, why dear Sieur Carcasse? Why do you open your guts to the lance so purposefully?'

A voice whispered in my ear: 'Open your sack for the answer! Have you forgotten what's in your sack.'

'No,' I said. 'No, God pity us.' And I spread my tricks on the frayed mat of my mind.

'There's a rose, Little Beast. Here! You have it in your left hand. Now press it to your nostrils. It reeks of musk and woman's love. A false thing is it, Little Beast? But it throbs between your fingers with a drowning passion. And the thorn pricks your fingers. And then what do you have? A cat creeps mewling from the sack. Look out! It claws your hand. Watch how its four flailing claws plough into your skin like strokes of red lightning. A mangy thing it is, but full of spite and curiosity and envy. One ferocious paw strikes out! Strangle it first. No, let it live. It stretches jealously to the star. Yes, the star, Little Beast, that glitters deep in the recesses of your sack. It glitters. How it glitters! Reach for it. Fast, before the cat tears loose your muscles. Watch the claws, they'll drag you from the star. The cat will swipe all the little fishes from the pool of Heaven. Reach for the highest star, Little Beast!'

. . . If mortals could just give a kick in the pants to gods and devils, eh? And to hopes! Aie, what a treat! If I could abolish dreams; stick a poker into my skull until they fizzled out. If I could boot this swelling hunger, and my mean pitiful hopes high into the sky, and watch them rise, rise, and fly out of this rusty sieve in which men rattle so; fly out like a bunch of neat, slithering skylarks. I'd manage without the skylarks in the future. Wouldn't give 'em a second thought. Let 'em go, say I, so long as they take off with them all the rubbish in our heads!

Well, Sieur Peire, I'd really be free then, by God! Really free, wouldn't I . . .? We could both be free dear Master. Just think. Abolish skylarks, and there you have it!

'And the songs . . .?' a voice whispered to me, 'and the singing. Who would sing?'

God, you're complicating matters, and you don't even keep an eye on my Master! Yes, I know he's got to sing his songs. All right, I admit that. But you want him to chase after perfection as well? Tickle the keys in the locks of Paradise, and sing about that too, I suppose . . . but God, he's only human . . . yes, I apologize for that last remark. But is it necessary to send him on such a wild goose chase? You know, and I know, saving your presence, that with his last breath he won't have found it, and that he'll still be looking. It's not enough, God, I'm sorry, but it's a shocking bargain.

Then in any case everyone will be misunderstanding him and his songs afterwards, talking of keys and secrets, this and that symbol, when he was perhaps only referring to the panic (if you follow me) of hunting his own end, and to the wonder and misery in him, that he tried to release, and to that wretched skylark of yours; that stupid, formless shapeless perfection he was after. If you could perhaps let him grab a tail feather—only a tail feather—to calm him a bit. Wouldn't that be at all possible?

But God must have had other business on his mind that day. It was the thunder that answered me, and the driving, icy rain, which we couldn't avoid. There was no protection under the heavens.

The storm thickened, and my last sight of the sea before we turned inland was of hundred-humped dragons ripping up the water, and flailing the beaches with their dangerous tails. Grey spray, sea-spray, mist and sky merged. The sky rolled over, heaved and split with white sword thrusts—now farther, now closer—so that the horses reared and neighed with alarm.

All day we continued, pressing our necks into the driving sleet and wind. Night and day were abolished in that thunderous, murky clatter.

My Master neither turned leewards, nor called a halt to our winding, desperate progress into the Corbières.

Towards the hour of dusk, he began to speak. Disjointedly at first, and it's true that he spoke more to the elements around him than to me. I understood little, and what words I laid a-hold of seemed to lack order and sense. The rock-faces gleamed white and threatening through the dark. But when we reached the brow of one hill it was only to find that the harsh slopes fell away in twisting right-angles, and that our path doubled back before creeping higher into the maze of mountains. We were truly in the Devil's country now.

Peire spoke. At first I could barely hear him.

'Death stalks out of his cave,' he croaked. 'I can see him before us, and he's dancing with the Devil arm in arm. Today they come with loosened hands. Their hounds, too, are loose in the storm, and I can hear their baying. The foam from their jaws flecks the wind. They run sometimes separately, sometimes together in the pack, gathering speed and stamina for their descent upon the refuges of men.' His voice drifted away and then came back more distinctly. 'Where they go we reap the whirlwind. Where the Devil sows his bitter seeds, there shall rise a crop of deadly blades. Death waits beside him, arms crossed, to memorize the fields for harvesting. Does he see us, Little Beast?' The spattered face turned to me. 'Does he let us live to watch his work, mocking our horror? Or will he destroy us from behind our backs, with a cowardly stroke, as we approach eternity, having learnt to open our eyes? When my lady leaps to me with real laughter; when your uncle's son holds out his hands to you? Will they come for us when we have learnt to open our mouths, when we have learnt the real words to warn our neighbours?'

'I don't know. How should I know, good Master? But if it's the hereafter that we're after—if you follow me—shall we not rest a little to give us strength?' I squeaked back in the teeth of the gale.

'Rest, my poor companion? Where shall we rest with this rattling at our hearts' gates? Don't you hear it?'

'I hear the Devil's wind through the rocks, Messer, forgive me.'

'It has the same purpose,' he continued wildly. 'We mourn so many deaths. Beauty's downfall, the death of justice, courage, love. But you *still* dream falsely Peire Carcasse!' His voice broke away. 'My God,' he cried, 'tell me the truth! And if we must abandon hope too—this vest we wear so close to our skins—why, damn your skies, we'll cast that off as well. Is that true poverty? Is that the truth at the end of our travail? My God and my Destroyer, strip me naked if it must be so. And if it must be so I'll learn to bear the cruellest pain. And if it must be so, I'll suffer the most terrible joy you hurl upon me. And my God, I'll promise you to tell other men about that agony. So that they won't be so frightened by the pain and the joy, so that they can say to themselves: Look! That minstrel, that vagabond, poor what's-his-name walked through fire and water, and he's still laughing. So can't we too? And they will, God! I promise to laugh until my entrails drip out of my body so long as you tell me the

115

truth about hope. I'll laugh at all your minions, all your agents of destruction—the Devil, the Pope, the King of France—I'll promise to laugh in the dungeon, at the stake. I'll swear to laugh on my funeral pyre until it hurts too much. Then I'll be silent. I swear it if you tell me the truth. Because afterwards it won't matter. It will be straightforward to die ... Little Beast, here, and I, we'll become brave cowards. We'll show our countrymen how to pluck courage off the wind's back; how to grow strong and hungry in rebellion; how to wax boldly to the fierce state of bastardy, so that blood courses through our veins, not borne on water, but on molten flame.

'So that we'll be ready and willing for the new age. And when that new age comes we'll thrust it forward like a rolling boulder, or pull it out of the old by its bloody feet, kicking like a new-born boy—so that it comes more quickly, so that the stench of our present dying does not linger.

'My God, let's have no more juggling for balance on the rim of this putrefying age. We'll throw wide our arms, we'll strain on tip-toe, and we'll hurl the hopes of all our souls into the chasm of the future!'

'Master,' I cried in distress, 'don't say such things. Not even God asks that from a mortal. Don't say such things! We'll be trapped with your words, and destroyed.'

'Little Beast,' he answered me, 'I'm a coward too. But once out, the thought cannot be undone. We are surely trapped into the future.'

'Sieur Peire, I couldn't do it. I'd like to be brave and that, but I'm not made for the future. My brain wobbles over the rim and I'm done for. Please, Messer, don't tempt Heaven and Hell too much. Perhaps if we're patient, you'll grab the skylark's tail feathers. And we'll have a little peace.'

'It's not enough, Little Beast. I want more.'

'No. That's arrogance, that's competing with the gods! Lightning will strike us, or a thousand devils, with their pitch-forks ready to toss us into the blaze, ass over tip. There's no escape from there!'

'I want more,' he cried. 'Occitanie needs more from every one of her sons and daughters. I want the lightning and the flame. And even what's beyond!'

'There's death beyond,' I stuttered. 'There's only death. Like you said about the Devil sowing, and Death reaping. There's only death. It's true Master. How can a mortal dare to go beyond?'

'We'll pioneer the pilgrimage,' he bellowed in anguish.

I opened my mouth to shout hold. But it was useless. My Master was beyond me. What he said, screaming at the elements, was beyond even him. He was rolling in his own terror, like a dog in its dirt, to soothe his sores. He frightened me. I wept for him, wiping my sleeve across my face, and for myself, because I didn't know us any more, and there was no light, no light. Only the weight in my skull, which crushed down over my eyes.

'Messer, I can't hear you. Did you speak to me? Sieur Peire, come back to yourself.' I called, teeth chattering like pebbles rolled together. 'Messer, I'm afraid. I can't go on much more. Peire, do you hear me? My hump is slipping . . .'

It was then that I think my wits finally abandoned me. And then I saw Peire's face close to mine, and I could smell the horses. I lay between them.

'Be still,' he murmured, trembling with tears. 'Forgive me.'

'For what, Master?' I whispered. I could hear the rain, softer now, falling, falling . . . 'Master?'

'Be still,' I heard.

I was beneath a roof. It was still dark. Pools of water eddied off my clothes. There was straw, sweet-smelling straw, and a smell of chalk, and cattle. I started. But it was only the noise of the rain without, and I slept.

It seemed to me that my Master was tuning his lute. And that he dipped each string in his own blood, dipped and drowned each string in his heart's blood. There were eight strings to stain, eight primal chords to wring out of his heart. And then, when the strings were strung, red and glistening wet on the wood, the notes cried out, like eight quivering mortal wounds . . . I cried out to him, but he held his hands up against me, shaking his head.

Sometimes I awoke, and the rain had stopped, but the chill had passed through my sinews, and my hump was heavy with rain and sharp hailstones.

Later I saw flames leaping about us. My mind was clear, and I was afraid that the straw would catch fire. 'Make haste to fly,

Sieur Peire!' I called out. The flames jumped away from us, my Master held me, and the fire reached me not.

I saw Peire. He left me, came back. I saw him in many places. But it was hard to follow him. His face had changed. All the colour had ebbed away. I leant out to touch him, but he burnt like ice. 'Master, what ails you? Your face grows like mine.' I was fearful for him . . . and then sometimes I was alone again.

Once I caught a glimpse of Bernard. 'The sack!' I cried to him, 'they're in the sack, your britches. I kept them!'

Tears crept down my cheeks. He shook his head at me. 'Keep them still,' he murmured.

Other people came to me. There were days and days of people. Priests, burghers, usurers, and merchants, mountebanks and clowns. There were many people, and they crowded about so that it was hard to breathe.

'Sieur Peire, are you there? Please tell them to leave.'

'He's gone,' they whispered to me. 'He's gone to string his lute with eight bloody strings ripped from the bellies of seven devils and an archangel!' And they tittered.

'All inside him, I know, I know,' I burst out. 'But it's not true that he's gone.'

'He's gone to make his peace with the Count of Toulouse.'

'He sits mouthing pleasantries at Pope Innocent's feet.'

'He's gone to kiss the hands of Dominic Guzman, the Spanish preacher.'

'Who is that?' I cried. 'No, you're all lying to me!'

'He's thrown away his lute. He's sworn never to sing again. He's gone to his father and kneels, like the prodigal son, at his shop's doorstep. And all the people of Carcassonne are jeering and mocking him . . .'

With a terrible wrench, I pushed the intruders away, and sat up. I stared wildly about me. They all melted backwards. Farther, farther, and then on the far side of the room he was there.

He held a finger to his lips, and slowly the trembling in my bones ceased. I became still. It was my Master. But how he'd changed. His features were pale, pale, and sharply etched. The flesh had slunk off his bones. His wrists looked hollow and brittle, and his eyes seemed to have sunk deeper into his skull. Even his tumbling, matted hair was threaded with white, and fell dark against the sharp jawline. The broken nose, thinner now, jutted more voraciously from his face. He reminded me of someone whom I'd once known well.

He told me that I'd been on a journey which had lasted a long time, that I would be well again. 'I nearly lost you, Little Beast,' he smiled wry and gentle. There was no stutter in his speech, and though his voice had something of the harsh timbre I remembered, it was deeper and issued from him more reluctantly, as though speaking had become an unnatural exercise. He told he that he too had been away.

'Where did you go?' I asked him eagerly. 'I knew you had.' And my disappointment must have shown. He smiled again.

'You were in good hands. My nursing was a very rough and ready ministry. There were more capable doctors, and I could not spend all day locked in with you!'

'No, forgive me, of course not, Messer Peire, but . . .'

'I travelled, Little Beast, into the villages, through the shaky crofts, and stone towers that rattle on these dusty pinnacles about us. I listened to the Devil's wind, and the wind of men, and I muttered for hours to myself, perched on my heels in a cave on the hillside.'

He pointed to my sack. 'You've all your secrets tucked into your pillow there. You can take them out—one by one—your silver balls, your stars, your withered roses with their faint perfume still lingering, your ropes, and gewgaws. And at night they're all tied up safely beneath your head. You can take them out one by one, turn them over in your hands, and so remember who you are. You're a wise man, Little Beast, but I never acquired a sack. Vanity told me that I would remember . . . but you see,' he shrugged with a chuckle, 'my memory began to find it easier to lie. When you were ill, the lies began to sound hollow even to my ears. I had to pick through all my tricks at last, ferreting through my own brain.

'Strange things I found too. A Unicorn full of silence tapped my forehead with his horn, and bade me cease my windy words. A gate opened, and out of that gate rushed a tempest, bearing bits of tinsel, gold charms, worthless baubles, tossing conundrums at me and the tail-ends of a thousand mysteries. There was so little time to catch the matter rushing out of my head, and then I too was carried off.' He paused, tilting up his head to look at me. 'But that's not interesting. Look, Little Beast!' he pointed. 'There's a sparrow on the window-sill. He's bidding you awake from your long sleep, and your dark dreams.'

It was true. Perched on the casement, against a blue sky, sat a tiny bird, tweaking its head now towards Peire, now towards me, and occasionally releasing a chirrup—a little angry, impatient burst of argument: as though to say we were a couple of lazy fools to be sitting there, and that he considered it his duty to remind us of the fact.

'He's come every morning for the past week to see how you were progressing. We'd discuss the patient in whispers, so as not to waken you. He's a wise bird. He's told me many things about his wandering life.'

Peire whistled, and cast the crumbs in his hand on to the floor close by him. 'He's a scout, reconnoitring the end of winter for his brethren, and a bit of a vagabond like us. He always comes first, he told me, to test the temperature, and then, if he so much as sniffs spring in the wind, he passes on the message through the relays awaiting his orders.'

'Winter's gone, Master?' I gazed about in astonishment.

'Look at him!' The sparrow fluttered from one crumb to the next, and then, with a bustle of feathers, hopped on to Peire's knee, and cheeped furiously at me. 'Do you doubt my word?' he seemed to proclaim.

I shook my head. 'Have I been a-bed so long?'

'Some weeks. The moon has grown and waned many times. You were wrestling with the fever, and fighting for each mouthful of air. Sometimes you'd cry out with pain, and a rage I wouldn't have believed of you. At other moments you'd shrink into a corner of your bed so that all I could see of you was a pile of jagged chicken-bones sticking up from beneath the blankets. Sometimes I had to straighten out your limbs. You'd lie so tense, as if waiting to pounce on the fiend who tried to drag you to the Styx. I wiped your temples with a damp cloth, and you told me of a strange man that I did not know at all. So many stories you had about him. So many facts!'

I blushed. 'What did I say? Did I say many foolish things?'

'No. Your tales weren't foolish. You spoke clumsily—that's true—in fits and bursts. Now wildly when you saw danger, now in whispers, like spring air in the poplars bordering the Aude, when your pity made you look for sense in this character's rashness. You spoke of a man who was sometimes a giant, with feet of wet clay, sometimes a dwarf perched on the other's back, and staring into the future. I learnt to know him through your storytelling. Often I hated him. I had a grudging sense of kinship with him too.'

'What happened to him afterwards?' I asked.

'Afterwards he travelled up the rocky precipices. He threw his velvet cap and silken doublet away, from a peak that overlooked the citadel of Peyrepertuse. The bright rags fluttered over the valley like a knight's gage knotted to a shaft of wind. Trumpets sounded distantly, it seemed to him, and he ripped the strings from his lute.'

Peire looked at me. 'I believe he said that the eight strings had not nearly enough blood on them, nor love, nor tenderness to let loose the real spirit of a song.'

'What does he have left? How shall he live now?' I asked, swallowing nervously.

'From the beginning once more, so it was said. From the beginning. He'll learn to listen for the footsteps of the eternal ones, the Princes of Light and Darkness, and perhaps he'll learn how to tell them apart. He has more silence and space around . him. There's little left to trammel up his fluttering spirit now.'

'And . . . and what shall become of the Little Beast?'

'You're alive, and soon you'll be strong again. We'll set out into the villages and towns. We'll play the songs of Occitanie. And we'll listen. Our people will have to prepare themselves for the iron men, perhaps also for new masters. Their own are brittle, like dead wood. And we'll slowly learn how to dance again, and how to follow the path to the magician's star—like moths to the flame—Little Beast. There's no help for it.'

'Which iron men are these? I don't understand. Shall we be going on a crusade? Saving your presence I'd as lief keep my distance from the iron men. I'm not a brave man, and those bully knights practise their sword-swipes on anything that moves. I don't move very quickly, Sieur Peire, with my sack and . . .'

'Save your fear,' he broke in laughing, 'we haven't sunk to such a pitch as yet.'

Scratching my head, I looked across at him. I thought again of the heat which sustained him through so much self-destruction. I also thought how good it would be if sometimes he'd just

talk of ordinary things I could see and touch. I shrugged weakly
. . . of a place to stay, to live, of a piece of land perhaps to plough,
till, reap oneself; of a garden where berries grew along the hedges,
where there were flowers, and a few sticks of corn, beet, green
vegetables, and fruit, where a vine would curl up to the roof,
where friends would come to see you. Messer, one day might
you not like to stop still, watch the same sky turn over your
head, and the same fields grow ripe round your feet? Might you
not want a home with a small hall, a minstrels' gallery perhaps,
with a big kitchen, rushes scattered on the floor, and good smells
tumbling out of the grate? And a son growing to manhood with
great wondering eyes, and his father's build? Have you never
wanted such things? But I asked in silence, staring at him with a
sudden yearning. It doesn't matter now, I thought. I knew the
answers to my questions before I spoke. He was waiting for me.

'Messer, I've been wasting your days lying here,' I murmured,
and then with a grin said: 'Time's round like a millstone, and it
rolls quickly. Here's a dried up pea shivering in its pod, but the
pea's alive and rattling again!' I looked about the room, and it
dawned on me that I had not the slightest notion of where we
were.

Peire glanced at me, understanding my bewilderment. 'Yes,
we're in a monastery, Little Beast.'

And I couldn't keep the grin from escaping into a chuckle.

I'd been lodged in the sick room, which was a separate hut
adjacent to the main buildings. It was the farmer's wife who
daily attended me. She came in one of those first days. I'd tried to
hide my nakedness beneath the covers, and she'd smiled. Tall,
dark-haired, and well-made, she stood for a moment in the centre
of the room with her hands on her hips, looking at us.

'Our friend's awoken from the dead at last,' she said. 'I was
becoming impatient.' She attempted severity, but her eyes were
compassionate and merry. She was a beautiful woman, of twenty-
five or thirty summers, with a strong generous mouth, and wide
forehead. She was dressed in a fluttering grey shift, with an apron
tied about her high waist.

Peire linked his arm in hers affectionately. 'You'll make him
strong again. But don't forget his stomach is a pit larger than the
crater of Vesuvio, and needs frequent sustenance!'

'Messer, I hadn't even noticed I had a stomach until you talked of it,' I protested.

'And you, vagabond,' she pointed sternly at Peire. 'You, sir, are doubtless off to the woods and hills again, with a pocketful of nightmares to keep you company.' She sighed. 'You'll drive my husband mad with your tales. And who'll look after the farm when he takes off with a rusty pike to defend Terre d'Oc? Will you leave me your jongleur as a replacement?'

'No Sieur Peire,' I cried out in sudden alarm. 'When I think about it I'm really not cut out to be a farmer.'

'I don't know . . .' he said with a hint of malice. 'Perhaps . . .'

'You wouldn't let such a fate overtake a sick man,' I laughed.

'Away with you,' said my nurse, 'I'll tend your empty jongleur better without you.'

In truth my Master looked like a wild boar let loose in a bed of small flowers, and unsure where to put his feet. He bent his head to kiss her cheek before she could draw away, and was gone.

'It's him who needs a cure now, not you,' she declared briskly, approaching my bed.

'Why do you say that?'

'Sometimes he's in the monastery, or stays close to the farm. Then he watches my Guillem at work with his men in the fields. He tries to help. My husband tells him to go and pen his songs, but he shakes his head foolishly, and sticks a finger to his lips. Sometimes he prowls about the house, or follows me into the garden. Other times he disappears into the high Corbières for days on end. He goes dancing in the villages, telling his tales, listening and talking to the simple folk, growling about the need for songs, and sons, and faith. The monks here are patient, but suspicious of him. They don't like minstrelsy too greatly. He speaks little to them.' She stopped. 'It's true that he's broken his lute, I overheard your talk.' She blushed, without regret. 'Often he'd come and talk to you for hours, even though you were unconscious. It quietened him. I'd listen outside now and then to be sure he wasn't about to frighten you . . . You know, he wouldn't let anyone else wash you.'

'My Master washed me?'

'Yes,' she said shortly, as though regretting her words. 'I could have done it but he was obstinate.'

She gave me my clothes.

123

'Mind you don't stir out of the house. You're as weak as a landed trout, and the fever only left you on the feast of St John. You nearly died.'

I nodded slowly back.

'Come down when you're ready.' She patted my head, and turned to go.

'Thank you, Ma'am, for your kindness to us both.'

'Why do you thank me for him?'

'Because he's grateful too.'

Her eyes crinkled slowly. She looked older when she smiled. She made a sign over her breast. I didn't know what it meant.

The spring of that year was a fair one. Rain fell in good measure. The grain, fruit and vines flourished. It looked as though there would be time to sow an extra crop. The monastic livestock had plump shanks and girths, and they thrived. The shepherds, surly, close-mouthed fellows though they were—it's in the breed—brought in good news of ewes lambing early in health and plenty. There was never any shortage of trade for the monastery, with the villages and the coast.

Esclarmonde, my gentle nurse, gave birth to a boy in the first days of May. Peire, once armed with the news, insisted that a barbarian born at such a time of year was truly a relation of his. He stood godparent to the mewling, wide-eyed brat.

'You say he's born in sin,' he told the parents, 'I say he's born out of it, and brings fresh blood to mix with our milkish fluids!'

My illness had left me paler, if that was possible, and so bony that my hump weighed down like a mountain. But as we began to move about, the muscles thickened once more in my legs, and back and arms, and I accompanied my Master more frequently.

Esclarmonde and Guillem belonged to the sect of Cathari, but everywhere we went it seemed that the people were adhering more and more to the heresy come from Hungary, and listening to the 'Parfaits', and 'Good Men', who brought them God and Death to end their earthly suffering.

For my liking they believed too hotly in Messer Death. My Master saw in their yearning a terrible sense of defeat, and powerlessness before the raging times.

The village curé, also a follower, argued the case with Peire secretly, for the monks had many spies. There were those who listened. Simple people whose eyes lit up briefly when Peire goaded their hearts with his dreams of independence and faith in the secret well of human renewal.

'It's in all of us!' he'd cry, 'you *can* stand straight. You can raise your own vines. You can raise your children to a full belly and belief in themselves. Look into yourselves. It's not death you'll seek but life, and in that life a sprig of eternity. Eternity first in strong sons trained to a pride for life, trained to the disciplines of freedom, and the thrusting value of their own spirit. And then eternity beyond this world, if we're brave enough to look for it.'

'Man is drenched in evil,' harangued the curé. 'All coupling, copulation, fornication is wicked, and disgusting.'

'Long-winded humbug,' I murmured. 'Even in wedlock?' I suggested timidly.

'Worse still in wedlock, because men have a natural licence to pursue their lusts. A new-born baby is full of the stigma of his parents' act, and full of the evil they engendered in him.' He spat the words out like bitter lemons, staring at my Master, his cow eyes protruding from a face still good-natured and youthful.

'There are some,' he went on, 'who say that the soul is just blood, like in animals. Even if it's not true, God despises Man in his present state, and waits patiently until Death cleanses the body, so that he can pick out the rare ones who deserve resurrection. Life is nothing except the path to Death. The more we fornicate, the more we worship the flesh and our lusting, the shorter is our road to oblivion. Life is nothing but decay!'

Peire gazed at him. 'You look at d'Oc. But you see only the nobility who wring the blood from you to feed their dissipation. Look farther. Break the blinkers to your vision. There's another Occitanie. There's a future Occitanie. Don't waste the tears you've spent, don't make obsolete the fathers and grandfathers who carved out this land, and made it flower; don't cut your wrists so easily in surrender. This is your land. Make it yours. This is our land, and we must make it ours! Yes, life is nothing,' said my Master, 'except the path of stubborn, real men to immortality, except the path of stubborn, real men to independence, to knowledge, and the joy of it . . .' He turned away muttering. 'If there was less truth in these starved fanatics it would be easier to blow heat back into their ashes.'

And the rumours in those days began to blow slowly, poison-ously through the land. They reached even into the Corbières: that a skin-sickness had crossed the Pyrenees which flailed the hide off a child's body, with ugly weals at first, that would run with pus. The curé called it, needless to say, a plague of God's for the heinous sins of the Roman Church. There were other menaces too. Pirates were raiding the coastal towns under Raimon's nose, and the nose didn't even twitch. Folk were saying that chaos was coming, and the age of the Apocalypse.

There were also many shave-pates abroad on the highways: mendicant friars who were not like the well-filled and well-lined ones we had hitherto come across. These men were lean, they too were hungry, lusting for God and the souls of men. They travelled barefoot, seeking out the 'Good Men' for public debate in the village squares. They came, often as not from Aragon and Castile, perhaps because in those lands a tongue similar to our own was spoken. And there were some who claimed that a monk called Dominic Guzman had inspired them to preach, and that he too would come, bearing fire and sword for when his words fell on deaf ears. But their effect was not great, nor their conversions numerous, nor were they treated with more respect for their poverty, because they came at Rome's behest, and as instru-ments of that defiler of faith and truth, the Pope. Nonetheless they frightened many people, women and little children. From the Black Hills north of Carcassonne, and down through the desolate paths of the Corbières to the Pyrenees—back and forth they passed, these ragged monks.

They preached to silent audiences in the market places, strid-ing out of the empty churches with dark faces, and sorrowful countenances. They preached, with threats of excommunication, and torture for the heretical, the dissident, the rebellious, the blasphemous, and if there were one or two brave, foolish souls who laughed, there were many more who shuddered with the chill in their hearts.

The 'Good Men' spoke up against the Church's greed, and the wickedness of her priests. Freedom, they said, was not the ele-ment that surrounded a man in his mortal state, but a prize that, once achieved, had to be grasped tightly and courageously, like a swimmer who bears a lighted beacon above the water.

Once we had come to Arques on a market day. Guilabert de

Castres himself was there—the greatest of the Cathari preachers. He quoted St Bernard—I remember it exactly—saying: 'The Churches are without devotees, the faithful are without priests, the priests without honour. There exist but a few Christians, and they without Christ.'

He said that it was for new warriors to take up arms against the spiritual evil of the Roman hegemony, and to scourge clean the land. His words stirred the townspeople into murmurs of applause.

'Our fathers and grandfathers fought to give us life, they gave us also the beacon of freedom to carry, and now we shall fight for it, for truth, and for our faith,' he declared. 'But we must also fight to ward off the grasping jackals and infamous barons who seek to enslave us. Remember your faith, and our free communities, our thriving democracies, and townships shall not come under the heels of dissipated thieves and hypocrites!'

Peire spoke that day as well. He was quiet, and the words forced themselves out of his mouth, with the restraint of desperation. The little tavern was full to bursting, his reputation was known, his name had gone before him, and the people wondered why he had no lute. 'The last freedom,' he said slowly, referring I think to Guilabert de Castres' words, 'the last freedom which a man throws away before his enslavement is the freedom of his body. The freedom to use it as he wills. The freedom to slake his desires.'

A plump, chubby-faced woman, no longer young, but painted artfully for her evening's business, laughed in his face. My Master suddenly leapt to his feet. His stool fell behind him, and the woman blanched. 'Don't look on yourself, but rather at the manner in which men wreak their will on you. Does it have affection? Answer me! You must answer me,' he cried.

'Not much,' she whispered.

'Does it have pity?'

'Not much.'

'Is there a jot of kindness in their thrusting?'

She shook her head, and tears drew comically into her painted eyes. 'They make you crawl on all fours like a dog bitch,' he said with anger, 'so as not to see the body, the human creature they mortify; so as to be better able to release their fury, their impotence, and the last animal flecks of life-lust into this

127

vehicle of "Love". Love!' He laughed aloud. 'We still call it that!'

She stared at him, her breasts, old with wrinkles, winked and fluttered behind their flimsy barricade. Pushing aside his listeners, he went up to her.

'But you're braver and stronger and more full of life than the men who try to resurrect themselves in you,' he said clearly. 'It's true!' Turning towards the older men, the merchants, scribes, and two priests standing at the back, he began again.

'When a man, be he prince or pauper, and today it's more often our princes,' he added bitterly. 'When he chooses the animal in him, living on his instinct for humiliation, he becomes an animal, and makes outcast of his spirit. He is become desperate. When we do this, we destroy the vessel from which we can assuage our mortal thirst. And we have nothing left to aspire to. Our desperation has become the reality of impotence. But let a man make his journey, let him hold the sap within him, and, at the end, whether he take whore or virgin, the gift, the potency, the love is greater, and being more cherished, has the value of inspiration. Love cherished is love earned. Love earned gives us the freedom to challenge cowardice, wrong-doing, hypocrisy, with a flame of faith and bravery in our hearts . . .'

He said more afterwards. I watched him attempting to rouse his listeners. A few thrust closer, pleading that he would go on. A few called him a vicious madman who spoke evil parables. More shouted insults, saying that he was a notorious lecher, and a public blasphemer.

But the majority of heads were already turning feverishly. Peire's was a lonely voice amongst the visions of Hell offered to them. These peasants, serfs, shopkeepers were being tossed on a sea of troubles. Scorpions and viperous thoughts filled their ears, and their unease knew not—so it seemed—where to assuage itself.

One morning, I was hobbling about the cloisters behind my Master. I still needed a stick to support me. Peire was listening to a young monk who had befriended us on the sly. He'd discovered who my Master was, and the secret, coupled with the fact of having a troubadour at his call, had inspired the ribald, yearning elements in him to confess themselves.

It was shortly before Matins when the Roll-caller arrived, and the monks eagerly anticipated his messages from the outer world. It was a rare occasion for them, and to make it rarer still, he'd come with a parchment a good forty feet long. It heralded a fine morning's entertainment.

He must have been travelling many months to have collected such a number of messages from the brothers of his scattered order. Our friend was himself a keen listener. He told us that he'd been writing to a colleague in Rome, and expected answers. The Roll-caller had much news and information to disseminate, and we listened awhile.

Many of the distant brethren referred frequently to the corruption that Holy Orders had first to stamp out within their own chapters, before turning their attention to the lay folk. One monk thundered in his epistle that moral corruption in the broadest sense was inseparable from absolute power, and that the Holy Church would do well to review the question of her economic abuses. From the shocked faces about us, it seemed a brave statement to venture.

There were conflicting accounts of the effects and successes of the crusades, and on the horrors perpetrated by Saladin. There were references to Richard Cœur de Lion's mighty defence of Christendom, and to his weak brother, Jean sans Terre, who now reigned in England. A number of those penning letters spoke of the latest drastic edicts to the faithful. Pope Innocent himself had denounced the vices and dissolute behaviour of the monastic orders. At this there fell a weighty silence in the cloisters.

'This state of things,' had declared the Pope, 'affords heresy great encouragement.'

Our companion's eyes twinkled, the shave-pates about us glanced at each other mistrustfully, as though they feared spies on their own activities.

The Roll-caller's voice grew hoarse, his eyes watered as he sought to make out the fine small letters which his fellows penned, for parchment was precious, and space could not be wasted.

Peire, with one ear cocked in the reader's direction, listened carefully, his brows contracting. Sometimes he'd nod at a phrase that touched him. I crept up to the messenger to get a squint at all those fine letters, but he elbowed me off. One piece of information I particularly remembered. There was no wind and the sunlight sparkled in a shaft of silver scales on to the well in the centre of the courtyard. He'd almost reached the end, and tired from his journey, now sat on a bench under the arches, reading slowly to conserve his voice.

'Is it not balm,' he read, 'to our beleaguered brothers, that the work of our inspired colleague Dominic has now been blessed, and given free rein by our holy father? He will follow our Roll-caller's steps to your fair Occitanie propagating the message of salvation. Brother Dominic speaks persuasively. We have heard him ourselves in Rome, but it is rumoured that in case of failure with the Word, he advocates the sword, and the stake. There are many who listen attentively to him.'

There was more to it, but I forget now. I heard my Master murmur beside me.

'Occitanie, wake up, for time drips away like a spluttering candle. Too rich, too proud, too gay, you'll suffer more deeply than you dare imagine for these sins of past forgetfulness and carelessness.'

The monk beside us looked curiously at Peire. 'Messer Carcasse,' he whispered, 'who's in the greatest danger? The priests, the people, or the nobility in our land?' He put a finger to his nose, and waited slyly for an answer.

Peire jerked his head round to look at his interrogator. 'You speak lightly,' he said, and the vein began to bump on his temple, 'but, in some measure, it's because of careless priests who have relinquished both their vows and their honour before God and men, that Terre d'Oc now learns to suffer. You neither pray, nor study, nor minister to those who sweat to feed you.'

'If I could sing like you,' muttered the acolyte uncomfortably, 'I'd become a singing friar, and preach my sermons with gay, merry refrains, and tell my flocks how to climb to Heaven dancing! That way they'd pull me up too,' he added grinning.

'That, my bold priestling, is if the people don't first rise up and take to blocking up your mouths with chalk,' said Peire, loud enough for those in the vicinity to turn their heads in alarm. We chuckled softly.

'I swear to God I'm not made for studious monkery,' grumbled our companion. 'It gives me the mumps. And a song is as holy a hymn to Heaven as rattling about on one's knees in these barren cloisters.'

'Squeak much louder, and you'll never get the chance,' I winked at him.

'*Magis magnos clericos non sunt magis magnos sapientes*, if you catch my Latin, Messer Carcasse.' His voice had dropped to a stage whisper.

'I don't,' he said with wry amusement, 'but it's as easy to be a faithless minstrel as it is to be a faithless priest!'

'I mean that the greatest clerics are not necessarily the wisest of men. And all that work, running about the cloisters, in the garden, digging into monstrous heavy tomes. It's rotten for the constitution!'

'This is a poor lost soul indeed, Messer Peire,' I grinned at my Master.

I began to have the notion that my Master was preparing himself for a confrontation. And I can't explain myself properly. But he was calm in those days. He listened more than he spoke. His eyes penetrated those with whom he found himself. He sought to extract their marrow. He gave me the impression that there was a force in him which he nurtured painstakingly: that he was battening up his defences, stone by stone. When I asked him when we would be leaving, he told me when I was recovered, both from my illness, and the blood-letting which had come afterwards. He was kind to me. He allowed me to be with him, and I heard him speak his mind. Nonetheless there was a part of him concealed from me, and I wondered mightily for our future.

I found that I missed the company of Agnes, my little scullery maid. I missed her plump good-natured cheeks, and her visions of grandeur. I missed her strapping brown arms, her firmness from navel to chaps, her shyness, her suspicions, her gentleness with me. And to relieve my heart, I started practising my juggling and acrobatics again.

There was a paddock behind the chapel, and in the late afternoons, when the monks were at Vespers, I used to go there with my tricks. It gave me much pleasure, to be there with the sun striking on to the stained glass windows, and the solemn chanting within, which seemed unknowingly to condone my act of worship under the heavens.

I would do my turns in careful order, starting with the silver balls, because the sun was still high enough to reflect its rays in them. Then I'd continue with some acrobatics on my stool, twisting and leaping on to my hands, better, and each time more daringly, as the strength returned. And then to finish I'd do my turn with the hangman's noose, allowing the cord to slip to my neck as I hung upside down from a tree branch, belching out the Greek flame, which had always been the climax to my act.

There are many jugglers, and many arts has the mountebank, but I knew that what I attempted was special to me. I found myself hoping that He whom men worship in his hundred disguises—there are a limit even to his disguises I decided—would recognize that I offered him praise.

But it wasn't long before my outdoor ceremony was brought to an end. A monk, who should have been mumbling his prayers, and not staring out of the window, caught me at it. My disguise, at least, was revealed, and our days at the monastery became numbered . . .

In the next days there came news that a great tourney was to be held in Toulouse, at the bidding of Raimon himself. My Master sprang to life, and I watched him with trepidation once more, the thoughts of my rash display banished from both our minds.

'Damn these thoroughbreds!' groaned Peire, as he attempted to bring his frisky mare to order. 'Their blood's so refined that a blade of grass twitching in the wind is enough to frighten them hysterical, but if they put one foot over a precipice they wouldn't have the sense to draw back!' He grinned at me. 'Ah! Little Beast, you look miserable. But by the time we take part in the jousting, you'll have mastered the art of companionship with these beasts again!'

Esclarmonde and her Guillem watched us leave. Even young brother Anselm had slipped out from his gardening duties to bid us farewell.

We'd paid our dues and thanked our hosts, who'd refused, nonetheless, to touch either our hands in parting or the silver which they'd claimed from us. Esclarmonde—it's hard to credit —was made to wash each coin under the pump which she had then to hand to the purser. These shave-pates may or may not be

God-fearing, but they feared contagion from us more than they did the Devil's lucre.

We turned north-west. I waved to our mournful monk, whose enthusiasms and ribaldry had decreased with every moment that had brought our departure closer.

'What shall I do?' he'd spluttered, close to tears.

'Hush! You'll be released into this gay world soon enough,' my Master told him. 'Prepare yourself for the maelstrom!' And so we were gone.

Peire was brimming, full of hurry and intensity. It boded ill, but I didn't see how. Grasping my sack more firmly over the pommel of my saddle, I stopped trying to thread my slow brain to the needle. Instead I concentrated on getting to Toulouse, despite the ill-mannered monster to whose back I clung.

We passed some miles east of Carcassonne, but Peire sent messages to his family, and heard from a merchant we overtook that his father thrived, doing brisk business with ecclesiasts and nobles alike, though the weather was hot.

The third night we sought shelter at Castelnaudary. From there we rode hard, breaking our fast the next midday at Montgiscard, and hurrying on to Montaudran. If he'd been alone my Master would already have gained Toulouse. But the roads were bad, dusty and deeply rutted. The jogging gait caused me pain, and the fine white dust seemed to make pools of glue in my lungs. I reached the City of the Rose in a state of exhaustion, Peire in a state of transfixing eagerness.

Clattering through the Arab quarter, I sniffed the aromatic odours, the spices and roast lamb, with renewed enthusiasm. The stalls and bazaars, with their wild striped awnings, and the drifting confusion of a dozen guttural dialects cheered my ears and nostrils. The children's squeals, the braying of donkeys, the barking of the dogs and human laughter made a happy change from the silent villages we'd journeyed through. Sailors, merchants, tailors, weavers, silversmiths, usurers, urchins, whores, shopkeepers, hawkers, priests, Jews, beggars, cripples, cross-legged Arab sages, and strutting pageboys from the court thronged the streets—to buy, to sell, to steal, to look at life beneath the pink walls of this most capital of cities. I was glad to be back.

In the Christian sectors of the town, banners decked the streets, flags flew from the housetops, carpets hung, flapping festively from the balconies. And from the palace itself, fine tapestries drifted over the battlements with rich oriental hangings of silk and samite. Over the main gates, as was the custom for a tourney, there dangled a particularly splendid tapestry, depicting a unicorn with a golden bracelet about its neck, protected by a night in full armour on horseback, bearing his lance towards those who sought to attack the symbol of 'love' and purity. Peire pointed to it silently as we rode beneath.

Many knights had already arrived, and had established their pavilions on the sward beneath the palace walls. Those of a higher degree, or those whose fealty Prince Raimon counted dear, would be lodged within.

Varlets, scullions, and wenches raced about making preparation for the guests. Beneath us, and outside the town, the burghers would be supervising the construction of the lists, the pavilions for the ladies and principal guests who came to watch and spur their champions on, the tents where the wounded would be attended, the stables, and the retiring areas for those waiting to display their chivalry.

I pondered with a chuckle on how the Church deplored all such amusements, issuing frequent edicts on the immorality of fighting.

It was late afternoon when we dismounted in the main court-yard. My Master was anxious to see if the Sieur Blacatz was present. 'And perhaps Lord Gazanhat and his lady?' I suggested impudently. I awaited him outside, listening to the squires boasting, and learning that the prizes were great this year, in money, metal, and titles.

There was talk, as always, of knights attempting to buy off their rivals. Bribes, deals, promises continued to be made even as the parties fought, even as one knight laid into his adversary: promises of a very small ransom if the other acknowledged defeat quickly; promises to let the other triumph on the next day; promises that were broken and mended, as often as the tide of fighting changed.

A group of squires were bemoaning the arrival of a bunch of ruffians who were trained specialists in their fields—mace, broadsword, pike, lance, tilting. These would band together or sell themselves to the highest bidder. There were many ways of being declared the victor.

Still it promised to be a glorious entertainment. I thought nervously that Peire had no cause to press me into service as his squire. It would be a mockery of the rules. A mockery, I repeated firmly to myself. 'He just can't.'

Strolling players and mountebanks had their carts drawn up outside the walls, and I hopped out to look. What a confusion met my eyes! Little booths clustered next to each other, cymbals tinkled, children howled for their mislaid parents, and everyone appeared to be selling something to his neighbour. I hollered out a greeting to a group of jongleurs from Carcassonne, and they joined me, railing and joking.

'Carcasse comes to fight?'

'What do you suppose, imbecile?' I nodded fiercely.

'It's unfair,' shouted another. 'He's got the Devil fighting for him!'

'Would he take a bribe to lend out Lucifer for the first day?' said another in a melodramatic whisper.

'Lord Gazanhat is here,' said one slyly.

'And his lady?' I asked eagerly, falling into the trap. I got a shrug and a roar of laughter for my pains.

'Little Beast,' I heard my Master. 'We stay in the Sieur Blacatz's rooms.'

'Only fitting, only fitting,' I grinned nonchalantly at my persecutors.

'What are you muttering?'

'That my Master sleeps within the walls, unlike you riff-raff, as guest to Prince Raimon,' I said carelessly.

'Sturdy bedfellows will they surely make!' roared the joker. 'An impotent, half-excommunicated Prince, and Lucifer's second cousin should keep each other warm!'

'Tuck your cleft tongue back in your throat, or it'll rot off,' I shouted back.

Peire grasped me by the arm. 'Little Beast, it's good to have you here with me.'

I felt the colour creeping into my cheeks.

'But you don't have to rise to my defence so furiously. There'll be better occasions!'

He grinned at me, and I hung my head, because I'd spoken out like a boaster.

We rested, washed, and changed. At the ninth hour Peire was

called with the whole assembly to meat. I took an appetite along behind him, and my sack of course. After greasing my stomach in the kitchens, I followed Peire into the great hall where the feast was spread.

When the guests had washed their hands in chased silver pitchers, they sat, not on bare benches, but on cushions woven with fine threads, and the napkins on which they dried their hands were of damask. Climbing up to the minstrels' gallery I noticed many beautiful ladies, young boys, many richly decked knights, and a number of greybeards clustered round the empty seats of honour at the high table. These last, ignoring for the most part the bubbling laughter and conversation about them, conversed one to another, with ponderous mien, and much scratching of their venerable pates. Looking for faces I knew, I came across Blacatz, over to one side, momentarily alone beneath the tapestries and armour hung on the walls. He was stroking his lean, clean-shaven jaw, and looked on the celebrations from a careful distance. I watched him nodding his head at those who came to salute him, his manner obsequious, his voice always soft, his glance touched with the usual subtle mockery.

The Lords of Foix and Fenouillet, Trencavel of Béziers and Carcassonne, the Counts of Ventadorn, Baum, Marseille and Roussillon, the Lords of Narbonne and Cominges were there, and many lesser nobles. I saw our old host Gazanhat, and searched about for his lady wife, but there was no sign of her. The Princes of the house of Toulouse moved amongst their guests, now grasping the elbow of an old courtier to lead him to his place, now joking with a group of squires who would be dubbed on the morrow before the sport began.

The sergeant-at-arms sounded the horn, and there was a hush. Count Raimon of Toulouse entered. No, I should rather say that his wife came in first on the arm of Pierre, Prince of Christendom and King of Aragon. Behind him came our lord, walking a little mincingly, and scattering little high-pitched laughs and asides to his guests as he moved. On his arm he bore a lady. Her lily-shaped sleeves fell deep, bordered at the wide cuffs with ermine, and the waist was pulled in high under her swelling breasts. The neck was bare of ornaments, and her black hair was piled beneath the cap she wore, from which flowed a long veil. Her expression was proud, her chin high, the eyes gazed straight ahead. There was melancholy, though, in her pride and grace. It was the Lady Azelais, Aniara.

Heads turned. The greybeards rose with their eyes downcast, and hands over their hearts. Raimon welcomed his guests in fulsome terms. Pierre of Aragon responded in kind, and they sat down to meat. Eyes moved to feast on our lady of Gazanac, and on the scarce damoselles who rivalled her. But it wasn't her beauty, I thought. Her features were too strong to be accounted very feminine. No, it was a sorcery she had at her command. A lonely, unreachable magic.

I soon saw my Master close to Blacatz. He laughed and was merry, eyelids half-closed against the light of the many chandeliers, but the severity of his features was increased by the light and shadow; the grimness in him was closer than ever to the surface.

Delicate soups and broths were brought. And then wild boar, hares, pheasants and venison of all kinds were borne in by the varlets, on gold and silver plates. And then five swans, with all their feathers artfully stuck in place. There came duck, and heron, plovers, and, last of the fowl, a peacock in its splendour. Each guest had his own pewter plate, though they shared the goblets between two or three. Blacatz and Peire drank from the same cup, as was right.

The huge repast continued, and our music began to be drowned by the belches of the men, and much juicy sucking of fingers. Wine was circulated liberally, and those who had appeared most neat and dainty at the start, now stretched the most eagerly to cram food in their mouths, reaching across the tables to seize a chicken leg, a piece of salmon, the salted shark's tail, or to suck greedily at a plate of oysters. The sap, the juice and cooked blood ran from their cheeks, and trickled on to their clothes unattended. Conversation was pawned to the food, and the noises that issued from these halls of chivalry were the noises of animals. There was no merit in performing our jigs and pastorals. Instead we watched grave seigneurs, knights, and noble ladies turn into swine.

Me—even the gluttonous Little Beast—I turned my eyes away from their display. The cheeses came, and then the cakes and sweetmeats, tarts, spiced bread, and the honeyed almonds,

137

crystallized fruit from the Orient, with apricots, melons, dates, oranges and figs.

Two tasters sat behind our lord, and chief guest, who had taken such advantage of their sought-after duties that they were rolling off their chairs. Food spilled over their raiment, the vomit spewed in drops from their slack lips. Though they had more practice in eating, their masters were not in very different state. Guests, male and female, stumbled behind the tables to vomit up their indigestion, and the servants and varlets hurried behind them with damp straw and water to clean up these noble droppings.

Toasts were pledged, oaths were sworn, the Dame of Love was heralded in a dozen drunken speeches. Honour for the morrow's jousting was boasted of, Courtoisie was proclaimed the soul of our festivities, and a few younger knights, less used to holding food and liquor with continence, slipped beneath the tables.

My Master's eye stole towards his lady. The look they cast each other was careful, and wretched.

The sergeant-at-arms clapped his hands, and in a short time a host of varlets came running in, sweating and broken-breathed from their evening's exertions. They bore small oval mirrors which they set before each of the guests. Without more ado, these latter set to busily, resurrected from their stupor by the vision of themselves. Feverishly you could see them arranging a curl, smoothing a wimple or a bodice to better advantage; or re-dressing a shirt, a cuff, or a bonnet. One pulled his surcoat down over his heaving stomach, throwing water on the food stains; a lady scooped furtively at the crumbs before attempting to squeeze her breasts still higher, and the ill-treated material down farther. They poked fingernails between their teeth, sucked their lips, or made ridiculous grimaces to tweak away a string of flesh or fruit from between their gums. Like peacocks, they squabbled with their reflections.

Blacatz was murmuring something in Peire's ear. My Master nodded, and the two of them smiled faintly. At that moment we were called again and each jongleur did his mightiest to prevail above him who'd gone before.

The next day was given over to the final preparations. Squires burnished their knights' armour and coats-of-mail until they shone; helmets, shields and swords were scrubbed with sand. Heraldic devices were refurbished, crests repainted and unbent, so that the jousters could be recognized in the lists. The lances, axes, maces and other offensive weapons were cleaned and oiled; their grips patched up with new chamois leather, their blades and points honed to fine edges, although Raimon had declared that those who dealt combatants severe wounds would be banished from the sport, and severely fined.

To my dismay I learnt that my Master would fight. He had the right, having been dubbed knight by Raimon himself, in a fit of affection, some years before.

'Your armour, Sieur Carcasse?' I asked him. 'It was left at Gazanac.'

'But my armour has travelled too, I believe,' he said lightly.

In effect, that evening it was Aniara herself who brought his helm, the rest being carried by a servant. I gawped at the two of them. She paused, inclining her head away with a sudden shyness, before turning to look at him. In her hands she stretched out the gleaming steel, bare of a crest.

'Sieur Peire,' she said. 'We parted last on miserable terms. There was bitterness in you perhaps, as there was in my heart. Strange reports have since reached me of your wanderings. Has Peire Carcasse become an honest man?'

'Surely not,' he smiled. 'It would be a sacrilege to the Carcasse, my lady!'

'Fulfil your duties as a knight in these days. As you have boasted in the past,' she said quietly. 'And knowing there is one who encourages you.' There was a pause. 'Even in her heart.'

'My lady, thanks,' he murmured bowing his head. 'But I have no gage to fight with.'

'Are you sure?'

She smiled faintly, throwing her deep gaze on him, before gliding away. Tucked in the helmet, between steel and padding, was a cornflower blue silk scarf, with the 'A' embroidered in tiny blue flowers in one corner.

That evening at the banquet there was much grave talk between the princes and councillors. It was clear that Raimon had other schemes to pursue besides the jousting.

Never in my life had I seen such an array of chivalry, nor heard so much talk, nor been an onlooker to so much whispering of secrets. Never had keyholes seemed so small, nor doors so thick against the ears of spies. Peire told me that we were only the doorkeepers.

'When those who've gone in, come out again, we'll look at their faces, Little Beast, and know whether to run for our lives.'

'I hope so,' I growled.

The tourney commenced after offices at Prime, and continued through the day, co-ordinated by the heralds. They cantered up and down the lists, announcing the various deeds attempted, the hits scored in the mêlées, trumpeting when fouls had been done, dispatching offenders from the field, and maintaining rough and ready order. So it was to continue for eight days.

In the evenings, Peire doffed his armour, and I, relieved to find him still alive, feverishly unlaced his tunic and mail, muttering over the scratches and tears which he'd received. I was glad and not glad that he shared a squire with the Sieur Blacatz.

Tired and torn though he emerged from the lists, he would still sing with more gaiety and wonder than I'd ever known in him. His voice blazed down from the gallery, caressed and stung his listeners. He had a new lute, bought in the rue de la Pourpointerie, from an ancient Arab instrument maker, and it was as if his abstinence for all those months had given him back his voice twofold, to play with all the honesty, passion and vitality in him. His lays were sometimes fierce, rippling with the tides of battle, sometimes tender, full of druery and pity.

He sang for Aniara. He clothed her in flame, and his songs adorned her with priceless jewellery. Each night he made of her a comet in travail through the heavens. And in his praise of her, in his bounteous mockery, in this prayer he sang for her, she writhed beneath, staring up at the spirit who claimed her, proud, pitiful, wide-eyed, and triumphant; staring at him, at Raimon, until all three must have understood the nature of the web in which they meshed themselves.

To a hunchback juggler watching, it was like being spectator to a feat of arms, more terrible and warlike than the battles of the tourney. The one, my wild Master, consumed in the furnace of his own leaping spirit, shivering Raimon, and the other, caught like a flying fish in the arc of her desire.

Her gaze sought out my Master's time and again. A pale violent hand would flutter up as though to banish his regard. Sometimes, when she was sitting amongst the cushions by the fire, with her maids, she'd stoop to her heel, gather the foot up, and arch backwards, as if to release the emotion and bewilderment out of her body, like a stone from a sling.

The guests became aware of the duel. For the trobar clus had been abandoned, and it had become too easy to recognize the original for Aniara. That itself was not extraordinary. Extraordinary was the persistence, temerity and explicitness of Peire's songs. He touched forbidden ground, not only in the songs of love, but in the sirventes which harped on the decadence of Occitanie's princes, on the evil in the Church, on the rumbling thunder racing through the villages. I held my heart and waited.

Reaction came soon enough. One night Count Raimon stirred in his chair, so that the legs jarred on the flagstones. His forehead creased in anger, and he raised a clenched fist. He stood up and ordered another troubadour to take Peire's place. The King of Aragon, who'd always been generous to my Master, and had, so it was rumoured, put up with many of his fits, caught Raimon's arm, and there was no more said on that occasion. But Raimon dispatched a squire to whisper something in Aniara's ear. She started, and glanced towards the Count. Her lips moved, but only in the shape of a smile. That was all.

Much was sung and spoken. Much was dared in the lists, and Peire Carcasse was not the only troubadour to tackle gritty problems in verse, and to the discontent of more puissant guests. Uc de la Baum, and the younger Ventadorn took to the floor. The former, who was as good a warrior as minstrel, made slighting reference to the lazy nobility who grew lax, unwatchful, and a prey to those drugs of love, liquor and gluttony. He sang the song of the sword, using the old ideas of chivalry as symbolized in the knight's weapon: courage to be gained from the cross at the hilt, knowing God supports him; loyalty and justice to be remembered from the two-edged blade, because knighthood must sustain the weak against the strong, the poor before the rich; humility from the first stroke which the blade delivers, because the sword is used against its own master when he's dubbed knight, and he may not retaliate or take offence

Bawdy songs, too, were sung, inveighing against the falseness of chastity, the hypocrisy of moralizing. The priests were often the butt of such lyrics.

Peire took up his lute again, the night after his dismissal by Raimon. In the latter's presence, pressing his luck, and my nerves to the limit, he sang of his preference for Pierre of Aragon, and made slighting reference to the war-cry of the Toulousains— 'Bear and Snake'. Many in the hall lisped and fell silent, until Peire suddenly made volte-face and spoke of the saving qualities of the two heraldic creatures; the bear's huge reserves of strength, the snake's cunning, his healing powers.

The night wore deeper, until the last twang of a lute string called us to bed. As the throng separated, Raimon brushed close to my Master, and, with his back to him, called out clearly, so that all might hear: 'Carcasse should have a care not to overstep the boundaries of our dignity. His songs are pretty, we have been generous to his faults, but even courtoisie and love have frontiers!'

'Perhaps we should extend those frontiers,' my Master called out gaily, 'and my ditties will grow still lewder!'

I tugged on his doublet so that he'd stop. 'And if you end up on the wrong side of those frontiers?' I hissed.

On the eighth day the jousting came to an end. Fresh knights had earned their laurels, tried soldiers had retained their reputations. The mercenaries and professional jousters were splitting up their spoils and preparing for the next occasion. That night we had a new guest in the palace of Toulouse.

The lithe, copper-haired spitfire whom I'd met that first time in Carcassonne, and who had told me of Peire's whereabouts, arrived with her betrothed. At least I presumed that the gangling, lank-haired youth, with spots covering his jaw, and the nervous disjointed hands, was her betrothed. Perhaps he owed his luck to a lengthy pedigree.

'Na Louva's here,' I told my Master, pointing to her. Her eyes glittered, big at the unaccustomed splendour about her.

'She came on the right day for surprises,' he grinned.

It was Blacatz, with his usual penetrating eye, who sought out the little group. 'Our she-wolf!' he chided.

Her reputation had clearly travelled farther than the Little Beast. Her skinny clerk of a father stood beside her, looking askance at all these nobles whose charters of rank were doubtless older than his own, and whispering heatedly at his daughter.

'Be quiet, father,' she said, beaming radiantly at the Sieur Blacatz, and taking his arm.

He it was who escorted her among the guests. She'd grown to lusty roundness, to beauty, to pride in her youth, to rejoicing in the loving, licking eyes cast on her. She noticed me, and tossed me a stray smile. I admired her in surprise.

'Look, even the Little Beast is here!' she noted to her mentor.

'As jongleur to Peire Carcasse,' answered Blacatz.

She turned sharply. 'Will you make him sing for me?'

'It's early yet. We must first sit down to meat.'

'No matter,' she whispered urgently. 'Make him sing an angry sirventes or a cri. Something to frighten all these noble people.' She was flushed and full of excitement. I wondered if she'd forgotten her hatred of my Master.

Blacatz laughed. 'He's been doing just that for the past week,' he said. 'And it's hardly in my power to squeeze the music out of Peire Carcasse. But you could try!'

'Oh no,' she replied very seriously. 'That would be impossible. I bear him no regard. He's not an honourable minstrel.'

Blacatz told her that she was surely right in her opinion, but he was unable to restrain his merriment. Peire had overheard their conversation and, seizing his lute, he leapt up to the gallery alone.

Who seeks to love a damoselle,

he sang with a chuckle in his voice,

> Will tame her gently and with time,
> Just as the wild she-falcon needs
> A magic hand—no less she heeds,
> So does the virgin mistress bide,
> Untried in Love, but loathe to hide
> Her mysteries—then tamed to Love
> She flies more perfectly than any dove,
> Than any bird who seeks her prey
> Upon the roads of Amor's way!

'But it's the lady who tames her lover,' pealed Na Louva. 'Not the other way round!'

Her face puckered in annoyance. Knights and ladies smiled at this novelty, and Blacatz cozened her merrily.

143

The company sat down. The guests of honour proclaimed the victors of the jousting, and crowned them with laurel. My Master, although he'd fought courageously, and had suffered a severe shoulder wound, which he'd not reported, was not among the trophy winners. But his deeds had been mentioned by the heralds on more than one occasion. That was enough for me, and for Aniara, too, I'd begun to suspect.

Peire ate next to nothing, and was withdrawn throughout the meal. As the sweetmeats and fruit were brought in, he rose and, striding to the centre of the hall, begged that he might be allowed to sing a cri that he'd composed, dedicating it to his friend and patron, the Sieur Blacatz. This last, cast an uneasy glance at my Master, but refrained from speaking, or accepting patronage of the composition. Permission was granted, and Peire ascended to the gallery.

'Little Beast,' he called. 'Do you come and keep me company!'

His instrument and mine tuned, he turned to the guests. I began to have an inkling of the next moments, for I'd heard snatches when he'd been practising.

'Good Prince, fair Lord of Occitanie, dear chatelaines, damoselles, my gentle knights,' he cried. 'We've come to sing farewell. If our gracious host wills it, let the sweet wines be brought in so that you have nothing lacking. Let the mirrors be brought you too, so that you may freshen up those sagging curls, those poor dried cheeks and faded lips, which smile so fulsomely upon us.'

It was done. The varlets hastened in with their glittering burdens. The burnished steel cast a thousand splinters of light about the high, arched hall. Each turned his mirror to his best reflection.

My Master continued: 'Tonight we wish, fair brethren, to seduce you towards a new madness! What shall we call it, Little Beast?' His eyes danced over me.

'You'll tell me doubtless,' I muttered.

'We'll call it survival,' he paused. 'Yes, the madness of survival!' And he sang . . .

> Fools reflections linger
> In the mirrors you so prize,
> Painfully reflecting
> The features you disguise.

144

Like our Damoselles pull faces,
Like they squander love and pain,
Your candle-lit reflections
Tell men the world is vain.

The wheels of change turn slowly,
But the candlewicks burn down,
Our Hall of Mirrors darkens
Do you now begin to frown?

You cripples dancing gaily
To your liegemen's freedom cries,
Your souls like broken vessels
Shall be tossed in blood-red skies.
And Peire Carcasse before you
He stares down empty halls,
He weeps for your reflections,
Their death, their dying coils.

The wheels of change turn slowly,
But the candlewicks burn down,
Our Hall of Mirrors darkens,
Do you now begin to frown?

An age of ease is ending,
Your knights shall be cut down,
Their windy gestures fending
Off a foreign prince's crown.
All your daisies are beheaded,
All your games have no encore,
Death holds his hand to heaven,
D'Oc weeps for evermore.

The wheels of change turn slowly,
Now the wicks are all burnt down,
Our Hall of Mirrors darkens,
Do your smiles still hide the frown?

A voice rang out.
'Peire, enough!'

145

It was Blacatz who, letting his mask drop for an instant, released his own fears into the public air.

'You're too late,' I murmured to myself.

'On this last day of jousting and bravery,' Blacatz continued, 'we need more cheerful panegyrics to . . .'

He hadn't time to finish before Count Raimon rose to his feet. 'Minstrel and knight,' he said in ringing tones. 'We have listened to much from you. We have born blasphemy, falsehood, traitorish words, and knavery at your hands. We have listened to your discourtesy, have noted your unchivalrous behaviour, and have regretted the death of your honour to lady and lord.'

There was a short pause.

'Honour has no place when you fight for survival,' said Peire bitterly. 'And chivalry, true chivalry to God and Beauty, was dead long before I came to watch your knightly hogs swill themselves to stupor at your tables. Oh, my lord,' he cried out, 'teach us to live, to fight. Shall we stand upright in our hoggish nobility, and wait to be mown down by iron, greedy, foreigners?'

'Messer Peire, you've thrown your life away with those words,' I whispered, but he did not hear me.

'Mercy and thanks, minstrel, for this advice! Carcasse!' Prince Raimon shouted above the growing tumult, and his voice became high-pitched in cold fury. 'By right as lord and ruler, by code of knighthood and chivalry, by the blood in you, by your life, I herewith order and demand your banishment from all our lands in Occitanie. You shall be banished from our courts, from our realms, from our brethren. Those who succour you will do so on pain of death. If you are found still in these territories seven days from dawn tomorrow, you shall be hung, drawn and quartered like a common felon. You shall take you on pilgrimage to the Holy Land, there to make penitence for your crimes. Return with the proofs of your conduct, and you may yet die at peace in your own country. This is my word. Who hears it and obeys it not, suffers death.'

Raimon turned on his heel, his royal cousin of Aragon awaited him, and without a backward glance they left the place. Two greybeards followed each man out. It had been rumoured that there was a secret council that night. Behind them they left a deadly hush.

Peire turned away. Feverishly I signalled to the jongleurs

behind us. They at least had their wits about them, and struck up a measure. It turned out to be the worse thing they could have done. Their leader stepped to the balcony's edge, announcing a dance. Voices responded from below. My Master lifted his lute over his head and passed it to me.

'Guard it well,' he muttered. 'I don't think her strings will shiver to a cheerful tune for many a day! Oh, Little Beast,' he grinned tightly at me, putting an arm about my shoulders, 'I wish we knew another way to live, not spread-eagled on the thorns of our hunger.'

'I wish you knew, Master . . .'

Peire ran down the steps to the hall, and I tumbled after.

'I'm not banished until tomorrow,' he shouted lustily, 'so may not a skinner of songs lead the fair Azelais to the dance?'

'Sieur Peire,' I grabbed his arm, unable to control myself. 'On top of everything will you dance with the chatelaine of Gazanac? Look at all their faces about you!'

'Yes, my friend, if it please you, I will.' He fixed me suddenly with stony eyes. 'One last dance before the jackals are on us—if you will allow it.'

The sarcasm made me wretched. I dropped my hand. 'Forgive me Messer, I would not interfere.'

'That's wise Little Beast.' His voice changed. 'You see, dear friend, the hour of jousting has only come for us now. And we must step bravely into the fray, to the music we've invented. Isn't that right?'

I stared at him.

'But the road afterwards is truly a lonely one.' He shook his head. 'Would you rather stay? I make you free of me. You shan't lack a stomach's fill, nor an audience to gaze on the mysteries of your sack.'

The dark head stared back at me. Over one angular shoulder I could see through a chink in the wall bright stars against the dark.

'I can't turn back now, Sieur Carcasse. There's nothing behind me.'

'There's still time, Little Beast. What will you do with all our fears, an empty stomach, a fugitive for a Master?'

'Hold on tight,' I muttered, 'and hop behind in the madman's footsteps.'

He gripped me close. I watched him turn lonely across the

147

empty floor, with the slithering music rippling behind us. People were turning their heads away already.

Blacatz caught up with him. 'You risked more than your neck, you crazy fool,' he hissed. 'You risked mine. Why did you do it? You've already seen the consequences.'

'The time had come to do it, Blacatz.'

'How did you know so much?'

'Holding the portals wide, and watching who came in to feast, good patron. But I know nothing. Only what I see.'

'I can't help you any more, Peire. I can't protect you.'

'I know, so good-bye Blacatz. Fare you well. Now you must release me to the dance.'

He strode on. I saw him lifting Aniara from her seat. I saw her mute appeal, but there was nothing for it. I saw them sweep on to the floor, her white hand knotted in his, at arm's length. And opposite me I also saw Na Louva's copper hair. Her eyes followed my Master. Was this a small revenge for her? You've had your cri, spitfire, I thought.

The sweep of her gown, and my Master's scraping feet, the glinting hair tumbling from her coif, the eyes which didn't look any more to escape, their two hands clasped, their feet in stately measure—yes, they danced—Aniara and Peire Carcasse, they danced together and alone.

That night he stole upstairs into the gallery where the ladies and damoselles slept. He unfastened the chamber door where Aniara lay. First he glanced long upon her. He kissed her uncoiled hair, the smooth forehead, proud nose, her eyes. He kissed her red mouth many times until she awoke. Half-asleep and beyond endurance, she plunged fierce arms about him. He cast the stiff linen sheets back, and drew her body to him. He traced fingertips the length and breadth of her; down breasts, abdomen, thighs, down to the strong wench's ankles, and her high arching feet. He took her and loved her, as she did him, and her cries grew heavy on the silence.

'Is there honour in us now, Peire?'

'I know not!' He howled like a wolf.

The house woke stealthily. The varlets scuttled up with torches to illuminate the keyholes down the draughty passages. Peire kissed her.

148

'You've given me earthly communion,' he said. 'And Carcasse will wait for you on the edge of the world.' He was gone.

Varlets retreated back into the yawning stillness. They talked of that 'kiss' for years to come. Who had given it? Was it him? And the lady?

The following morning our bags and accoutrements were packed carefully on the extra mule. My Master's armour was tressed up behind his saddle, and the victuals behind mine. He gave me what money and silver we still had to guard. On his right shoulder I stitched the cross, and another on his mantle. The sun crept up across the rosy walls. Toulouse was awaking, and the bells of St Sernin rang out the Prime.

'We take ship from Marseille,' he told me. 'God help the Carcasse and Little Beast.'

6

It took us ten days hard riding to reach Marseille. Every night when we stopped at a hostel, Peire would hand me the reins and, with his lute on his back, take himself off to the village square. The people listened to his songs, his hymns to survival, he called them. In frightened, hesitant voices they'd also ask him what was happening in the palaces, in the capital, in the nobles' halls. With wonderful confidence they'd beg his answers to why the plague of boils was sweeping up the coast, and why the priest had seen vultures hovering for days over the village church, and why seven ravens had come screaming from the north and in each village they passed over, a man or baby boy had died.

I was amazed to see how far his name had travelled. But no, he told me: 'This road from Toulouse to Marseille has often witnessed my hasty passage.'

It was a wry, sad ache of a grin that accompanied his words. I thought of this fugitive of a Master. So many fugitives wrapped in one, I told him.

The consummation with Aniara had perhaps given him new fury, even some magic kind of courage. But it had also taken something away from him. In some way he had given in to the anger and frustration in him. And then I remembered his having said to me roughly, jokingly once: 'Save your sperm, and when you finally sow your seeds, they'll spurt deep into the womb you choose, ripen faster, and give up a crop of heroes!' But then, I told myself, what other woman was there for him in life? What other womb?

He listened to the peasants too. Often I'd go to bring him to bed, and he'd be asking an old knife-sharpener on his donkey, or one of the shepherds in the square about themselves. How could they answer his questions? They'd stare back at him, as lost as he was.

'Tell me who you are, what you believe,' he'd plead.

'It's plain enough,' would be the gruff retort.

'What will become of you, your life? Tell me, and perhaps I can learn too. What will you do when the iron men come to raze your houses?'

'I'll stand here with my scythe, and chop the horses' legs off, till they get me,' grunted one.

'And your wife and daughters?'

'When the bullies come, I'll tell you then.'

'And if they rape your children?'

'Sieur Carcasse, you may be a fine minstrel, but I'll knock your block off if you talk about my women that way!'

Peire would smile despite the harrowing misery in him.

'Organize yourselves; you could live in the forests, attack their stragglers, the tail-enders. You could protect your families, hide them away, hide the corn. Think on it for Christ's sake! The plague's come, the omens have come. How much longer have you? Will you wait and see?'

'What else? We have to live.' And they'd shake their heads at all the strange questions, preferring the songs.

'And then,' muttered another, 'it's safer to flee. What are we to fight the iron men with—pitchforks made of wood? Better to hide away until they've gone.'

'They won't go away.'

'They always go on. They always move somewhere else. When they've plundered all we have, what else is there to stay for?'

'Your land, your forests, your lakes. This patch of sky here,' said Peire. 'And you. All of you, men, women, babies. They'll stay to rule you, and I know their rule a little. I've been to their lands. They rule well, in their fashion.'

'What's the difference, then, between Count Raimon and these?'

'They'll want you to break your souls, as they will your bodies, to their bit and bridle.'

'Like Rome?' they asked.

'Like Rome,' Peire nodded. 'Because they know that power over a man's body can be exchanged or transferred, but that once you've got his brains, and terrified his soul into belief in their authority, he's theirs for ever.'

'Hasn't Raimon got us body and balls?' cried one hefty giant. 'We toil from dawn till dusk for the scraps we have to eat.'

'No, friends. If you lift your head from the plough at daybreak for an instant, if you stop grinding your millstones for a moment, and stretch your muscles, you'll know that Raimon does not own you. He's too weak, but more important, he is one of you, one of us, a man of Occitanie. Those who come to take liberty away are not of Terre d'Oc, and have neither love nor knowledge of the land.'

'People tried to organize communities, and make guilds, town guilds, up north. The ringleaders were burnt as heretics!'

'Go on! We must go on. The men who come will burn all of us. These are disciplined, and more cruel than any men you have yet encountered,' said my Master wearily. 'They rule with iron fists, terror, fear and spies. They will lash you to the ploughs to increase their yield. They will take away your children to teach them to be good foreigners, and your children will return as traitors, to tyrannize their parents and villages. These men will make the rules. They will tell you what to think and believe. Those who resist will be tortured before their families, until they repent and are like broken reeds in the wind. You will be put in stone quarries, like prisoners, to till the rocks. You will be castrated, and blinded, and there will be no more sons in Terre d'Oc, unless you throw off your fatigue. Forget your impotent lords. They'll most surely be destroyed first of all. But you, you can be free men!'

'What if they don't come—these Iron Men?'

I'd tug his sleeve more insistently, until he turned.

'I tell them what will be. Perhaps I'm wrong. What if I'm wrong, Little Beast? I don't understand. How shall I learn?'

The last night before Marseille we stopped in a bigger village. If my memory is right it was after Aiguemortes. Yes, a good way after. There was a fair camped on the outskirts in a big field, and a few down-at-heel jugglers and mountebanks, hawkers and booth-keepers in their torn huts, selling sweets and quack herbs and trinkets. The tooth-puller sat on a mat with the bloody proofs of his successes laid out neatly in rows before him. His own mouth which gave off a foul stench was almost empty. There was a clown, too, putting up his tent, and we stopped.

He laced the fabric on to the back of his cart, thus making the backdrop for the little arena in which he'd perform. His props were pulled out. He attached a great white cardboard star to a pole, which he then buried in the centre of the stage. It reminded me of our show—my uncle and Fiametta and Bernard—and I stared bewitched.

'Wait Messer, let us wait, please!' I asked.

So we stayed. He painted his face white with chalk, climbed into his motley, and then strutted about, beating a tin plate with a stick to announce the show.

People drifted towards us, and soon a small crowd was standing in a semi-circle. The older ones squatted on the two benches he'd placed in front. We watched his antics, listening to the stray popular songs, and the poor topical jokes. It was a sorry performance, and I shrugged at Peire. He bade me contain my impatience, and I fidgeted next to him, ashamed of this colleague's undiscipline, and lack of talent.

The clown mouthed his ditties about monsters, kings and princes who all breathed fire and brimstone, of priests who breathed garlic and onions to disguise their foulness, of Frenchmen who breathed viperous avarice and lust for Occitanie. The audience cackled now and again, principally to see the puissant made so small. The actor then girded on a wooden sword, making a great show of bravery in the face of the cardboard foes he waggled in the other hand. There was a crusader with a black beard, on a horse so small that his feet touched the ground, and a painted devil with a long tail, cloven feet, and horns sprouting from his head. The clown strutted and fretted against his imaginary assailants. The plump girls and wide-berthed matrons chattered in noisy whispers at his pictures of chivalry, and the travesty he made of courtoisie.

All of a sudden, the clown ceased his pirouettes. The wooden sword, with the cardboard images, clattered to the ground, and for a second he stood still, with his white-painted face immobile and sad. The audience grew still too. A shiver of the chill evening air touched my shoulders. The benches beside us creaked with the weight of easing cheeks and thighs.

The clown flopped to the ground, pointed to the rising moon coming out over his cart, with a wide gesture that bade us look at this mystery as well.

At last he had us in his hands. With slow high steps, pointing his toes to the ground, as though each movement was an experiment, he moved to the pole in the centre. With a careful gesture, he held his hands cupped towards the star, and slowly turned his gaze. There were tears glistening on his cheeks.

We watched him, holding our breath, as he climbed slowly upwards, wrapping his feet and hands about the pole, so that his

153

body seemed to arc away from him, like a monkey's, or a cripple's. We watched him climb into the sky, his arms stretching out like a dwarf-Christ, when his feet had found their hold. I began to feel the unease of those who watched. Higher and higher reached the silent mummer, stretching his arms with a desperate restraint towards the star. He slipped a little. There was a gasp. He climbed on upwards. Now he swung close to the summit, and his hold looked infinitely precarious. A hand reached up. The fingers quivered on to air, and then stretched, stretched to touch the star. Amazement dawned on him, his eyebrows started, as though he'd been scorched by the heat of the celestial body. For an instant he was paralysed in space. He hung on nothing, and then with a quick, broken gesture his limbs slackened, and he slid to the ground. It seemed, in the stray moonlight, that it was only rags which had fallen back to earth, and that he'd vanished.

Briefly we stared, and listened. The clown's face looked up. He laughed aloud, and held his hand out in a jerky movement for the coins. The spell was broken. 'That's a clever trick,' someone said. 'He must have joints like soft paste!'

Marseille greeted us with its red and pink and grey stones, its pines and cypresses, its strange languages, its strange clothes. There were many Moors and Arabs in the streets. A man who'd come from China was pointed out to us, and there was no boat, we were told, for a month.

The port was full of pilgrims. Some who'd come from St Jacques of Compostela, or who were going there, others bound for Jerusalem, or Rome, or Saintes Maries. There were many also who had no place to go, and who moved, it seemed, in a state of trance from St Jacques to Rome, to Le Puy even. They'd set out sometimes ten years before, for a vow, for the death of a brother or wife, to expiate a sin, and finished by taking up their wandering life, because they had lost their place in the other.

We tried to get beds at one of the hospices. They refused us, thinking that minstrels would give any lie for free hospitality.

'Thieves for all your fine clothes,' they cried, looking at my Master and his lute.

We left our mounts at the stables of the big inn because we could not afford to take them to the Holy Land, and walked down to the port.

It was an old man who sold salted fish who took us in, out of charity, he declared, though he was not rich and clamped his paws on the deniers we gave him with great alacrity. It was always the same fish he brought back in the evenings, swearing and cursing at the pilgrims who found that his wares stank. 'What do they want my fish to smell of?' he'd shout at me, wiping his chapped face with a dirty hand. 'Roses?' And the next morning, he'd leave the evil-smelling house again, always with the same wares it seemed. To avoid the sickening odours, Peire, too, would take to the streets.

He'd changed his clothes. He wore now a grey pilgrim's tunic, but without the cross sewn to the shoulders, and of his armour all he kept was his sword, which was thrust between the knotted cords about his waist. He'd cut his hair, and had lost some weight. It was colder now. The time hung heavily.

One day he took me to the great cathedral. He said he was going to show me the relics of St Mary and of St Lazarus. 'Christendom is lucky,' he said. 'We have enough relics scattered about to remake at least two Saint Marys, bone for bone!' His joking made me uneasy. It wasn't that simple to throw off superstitions of the faith. I'd mumbled before a good number of relics in my time. They'd served many people. People whose own faith had given holiness to those old bones. I peered behind the grill where they were, listening to the spluttering candles, feeling their heat close to my chin, while Peire strode about the dark naves, with his head sunk on his chest.

I often used to wander along the quays, peering at the fishing boats, and at the long blackened breakwaters thrusting deep into the sea. The wind was strong with the smell of seaweed, salt, stale river water, and fish! Live fish, dead fish, salted fish, but fish, always fish!

And my Master? I'd ask myself, what's he sniffing? The humiliation in him, and the horror, and the pity? What could I do? I'd stare out at the green waves until my eyes became glassy, and I'd lose myself on the sea's horizon with no more thoughts in me. A shell was like my hand when I tucked it round my ear. It brought stillness with the noise of distant waves. I tried to calm my anxiety. A picture of Bernard would run into my head. I remembered what my Master had said about the Iron Men taking the children away, and sending them back traitors to their homes, to tyrannize their fathers . . . 'If you can't swim you die faster,' I said to myself, watching a vessel wobbling into harbour. 'And death enriches the sea as much as it does mother earth!' I grinned.

Cease wretch to mourn, to weep, sip up the sun,
We dance along death's icy rim, but is the dance less fun?

And Peire was alive, and of course he would return to Terre d'Oc!

I awoke one morning to find him already up, and preparing to leave. I asked him whither he was bound, but he ignored me, pausing to unbuckle his sword and throw it on the pallet. I crept after him.

He walked steadily, deliberately, now and then turning his head this way and that, as if to keep his bearings. He looked so thin. The flesh was wearing off his bones, and the wide shoulders, stuck out at right-angles to his body, were like the sticks of a cross. Even his head sometimes looked too heavy for his body. He turned round, stepping backwards, and I caught my breath. But no, his gaze was not on me. He seemed to be listening to the wind. Snatches of a song, a few words, or the melody hummed in splinters, reached me. I dodged behind the wine carts, and water-carriers, keeping close to him. It was dusty work. 'Little Beast,' I grumbled, 'you'd have done better to mind your own business. What concern is it of yours if Messer Carcasse chooses to fly around in half-holy rags, and scare good folk out of their wits?'

We'd reached the cathedral square. It was still early, and there were few pilgrims, or any souls about for that matter. Peire sat down on the bottom steps, cross-legged and as calm as you make them. As if he'd been a professional pilgrim all his life. 'What's he got in his head? My heart dropped straight into my stomach, and I became aware that the latter, far from the whiff of rotting fish, was experiencing pangs of hunger.

Peire sat motionless, with his hands knotted on his knees, and his head bent down. A donkey stopped, and a burly peasant leant down. He must have mistaken my Master for the real thing.

'Watch out,' he wheezed, 'or you'll be catching sunstroke on that ill-shaved pate of your father!'

Peire's head jerked up.

'No irreverence meant, your worship!' The peasant added hastily. 'Would you be going to the Holy Land?'

His question was overheard by an old woman, perched high on an ancient donkey.

'The Holy Land!' she squeaked. 'Holy father, will you take a prayer for my son with you?'

The donkey managed a brief burst of speed which carried it some yards past my Master. Flailing the beast, she turned his head about and brought him back.

'Would the good father accept a pitcher of fresh milk, and a new-baked loaf? My sister's house is not far,' the old lady wheedled. She knew that pilgrims, especially monks, had large bellies and small purses. She also knew that if she could impress her message on a holy traveller, it would be brought to the Holy Sepulchre, and serve greatly towards the remission of her sins.

Stray people were beginning to tarry about my Master. A couple of sailors approached, and three or four urchins on the look-out for a squabble and a few coins. The woman kicked her donkey closer.

'If the good father might even be willing to have a word with my son. He's in town, at my sister's,' she mumbled slyly. 'He's all that's left to me.' Her face squeezed into a thousand wrinkles. 'My boy's a blasphemer. He talks of nothing else except "joi d' amour" and courtly ladies, as if they were for the likes of us. He's gone and got himself mixed up with those "Parfaits" too, 'though he only does it to meet the knights and that. The priest in our village has already reported him. What can I do? I fear for him!'

Peire looked up at her finally. 'Is your son a blasphemer from hope in his future, or from hatred of the man he is?'

She gawked at him uncertainly. 'Don't rightly know, your worship, I don't think he hates anything much except work—with the vines or the olives you see. He calls it demeaning to noble spirits.' A mournful cackle rose out of her chest.

'Your son, good widow,' Peire said gently, 'is a bit of a scoundrel, I think. Let him loose in the world, and if one sturdy thrashing doesn't bring him home chastened, perhaps the second or the third or fourth will persuade him he's a man!'

'Won't you speak to him? I couldn't say those things to him. And then he wouldn't last two minutes on his own. He's that

157

useless!' She began to weep. 'He says he's waiting for something to turn up. He says a knight'll ride past our door, and take him off. He says that the most famous minstrels came from poor stock, like that one—what's-his-name from Carcassonne? The only person he'd give a beating to is his mother, when I bid him to help me in the fields.'

'Your son wants to live,' Peire said, 'but without the effort which makes good the enterprise. It were better to throw him out, bar your door to him, and let him die, good woman. Your son is impotent. There are enough of his kind in Occitanie already. Yes, better to have him dead. He'll shame you less.'

'What's this, what's this?' grunted a plump, sweating merchant, astride a tall mule, who was pulling two pack animals behind him. 'Occitanie's the best place in the world. More freedom, better prices, good living conditions, if you're prepared to work. If the poor weren't so lazy they'd be as well off as I am! And what's this about impotence? Plenty of babies being born, eh?' He stuck a finger in his collar to air his sticky neck.

'How can you say he's better dead,' wailed the widow, 'he's my son, he's all the child I've got.'

'And Terre d'Oc is my land. It's all the land I've got,' Peire said sweetly, staring into her face. 'If the real cowards are dead, perhaps we'll be brave enough to survive.'

'And you'd have my boy killed. That's worse than the heretics. It's not true. You're a priest, no? Help him.'

He burst into laughter. 'Oh widow, what a man you chose!' He glared about him, and I crept closer. 'For your son, however, I shall be a kind of death.'

'It's not as if my boy's a thief or a murderer,' whined the old woman, 'and there's many a rotten fruit among the clergy, what's more; 'mong them trying to chase us into Paradise before we're ready.'

'My friends, do you doubt me? I promise you that a wolf in priest's clothing may be relied upon for his wit, his cunning, and his sharp teeth!'

'What's that supposed to mean?' cried the hefty peasant who'd first accosted Peire. 'And who are you, if it comes to that? I bet he doesn't even know his Ave Maria. Tell us a prayer, quick!'

They jostled closer.

'I've sung my prayers,' he cried into their curious faces,

'beneath a thousand silken counterpanes. I've worshipped the divine incarnation in womanhood at a thousand bed-rails. I've never wearied in my zeal!'

'It's not true, Master,' I whispered. 'Why do you tell them that?'

'. . . Not like that plump merchant who labours to his heaving bed already asleep, for want of spiritual ardour!'

The burgher started. 'An ill-mannered priest,' he declared with ludicrous surprise.

'And I've sired also many bastard ditties to the glory of love and druery. My soul picked out the queen of Heaven.' He stopped suddenly, staring a little wildly at those pressing in on him. 'I cast the seeds of desire into her womb so that they might be fertilized into well-made bastard beings! And I donned the vestments of holiness . . . don't you understand, don't you see?' He groaned softly, rocking his body from side to side.

'Blasphemer! Blasphemer!' hissed the widow.

'The fellow's dangerous,' shouted the merchant. 'There's a heretic here. He's no priest. He's lost his wits and insults the mother of God!'

'I have not lost my wits,' my Master cried, and, jumping to his feet, seized the mule's bridle. 'Madness, brother merchant, is the oil in which men fry sanity—without it life has no taste, and burns to charcoal.'

The trader became frightened by the scarecrow's antics. The mule reared, unaccustomed to the strange hand tearing at the bridle. The rider drew his whip. 'Let loose, let loose, maniac!'

But Peire gripped tight, letting his assailant's blows rain down without hindrance.

The old woman slid down from her donkey in a flurry of black skirts. Crying out that the Devil was in their midst, she took to belabouring my Master from behind, slapping and pulling at his garments. 'This for my son whom you'd murder, and this for deceiving a hapless widow,' she squealed.

People stopped. I crept up behind them, gazing at the mêlée round my Master.

'God, what was wrong with the man? What's he trying to do? Invent a new murderous variety of misery?'

I'd grown sick of trying to understand. Swinging my long arms about the widow's mighty waist, I heaved backwards, and pulled her away with a cracking noise; I had all the breath knocked out of me. He turned, and, catching sight of me beneath my catch, bade me desist.

'A blow to echo each song I've sung! That's a good price. But you, what are you doing here? You've betrayed your trust!'

'What trust, Messer?' I said bitterly. 'A dog follows his master. Have you sold me to someone else?'

'No witnesses!' he whispered, and then raising his voice furiously: 'I want no witnesses. Go away from me!' His words were forgotten as the stout widow turned on me with flying fists, and raking fingernails.

Out of the tail of my eye I saw a stocky, raw-boned peasant approaching. He bellowed to know what was amiss.

'A false clerk from Rome,' cried the woman. 'He slides into honest folk's beds when the men's backs are turned!'

'We'll teach him a lesson to remember, widow Maury,' answered the other. He elbowed me out of his path, and, detaching my Master's hand from the bridle with one huge paw, he seized Peire by the throat.

'So you've come to preach lies and threats from Rome. Bed-prelate scum!'

'Not from Rome, friendly ogre,' said Peire, with a bloody grin, 'but to preach—yes, perhaps that's why I'm here!' He raised a haggard face to his captor's, and with a jerk shook himself free. 'I'm here to tell you to beware of priests, and not to hearken to the salvation offered you by foreigners. You shouldn't be taken in by appearances. Holiness is not the clothes on a man's back, nor the texture of his skin, nor even his unctuous words. Open your eyes!'

The merchant hit him in the eye with his crop. It was a vicious blow, and my Master's head jerked back. I ran towards him.

'That'll open yours maybe,' laughed the fat burgher.

'Yes, yes, aim well your blows, clout lustily I beg you, before my holy sense of independence gets too uppish!'

'Stop it,' I cried to them. 'For pity's sake, he doesn't know what he says.'

'But remember,' cackled Peire, 'though appearances leave a lot to be desired, you must first live and breed lustily to earn your salvation hereafter. But raise your sons to potency, not dreams; forge them with fury and pride, not despair; groom them with harsh love, and independence, and respect, but not fear nor subservience nor awe, nor sly comparisons with those around them! For you are cowards, all cowards, but there are heroes swelling within you!'

The thick-set little fighter, his mouth gaping in a mixture of frustration and anger, dispatched one mighty cuff which caught Peire on the side of his head, and sent him headlong to the ground.

'To survive we need real men, not shadows imitating each other.' He uttered the words faintly, passing a hand across his bloody temples. 'Our nobles have dried up, our peasants cringe, our women yearn for new yeast to swell their loins. Get to the sowing!' he shrieked. My Master was delirious.

'Punish him no more! He's no priest from Rome. Have pity on his folly.' I fell at his side. 'Messer Peire,' I whispered, 'Speak no more.'

The others stared down at me incuriously. An urchin crept between their legs, scurrying dirty paws into my Master's clothes. I brushed him away. Dumbly I listened to the noise of the wind, a bird crying, the carts rattling in the streets. Although my eyes were not focusing it seemed that the sky flew away over our heads, taking with it this moment of blood and pain. My heart refused to let it all depart, and there was still more loneliness in me for the two of us.

I heard their breathing. The merchant had taken up his reins again. The widow was mounted on her donkey. The wild red peasant who'd beaten my Master had his scythe over his shoulder, cutting the sky, immortal and stupid. I turned back. There was blood, sweet and sticky, on his face. Gouts fell from his lips. The eyelids stirred, and then his eyes had plunged into mine. 'Little Beast,' he said, 'poverty means living without hope.'

. . . There was a ship—a neat, high-prowed three master. She crept out of the light pink mist early one morning, laden with rosewood, cedar, copper, mercury, precious metals, and paper, and a cheerful bunch of returning pilgrims. My Master was one of the first to board the vessel. The captain, a violent, barrel-chested Dutchman, and very lousy, spoke execrable French, loved music, and gave us cheap passage in return for entertainment. We were rescued at last from this town which had imprisoned us. At that time I felt eternal gratitude.

Our voyage in the vessel's hold was a month-long nightmare. Peire was almost speechless. I suffered permanently from sea-sickness. At night, the stench of human dirt, and the rats, with which we all battled, reduced sleep to a slipping mirage.

There were twenty-five pilgrims in the hold. The women and children had the worst of it. At dusk, when the sailors had finished their chores before the night, we'd pull the weaker ones up on deck. It was hard but we did what we could. The seas were heavy though autumn was just started. The pilgrims, even Peire, would chant the psalms on Jerusalem to pass the time.

Sometimes the captain would let us walk on the bridge, though he disliked having a hunchback on board. It would bring ill-fortune he said on many an occasion. During one heavy storm, one of the sailors had offered to throw me overboard, as an offering to the sea. But afterwards the wind had abated. I was glad that my Master had only told me when we reached land.

I'd cling to the ropes by the main mast, staring up at the great, yellow-patched sails, sewn with crosses, and the multi-coloured insignia which ships bear for recognition, and pray for calm. For hours I'd watch the swell, washing over the decks, and the sea, blue and green during the day, and turning white at dusk; white and gold, then sometimes red with the sun, and strewn with diamond lights.

We put in to Cyprus for stores, fresh water, and news. It was there that I asked Peire why we were going to the Holy Land. He looked at me slowly.

'But why?' I insisted rashly. 'We could have gone into hiding at home and waited.'

'Neither of us knows how to live, hiding, I think.' He shook his head. 'We would be greater parasites for it. And what should we have waited for, Little Beast?'

I shook my head.

'No, we'll stagger on to our end, better for knowing that a lance pricks our backsides when we pause.'

One morning the Holy Land was sighted. Since three days the seagulls had been circling overhead, swooping out of the dizzy, trembling horizons. Now they beat away towards the shore, and into the glowing blue skies of this Holy Land. All white it seemed to me this land. All white. The priests on board, and the pilgrims, all fell to their knees, and I heard many voices intoning the Te Deum. I prayed with the others, not knowing why except that I was glad to be reaching land, any land, after our heaving voyage. An hour after dusk anchor was cast in the harbour of Acre. Shortly afterwards we debarked.

I'd never seen such a white and shining city. In my wonder I forgot the uncertainty before us.

'Even the jewels they wear, Messer, even the jewels glitter! Aren't they afraid of being robbed? And the white churches with their tall gleaming spires. How is it they're so clean? What magic!' I shouted out. 'It really is a Holy Land!'

He glanced at me affectionately.

'Ah, but Master, you know it all. You've been here before. But a poor jongleur who's heard all his life of the mystery . . . who's watched men leave like beasts of burden to return with the light of the Holy Land in their eyes . . . it's something miraculous!'

'Little Beast, but you're full of miracles, with that white ramshackle face, and your bobbing Adam's apple like a bucket on a rope, and your head of dark straw, and your camel's hump! Full of miracles tucked in your sack, and woven out of your brain with your spider hands. I'm glad for it, I'm glad,' he said.

'It makes a change,' I mumbled, suddenly downcast. 'Perhaps a little sanctity will rub off on us! And we'll rummage back to Terre d'Oc with haloes round our pates, and be left in peace for a change!'

It was strange. I believed in it then. I believed that in this land there was perhaps enough holiness to burn away all the sins of the world. Precious things acquire sanctity from the faith of men. Isn't that true? And surely a man who touches such a holy thing as faith, with his lips and forehead, be it a tomb or a wall, or a stone, surely he too may be cleansed of his wickedness?

Peire said no more, but I was sure that he believed in miracles. He might laugh at the word, as he might laugh at his own grief, but he believed it.

We saw the vast cemetery beyond the walls of Acre, where the knights who had defended or attacked the town were lain to rest. It was a great field of stones, white and black. My Master said that the living who penetrated amongst the tombs were more ghostly than the shades who hovered by their earthly remains. He took me to the prince's palace, and we gazed on the dusty knights and squires, blackened by the sun, who flung through the portals on their mounts, but we did not enter.

Two days later, the pilgrims set out. Our road followed the sea shore, and before us rose up Mount Carmel, glistening red and sharp against the bright sky. There were cripples, children, two women borne in litters by their servants. Some rode, most walked, pushing their way forward, staff in right hand, and their hoods thrown over their heads against the sun.

We passed the town of Jaffa, and rested the same night in a small monastery on its outskirts. The cloisters were cool, the shade soothing. The half dozen monks who tended us were silent, and I thought, full of the light of the Holy Land. Their gentle smiles, and hands, cooled and uncreased many a weary brow. I saw the youngest of them padding amongst us late that night with a lantern over his head, watching out for sickness or travail. I fell asleep, feeling that it wouldn't be so bad to finish here, in the clarity of this hard country. I had an image of a stone rolling off the path and coming to rest in the shadow of a bigger rock.

The next day's marching was harder. There were no more olive groves, nor vines. We struggled through mountainous deserts, beneath a flaming sun that showed pity to neither man nor beast. It was hard to see that we advanced at all. The same mountains leant over us with their threatening shoulders, and the rocks beside our road all looked alike.

Peire bade me hold tight to my courage. His mouth smiled at me out of a dusty face. Sometimes his arm would be beneath mine, and he'd pull me along. I saw an eagle pull out into the blue, and pointed it out to my Master. His eyes narrowed suddenly, as though he'd remembered something, but we continued as before.

'What is it, Messer?'

'I don't know,' he said hesitantly, and then: 'Yes! Infidels, or rather Saracen knights, who watch our progress with interest.'

'Why?'

'The eagle was disturbed. You saw its flight.'

'What happens?'

'Battle,' he said grimly. 'We must warn the others.'

The midday heat was upon us, but the rumour of infidels produced swift reactions. Two Christian knights had also seen the eagle. Using a great boulder for shade and defence against the road, and with the mountain behind us, we crouched and waited. The women fluttered and chirruped like terrified birds. One of the ladies borne in a litter screamed at her servants to carry her on. They dropped the litter and she rolled out like an old onion, weeping and kicking. The women's would be the worst lot if captured, but their squeals touched others, and the party became slippery with fright.

Two things occurred simultaneously. A knight in white surplice, riding a small black horse, appeared on the crest of the incline above us, and one of the women let out a long piercing wail in our midst, which shivered like a blade in the heat. Suddenly the hill was covered with riders. Each bore a javelin with a coloured pennant fluttering from its tip, a short bow, and scimitar. There was no noise. A hail of arrows assailed us, and then the enemy was upon us. We were two score pilgrims, they a hundred armed soldiers.

A man fell next to me with a javelin through his neck. My Master drew his sword and jumped on to the rocks, hurling out his own name like a battle cry. 'Carcasse! Carcasse!'

But they were already hacking us down. Our few horses had been speared and killed, their throats pierced by the whistling arrows. There was no escape. By mistake or chance I found myself holding an Arab javelin. I thought I'd been hit, but the weapon had caught in my leather jerkin, only scraping my ribs. I sidled towards my Master, cutting and thrusting and jabbing at whatever dusky face approached me. Peire, foaming with rage, was whirling his sword in sweeping arcs about him with such speed that they had not found time to kill him. The fearful high-pitched cries of the Saracens mingled with the sobbing, and the rattling of our dying men. An arrow caught my Master in the shoulder, disabling his sword arm, and he toppled over. The battle, some lives, the threat of immediate death for the rest of us, were over.

In the space of a few moments we changed lives. Many, knowing what would come, bewailed that death had passed them by.

In a camp of tents, those few who would or could pay the ransoms demanded, were separated from the rest of us. One of these was an abbot from Narbonne. The younger women were shared out amongst the warriors. One of these was stripped naked in front of us. Her white buttocks shook as they turned her round. I could see the red marks where the garments had squeezed her flesh. Several of the younger men raped her from the back, while others took it in turns to amuse themselves by forcing their genitals into her mouth. She collapsed. A young boy of eight or nine was pulled from his mother, and presented to the chief of the band, who still strutted before his tent, wearing his gold-embossed helm and chain-mail beneath the djellaba. The boy would be fed properly at least, and kept clean as long as they were debauching him. The child smiled innocently at his mother, to relieve her tears.

We were to be sold as slaves. At sunset, they brought us a jug of water.

'Is this the end of us, good Master?' I asked gently. 'Saving your presence, but it helps to know . . .'

'Not quite the end, Little Beast. But nearly.'

The shoulder wound had sickened him. I hadn't been able to cut out the arrow tip. And there was a gleam of indifference in his face, which made me shiver with loneliness.

The night was icy that we passed in the Saracen camp. A man died. The next day, all of us excepting the infirm or dying were to be taken down to the plains, to be sold in the villages.

'We could escape from the *convoi* tomorrow, Messer Peire!' I hissed late that night.

'Wait and see,' he told me calmly.

It was as if he didn't care, or as if he'd abandoned stewardship of his life. I sobbed dry tears, and spoke no more to my Master.

Just after dawn the following day we were bound together, one behind the other. Where foot manacles were lacking, strong rope was used. My Master's lute had been taken away from him. He hadn't murmured, standing with his head bowed and arms loose, allowing the enemy to lift it from his shoulders. But when they tried to take my sack from me, a short burst of rage had seized him. Using the Arab words he knew, he told them, I believe, that I carried nothing dangerous to them. They then contented themselves with making me juggle for them. I was happy to. I'd been so fearful that they'd leave me naked. It was like being given back hope.

Our journey down into the plains was—I shudder to say it—a

path that led to Hell on burning coals. Some crawled until their knees were like raw meat, and the Saracens cut them out of their traces to die on their own. When I stumbled I'd cry out with the lashes from their whips. There were blisters and sores running all over my feet and ankles where the manacles grated the skin. Walking was not easy. The steps we took had to be small and fast. Each movement hurt. The worst thing though was the panic in me that I'd finish alone, like those cut from the *convoi* and left to die amongst white, speechless rocks, without any human comfort. Peire walked forward as though strolling beneath the poplars by the Garonne, his palms swinging out, his gaze straight before him. Nothing touched him, and I don't believe he even heard the cries of pain that accompanied our passage. He'd forgotten to pull his hood up. He looked like an evangelist struck dumb. He was beyond my reach.

The day passed. A man who'd sawn through his knots and had tried to escape was beheaded in front of us. Some of us were sold off quickly in the first villages we reached. It seemed that Peire was being reserved for a special fate, as he was big and strong-looking, and I, because of my hump, was a burden they had not discovered a remedy for. Thus it was that we reached the same destination and, in the end, were not totally separated.

By the evening I was close to the end of my will.

'My Master's left me,' I sobbed to myself. 'He's left me in heart, and mind and spirit. What shall I do alone?'

The cruelty of these men, the memory of my words spoken so innocently, at Acre, the insane fatigue that turned my bones to mud, and invaded my brain like soldier ants bent on destruction, made me start to laugh. The noise issued from cracked lips, and appalled me. I stared about, then realized that it was my own voice. I laughed again amid the low moans, and looked at my Master. He lay on his back, hands spread on the ground by his sides. His eyes were shut. He looked like a corpse waiting for burial. And again the mad laughter rose out of me. 'This was a man!' I thought.

I saw myself from a great distance, with my hump pushing me down to the red earth, until the stones and dust filled my nostrils and mouth. 'This is what a man becomes!' And I was filled with loathing.

We had reached a big village. The Emir had sent his eunuchs to look at us. They pinched our muscles, our legs and backs, and kicked us to see if our joints still had juice in them. One of the eunuchs spoke a little French, and reviled us, as he worked through our ranks.

'Three gods for the little Frenchmen, eh? What greed have these filthy unbelievers!'

'We are not French!' I croaked.

'We shall teach you nonetheless to worship the one God, and his sole prophet! That will be a happy revelation for you, filthy Frenchmen!'

'We are not French, and you lie,' I shouted.

It was very stupid. The open-handed slap almost dislocated my jaw, and he'd turned his ring inwards, which had taken a piece out of my cheek.

'Such things you will soon learn not to say!'

The eunuchs accepted all the last prisoners, and there only remained to haggle over the price.

The first days my Master was put to work in the stone quarries, hacking blocks to be used for rebuilding the Emir's fort, and I was put with the women and old men in the groves to pluck the olives. At midday I would crawl beneath one of the ancient trunks, taking advantage of the Muezzin's call to prayer, which echoed down from the village. A woman fed her child. The long pendulous breast flopped out of her dress, and I'd watch her teasing the nipple into her child's mouth. At night we'd be taken back between the white huts which led up to the fort, before the evening call to prayer. The cypresses trembled faintly in the whispering breeze. It was quiet except for our breathing, and the barking whine of the Muezzin. It was quiet inside us, for our memories were dying.

'But a bell would save his vocal chords,' I said aloud, trying to imagine the abbot of Montaudran tied to his monastery's belfry, and bellowing out the hours.

But I couldn't see his face any more. That was an old life that had been ripped off our backs. We were raw now. I thought no more of escaping. I thought sometimes of shade, of water. I thought of the mosquitoes in the pit where the Christian slaves slept, and of the stinging flies. The days passed in slow waves; it seemed to me that we were being pressed out on a sea that had no horizon.

At night, because his work was harder, Peire was usually there before me. His wound had been cauterized, the arrow-tip removed, and it was now healing slowly in angry seams.

Often he would be asleep when I got back. I'd stumble towards him in the dark, reaching out my hands to find him.

'Is it dawn already?' he'd murmur, trying to raise himself.

'No,' I'd stutter, 'no, it's only the Little Beast.'

And he'd put his arms round me, and hold me. Or he'd pass a distracted hand over my head, and pull me to his chest without a word. He was too deep in his own hell, or too far away, to notice who I was.

The olive-picking season was gone. Months passed. The rainy seasons came upon us—then winter. In the cold weather, Peire had been taken from the stone quarries. The building and repairing work had been halted. He worked now as a water-carrier in the Emir's garden. I worked in the kitchens. In the mornings I could see him trudging to and from the well with the thick stick across his shoulder-blades, from which hung the water-pails. The wooden bar rubbed on his bad shoulder.

The Emir hunted like a Christian noble. He, too, had falcons. His horses, though smaller than ours, were lighter and faster; beautiful animals. And he looked almost like a Christian knight; like my Master had been in his way, before . . . Why had this happened to us? Why to my Master? Did he deserve it? For what sins? Suffering for sins! The Christian phrase strangled in my gullet. God of Christians or Moslems or Jews, why do you do this to men? False, cruel God of suffering and mortal hatreds. What was Peire Carcasse now? A shell indeed.

When he slept I'd try to pluck the fleas and vermin off him. He ignored them himself. It was so bad that they'd even go in his nostrils and mouth. They blocked his breathing, and hearing him was horrible. Sometimes he'd grin at me. For a moment there would be hope again. A hope that fought against the other hope for an end.

One of the gardeners was called Amin. He was kinder to my Master than the others. He allowed him to sit against the well sometimes, and intervened when the other gardeners took to lashing Peire's legs with their whips to make him walk faster. For some reason the Musulmen hated Peire more than the other prisoners. Perhaps it was because they'd discovered he was a minstrel, or because of his grinning when they beat him, or because of his features which gave credence to the rumours that he was half Saracen himself. They'd spit in his face, so that their spittle would run down his cheeks in yellow rivulets, and then force him to his knees to recite the Litany for their amusement. The domestics working in the Emir's palace encouraged their children to throw rocks at him. Peire looked at them, or stared docilely before him, as though waiting to be told to return to his gardening duties. No amount of baiting provoked him to a sound of pain as far as I heard. He loomed over them, more gaunt and wild-looking than ever, until the burly Amin with his little daughter staring into my Master's gleaming face, would put one great arm about his shoulders, and lead him away. The girl's face often showed her fascination with this shell of a man, and would gaze with wonder, and a childish pity up at him.

His patience and capacity for work earned us both favours. We no longer wore manacles, and when we were not working had the freedom of the fort. For my Master this meant nothing. When he toiled not, he sat empty-eyed and still, or slept. But for me it meant that I could juggle my sticks and balls, even if it was before our captors. I helped him eat his scraps of food, and when there was nothing more to do, I watched him. He lived in his suffering. No, that's untrue. He lived on the other side of it, beyond the reality of our daily wretchedness. And the suffering seemed not to threaten him. It hid him from my eyes. Sometimes I asked myself if it was not me who was blinded by this darkness between us.

Peire's endurance finally caught the Emir's attention. He was called one evening into the audience chamber. They had removed his rags, washed him, and dressed him in a soft caftan. The other slaves who slept with us were all roped together and herded through the portals to watch. My Master was led, unresisting, before the Emir, where he was pushed to his knees.

The Emir told him that surely he must have Arab blood in his veins, and that as a special mark of favour he would be allowed to make love to his Christian bitch of a concubine who was barren. The woman was brought forward, painted and trussed up in her raiment. Peire stood silent and uncomprehending.

'But first,' declared the Emir with a smile, 'you must entertain us. A little dance perhaps, or a song?'

He glanced with amusement at the knights about him. When my Master made no response, he nodded to one of the guards. This latter stepped forward and brought a metal-thonged whip down over Peire's shoulders with all his force. Peire tumbled forwards.

'Sing or dance, cur of an unbeliever,' said the Emir coldly. 'Don't you wish to amuse yourself with a woman, after such lengthy abstinence?'

'I don't know how . . .' whispered Peire, barely conscious, ' . . . to sing.'

There was much laughter. Chiefly from the ragged, Christian slaves whose own minds were unhinged with fear.

'May I return to my garden?'

'No you may not. Sing!'

He raised himself from the floor with his hands, but had not the strength to stand. I watched him crouching there, and trying to turn his head round, looking at the rows of faces that confronted him.

'Sing!' ordered the Emir in a low voice. He rose from his seat, and approached close to Peire. 'You are a brave man. We must, I'm afraid, reduce you further in the eyes of both my knights, and these Christian curs who mock you with their laughter. Their docility depends on the humiliation of the only symbol of resistance they can claim.'

Peire's eyes stared back.

The Emir lifted him to his feet. 'You and I know we can no longer reduce you.' He shrugged faintly, and then bowed his head to my Master, in a momentary gesture of respect, before swinging back to the dais.

My Master propped himself on his knees, with his palms on the floor, and raised his head. He opened his mouth once or twice. No sound issued. He tried again, and this time a thin croak, more like a laugh, came out from his lungs. Pushing himself higher, he thrust harder with his voice. His eyes bulged with the effort, the vein on his forehead throbbed, as he gathered all his remaining strength. Around me I heard our fellow slaves crackling dutifully with giggles and snuffling smiles at this mirror of themselves. He sang . . .

> I newly found a garden
> which lately is begun
> to flower with blooms no garden sees
> beneath the sun . . .

It wasn't singing. It was a horrible echo. I felt a titter rising in my throat. Peire had exhausted his reserves. He fell back on his heels, swaying drunkenly.

'Good, very good,' said the Emir.

The woman was stripped before him. Her breasts shook out, shiny with oil and paint. She put her hands over the red nipples to hide them. She was smooth, well-fed and frightened.

Two guards raised Peire and lifted the caftan over his head. He stood between them like a dried-out mummy in his nakedness.

'Go to it, cur! Aren't you eager to lust?' cried the eunuch.

'May I go back to the garden?' he mouthed.

The woman was lain down before him. The guards held her thighs apart, and Peire was pushed on to her.

I turned my head away, hearing his faint laughter. The Emir's voice rang out once like a whip-lash. And then silence. My Master was unconscious. We were removed. Peire too. The Saracen knights had been amused.

Peire was returned to his garden, and the watering of the flowers. He touched their petals gently, and watched the blooms maturing and fading with untiring attention.

Winter passed, spring, summer, autumn. Sometimes they took him away from the garden, and put him back in the stone quarries. He reacted then, shaking his head.

'Unkind of them,' he murmured once. 'I work better in the garden.' But such things were only a mild form of torture, and affected him very little.

And then one day—it was spring again, and the shutters were open—I heard him crooning to himself. His voice was weak and battered, but I could hear the words quite clearly. He sang doggedly, thinking himself alone, and the pails of water rustled beside him as he moved . . .

> I newly found a garden
> which lately is begun
> to flower with blooms no garden sees
> beneath the sun.
>
> In the beds were neatly sown
> and ripened, stranger fruit,
> Aching broken bones were hoed
> By a gard'ner mute.

172

And as he raked those blooms decayed
Into the earth around,
I saw him smile, I heard him say
Death enriched the ground.

Oh gard'ner, why does God destroy
Man's dream – his bride?
He answered, 'Shackle not a wave of joy
But love her till ebb-tide.'

Again and again he repeated the words until they acquired a
rhythm to his movements. He paused at last by the well, staring
down into its depths. My heart was in my mouth but nothing happened.

He slowly lowered the buckets to the ground. With a cramped,
stiff movement he shrugged out of the wooden bar and harness. He
stood still, bent slightly, as though still weighed down by his
burden, and then cautiously, and with an expression of dawning
amazement, he stood erect, straightening his back and opening
wide his arms. He turned about, moving his feet tentatively. He
walked to the rose-beds which he'd last watered, and gazed at the
drops of moisture which still clung to the leaves. He raised his arms
slowly from the shoulders, until they came together over his head.
He looked up, and a deep, reverberating cry escaped him.

'It's true!' he cried.

His voice split at the edges, and I watched him standing there
with his legs apart, face turned up to the hard sky.

'It's true!' he said wonderingly. 'The wax is washed from my
ears, and I can hear your voice! His words echoed into silence. He
began afresh . . .

'It doesn't matter that my world is upside down. I *hear* your
voice! 'You have destroyed me, but only in my downfall do I hear
your voice!

'You have taken life away from me, hope too; you have given me
a live death. But I hear your voice!

'A ravenous animal was chained inside me. I became a man. You
unchained the beast, let it loose in my entrails, in my mind, and it
wreaked havoc. But only when it had gnawed its way through the
walls of my despair . . . only then could I hear your voice!

'I was alive. You destroyed me not once, but seven times. But
only at the seventh death can a man hear your voice!

'Only in the impossibility of hope and life, exist the reality of you. Only in the valley of the impossible can a man hear your voice. All miracles are born from the womb of despair and impossibility.

'I have lived in my hurt. I have succoured my suffering, and watered its flowers, to hide myself from this Word.

'But I heard your voice. You spoke to me, and the Eternal Word shivered like lightning in my temples!

'I sought causes, my God. I sought Eros and Thanatos. And you isolated me within those causes. Those causes withered me, and bade me tramp upon my isolation; tramp it into the dust of my buried soul, and to forget . . . but you murmured to me out of the whirlwind, as you did to Job, and your hand and your chain smashed my world to fragments on your anvil!

'My God, oh my God, you *have* destroyed me, yet I am happy. All is mystery, growing wonder, and terror before your infinite strength in me. But I have heard you. I hide no more!

'My God, I have spoken of great things which I have not understood, things too wonderful for me to know. And I knew of you only by report. But now, though I have not seen you, I have heard you with my own ears, as the minstrel harkens to the wind for inspiration. And therefore I am melting away.

'My God, the glory of the whole is nothing. The glory of my fullness is emptiness. The glory of completion is in encompassing the vacuum!

'Oh my God I have heard you, and you have delivered me from all the gods worshipped by men, and sealed in caskets of doctrine and theology.

'Oh God, you have delivered me from God, for mercy pulls at your sleeve, even in destruction.

'My appetite, my hunger of mind and body, have hidden my spirit from me. But your voice reached through to me. And these things are now one in me amid the chaos, as you are One.

'Oh my God, I have heard you, and I shall fly no more. I shall escape no more, because my freedom is here. Always here in me. How may I run away?

'My God, I have heard you . . .'

The Sieur Carcasse pranced about the well, raising his arms out to the sun. His steps were at first slow. His feet seemed to approach the earth as though the rough grass, already mottled by the heat, was a carpet woven with threads of fire and wind, of ice splinters and rays of gold, on which the greatest prince on earth would tread with awe. He gained courage. His movements grew faster, until he whirled in shifting patterns, dancing, dancing, and crying out in his hoarse voice, with surprise and joy.

Amin, the gardener, drew close, and stopped, his round, friendly face dropping in astonishment. His daughter Fatima was less disturbed, and tripped up to the leaping scarecrow. She held up her arms. My Master paused to understand the creature's gesture, and then swept her into his arms, so that her laughter echoed with his in the garden, with the noise of the ravens, and the doves cooing, and with the noise of water slapping against the stones.

Tears slipped down my face. I threw down the bowls I'd been wiping, and hobbled outside, as fast as my legs would bear me. I had a piece of red cloth about my waist, and bits of old sacking binding my legs tight, which served as bandages. I almost fell down the steps, and Peire started.

'Little Beast, my wisest of companions!' he shouted.

'That's because you don't have too many to choose from,' I grinned.

'You look like a ship's flags, knotted out to herald a battle! Where have you been?'

'Sieur Peire,' I stuttered, 'saving your presence I've been waiting.'

'What in the Devil's name have you been waiting for?'

'For you, Master, just for you. I had my doubts that we'd ever meet again.' I stared at him, with my hand tucked round my ear, still not quite certain that I was talking to, really seeing my Master before me. 'And seeing you at first glance,' I muttered, 'is not necessarily to be bitten by reality, saving your honour's presence!'

It was my Master though. I dug him gently in the ribs to make sure. He was with me again.

Some days later we were on the ramparts. The sun was falling down the sky like a scimitar, and the dusk was full of fluttering bats, the creak of the cigale, and a nightingale's passionate voice. I could hear a jackal now and then below.

'They told me that the river sparkling over to the west is the Jordan,' I told Peire. 'Where John the Baptist anointed the Christ. Is it really the same, do you think?'

'There's one river Jordan,' my Master said with a smile.

'Many of the Christians here have been taking on the pagan faith,' I told him. 'The Emir's Christian concubine goes about exhorting us to betray the scriptures.'

'Holy men, real holy men,' he said softly, 'are all the same whether they're Christian, Moslem or Jew. If you look at them I think they have the same lines, the same eyes, the same stillness. Reason in the end must learn obedience to the spirit's imagination.'

'But many do convert, Sieur Peire, and then if they escape afterwards, they do a little penitence, and all's well!'

Peire was silent for a time. 'We must go home,' he said at last.

The night we escaped there was a cold, perfect moon. It hung in the heavens like the unblinking eye of our destiny. I hoped fervently that its light would be to guide us, rather than to betray us.

My Master had been putting the stray pieces of himself together, searching round for the bits of the Peire Carcasse he'd once known. I supplied him with my memory, and he availed himself of it with a humbleness that embarrassed me. He asked many questions. In the months I had toiled beneath the fruit trees, and in the kitchens, and he in the quarries and Emir's garden, my Master had relinquished all the facts and figures that had marked his life. Now he waited on me to tell him everything. At first I'd had to show him his food, help him to drink, and to nod reassurance from the kitchen windows when he worked. I was filled with both joy and sadness. It was like watching an old man become a child again.

And then he had determined on our escape.

It was not hard. We wore no irons, and the ropes were soon severed. I only feared a little for his lacerated back, and my feet. I'd stolen bread, the flat, bone-hard bread which the pagans eat, some dry figs, and a handful of wizened olives. We had a gourd of water.

There was a place on the ramparts, still broken and unmended, where it was possible to jump down. My Master went first, and I followed, for him to catch me. Our bodies cast huge shadows before us, as we tumbled through the gorse bushes. I hardly believed that my limbs were no longer bound, that I had my Master, and my sack. Hunger, thirst, sleep? I believed that I could endure anything for this liberty, which filled my nostrils when I sniffed the air.

Peire told me that we had to reach the great road to Jerusalem as fast as possible: and that once on it, our only hope was to pick up with a group of pilgrims either going to the Holy Sepulchre, or returning. Otherwise, he said, we could be picked off by any stray horseman.

'The possibilities don't seem stacked in our favour, Messer, do they?'

'They're all we have. We must get home to Terre d'Oc.'

'Humph!' I said to myself, resigned. 'Peire Carcasse's race begins again, and Little Beast pants on behind!' I shrugged my shoulders. But how glad I was, and how full of gratitude was hard to speak of.

The sun rose, and for every hour that it climbed up the sky, my head swelled more, until it weighed on my shoulders, heavy as a bell. When I moved it, the brains rattled inside like a broken clapper, and I only saw black spots before my eyes. Where it was rocky, my Master would haul me on to his back, and stumble forwards, brushing his way carelessly through the thorns. I protested each time, but he'd grab me round the legs, and I hardly had the strength to argue.

Often a shepherd's head would appear over the hill, and we had to fall in our tracks until he and his dogs passed by. We stopped exhausted that night. My Master was a little desperate with uncertainty. 'The stars are right,' he muttered, 'this must be the right direction!' I used a little of our precious water for his back, and he'd stifle a groan as we lay down. But sleep was a foreigner to both of us. It became easier to move on.

I began to imagine infidels crouching behind each rock, and when a jackal came close, eyeing us warily with the moonlight catching its evil face, I jumped and cried out.

The nights were bitterly cold, and the chill enveloped us, so that we proceeded, shivering in our own icy sweat. It was the Chariot star we followed, up the desolate slopes, over boulders, through thorns that made tatters of our clothes. After skirting a great hill, we found ourselves in a ravine, where our footsteps echoed, and each step we took reverberated off the cliff sides loud enough to wake up a Saracen fifty leagues away. I reached forward to cling to the hem of Peire's mantle. He was bleeding from a dozen different places, and his legs had long cuts about the shins and ankles. Thirst tormented him. He'd rub a thick tongue over his lips, and the rattling breath would flee from him. But he wouldn't drink. 'Save it until morning,' he croaked. 'We must wait until daylight.'

The stones and trees that loomed about us seemed to move. I

began to imagine they were coming alive, changing into monsters, and I tried to hobble faster, jostling my Master.

'What is it, Little Beast?'

'There are ghosts and wild animals,' I panted, 'we must run faster!' I stumbled on a few steps, and fell headlong. Peire reached me, and raised my head. I looked over his shoulder. The sky was no longer dark. It was grey, then pink. We both drank.

The first night, the second night, the third night. We had only a few crumbs of bread left, a dribble of water.

Stones, cliffs, dusty bushes, with the colour blown out of them. Stones, stones, stones. When we stopped, I saw cactus about us, and I hacked at one with my fingernail, but the liquid that I tasted was like pus and stung my mouth. Thirst grew. In the daytime we were stung by flies and there were often vultures overhead, much bigger than those in Occitanie, and I felt their eyes on us. When we stopped, they flopped to rest, like bald priests in their cassocks, on the rocks round about.

'Bald priests!' I cackled. 'Bald priests and vultures!' The laughter hurt me. I doubled up. 'It's all right, Master, but the priests . . . can you see them?'

'Hush, Little Beast!' He held me to him, forcing my mouth open, and emptying the gourd's contents on my tongue.

'Save it, Master! Now there's none left. We're lost!'

'No, my friend, we're on the road home at last. We've found the road to Acre.'

'And the Holy Sepulchre? All the way to the Holy Land, and not even a glimpse of the Holy Sepulchre?' I shuddered.

'Still chasing facts, Little Beast,' Peire chuckled down at me.

'It's true.' I slumped back. 'But Messer, I think one pilgrimage to the Holy Land is all I'll manage for the time being . . .'

'Saving my presence?' he whispered.

'Yes,' I nodded, and slept.

We both nearly died of thirst, however, before those confounded English pilgrims picked us up. A bunch of more sanctimonious, arrant numbskulls it would be hard to find. England was rich, holy, democratic, righteous, religious, rampant, and the only suitable place of abode for a right-thinking, upright, God-fearing man, who took things, and most particularly life, with the proper degree of seriousness. They couldn't even speak French properly, that coarse

178

tongue which any monkey in Christendom knows how to mutter in. They took umbrage—a favourite word of theirs—every time my Master even mentioned Alienor of Aquitaine, that famous patroness of troubadours and chivalry. 'Another foreigner,' they'd say with a curl of their lips, 'not a real Englishwoman, we're afraid to say.' But they brought us to Acre. God bless their skinny souls, and keep me away from such a race.

We had but a wait of two weeks for the last vessel leaving the Holy Land until the autumn. The last thing my Master did before our departure was to go out into the countryside inland from Acre. He picked a branch of young pine, and a branch from a cypress tree, and bound them together with a faded piece of blue silk, whose colour had once been cornflower. Bending the young twigs, he shaped them into a star whose edges were held in place by the blue ribbon. Threaded through the green were bright wild flowers. This he hid in his tunic.

We took ship, and then, as if to balance our fortunes, were blown about the Mediterranean from one port to another for the best part of three months. Cyprus, Crete, Palermo, Rome, Genoa greeted our heaving legs. Out of the vessel's bowels we were spat, to linger in a frenzy of impatience, until the captain chose to haul up the canvases once more, and sail. There was one advantage to this rolling life: my Master's limbs knitted back together. One shoulder, it's true, would always stay bent, and he looked more than ever like a wild hermit returning briefly to the world – thin, angular, and lonely. Not lonely perhaps in himself, but lonely when looked at through other men's eyes. My sores had healed too, but my miserable feet had suffered too much to serve me as they'd done before, and I limped badly.

We sailed into the port of Marseille, almost three years after we had left her harbours. Occitanie was trembling on the slopes of a moving volcano. By chance, we heard that the Sieur Blacatz had departed to another world. My Master, as though with the act of touching land, had become illuminated with a flame which drew more and more people towards him. The flame burnt steadily, perpetually, for he could not restrain it. And I watched over him secretly, awed by his symmetry, but at peace in my heart. To be with him now was to lose fear. I felt truly home.

7

Occitanie lay under threat of the Interdict. Count Raimon could not even speak to the Papal legate. He had been excommunicated, as had Lord Trencavel and others. Had he been reinstated? Was it possible that Pierre de Castelnau had been murdered? The rumours flew in all directions. What was true? The Spaniard Dominic Guzman, had been preaching throughout the land. It was said that at Prouille, where he had made oratory before a large audience, he'd had numerous confessions. A Cistercian monk who we met on our ride west told us that he'd been there himself. He repeated what he remembered: that Guzman had preached, begged, wept, since many years, that he had an expression in Castile—where a blessing avails not, avails a beating.

'Thus,' said Guzman, 'will we come against you, your princes, and your renegade prelates. My masters will bring whole nations against you, and many thousands will perish by the sword. Your towers will be destroyed, your walls overthrown, and you shall be reduced to slavery. So it is that force will prevail where gentleness has failed!'

Nothing could be heard with certainty. It was said that the Pope Innocent had dreams of bloodshed, and that he was afraid to sleep for them. It was said that he had ordered Philippe-Auguste, King of France, to prepare himself with arms, and to enlist his knights and nobles for the quarantine—the forty days of military service liable for every man at arms. Since early March, people had not known what to believe. Everywhere we stopped, men and women, seeing our garb, would run to our horses, for news. We had little to offer them, and when we questioned them in turn, their answers were confused and tentative. At night, serfs, yeoman farmers, and even knights, armed as they could, had to guard their property most watchfully. Fires were lit throughout the country to ward off thieves and pillagers after dusk, but these last grew in daring, as the unrest and ill-ease spread. Women were violated, men killed. And these crimes were only a warning it was said.

My Master thought at first to press on to Toulouse to gather what truth he could extort from the royal court. But then, a day out of Béziers, he turned his mare's head towards Carcassonne, and I was glad.

A west wind blew in our faces, chasing the pink and grey clouds from the sky. Peire's gaze followed the Aude. He dismounted, and led his horse by the reins, tugging it impatiently now and then when its head swung down to graze. The wind had died away, and he bade me dismount to prepare our victuals. For a few moments he watched me, with his hand shading his eyes, as the sun reflected sharply off the water, and sparkled on his face. The jaw was clean-shaven once more. In Marseille our beards had been scraped off painfully, and my Master's features had grown harder, as though the bones had swollen beneath the skin. He stared down at me, his hair short-cropped, like a gargoyle—half-man, half-beast—from the flying buttresses of some lofty cathedral.

'You're glad to be home?'

'Yes, Messer Peire.'

He was searching for words.

'You've been a sturdy vagabond!'

'I'd a master to follow.'

'And now, whatever things are done, you'll stand with him?'

'To where should I draw back?'

'You still trust him!'

He sounded full of surprise. I grinned, pushing the prickly hair from my face, and his stern features relaxed.

'We return to nothing, again and again, Little Beast. Your spirit and fantasy have kept us alive!'

'My Master's gone off his head good and proper, saving . . .'

He laughed. 'Perhaps that's true. But it's also true that you'll go on, cool as this river beside us, whatever happens, towards the sea. A sea of juggling waves, of minstrel's music, of lights, and leaping embraces. A sea of silences. But you'll travel on to the hereafter, with that mournful face of yours sniffing the wind to make sure of the right scent, and there'll be no fear in you.'

'Are you planning on leaving me?' I asked carefully.

'No, no, Little Beast,' he said distractedly. 'But you'll remember that spark of yours, will you? And that fantasy? It's a quirky, fiery creature which knows many devils, which knows beauty, human joy, the gifts of survival; which knows that faith is discovered in the maddest hope, which knows its own *will*. You do have that faith,

Little Beast. You won't forget? A faith hidden like a flame in your entrails. Remember the heat at your centre.'

'And you, Master?'

'And me? I'm going to sniff my country once again!'

I stared at him.

'But don't worry, Little Beast, it won't be dangerous!'

He stepped through the tall grasses down to the water's edge and cupped his palms to drink. I watched him crouching by the river, taking the dry mud between his hands, and rubbing it against his cheek, so that it crumbled into his lap. He began to take off his clothes, hurriedly peeling them from his back, like a snake shrugging out of its old skin. He hopped from one foot to the other, pulling off his boots. He was naked, striding into the water.

'Come and wash the salt and dust from you,' he called, 'we must return home as clean as babies!'

But I was ashamed, and shook my head.

He splashed deeper, dived beneath the surface, and his head reappeared a few yards upsteam. For some time he swam, beating up against the current, before leaping out and throwing himself in the grass. He laughed like a child, throwing his head back, and opening his throat wide. Around him, half hiding him, the wild flowers shook. Periwinkles, anemones, daisies, buttercups, and rosemary in bloom. His fingers reached out to them.

'Will you be plucked, little flowers?' I heard. 'But not here.' Above us a flock of swallows screamed, flying low through the trees. 'Aye, Little Beast?'

'Yes, Master?' I answered, not understanding him.

He clambered to his feet. 'If we're not permitted to pick a bouquet of flowers, what shall we bring my lady mother?'

'Your love and wounds,' I said, looking at him. 'They're the most precious for a mother.'

His head turned sharply, and then he nodded.

'Words are very narrow,' I thought. 'Hearts very wide. There's room to share the worst hurts, the best loves.'

I sighted first the walls of Carcassonne, and pulled Peire's arm. 'We're almost there,' I cried. 'Even the vines are beginning to ripen. Is it a hundred years since we last watched autumn in Carcassonne? At least!' I shouted happily. 'What will have changed? Who'll have been whisked off to stew in the Devil's cauldron? Will the children whom I played for be women and lusty youths?'

For a moment I forgot everything except the sight of those old brown baked walls, the high towers.

'And the doves, Messer Peire? Are there still the doves flying from her battlements? Can you see?'

'I see doves,' he said, 'and ravens.'

Our path wound up to the Dame's Gate. The horses plodded slowly. They were tired, and lathered with our riding. The fields on either side of us were turning yellow for lack of rain. As we came up to the ramparts, the sentries bade us halt and declare ourselves. The town was in a great state of activity. I noticed there were more soldiers than usual on the battlements. My eye moved about, becoming reaccustomed to this familiar setting. I saw a white bird fluttering beneath the gateway, and while Peire was talking to the sentries, I hopped down and went over. The warm body trembled between my fingers, beak opening and shutting, and the red ruby eye glinting in fear. There was no visible wound on the body which lay pristine and quiet. I lifted a wing, and there under the wide quills was a dark festering patch of blood. Ants and maggots scurried in the blood, sucking and penetrating deep into the flesh. The dove neither knew nor could believe that she was dying, as she looked at me. The red eye winked quick and cold. Running to the wall, I raised the white bird over my head, and cast her gently down towards the water. Her wings bent open, the breeze bore her slowly, slowly, the water rose to meet her, to cleanse her, I thought, as if water would wash the wound away . . .

We reached the house. After tethering the horses, Peire took me inside. It was very still after the clamour in the streets. Light filtered dustily through the hall. From above we could hear the faint tap-tap of the loom. My Master listened for a moment, nodded, wiping the beads of sweat from his temples, and moved in easy, loping strides up the stairs. The shuttle of the loom paused. There was the creak of wooden steps, and I followed him.

The room was deeply shaded. The smell of musk was as I remembered it, the bright cushions, rugs, and tapestries scattered in the same peaceful disorder. She sat at the far end of the room, by her loom, and her hands were clasped in her lap. Her stillness was full of intensity and expectancy. She turned her head slowly, and I saw, with a start, that her hair had gone completely white. For a long moment she stared at her son. Tears were rolling, unheeded down her lined cheeks, but she made no noise. Then, with a sudden movement, she rose, straightened, and ran nimbly to Peire.

'My child! Is it truly my son?'

Peire tried to hold her in his arms. She caressed his hair, his cheeks. With fluttering hands she grazed his wounded shoulder, and bent to kiss his hands.

'No, mother,' he whispered, drawing her back to him.

She gazed at me, shaking her head.

'Little Beast, he was in your care. You've brought me back a tattered skeleton.'

'It wasn't him, lady mother, who was the cause of it.' He smiled. 'But he did bring me back!'

She lowered her head. 'You wear pilgrim's clothes. You've been to the Holy Land, to the Sepulchre of Christ. Oh, I've heard too many rumours!'

'Yes, mother, we were p-pushed to the Holy Land, and . . . and almost lost our way coming home. I heard a voice there, on the world's rim, which mocked me as no mortal has ever done. There was no escape from it, and . . .' he stopped.

Staring at him through her tears, I watched her learning to recognize her son again.

'Yes,' she said at last, 'I see it in your faces. He has spoken to you in some way, but He did not heal you.'

'How could he?' Peire whispered. 'It was not to heal me that He spoke.'

'Peire, my son, but you've come back!' she cried, still bound in her amazement. 'You brought him back, Little Beast, when I didn't hope to see him again. I forbade hope. Every morning I prayed to obliterate hope. But he's here, alive again, and there's no more need!' Encircling one arm about Peire's neck, she brushed my head with her other hand.

Kneeling, I reached for the hem of her dress, and kissed it, biting my lips.

'Good mistress, we come back to much sadness, but give thanks for your safety and well-being.'

'You've returned too soon,' she said with more composure. 'And as for my safety, it's but a prison looking out on to fields devoured by a plague. Occitanie quakes in her slippers!'

'Why too soon?' Peire asked. 'Would it be better to stay away, or fly to a corner of the world that's safer?

'Many try; many of the rich are flying to Castile and Aragon, taking with them the gold, jewellery, and wealth that they've amassed in easier times. Those that stay are full of Ave Marias, donate to both Church and State, and their public words whine with self-justification. Thus they hope to avoid the consequences of their faithlessness, their lies, and their treachery to this country. Thus Castelnau was murdered. An evil, foolishly rooted out. There are many similar cases. Even the people are now substituting old faith, real knowledge, for barbarous superstitions, dredged from the wells of their alarm. And no one helps them. Women are burnt as witches, chatelaines stoned for their vices, priests drowned in their fonts. Every vulture, every deformed birth, every fallen cross, every stray tempest, every shooting star, has become a portent of truth, a portent of terror. And Occitanie rocks closer to perdition in her cradle of last-minute hopes. There is no *will* left in people. Will has been thrown away. Instead we live on straws caught floating on an evil breeze. It's to such a land of fairy-tales, that you've returned.'

Her voice was rippling with cool disdain, and something of the old hauteur I'd known in her.

My Master bowed his head. 'We've done nothing, nothing for our land. We've done nothing to help. What arrogance to believe for an instant that we could.'

'But human and right to do so!' I growled furiously.

In those days at Carcassonne, we gathered news like stale crusts of bread, with starving eagerness. And the rumours, like water, trickled through our fingers.

My Master's name had travelled before us. Name, reputation, life, I know not which it was. People would come up to him in the streets of this town which had so often cast him off. They'd touch his clothes, reach for his arm, pull on his mantle to attract his attention, and then, when he turned reluctantly towards them, the pale, swarthy face lifting haggard eyes into a real smile, they'd nod, tap their noses, grin foolishly at him and murmur thanks with a little awe in them.

'Thanks for what you've done, for what you've said, for what you are! We know of you, and that's good, Sieur Peire.'

'Thanks for what, poor friends?' he'd ask in slow surprise. 'What have I done for you? Nothing, nothing!'

'You were banished for speaking out for us,' muttered an old fellow, with more temerity than the rest. He glared at my Master out of watery eyes, and I had the notion that he didn't see the tatters hanging on Peire Carcasse, that he couldn't see the sloping, wounded shoulder; that he couldn't see the deep furrows criss-crossing the skin about his eyes; that he couldn't see the bony, wasted body who stood, quite humbly, before him; that he would never see those things in my Master again.

'I was banished for insulting the virility of a few nobles,' Peire declared, 'and it wasn't even what I intended!'

'Ha, ha! Sieur Peire, you can't fool us,' screeched a tubby widow. 'There's hardly a soul who doesn't mutter your ditties when the pig bailiffs come, or when the Legate's retinue trots past.'

'As for Peire Carcasse in the Holy Land!' said another slyly.

He stared about him, hardly comprehending their words. 'You're mistaken. I'm more full of fear than you.'

'Facts!' I chuckled out loud. 'Facts, Messer Peire! You'll never change people into believing they don't exist!'

'Will you tell us Sieur Peire, that you didn't fight off those Saracens before Jerusalem?'

'Or that you haven't worsted the Roman shave-pates at their own debates?' said another.

'That you didn't let yourself be beaten to pulp in the market place at Marseille, to show them any man can do it, and still be a proud fellow?' 'Or that you haven't kicked a few knights hard in the arse, so they'd ease off on corn rations, and their rights to us, body and soul?'

'Will you tell us straight out, that you haven't taken your own victuals to feed the needy—shepherds, peasants and the like?'

'Yes,' cried Peire. 'It's not true. If it is true, I stole the food first myself.'

'Even better,' hollered one young scamp.

'But those weren't the reasons . . .' my Master shouted. 'There were no noble reasons!'

He turned to me. 'Where have they learnt all this?'

I swallowed. 'First of all, by looking at you, knowing you better and knowing themselves now a bit desperate, maybe. And then, Messer, every time we talk to a man, whether it's at Marseille, in Acre, Toulouse or Carcassonne, a seed gets whisked off on the wind. You know it better than I do. How many banished minstrels known by a couple of great princes, and sworn at by half the country, go shipping off to the Holy Land, and get back in one piece more or less?' I was blustering it out. There'd been plenty of occasions when I'd opened my mouth about him, if only to get the worst off my chest.

Often there were children about us, whether we were by the Aude, or on the ramparts, or tumbling through the narrow streets. And it seemed—to Peire's relief and amusement—that my predicament was not very different from his own. Little Beast's name was bandied about too; Carcasse's hunchback with his magic sack! It didn't matter to me, and I was happy to juggle for the little ones.

It dawned on me slowly. Ever since we had debarked at Marseille and I'd noticed the way my master drew people to him, stories and news had fled before us. Peasants, shepherds, tinkers, even shopkeepers and merchants, old widows and young children talked of him with affection, and gentleness, as if they'd got to know him intimately, as if he'd stepped out of a nightmare and told them there *was* a way to live through even nightmares. They recited and embroidered what was known, so that he grew to the shape of a mystery, but a mystery whose closeness to them was both a warmth and a hope.

The ne'er-do-wells and lute pickers, who'd once followed Peire about, laughing at his tricks, applauding his outrages, and copying his songs, were, at the same time, the most timid before him, and the greatest scoffers. I remember one in particular.

He swaggered up to my Master as we were making our way home one evening, with a bunch of friends to support him.

'Look whom we meet! What luck, the Devil's preaching minion himself!'

They jostled us, and I eyed them anxiously.

'How did you manage to invent such a number of lies about yourself?' another shouted.

'Tell us, Sieur Devil, what gives you this right to champion Terre d'Oc?'

'Nothing,' Peire answered hoarsely. 'Nothing.'

For a moment they were silenced, and his first assailant then said: 'By Christ's wounds, Carcasse has filled his belly with piety, and become a renegade to anarchy!'

There was much laughter.

'My belly is emptier than it ever was, my friends,' Peire had suddenly grown angry. 'I see too easily the red holes out of which your

187

entrails will slop, unless you turn your brains to other pastimes.'
He paused, and raising the great head from his chest, stared back at
them. 'My hearty rogues,' he cried out loudly. 'Make your pil-
grimages to Hell quickly. Choose fast, while the minutes are still
here. Choose fast, so that, on returning, you'll struggle for this
future of ours with *real* will, real courage, real fear, and real affection . . . but hurry!' His eyes bored into them, and they were quiet.
'Hurry!' he urged again.

The first gallant pushed the others back, and stepped up.

'I'm Andrea, do you remember me? You taught me how to
play.'

Peire glanced at him, and then grinned. 'You've grown into a
great layabout minstrel.'

'Sieur Peire, why did you say "choose". Choose to make a
journey to Hell?'

'Choice never lasts very long, my pupil. Choice gets taken away
from you; by age, by a wife, by fortune, but above all, by servitude.
And he, my fine companions, who makes no choice and drifts
becomes a slave first to his indecision, then to his weaknesses, and
last (but very speedily) to the first man who frightens him!'

A mouth or two hung slack. Peire swung his mantle about him,
despite the heat, and strode down to the square. 'Work that miserable conundrum out,' he muttered, 'and you have a key to your
futures.'

I wondered if he was mocking himself. Maybe not anymore. I
nodded warily, and hoped that I'd understood him.

One morning there came a knock on the side door. The servant
went to open, and returned to tell Peire that a young woman
wished to speak to him. He glanced at my Master. 'She's . . . um
. . . with child,' he mumbled with embarrassment and a shrewd
look darted from his eyes.

'Bring her into the hall. I'll go down.'

He smiled at his mother. 'No, it's not my seed she nourishes.'

The girl had pale hair, and her exhausted grey eyes flitted over us
from the depths of a thin, drawn face. Her belly was soft, and
swelling big beneath the black dress she wore. She hovered on the
doorstep, twining her hands feverishly, and unable to open her
mouth.

'I used to work for your father,' she suddenly burst out. 'He said
wicked things about you, but then I heard you sometimes. I never

188

believed what he said . . . it's about my child, Sieur Peire.' She stretched her hands across her belly.

I tried to sit her down, but she moved away.

'I hated my child. At the beginning I beat my belly with a stone to make it go away.' Her eyes reddened, and she ducked her face into the dirty apron.

'Hush, woman,' Peire said gently. 'Tell us what you will.'

'One of Lord Trencavel's young squires had me. There were two of them. They said they'd be protected even if they killed me. My husband was in the next room. Afterwards I hated him too, but the baby was worse. It sounds a good joke perhaps,' she murmured bitterly.

But Peire only shook his head.

'Now,' she whispered, 'I don't hate this unborn child any-more.' She peered towards my Master. 'Because of what you said, Messer Peire. Do you remember? About bastards?'

'How can we help you?' he asked.

'No, no. I didn't come for anything like that. You see, I often thought about what you said . . . in the night when it was cold, and my belly hurt so, and when my man wouldn't touch me. Of course it was being hungry too,' she said, 'and wondering if the brat wouldn't die on me in any case.' She stared at us both. 'Then I began thinking that he might be freer, just because he'd been made like that, and fiercer. He's still growing fine, after what I dished out to him,' and she patted her stomach.

'And I thought that I *wanted* my baby to grow up knowing what he is, and not afraid of it. If I'm not afraid nor ashamed, he won't be will he, Messer Peire? Because he'll have to believe just in himself, won't he? Not in his kin because they're rich, neither in his folk if they're starving wretches like us, because they're slaves. And then that way maybe he'll catch a piece of God's spirit out of all the loneliness, knowing that he belongs to no-man, so he'll be strong enough to stand up on his own feet.' She stopped breathlessly. 'That's all, Messer Peire . . . because I did understand, didn't I?'

'Yes,' he whispered, 'better than Peire Carcasse.'

Before he was aware of it, she'd kissed his knuckles, and reached a red hand to his cheek. 'You poor man,' I heard her say before she disappeared through the door.

Lord Trencavel, now a man of twenty-four summers, had ridden into town with his knights and courtiers from Béziers. He looked fifteen years older, and anxiety riddled his features. Peire was told that the Pope had begged the King of France to pick out a champion, who would lead the knights of Christendom 'in their Heaven-blessed cause' against the heretics. The suave calumniator Pierre des Vaux de Cernay had spread well his lies to the effect that Raimon had been married five times, that he'd fornicated with his own father's mistresses, then he'd admitted in public that the Papal Legate's murderer was a good friend of his. Was it false? It was true that he'd recanted.

Some said that he'd recanted out of desperation, others out of foresight for his country's peril; others again said it was from despicable weakness of character, out of indecision, because he knew that his country was divided, quarrelsome, undisciplined and impotent to defend herself. But even Trencavel said that Raimon's act of renunciation at St Gilles was pointless. Innocent III had him in a cleft stick. If Raimon renounced heresy, he must then fight it in his own domains. How could the Count go to war against his own vassals? He had not the men to do it? And if he did not, then the Pope would fight himself against the blasphemers.

'Attack and destroy them one after the other,' he'd said. 'And if, which is probable, the Count does nothing, leave him in peace!' What peace? He would be destroyed either way. A crusade against Occitanie. What would it mean? The same things as did a crusade to the Holy Land? Indulgences for past sins? Reduction of sentences in Purgatory for each thousand slain? Plundering, rape, pillage, theft, all at the Church's blessing? No, it wasn't possible! That was ludicrous war-mongering! Such things could surely not happen here. They wouldn't take our land away from us! They wouldn't destroy Occitanie's heritage. These foreigners—not even the French—would steal our fiefs, our treasure, our castles, towns.

'You were right,' Lord Trencavel told my Master wretchedly. 'If you put importance on it. They do want our land.' He grinned wearily. 'But perhaps there's still time, eh? Do you honour us tonight at our festivals? Love after all, and Courtoisie, are not subdued by barbaric noises such as these.'

The couriers from the north thundered up and down the valley of the Rhône. The country stared, open-mouthed, too startled even to shift its feet out of the flying dust, and, therefore, saw nothing.

Peire's father had made out his last will and testament. This priceless document had been left behind, before his departure to the coast. His goods were to go to the Church. His wife would have nothing, and was ordered to retire to a nunnery.

'Where's the worthy merchant gone so hastily?'

'My lady mother says on pilgrimage.'

'And he didn't even leave a fare-thee-well for his son. He must have been in a great hurry to patch up his soul.'

'He took a coffer of gold with his mules. I doubt he'll return. He must be a lonely man.'

'He'll certainly be relieved of his gold before he reaches Jerusalem.'

The picture of this avaricious merchant hastening to Paradise with a box of precious metals clutched under his arm was too sweet a caricature! I scratched my bristling pate, and chuckled. Peire looked at me sidelong.

'I know, Master, what you're going to say any minute.'

'What's that?'

'That you'll be wanting to leave for Toulouse. What a life!'

'Little Beast, you've become a prophet!' He burst into laughter. 'Yes, we must go, to gather what truth, arms, and support we can,' he said slowly.

'Has the edict of your banishment been raised?' I coughed faintly.

The dark eyes hardened, and sunk farther into their sockets.

'I neither know nor care.'

Still it had not rained, and the sky glowered over us, heavy as lead. The farmers had been forced to bring water down from the river to give to their livestock. Through the night there had been flashes of lightning, but no thunder to herald rain. It was a hot sticky heat that the early-morning sun cast upon us.

'The rain must come tonight,' I thought.

We passed outlying farmsteads, and mounted into the hills. At one croft, I saw two peasants working at the plough, the man hauling it, and his wife, a thin scrawny creature with bandy legs, directing it feebly. I dismounted to ask for water, and stumbled through the furrows towards them. Their shack I saw was burnt black on one side. The woman turned and took a step away from me. The man stopped in his tracks.

'Good people, could we beg a little water?' I asked.

'There's hardly enough for us, let alone the sheep,' she whined. 'Go away and let us in peace!'

'He's a minstrel, that one mounted. He's got a lute on his back,' cried the old man. 'Children of Satan, leave us alone!'

He turned, and picking up a clod of earth, hurled it towards my Master.

Peire dismounted too, and approached. 'Forgive us our trade,' he called to them, 'but give us a drop of water.'

'Go away you vultures! Get away I tell you,' cried the woman.

With a kind of organized madness they started throwing lumps of earth and stones at us. I stared at the remains of their house.

'Master, they've been pillaged. There's nothing to do.'

Loose earth splattered my face, and I turned away. Peire stared at them for a moment. 'Forgive us,' he muttered. 'We can't help you.'

Not long afterwards, by the forest's edge, our road was blocked by a score of burly peasants, brandishing scythes and pitchforks, who stood in angry groups muttering to each other. Two monks had also been held up, and waited with the patience of shave-pates attending the second coming. Now and again they'd cast their eyes to heaven, as though seeking consolation for the bestial world they suffered in.

'The Revelation of St John will soon come to pass,' quavered one. Miracles have been accomplished, and the world of Satan will be overturned. The beasts shall be harnessed to ploughs of servitude—mark my words—and the godly shall have sway again!' He wagged a finger at the peasants, and shifted round to his colleague. 'Look at these slavering animals here, waiting to commit murder!'

'What are they going to do?' I asked timidly.

'They claim that some idiot is hiding up in the forest, and that he's the cause of their wretchedness. Their mates are at present trying to flush him out.'

'Why aren't you using your spiritual authority to bring them to heel? Now would be the time to dispense a few bulls of excommunication!' said my Master with some bile.

The monk shrugged. 'The problem of spiritual and temporal control is an interesting one,' he declared with the air of a pedagogue discussing Aristotle. 'But then this fool is probably as wicked as they . . . you see?' He smiled arrogantly.

The other broke in. 'My good brother Raoul is not advocating wanton cruelty you understand, but a minimum of intelligence. These louts outnumber us. If strong in zeal we're short of arms. And as the apostle said, "I was astute, and conquered you by ruse and division". A few of them will be killed off in the struggle, all being well. God will doubtless know his own, and save the righteous. Who are we to intervene? Indeed, when I think on it, this is surely to be taken as a sign. You agree, brother Raoul?'

Peire, without more ado, jumped from his horse and approached the noisiest group of men. 'What's happening?' he asked. 'Are you going to do away with some hapless fellow as the scapegoat for your own misfortunes?'

A huge gangling man, with narrow eyes, and wide shoulders, pushed his way forward. 'You'll do best to attend to your own affairs, Sieur minstrel. No disrespect meant. This man's cast the evil eye on our villages. We've got proof. He tells us that our children will be born crooked, that our crops will fail. He's said in his filthy rimes that no rain will come until the foreigners have razed our homes to the ground with fire and sword. It's more than a man can take. We must have him, and put an end to him.'

I started . . . his rimes! His rimes! Was it our one-time companion? The peasants stared hostilely at my Master. I watched their hard, cracked faces, like leather, like burnished copper, with the rough, ill-cut hair falling greasy and tangled about their ears. The sharp thin stench of their bodies, sweating freely, and the hunger and helplessness in their eyes—it was a bath they wanted, a bath in satiety. All that held them together was the comradeship of their misery and suffering.

'Do you think salvation will come like that?' Peire's voice rose.

'What's salvation?' jeered one of them, his eyes flaring red and raw. 'When we're dying of hunger!'

'There was rain up round Hautpoul,' shouted another. 'After they'd burnt a witch, it's said!'

'I mean salvation of your hides, wretches! It won't bring rain, or plenty, to kill one lunatic. If you speak of the man I've known, you know better than I that he suffers more than any of you.'

'Then he won't mind departing this life, eh?' said the narrow-eyed spokesman slyly.

'My Jeanne swears she saw a devil come out of his mouth,' cried another. 'The size of a rabbit, but black and slimy with blood and vomit.'

'Then your Jeanne,' said Peire distinctly, 'needs help worse than this poor idiot!'

There was a growl of anger. The peasants hemmed my Master in. I looked at the priests but they carefully ignored us.

'Here,' cried my Master desperately. 'Take the silver I have.' He threw a pouch at their feet. 'And buy food! Or better still, go storm your lord's castle. Speak to the burghers. Demand the corn hoarded from you in their bins. Demand your wages for work, like men, not dogs: like men, not slaves snarling with impotence and despair . . . but you won't,' he looked steadily into their faces. 'You've forgotten . . .'

The money lay untouched on the ground. A head turned.

'He's there!' someone shouted.

All heads craned to see.

In the pause, Peire grasped his sword and dived ahead of them, running up the slope to where the idiot stood, clutching his stick with both hands, and staring about him, eyebrows dancing in astonishment and glee at his reception.

Dusk was falling, and a few men had run back to the village to collect torches. The sun had rolled to the sky-line, like a bloody head, and heavy, pale-grey clouds lay like scars over our heads, hiding the first stars. The torches bobbed here and there, crackling and smoking in the stillness.

I was still fixed in my saddle, but now I hopped down, and tried to push through the men. I was caught between two hefty brutes. The more I struggled and shouted, imploring them to let me go to my Master, the tighter they held me.

From the edges of the forest, a thin line of men emerged. The two figures jolted forward too. I saw Peire saying something to his companion. Then the other shouted something about the final celebrations at the Court of Love. Peire was pleading with him.

'But we met again, there's still no rain,' cried the lunatic. 'And Paradise is nice!' he screamed louder, hopping up and down.

Peire tried to restrain him.

'And I'll show you how to dance in quick!'

'No rime there,' I muttered mournfully.

Pitchforks and scythes gleamed. Those behind were attacking. My Master's sword flung high over his head. There seemed to be fire all round them.

'Let me go!' I bellowed. 'Don't hurt my Master. Why don't you kill me off instead. It'll be easier, less dangerous. Let me go!' I was mad with rage and frustration.

But at that moment, the idiot, breaking free of Peire, leapt down the hill. He'd thrown away his stick, and was shouting snatches of a song. For a moment that seemed as long, and as short, as a dream, the men around me stood as though turned to stone. The idiot approached closer, dancing and skipping, with his hands out. The weapons hovered, their tips waving like a crop of maize in rank and file. There was one quick movement, a scream, and then the stabbing and stamping of many shadows.

It was over. Our mad rimer had kept his promises. He was dead. Weapons were thrown down carelessly. Men turned away from each other, breathing fast and heavily. No one looked at his neighbour, and I heard a fellow sobbing.

Peire stumbled down the hill.

The slopes were deserted except for us, and the two monks. The peasants had melted away. The one called Raoul knelt beside the body. He was intoning the last rites in a ponderous voice. The other monk stood holding the mules' heads. 'The least we can do, the least we can do,' he kept repeating fearfully.

My Master stared down.

'But he wanted it, Sieur Peire.'

'I failed to make him want it less,' he said. He turned to the priest, and gently taking him by the collar, hauled him off his prey.

'Leave him. Your prayers are less sincere than his desire for Paradise. You've no right under heaven to desecrate his progress there.'

The gaping monk scrambled away to join his colleague. 'I've never seen a man killed before,' said the younger.

One last torch flickered by the crooked feet. I heard bats squeak, and I beat the air to frighten them away.

Toulouse glowed in the sharp, transparent light. I'd hopped out of the palace to get a breath of air. The night before we'd juggled before count Raimon himself in the great hall, and he had complimented me. Now I heaved the cold breeze into my chest, flaring my nostrils, and stretching lazily.

I moved slowly through the Arab quarter, sniffing the mysterious fresh smells inquisitively, with the winter sun on my back. It was a relief to be away from the atmosphere of the palace.

They made less and less sense to me, these nobles. They were worse than the women, with their scented hair and cheeks, their eastern gowns, their tight buttocks encased in velvet, mincing through the antechambers, and insulting the weary couriers who brushed past them hastily.

How they bickered amongst themselves! How they snarled over whose falcon was the best, whose horse or damoselle was fairest, who was bravest! How they tittered at the women, blowing kisses on their delicate white hands, pursing up their mouths, and then running off to make their conquest, fornicating in the private rooms, in the laundry, in the stables, with whatever fodder was served up to them. These nobles were driving my Master to a frenzy.

Our return had been different from what I'd expected. No open reference had been made to Peire's banishment, although many had wanted details of our adventures. Peire was speechless on the subject. I less so. Garbled versions of fighting, capture, torture, had of course reached Toulouse. But my retelling of the stories was more a source of irritation than interest for those—the majority—whose fantasies provided them with all the material they needed. Still, they eyed my Master with jealousy, greater respect, and when he moved among them, would step away, subdued by his burning, emaciated features, and his questions. They no longer called him mad, nor a demented vagabond. They no longer dared. But they grew tired and frightened of him.

'How many men owe fealty to you? In what state are your castle's defences? Are your ramparts reinforced? Can you supply arms to the surrounding villages? Do you have water supplies?'

'By the Virgin! Give arms to the peasants? They'd probably attack us first!' said the Lord of Hautpoul.

'You wouldn't be undeserving of their attentions,' answered Peire coldly. 'But they'll doubtless wait until the danger from without has passed before turning on you. They'll fight for you, fearing more the evil they don't yet know.'

'And afterwards?'

'You might have learnt to rule men more honestly by then.'

Peire sought for men, men to resist, men who could be warned, who would fight. Every knight, squire, sergeant-at-arms who had some authority, or possessions, or a reputation, in the vicinity of Carcassonne, was confronted. Some respected Peire, and reached to him. They were very few. After a time he had ceased to approach the state counsellors for honest reports, and clear information. One grey-beard, close to Raimon, could regularly be found, either attempting to copulate with a young whore he'd introduced into his chambers, or gliding up and down in the great hall, with his pointed fingers tapping together, and reciting to the masks about him that there would be no war.

'Ridiculous. We have a firm peace undertaking already in the offing. No question about it. My reputation's on it! Useless anxiety. Foolish rumours. Count Raimon is even now making the final additions to the text.'

'Who is this Count of Leicester? What's his name—Simon de Montfort? Hasn't he already left Paris?' someone asked.

'Ah yes, indeed,' said the counsellors. 'But an empty threat!' He cleared his throat, and spat slowly into the bronze spittoon brought to him. They nodded about him, relaxing into smiles.

'And then we're too strong to be attacked,' said the Count of Foix on one occasion. 'Our cousins and allies in Brunswick and Aragon stand beside us. As Horace put it, "Their interests are at stake when a neighbour's walls begin to burn . . ." The French, loutish though they may be, have possibly read the Latin poet too!'

Peire would stare at them, his eyes gleaming heavy with frustration and disgust, but he'd only shake his head grimly as though to wash their cloying lies from his ears. 'We waste so much time in lazy anguish, and lazier pleading,' he said to me, 'but how I miss the Sieur Blacatz! He was not a foolish man. He could have helped us now.'

It was rumoured that the Count's brother, Baudouin, who'd been brought up at the French court, would fight against his own people. It was seen as yet another evil omen, and people threw themselves more frenziedly into the tremulous gaiety, the wild licence of court banquets, pastimes, and love-games.

Our lord, Raimon, was a nervous, ageing shadow of the man we'd known. He was afraid to be alone, afraid of the faces around him, afraid even of the darkness. Two pages always walked before him bearing torches, in daytime too, so that no nook, no corner of the palace would remain hidden from his eyes. Fires roared high in all the chambers. Raimon would stand for long minutes, fingers stretched to the blaze, with his counsellors murmuring behind him. He stared at the leaping flames as though looking for the conviction to put his hand out and pluck his withering heart from the embers. The varlets whispered that he had ordered all mirrors to be destroyed, because he could not bear to see his own reflection. It was said that he could not look his own son in the eyes.

I bought an orange and sat on the steps of a merchant's house, peeling it slowly, and licking my fingers. A tremor of excitement and anticipation fluttered in my stomach. Unconsciously the finger curled round my ear, rubbing, rubbing. The orange was sweet, and full of juice and pips.

I'd had a dream that night. It perplexed me. I'd dreamt of Bernard grown to manhood. I'd never imagined him fully grown. He'd always been a child without britches. He'd come close to me in my sleep with a finger laid against his lips, and he was a man. He told me in my dream that I would have a good death.

'What's a good death?' I asked him. 'Quick? Unconscious? Brave? Hopeful?'

He wouldn't answer.

'Will I die before my Master?'

'Your Master is God!' he said fiercely with his brows pressed together. And his god frightened me, for I straightaway turned my head from him, and Bernard vanished.

I let my gaze wander to the stalls in front of me. Two women, like black beetles, were bargaining over the fruit, their voices high and echoing. A young page-boy from the court, with a sword and scabbard in his hands, had stopped to stare at a peasant girl who was mounted on a donkey. The beast refused to move. The girl, flushed and pretty in her anger, was belabouring the animal's flanks, and glancing at the boy with irritation. He didn't budge to help her.

Suddenly I thought to myself that there would be fighting, that the war must come, that my Master would still be alone even amongst the betrayed and desperate, and that there was no help for it.

'War,' I said aloud, in dawning surprise, 'war in Terre d'Oc?' And my heart plunged already—so it seemed—in despair. All their words were talk. All the counselling and couriering were but the frantic scurrying of ants, whose hill trembles with the echo of approaching feet. And ants hide their eggs at least, when danger threatens. My Master was right. Peire was struggling with these numskulls, shaking them to a semblance of energy and initiative, and the minutes were really escaping, escaping too fast, like black notes of warning from the Devil's sack. And then I thought it would be better if the minutes had all fled, so that we would know the Time had come, so that there would be no more scurrying, and lies, and no more straws to catch. My head sank into my hands.

'It's true,' I shuddered. 'And Sieur Peire will leave me. Only the devils and traitors in my brain will be left, and the ones outside as well. Terre d'Oc, who'll know you then?'

A shadow fell across me. I started. It was a young monk with the tonsure. He had a gentle face.

'Aren't you he who is called the Little Beast?'

I squinted up at him, and nodded.

'It would be wiser and safer for you to keep away from Peire Carcasse,' he said penetratingly.

'Why?'

'You know why.' Turning he walked swiftly into the crowds.

'Stop. Why do you tell me this? Who are you?'

Tripping to my feet, I craned my head to catch a glimpse of him. I gazed about hopefully for some time, before turning my steps back to the palace.

'That's surely another omen of sorts,' I said. 'A plague on omens!'

I found Peire talking in a corner of the great hall with the Lord Trencavel, who'd galloped in from Carcassonne.

'No more words, my lord,' my Master was saying.

The other eyed him impatiently.

'We'll employ the flesh—our blood and sinews. What else have we? They can eat our meat, drink our blood, my lord, at some cost to their own hides, but they can't devour the spirit so swiftly. And if the spirit's strong, even in few of us, and burns brightly, perhaps the dry tinder that lies around will catch flame too.' He spoke more gently now. 'I think that's what's meant when we say the Phoenix rises perpetually from her own ashes.'

'Peire, are you so sure that your spirit will not be eaten alive? There are cannibals even amongst our own forces.'

My Master stared at the other thoughtfully. The hard lines about his mouth creased with a smile, but he said nothing.

'Now we must concentrate on preserving the flesh, Peire. You once sang a song about survival. All Occitanie sings it today. Have you forgotten?'

'I wish they did sing it, but no, my lord, I'm dreaming of another survival. I see a flaming gauntlet pointing to the future. And I see men overtaking the Black Archangel in their eternal progress, without even turning their heads, and riding on, holding high torches against the enclosing darkness.'

'Don't see too much. Don't look too closely,' muttered Trencavel. 'I don't want to see my deathly shadow.'

Peire stretched to his feet, caught sight of me, and called me. 'I've been looking for you,' he said. 'We must knuckle back to Carcassonne. Our stay among these hyenas, and mangy wolves, serves nobody.'

'I doubt you'll leave quite yet,' chuckled Trencavel behind him. 'Lord Gazanhat and the Lady Azelais are come to Toulouse, for better protection, they say. And they bring their family.'

With this as a parting shot he clattered off to his uncle's apartments.

Peire stared at me opaquely. His face had lost all expression, and was suddenly full of lines.

'What must I do, Little Beast?' he whispered finally. His gaze fixed itself to me, and I felt cornered in his dark eyes.

'You haven't mentioned her name for months, Sieur Peire.'

He nodded. 'It seemed that I heard her speak it herself often enough . . . and that I only had to listen.'

'Master, if we hop off quickly . . . there's Carcassonne to defend, and also, Messer Peire, I had a notion this morning that Toulouse could be a rather hot seat . . . for your seat, if you follow me.' I looked into his face, listening to my words leaking away.

'You'll see her,' I said trembling. 'You'll see her, and somehow the anguish in the two of you will be resolved.'

He shook his head.

'. . . Little Beast wishes it with all his heart. The God you spoke to in the desert will wish it too. The wheel must turn full circle,' I pleaded. 'Isn't that true, Master?'

That afternoon, before evensong, the Sieur Carcasse and I were called up to the ladies' gallery. A damoselle opened the door, and we were ushered in. Peire half turned, but the lock clicked into place. He stood with his back to the door, the great rumpled head down. He had many, fine streaks of white hair, I noticed. I became aware of how much, in the deepest part of him, he had awaited her for all these months. I was aware too that nothing more in the world could have loosened his courage and the agony in him from their sockets. For a moment I thought that he would still leave the room. But it was not so. He raised his head. At the same moment she had raised the veil from her face.

It was a pale drawn face that lifted up to him, the eyelids dark with fatigue. The cheekbones still rose, proud and splendid beneath the great eyes, now washed with endurance and suffering. The nose curved down with all its old grace and firmness. Her lips still had a stroke of cruelty in their control, still the secret generosity in their shape. But it was a face of mortal sadness which gazed unflinchingly into my Master's.

He stepped towards her.

'Peire, it *is* you?' Her voice quivered. 'What have you done to this face? Oh my God, what have you done to him?'

She drew closer, and raised her arms involuntarily, until her two hands, like a miracle, lay on each of the wide, bony shoulders. Her eyes strayed over his features, until at last they alighted on mine.

'I recognize the Master better through his servant,' she murmured. 'Oh, hail Little Beast!'

'Aniara,' he cried.

'Aniara,' she said back to him. 'Yes, Aniara.'

'Why are you here? Have you really come for Raimon's protection?'

She looked at him, frowning a little, and then stepped back, shaking her head. 'I came because I heard there was a pilgrim back from the Holy Land. I'm a great believer in sanctity. Peire Carcasse knows that!'

Peire stared through her.

'No, that's not true either,' she whispered. 'I came because I couldn't bear my hatred any more. I came because I couldn't weep any more on the flatterers who courted me; because I didn't want peace with God any more. I came because all the images of God were in your image, Peire. All the pain of him seemed to be your pain . . . I came because we've hated so much that there is only God left between us . . . because you were here. I came . . .' She ceased. A wrist pushed the hair from her brow.

'You've been ill?' Peire stared at her feverishly.

'I've been ill. Oh yes, I've been ill. I've been well, too, and living, Peire. Living a kind of life.'

She made a sign to the damoselle. A small door at the other end of the apartment opened. Aniara smiled—a curious, wry, rancorous softening of the mouth.

'I also came, wanting to present you to the future Lord of Gazanac,' she said.

She led the little boy of two or three years gravely up to us. He held himself straight and high, like his mother. He tilted his head up, so that the mass of dark curls shook, and his deep-set eyes stared slowly, and politely, into the widening gaze of the man before him.

'God greet you, Sieur,' the voice piped out. 'I nearly know all of your songs.' He blushed. 'Those that have been brought to me at least.'

In the pause, in the acceptance of something that I'd never believed in, that had always appeared quite impossible, I opened the door and slipped out.

For three days I watched over their happiness, with the jealousy of an old nurse guarding her infants. Three days aren't much. They're certainly not much for a lifetime, but it was a life they lived through in those hours.

The star made of branches and flowers, woven with the blue silk of the gage she'd once given him, hung over the child's crèche. When Peire had pulled it from his jerkin, telling its tale, the boy reached for it at once.

'Mama, it'll keep me safe won't it? It's the star of David from the Holy Land. I'm called David too. That *is* true, isn't it Sieur Peire?'

'Yes,' said my Master with equal seriousness. 'It's most surely the star of vagabonds, of dreamers, of wonder. Indeed it must be the star of David, and may it guard you, and remind you of all the miracles that a star foretells, and inspires a man towards!'

My Master treated her with the awe of a man who lays hands on the truth of his own spirit for the first time. She was always a little distant. With her ringless hand placed lightly on his arm as they walked in the gardens, she'd listen to him, looking straight in front of her. Only occasionally would she pause abruptly, to see into his face, with a mixture of hesitancy, wonder, and infinite surprise in her cool lighting eyes.

On the third evening after Vespers, she kept her seat in the chapel, when the service was over. The choir's voices had died into the vaults, the priests, monks, and legates had given the blessing, and departed after their gilded flock. I'd crept in at the back, as I often did, for I loved the smell of incense, the music, and to watch these noble people, all these noble people, turn into men, even if it was against their natures! As I stood leaning my hump against the wall, with my fingers tucked about my ear, it had seemed to me at last, that something much stronger than ambition, more persuasive than power, touched each of us when we came together there. It seemed to me that the richness of a prince's clothes, or the jewel-encrusted garments of the priests, were like my rags; and that the words spoken made no distinction for true man or liar, for hypocrite or saint, because—without any of us understanding the secret —the words were spoken to Man, searching for his own divinity; and that somehow, the God of Man, the one whom Peire spoke about, the God beyond all other gods, was reaching down to us and tempting us to holiness and wonder; tempting us through his own humanity, which he'd once put on, like my rags, like the count's precious clothes.

The door creaked. It was Peire. He stood for a moment, accustoming his eyes to the dark, and then to the figure of Aniara, who sat, leaning her head back, her face bright and sharp, lit by the candles. He stared at the great silver cross on the altar, and the lonely figure, who clung like a poor monkey to the nails. His eyes moved to the painted virgin, leaning dwarf-like from her pedestal, and then slowly through the spitting candles to the high window above the altar. As though he'd ceased to focus, his eyes peered upwards, abandoning all the baubles, the graven images, discarding them from his mind, so that the flame appeared about to leap out of him, penetrating upwards through the dark.

I could smell the rough odour of his doublet, the ointment Aniara had rubbed into his shoulder to ease the stiffness. I believed that I could smell the eagerness and the fire in him. It burnt in my nostrils, and I wondered if I was going mad, or if he was like that saint who stank of roses, but something else, something different.

Peire's eyes closed. I saw the Adam's apple wriggle in his throat. Aniara broke into a fit of coughing, pressing a hand over her lungs. The noise echoed, disguising my Master's footsteps. She must have been in pain. He stopped beside her, on her left side. She arched a little away from him.

'Peire, in a Christian chapel! But let me be now . . .'

'You weren't praying.'

'No, I was sleeping, I think.' Her voice swung like a chandelier. The cough came again. I watched the hand pressing against her neck. 'Let me be,' she said, and her eyes fell on him gently.

'I can't. I'm perpetually waiting for you. When I'm with you it seems that it will always be so. When you're not there, I think we shall never meet again.'

'You sound as if you should be talking to God,' she mocked softly.

There was silence.

'If I could touch you, and all the sickness would go away! Oh, Carcasse, what a fool . . .'

'If I could have *that* pain, like him on his crucifix,' she said fiercely. 'And then afterwards heal the wounds in Peire Carcasse!' She stopped to catch her breath, and then spoke again with a kind of ferocity.

'Peire, Peire, I'm dying for having lived without you. I needed the Carcasse by me, to house all our devils. I need him still,' she cried out. 'It was never enough to have either the dream or the hatred. Did you know that? It was flesh and blood, Peire, that I missed.' For a moment she leant her head back against him. 'The hatred made me your prisoner more surely than any love.'

The racking cough broke out once more. Peire moved. He touched her breast, her pale cheek.

'You held Carcasse so surely, Aniara, but yet you let him loose.' He spoke hesitantly. 'My words are all dried up. I have only two hands, Aniara, that take yours—so—and a song that I can't release from my lungs . . . which is only a single note . . . and a knowledge that this note rings so loud in me that it will last forever.'

'But I, Peire, where shall I go when you leave? Which God will succour me!' she cried.

Peire took her arm and brought her to her feet.

'Aniara, my lady,' he said. 'Forgive me if I speak foolishly. It is for the last time . . . we have seen and heard so many gods. Terre d'Oc has hunted them out as scapegoats, or as deliverers from the passions and evils of our age. Our people have turned their heads wildly, until their distress drove them mad, and they hid like ghosts from their mortal desires. But if there is a god today who must be destroyed, if there is a god whom men have placed above themselves, and in whose image they rule, it is the god of death.

'Once men ruled in the image of a power whose creative inspiration gave them light and energy. Perhaps in that time Occitanie was brought kicking to life. Today Death is our sovereign prince. His minions have bound up our sinews, dried up our manhood, perverted our minds with fantasies of pleasure, ease, and corruption. We debauch, dismember, mutilate and destroy each other for the smallest excuse. For faith! For the Church, for justice, for remission of sins, for revenge, for peace! We do this above all to prove that we're alive, to prove that although Death is our master, we, by dealing death, are not his slaves. If there is any god who must die to save our land, it is the god of death. And if there is no other way to prove to ourselves that there is the God of Creativity who awaits us, we must struggle past death, heralding the other's name through the regions of oblivion, until we are remembered.'

He had her hands clasped tight within his. They stood straight and fierce together, like two poplars.

'Aniara, where shall you go when I leave? Where shall I go? I'll tell you! My love, we shall take horse, and torch, and faith slung over our backs, like the Little Beast's sack. We'll gallop within the shadows of the horsemen of the Apocalypse, and we'll pass beyond this demon.' His voice rang out proudly. 'I promise! A vagabond's promise. 'But still a promise, Aniara,' he finished.

'Minstrel, God love you,' she said. 'My son needs raising until that time. May God help me!'

He bent to kiss her hands. With his fingers he separated the curls away from her forehead. She still held him.

'Peire,' she called. 'Peire!'

The great head looked down at her. She reached towards him, one white hand caught his neck, and she pressed her shivering body tight against him, crushing her face in his hair.

'We're alive,' she cried out, 'we *are* alive!'

'You will be dead!' said an iron voice. Behind me the chapel door had opened wide, and light poured in. Standing under the arch, with his hands folded in the deep sleeves of his robe, stood the

Cistercian abbot of Toulouse, with four sergeants-at-arms holding pikes behind him.

Peire was held at the Cistercian monastery in the town. I shared an Arab vendor's hut, with him and his family, just outside the main gates. He was a kind man with a gentleness in his heart that was stronger than his sense of persecution. He sold his spices and herbs to both the monks within, and to the townsfolk.

Peire's last words to me before being taken away had been to watch over his lady. 'They can't keep me for ever,' he'd cried. 'They have not the patience, and I doubt they'll kill me, for there's still Little Beast to carry on the tale!'

A rough hand was clapped over his mouth with such force that I thought they'd break his neck.

'Guard my lady,' he called faintly, and was gone.

But the Lady Azelais—Aniara—was gone. Lord Gazanhat had clapped her into a litter, and, with his retinue, had left for home. The last I saw of them was David, perched on the saddle before the pumpkin whose name he bore, waving fiercely at me, tears blinding his eyes, and piping: 'I'll never forget the songs. I'll learn them all. I'll never forget a single one!'

So there was no reason for me to hover about the palace any more. I took my sack, my Master's armour, and weapons, his lute, and rode down in the biting north wind to the town centre.

Sometimes I caught a glimpse of my Master. It had taken me many days to discover where they held him. With my viol, I'd passed beneath one window to the next, singing his songs softly, until one day I heard my name. He'd pulled himself up to the casement, gripping the bars, and I'd had a glimpse of his face.

'Little Beast,' he croaked with a grin. 'At least you're still kicking. You must forgive me for keeping you inactive. Where's my lady, Aniara?'

I glared dumbstruck at his features. The skin had worn parchment thin, the eyes hung gaunt in their sockets. His head had been shaved. I could see the dark bruises, and dried blood still adhering to his scalp.

'What have they done to you?' I whispered.

'They've inflicted pain,' he said reluctantly. 'They appear to want me to confess to a great list of sins, that half the bandits in

Terre d'Oc would be hard put to commit in a hundred years.' He paused.

'These priests have neat minds. They get desperate over the details of wickedness. I understand them . . . but Aniara, where is she?'

'They've taken her home. In a litter. She was not molested.' I stopped.

'What else? There's more, isn't there?'

'She's ill, Messer Peire. She's ill.' I avoided his gaze. 'What will happen to you, now?'

'Come back tonight,' he said urgently, and dropped from sight.

I waited all that afternoon, and until late that night when they brought him back. I heard a groan.

'Repent and confess,' a young, calm voice had repeated over and over again.

It rang a chord in my brain.

'Repent and confess. Only thus can you be saved . . . In the name of the Father, the Son, and the Holy Ghost, abjure Satan in all his disguises, and recant. It will be easier for you Peire Carcasse, and your soul will be eased from eternal torment!'

'Confess what, you fools?' he cried. 'My sins, God knows about already. We've pardoned each other for a great deal. And Satan, how can I abjure Satan when he lives in God too? The charges you bring against me? I cannot understand them!'

'But we understand them,' said the soft voice. 'Trust in God, and admit to them. You have fallen into depravation, into heresy, like a dog licking up another's vomit. Relieve yourself. Your own sins, and those we accuse you of, are the same. There is no difference. You know it poor minstrel. Admit to the crimes, and save yourself from Hell.'

'I can't admit what I don't believe!'

'You can, you can, and you must, if you believe in Holy Church, in us, in the True Faith. Obedience is faith. Faith is belief!'

Peire gasped for breath, but was silent, recognizing the trap.

'Peire Carcasse, listen attentively!' The gentle persuasive voice continued. 'There are three cells which will be your antechambers to eternity. Shall I tell you of them?

'The first is where you find yourself now. You have enough room to walk a few steps. You have a little air, even some light. The next cell allows you room to stand, and to crouch. There is no light because the cell is underground. You are chained hand and foot. There are rats, and the food is poor. In the third cell the door is walled up. You can barely move your arms, and you are in total darkness. No one on earth can reach you again . . . Abjure the evil of your life, confess the names of the heretical Cathari whom you know, and you shall be saved. We will all give praise together!'

'I believe . . .'

'At last!' whispered the monk.

'. . . I believe neither you, nor your Church, nor the god you desecrate with your words. God hears my words, and will succour me. Amen!'

The cell door slammed. I said his name, but he didn't answer me.

Christmas passed. The bells in the monastery, and all those in the city, rang merrily to herald the birth of Christ. There was a thin layer of frost on the ground, and the cold had gnawed into my hump, and my feet, and I found it hard to walk. I had not seen, nor heard my Master for many days, and believed that he could not last much longer.

One early morning, the monastery gates opened to admit a strange cortège. A number of defrocked shave-pates, whose robes had been torn off their backs, and who were only clothed with loin-cloths, tramped through the gates. They were escorted by soldiers and monks. One of the last to pass me was Peire de Vic, the bawdy Abbot of Montaudran. He stared at me with unfocused eyes, slobbering at the mouth, and rocked on. Behind him, walking alone, was the young monk who'd once accosted me in the Arab market, bidding me abandon my Master. I went up to him.

'Good monk,' I stuttered. 'You won't remember me, saving your presence, but you once addressed me concerning the Sieur Carcasse. What will happen to him . . . ?'

He turned to me. The gentle face looked gravely on me, but his eyes were bright and hard.

'I remember you, Little Beast. I remember you.'

He waited. I tried a different approach.

'Worthy monk, how do you know me? What are you called so that I may remember you?'

'My name is Bernard de Betaille,' he said smoothly. 'Brother Bernard in the order of holy Cistercians.'

My mouth dropped. I stared stupidly.

'Oh no. That's not true, no!'

He passed on, and the gates shut behind him.

I was back in the Arab's hut. I don't remember. I remember a young woman coming to buy rosemary and thyme. She spoke low, and the hard blue sky behind her seemed brittle unto breaking. It was his first transaction of the day. He pressed his hands together, and gave praise to Allah. For his daily bread! The woman smiled. She left. It seemed her smile stayed behind. It was still there hovering in the stall.

I didn't think of my Master. I found I'd forgotten his face. It wasn't important, and I had no desire to trek round the monastery walls in search of him. I was glad he was on his own, away from me, with Bernard; that he was nothing, nothing to do with me. Even of Bernard I hardly thought. Except that his features would sometimes pass in my mind, confused with my images of his childhood. MY images! Something had been left out, I'll tell myself. There's a link I've overlooked. When I find it I'll understand. I'll wait. Yes, I'll wait.

But first, first of all I had to empty my sack—that was important because . . . it was hard. So many things. Too many precious things!

The other voice answered: 'Nothing's precious. Destroy all the baubles of remembrance!' Remembrance is a funny word. Remembering and embracing. Members together.

I'd sit on the rushes close to the door. Rope coiled on the floor. My balls, my transparent juggling balls, my sticks, click-click. I reached deep, deep, deep, and touched the bottom of a dream. And I noticed that the little boy was dead. And quite silent. There was a man. Should he know me?

Souls may pass, and spirits go, nature is sad, heigh ho!

I looked out of the window; looked out of the window. But there were no colours in the sky, so I remembered the orange which had been full of juice and pips, which had been round and full of warm red tears, which had been in my hand when Brother Bernard had first passed me by.

Messer Delusion is an ageing suicide case, whom you stroke tenderly, and have no business listening to!

The Church had informed Brother Bernard that jongleurs and

minstrels were the perverted minions of SIN! And children's memories are short.

'Bernard!' I shouted at the top of my voice. 'Bernard, I put you to bed when you were a child, and juggled for you. My name is Adam and I loved you! I lived because of that.'

The noise shocked me.

'It's true,' I whispered. 'It is most true.'

The old vendor's wife, wrapped in her pretty Arab shawl, stooped down to me.

'Little Christian, are you talking to your prophet?'

Her eyes winked from a bed of wrinkles. They winked and winked until they looked like sticky sweets licked by her hairless eyelids. She smelt of basilico and thyme. Everything in the house smelt of basilico and thyme.

'Basilico has the strongest smell of all,' I told her, climbing to my feet.

Her face puckered up, and she turned away.

'No feelings, I'm sorry,' I muttered.

'Adam, not Little Beast. That was right. Bernard was his name, Adam was mine.'

But then a terrible doubt seized me. If Little Beast *was* my name? And if his name was Bernard the Cistercian? Who then was Peire Carcasse for example? I started wildly. No one at all?

'And Bernard was torturing him!' I cackled with laughter. 'Poor Bernard!'

I looked about, but there was no one listening. I opened my mouth. A bird squeaked. It wasn't me. It was a sparrow rocking cold and hungry by the window.

'I'm hungry too,' I said.

The tears poured down my face.

I dreamt one night that Aniara's tapestry was finished, and that it hung suspended by two huge lances in the sky above a battlefield. A rose tree grew in the centre, blossoming in changing shades, and two rearing unicorns guarded it. Round about there danced monkeys, cats, and wild animals, skipping on their hind legs. Outside the inner circle, there were men and women and children. And next to each human was a leering corpse, whose flesh hung in strips from his bones. There were half a dozen Popes in jester's bells; there were minstrels and lovers, knights, peasants, kings in parchment crowns, and beggars dressed in ermine, and they all held hands. Hanging by his heel from the rose tree was a mummy, and his entrails swept the ground. Devils with pot-bellies, long snouts, horns and tails, licked his blood, and poked nails in his face. Troubadours played lutes and flutes, singing songs like lullabies. They all danced about the tree. Messer Death was there, leaning on his scythe. His smile was wide, and from his shoulders dangled a hundred crowns, a hundred orbs and sceptres. Above, high above, hung a star whose light reflected off the horns of the Unicorns. I saw Little Beast with his sack, and Peire Carcasse, and Bernard, and Aniara kneeling on her heels. Some were being dragged down to Hell, while others reached to the beams of light.

The dream passed. I awoke icy cold. A grey light crept up the window. The old woman's eyes blinked at me sleeplessly from her straw pallet. Her eyes blinked and flickered with warmth, memory, and life.

'It's almost day, a new day,' she said in her sing-song voice. 'Allah be praised!'

'A new life, aye?' I muttered. 'With God's blessing and the Devil's curse, like salt and pepper to bring out the taste of it!'

My Master was released on Good Friday.

I waited for him at the gates, knowing that something was afoot. Swollen-tongued, sweating couriers and dusty monks on lathered palfreys had been coming in since before dawn. Rumours as usual were flying. Even my Arab protector was shaking. 'Now we shall have to flee once more,' he told his family gravely. 'Nowhere is there safety for us in this country.'

Peire appeared with a number of other victims of the Church's wrath. He looked like a tattered flagpole, a huge flickering reflection of the old Carcasse, in the light. But otherwise he seemed whole, alive; if anything, more eager and resolute than when he'd been captured. I held out my hands as he strode towards me. The monks were singing the Te Deum in the background, like hornets.

'If they'd kept me much longer, I would have confessed to murdering Christ himself!'

He took me in his arms, held me close, and then stared slowly over my face.

'My old friend,' he said wonderingly. 'Your white face has become smooth! The lines have slipped away. What did you find!'

I looked into the dark eyes calmly, and shook my head. Peire took my head and kissed me.

'It helped to know you were outside,' he told me.

'Messer Peire, what's happening? Why did they free you?'

He paused, and with a grim, hollow voice, replied to me.

'Eudes, Duke of Burgundy, Hervé, Count of Nevers, Gaucher, Count of Saint Pol, Guillaume des Barres, and Simon de Montfort, Count of Leicester in England, with the Archbishops of Rheims and Bordeaux, with the Bishops of Sens, Clairmont, Rouen, Lisieux, Autun and Chartres, and with Theodosius, Archdeacon of Notre Dame in Paris—who has assumed command of the engines of war —reinforced by German horsemen, and a horde of truands under their princes, have passed Lyon and Valence, have passed Montélimar, and now enter the territories of Provence and Terre d'Oc. A host of more than five hundred thousand men, under the banner of the Cross, now make crusade against our land and people. They approach even now to Montpellier, where the Pope's emissary, ambassador and spy, Arnaud-Amaury, Abbot of Citeaux, awaits them with arms outstretched, indulgences for terror in his hands, and a blessing on his lips.'

Behind us I dimly noted that the monks' voices had changed. The Te Deum had given place to a chant, whose words rose clear on the hot spring breeze . . .

> White was his naked breast,
> And red with blood his side,
> Blood on his tragic face,
> His wounds deep and wide.
>
> Stiff with death his arms,
> High spread upon the Rood,
> From five gashes in his body
> Flowed the streams of blood . . .

The words faded on the wind, and I hobbled off to get the horses.

'We're off in the right direction for the Resurrection,' I sang out, before shaking my head fiercely. 'You're beginning to sound like a dead idiot, Little Beast,' I muttered. 'Don't you hear yourself?'

8

Our journey home was a weeping pilgrimage. It was as if we heard a distant bell tolling our progress to an end. Stillness, stones, dust, and thirst. Our journey home was a riding through a land of shadows, of memories reflecting off a razor's edge.

The wells had dried up, the sun bore down on us with slow fury from dawn to dusk, and the nights were heavy with heat. The horses grew bone-weary as we did. The stones jumped from under their hooves, ricochetting off the bigger rocks to either side of the path. Sometimes we passed close to the stream's bed, hoping to replenish our gourds, but the earth was already cracked and dry. If there was water, it ran sluggishly, stagnantly, in rivers of sweat among the sand-banks, and had already been polluted by the cattle. With us, there was always the sun, blinding us, flaying us, bursting in bloody scything strokes across the heavens, and scorching the land, yellow and brown.

We passed Montaudran; we passed Montgiscard in the night, La Bécède, at dawn. Our beasts stumbled on into the torturing new day.

Peire wasted no words. When we halted it was to seek the Siegneur or Chatelain out, to avert him of the evil that war had come; and if necessary to haul with our bare hands, rocks, stones, and the débris at hand, on to dilapidated ramparts and crumbling walls. We even damned streams to protect what supplies still existed. The petty nobles through whose lands we passed gazed at us with foolish eyes, until our toiling suddenly took on a meaning for them, and my Master's fury acquired a sense for them, and his agony became theirs. With clumsy feet and broken flesh they'd begin to work like peasants, too, their liegemen bewildered and grateful, and we would move onwards, hunched over our saddles, sweating, stinking, dirty with blood, and endless fatigue. Peire treated me as roughly as he did himself, and would not let me pause.

About us, people began, with the logic of panic, to seek out the 'Parfaits', the Cathari, to stone them, to burn their houses, their livestock, and whatever the sun had not yet touched. These people too had death in their nostrils, and they struck at innocent and heretic, Jew, Christian, Moslem, and 'Parfait' with equal disregard. Man, wife, daughter, dog—had their throats cut. We saw an entire family thrown down a steep ravine, one by one, except for the eldest son, whom the ruffians held to watch. A bunch of roving murderers with rough crosses sewn hastily on their surcoats, first hacked off their heads, and then threw them into the abyss. Father, mother, daughter rattled noisily away. The last, her dress caught on a thicket, hung dangling upside down, until the stones thrown from above dislodged the body, and she vanished.

Another dawn had come. We'd ridden most of the night to avoid the sun, and now, to keep ourselves from falling asleep in the saddle, we walked by the horses' heads. The hill's summit was reached, and we paused for breath.

Beneath us a woman's body was hanging from an olive tree. The earth and grass was on fire. Her clothes were in shreds. She'd been stripped, beaten and stoned. A young boy of twelve years or so stood with a rock in his hand, staring at the body with disgust and hatred. When he saw us, he half turned irresolutely, before casting the rock away. He ran off, and then stopped to shout. 'Nail her through the heart, like for the owls, because she's a heretic witch— with a big nail.'

We ran down. Peire detached her from the tree. She wasn't dead, but moaned faintly, with the blood already blackening on her body. I stamped out the smouldering ashes about us. Peire pillowed her head on his lap. Smoke was still drifting into the pink sky. She could hardly speak, and lapsed frequently into her own darkness. Now and then a word did escape her.

'Mother. Horror. Dead.' Her hand tried to reach her temples. 'What do they want?' she cried. 'What do they want?' But her voice had lost all sound to it. A trickle of blood issued from her nostrils. She was gone. Peire shut her eyes.

'We must bury her.'

I stared at the body, already loose and slack in death. She was young. She reminded me of Agnes—plump, misty Agnes.

'Master, how many people will go? How many deaths? How much hurt will be needed before the end?'

Peire stared over the fields, rocking the girl. A hot wind caught at his clothes, at the tatters on her body. My hands flew over my mouth. I was crying with terror.

He was pushing the hair back from her forehead with a kind of bemused precision. 'Black hair for darkness,' he whispered to himself, 'red hair for sunlight, white hair for the turning of the earth, and for age.' He looked up. 'Until all the women's hair, all the women's long hair, their sleek locks are washed bright and sheared for mourning. Then the men may go home, for there'll be no more fathers and sons. But not until then!' he sobbed. 'Not until then . . .'

With Peire's sword, and our hands, we hacked a tomb for her in the hard earth. He wrapped her in his pilgrim's cloak, and we piled the heaviest stones over her, so that the crows and vultures would not reach her flesh. I knelt, and my Master stood beside me, for he would not kneel, and we made a prayer for her. Our faces were greasy with earth and sweat and tears. My Master stood very still with his hands clasped together and his head thrown back. He was tall and dark there on the hillside.

'Oh my God,' he finally said, 'we shall always fight you; preserve us from cowardice, and our attempts to escape that battle. We shall always fight you my God; deliver us from evil, and let us know your potency. We shall always fight you; give us therefore your blessing, guard us in our travail, and in our coming to you. Amen!'

We reached Hautpoul. The Lord Izarn told us that marauding bands were already scouring the countryside, out of Montpellier. My Master did not wait to hear more, but strode on to the pitiful ramparts which had been allowed to fall into decay.

'Protect your water, raise your walls, herd your flocks, your liegemen and families into positions of safety!'

The Lord Izarn shivered, and wrapped his silk stole more closely about him. 'What can I do? In any case, I'm a good Catholic,' he giggled. 'I've kept clear of Trencavel all these months. They can't accuse me of fraternizing with heretics. They won't, will they?' He pleaded with his soft doe eyes. 'In any case, what could we do? Even the Count Raimon supports the Crusaders. And the English can't help us, can they?'

'Count Raimon is senile, but his son fights for Occitanie. And Trencavel will be supported,' ground Peire through his teeth. 'Wrap your puny arms round a stone, and fight for your women who'll be raped and sliced to pieces, if you can't fight for your country!'

'Those rocks are far too heavy for me to lift. I couldn't possibly do that!' sniffed the Lord of Hautpoul.

Peire ran to the village, and begged men to help him patch up the walls, but there were few who came, and those listless, surly and already hopeless with the weight of gathering shock.

From Hautpoul we rode through Cabaret, and down past blackened olive groves, razed vineyards and cornfields, past dead sheep and cattle, towards Carcassonne. Many an old woman we saw whose sons had gone to fight, many a stray urchin who'd lost his family in the confusion. Many were the hands stretched up to our saddle-bows, clamouring for food, many the faces that turned away from us as though we had slapped them—because we had nothing left to give. The carrion crows accompanied us, and their cawing frightened all the other birds away.

There was a large piece of cloth flapping over the Dame's Gate as we rode up. From a distance it looked like a piece of tapestry thrown out to herald a festivity. But when we approached, my stomach began to freeze inside me.

'Master,' I blurted out, tugging his jerkin and pointing. 'It was in my dreams. I swear it's the same tapestry!'

He pulled on the reins and the horses drew to a halt. The two Unicorns were leaping on the wind, and the sun's rays were catching the gold and silver threads of the great star, and the devils were as I'd remembered.

'What future awaits us, Little Beast?' He smiled mournfully. 'Do you think there are brave men in Carcassonne?'

His voice, still hoarse with the dust from our riding, rose to the guards. 'Little Beast and Peire Carcasse bring rusty arms and worn voices to stand amongst you!'

It was hers. The Lady Azelais had made gift of her work to the city of Carcassonne. The town's crest and arms were embroidered on the four corners. Raimon Roger Trencavel himself had helped to fix it to the battlements.

The Lord of Béziers and Carcassonne was working amongst his shopkeepers, his peasants and labourers. With brick and mortar, with sand, stone, and gavel, axe and spade, he laboured as did his townsfolk to strengthen the walls, sealing up the broken passages, and reinforcing the watchtowers.

That evening when the council was over, Peire asked him the news. He stared bitterly and silently at my Master for a long time, then said: 'My noble uncle has not dared to give me either soldiers, or arms, or gold to buy the wherewithal for the defence of Béziers.

216

It is said that he prays much to the god of the Cathari, saying that the Christian god has let him down! It is said that he's lost his reason, and that he believes tragedy will still be averted. It is also said that he has no more couriers who will bear his protestations of innocence, purity and faith to the Legate at present in Montpellier.'

The young noble slowly covered his face with his hands. 'Peire Carcasse,' he said. 'Help me now!'

'I will,' my Master answered. 'We must indeed help each other.'

The work proceeded so slowly. There was so little time. There was only the thin rampart circling the town, and the towers were not (and never could be) properly buttressed against modern assault, and the war engines which Arnaud-Amaury and Montfort would throw against us. Water was scarce, although it was sworn that the citadel's well was deep enough to last a good six months, even with the drought.

'You're sure?' asked Peire.

'We're sure,' chorused those detailed to preservation of supplies. 'Of course we're sure. It's never dried up in two hundred years.'

There *were* brave men in Carcassonne. But as my Master said, there were mostly only men. Men whose crops had been destroyed, whose livestock had died of thirst; men whose farms had been burnt down, whose grapes had withered on the vine; men whose goods, whose stock, whose ships were barricaded on the coast, at Narbonne, Montpellier, even Marseille, and who grew lean and silent, who shrivelled in their bankruptcy. There were also the blacksmiths for example, who did a good trade, refurbishing arms, hammering out swords, and they were mostly very brave . . . with words, and with the prices they demanded. There were the young rakes who frequented the taverns, the brothel, who swaggered up and down the cobbled streets, and who brazened out the Abbé of St Nazaire in the square, with their brave boasts, with their jumping blades. Brave men?

There were cowards, though, and liars, and thieves, and weaklings. And I liked them better, for I understood them.

One morning I found a skinny boy and his red-haired sister cramming their mouths with olives and cheese which they'd stolen in the kitchen.

'And your pockets?' I asked. 'Are you stealing just for yourselves?'

217

They glared at me, terrorized. The penalty for thieving in a town threatened with famine was, for a first offence, the loss of the right hand, to be lopped off at the wrist, and for the second, death. The girl burst into tears, and from her apron fell a hunk of ham and black bread.

I watched the thin shoulders shuddering, and felt—as though it were in myself—the weight of fear crawling through her brother's entrails.

'Be off with you!'

They turned to run.

'And pick up what you've dropped!' I muttered, hobbling away.

Two days later I saw the boy again, but now he had a rag tied about the stump of his right arm.

Peire's mother gave away what she could. We were often hungry. Peire seemed hardly to eat at all. My stomach groaned in self pity.

Many people tried to sneak away from the town, with the excuse that they'd forgotten a cow, or a few chickens down by the river. 'We'll get them . . . to help in the general need,' they'd say, with their eyes cast down, pushing small children forward to play on the guards' sympathies.

Many people lied about the food they had, and would spend their days begging, so as to hoard more, when their arms could have piled stones on the walls more usefully and, more pertinently, to their salvation.

At night there was some looting. People suspected of heresy were beaten, thrown out of the gates, and their houses set on fire. Crosses were daubed on the doors to proclaim the faith of those within. Peire's mother dared leave her house no more. She was safe there because of her son.

A paralysis began to grip the town.

The energy and enthusiasm of the first days was drying up. I remember we had been standing outside the walls. Peire was watching a straggling column of families, pulling their overloaded donkeys down the road from the Dame's Gate.

'Too many people, not enough food,' he growled. 'Poor wretches it's better that they go.'

Beyond the line of refugees I caught sight of a horseman galloping alone in a cloud of dust towards the Gate.

'It must be a messenger!'

We ran to await him.

But it was a minstrel that my Master knew. A fellow known as Guillaume de Béziers. His right arm hung useless, slapping against the horse's neck. At his shoulder the flesh was hacked to the bone and the stuff of his tunic had mingled with the splintered muscles, congealing into a black hole. He was barely conscious, as he whispered: 'Béziers has fallen. They're dead. Clerks, women, children. No quarter. They kill Christians too . . . I rode out . . . couldn't see, hear a living creature. They're rotting in the sun, flies and maggots . . . Rome!' he screamed, 'you've decked your heads with infamy. Never was there such a monstrous butchery.'

Peire led him up to the citadel, propping the body straight. His head would fall, and then he'd pull himself up with ghastly eyes.

'They killed seven thousand people, seven thousand souls who'd sought sanctuary in St Madeleine's. The steps of the altar were wet with blood. The church echoed with their death cries. Afterwards they slaughtered the monks who tolled the knell. One by one.' He grasped my Master's head. 'They used the silver cross as a block on which to behead them. They violated the women. Even some of the children.'

Again and again he repeated the same things, never altering the words. When finished he began again. He was like an hour-glass. Once emptied, you turned him up, and the words ran out of him like sand once more.

Béziers; and then Capestang.

The army of the Crusaders moved closer, like an iron bull, pawing and razing the earth it traversed. The citizens of Carcassonne stood still in the streets, listening for their own heart beats. Footsteps echoed more slowly. The heat, the broiling sun seemed slowly to displace the inhabitants of our town. Their shadows withered imperceptibly, the flies crawled over their faces and they no longer brushed them away. They huddled closer to each other, quietened a little by familiar touch and smell. More fled away, but even the feet of these were weighed with lead, and they departed as though through water.

One night at the tolling of Vespers, a family of Cathari threw themselves one by one from the tower of St Nazaire. Half the town standing in the square beneath watched as the bodies toppled precisely from the sky to disintegrate at their feet. There was hardly a movement at first, no cry, and then small groups began to walk dazedly backwards, away from the fresh smell of death.

Capestang; and then Narbonne.

The air quivered over our heads, in our ears. The flies were worse. The heat closed round us, strangling the breezes.

The children had taken to following us about the town. Often he'd have one of the tiny ones cradled in his arms, and be hardly aware of its gurgling, childish noises as he moved hurriedly about. I think they followed him because he walked quickly, which meant that he was going somewhere. They scampered after him to see, because few men walked abroad, and fewer still with a purpose. They followed him because he usually recognized them, because he called them by their names.

'I follow you too, Messer Peire,' I said softly once, with a lump in my throat, but he overheard.

'But we know each other, Little Beast, we know our fears, and have each other to remind us of life and death,' he answered angrily. 'Do you know for sure?' I whispered.

One morning Na Louva, the auburn-haired spitfire, joined us: pale from dysentery, with the eyes hanging in her face like loose chips of marble. She was there; a dirty, swollen-faced little boy gripped her skirts in fierce ownership, and she became one of the troupe. When the dysentery seared like hot lead in her stomach, she'd hide in some corner until the worst effects had worn off, and then return to work, mixing the mortar, roaming the town vicinities for meat, vegetables, and grappling with our terrible needs, as furiously, as single-mindedly as Peire.

It was the last day of July. We sat in the smithy close to the house, cleaning and refurbishing the weapons, with the children playing about our knees. Na Louva was stronger, and tossing her dirty curls back still stared mockingly at Peire sometimes, out of dry puffy eyes.

'So in the end the Sieur Carcasse came back to Carcassonne,' she laughed, 'dirtier and more of a scarecrow than when he first left!'

The little ones looked up at her, wondering why she spoke to Peire so, and the older ones blushed in embarrassment for her. The steady sweep of his arm halted over the sword he was burnishing, and he looked at her doggedly.

'A scarecrow,' he murmured. 'Why not? Proud possessor of nothing under the sun.'

She giggled. 'Don't you still find me pretty?' Her bony forearm pushed the hair away from her face.

Peire smiled. 'I forgot,' he said, 'for a moment I forgot all our ugliness.' The haggard eyes passed over the surrounding faces. I watched his eyes catching at a memory, catching after his lady, Aniara.

'She is pretty, isn't she?' He raised his voice. 'Isn't she?'

'Yes, ma'am,' piped a dozen small voices. 'You're very pretty.'

Na Louva turned her head away.

Narbonne capitulated after two days. Narbonne; and then Carcassonne.

A sea of armour swayed in the plains encircling Carcassonne. Occasionally a rolling wave of pikes and lances would vomit forth a squadron of horse. These hauled the huge 'Cats' which, rumbling ponderously, inched closer to the walls, with their burden of archers, and knights, preparing for attack at close quarters.

The sun was pitiless, both to besieged and besieging. Montfort and his army of Christian knights must have been burning to hell in their chain mail. It was no better for us.

We stood helplessly on the ramparts all through the first day, watching the enemy setting up their positions, posting sentries, and platoons at all the strategic points about the town. There was no more escaping to be done. A thick cordon of many thousands of men was here to squeeze the juice out of us, and we gazed on them in silence, as they prepared their handiwork.

Carcassonne had lost her voice, and to walk in the streets, or along the battlements, was an eerie promenade, listening to the echoes of your own footsteps, and the reverberations in your own heart. In the town there was a stillness broken by nothing except the grating creek-creek of the grasshoppers, the whine from a bees' nest, or the slow flapping of a raven, beating lazily overhead in the white torrid sky.

That night we slept holding our breaths. When I put my hand round my ear, I imagined for a moment that it would be possible to suffocate in such a stillness, waiting for a heart beat that would never come.

There were many of us now in the house. In the darkness my Master stretched out his hand and found my arm. I clung tight to him. Between us we had the red-haired girl, and her brother, whose hand had been chopped off. A childish moan sometimes lifted into the heavy atmosphere. I'd see Na Louva, crawling towards the noise, lifting a brat on to her lap, and rocking the mite to sleep again, as her own head jogged on to her breast. Sometimes a sharp cry from the walls, the rattle of the assault towers creeping closer, would alarm the smallest ones, and even the throbbing heat brought on nightmares. A breath of fright released a scream, and there would be a forest of dark arms rising and beating against the darkness. Then Peire had to get up, pulling high the great boulder of his head, to murmur words or a slip of song to them, and to pass like a great wraith among them, touching heads, calling names, until the noise subsided, and the children sighed back into sleep.

Dawn came wearily. My Master slept at last, and I watched him. There were tears creeping over the dark lids. I brushed them away, and he didn't wake. About us, one or two of the children were awake, and stared patiently at us, mouths open, waiting to be told what to do. Na Louva jostled me. 'I'll watch him,' she muttered. 'You see what's to happen to us today.'

I crept out. She was gazing at Peire with dull, inconsolable eyes. I thought that no one would reach the gentleness in her. I was wrong.

War had at last begun. And a sort of miracle had occurred. We lived each hour in the throes of a delirium which kept us sane, active, and which gave strength. The threat of death had vanished. It had passed out of our minds; though it is terrible to say so, the threat had become a promise; a promise which permitted each of us a resurrection, if only for a few minutes, which guaranteed life to the exultation in our throats, even if only for a few seconds.

'We have life to resist,' shouted Peire. 'Don't you feel it? To walk, to shout, to succour the faint-hearted, abuse the lazy, to lift arms with a ringing curse for those who seek to destroy us.'

The delirium spread quickly. Soldiers, townsfolk, women and children hurling stones, arrows, burning oil at those on the assault towers; they began to mutter together, until the mutter rose and became a roar, until the roar leapt here and there, catching flame, building, developing its communal lungs and becoming the tumult of a town's defiance.

Peire with his ragamuffin army of urchins squealing about us, and I hopping by his side, had routed out every living creature that

222

could sing or play an instrument, beat a drum, or howl a song. With this bunch of strange musicians he mounted the parapets. All were spaced out at intervals along the walls, until each of us stood with an axe or a sword or a pick or a lance in one hand, a viol or lute or harp if we owned such, in the other.

'But we musn't only sing,' shouted Peire. 'We must also dance. Like this!'

He stood erect, with his arms at right-angles to his body, the lute dangling in one hand, his sword grasped in the other, and his toes stretched to the ground. He had his back to the enemy, of whom he appeared oblivious.

'Slowly, my brothers and sisters,' he cried. 'Nice and slowly you point your toes thus, bending your knees gracefully, so that your next step takes you leaping from the earth. Never forget your arms! Embrace the sky with your arms outstretched, and your weapons ready to attack. Now do it after me!'

His voice echoed along the ramparts. The defenders, and the assailants closest to us paused. Someone shouted above the din of steel that it was the Devil's rooster who'd come to perch on his fiendish nest. Another cried that it was the heretical minstrel Carcasse, crowing at the thorns of heresy which pricked the flanks of Christianity. Peire, hearing this last, threw back his head, and the laughter spilt out of him.

'So now, let's dance!'

He swirled about, facing the highest deck of the assault tower.

'But what shall we sing, my brothers and sisters?'

A brief hush fell.

'Let's sing for our futures,' he bellowed out. 'All our futures!'

And indeed we sang, picking up the simple words as he cast them from the leaping embers of his spirit . . .

> Sing for our mothers, sing for their babies,
> Sing for each new-born child,
> Sing for the loving, and sing for our ladies,
> Sing for the living we've thieved from the wild.
>
> Sing all of you yeomen, you merchants and slaves,
> Sing too, you farmers, and sing tavern knaves,
> And we'll sing us a song that'll climb close to heaven
> That'll shatter the anvil on which men are leaven.

Sing for your spirits that grow out of dust,
Sing for the fires that leap from our lust,
And I'll show you the flames that shall climb to the sky,
Which men will point out saying, 'Those did not die!'

Come sing all you yeomen, you merchants and slaves,
Sing too the tinkers, you whores and your knaves,
And we'll sing us a song that'll frighten their ears
For the song'll fly on, long after their spears.

Sing for our future, shall these scoundrels mock
The land of our fathers, our sons, this Terre d'Oc?
Sing for eternity, reached hand over hand,
Death sweeps us away, but not so our land.

So sing all you shopkeepers, citizen slaves,
Sing each of you children, you whores, you gay knaves,
And we'll sing us a song that'll whistle past Death,
And ring in God's ears like a prophetic breath.
We'll sing us a song that'll echo aloud
For our sons who'll remember, we lived hearts unbowed!

Peire sang for the life of Carcassonne, heaving the breath into his
quaking lungs—twisting, hopping, stumbling, bursting about, like
a wild animal released starving on to its prey. It was a horrible,
inhuman, cruel performance, whose appalling strength, whose
physical degradation screamed out to the seat of my being, even
louder than his words. He'd caught the dysentery, and his flanks
were shiny with his own excrement. The eyes were mad, bloodshot
and flaming mad. The heart of him was flickering like a whore's
smile, naked to any gaze. Not brave enough to watch, I wished to
hide him, smother him, to pluck away my own eyes so that it would
be over. What right had he to tear his entrails out in public — wasn't
there enough horror already? What right had he to laugh at his
deformities, at all our deformities? It was as if he laughed at mine.
What right had he to let this filthy stench of suffering out in public?
To make a mockery of it? To use the agony as a butt off which other
men could bounce their fears? It seemed to me that my eyes wept
blood and iron, and I still danced.

The sight of us with our miserable blades striking at whatever human obstacle imposed itself close to us, scared the daylights out of me. What effect it must have had on those dour murderers, God alone knows. Men dropped in our thin dancing line. An arrow nicked my arm, my Master was hit in the thigh . . .

But out of some insane, replenished well of hope, the will to live gave new sinew to our troops. Two of the assault towers were rocked and then toppled over. They smashed to the ground, crushing a number of horses and knights. A foray, led out of the Dame's Gate by the Lord Trencavel, imposed severe casualties on the enemy, and denied them the further aid of two of their generals, who lay dead on the brown fields. A woman's voice rose above the tumult towards evening. 'Sing, Carcasse, sing! As long as the voice goes on, we live!'

All day we'd danced, chopped and sang. Dusk came, and our band of musicians, like the real soldiers, like the women and children, fell in their traces. Limbs joggled and kicked, like the legs of so many newly-beheaded chickens. Night crept upon us, and those still alive crawled back to the wounded, with a few words, with strips of clean linen torn from the women's petticoats, with a drop of water, a thimble-full of wine, with a hoarse Pax for those about to die.

So it was the next day, and the day after, and the day after that. We sang blood, hatred and tears. Peire sang before us, dancing along the ramparts. Peire sang away his life, vomiting his soul through his teeth, and at last I approached him.

'Sieur Master,' I touched his arm gingerly. 'Why don't you fight like a real knight? With Lord Trencavel and the others?'

'Because I'm not a real knight.' He stared at me. 'Because I love you more than any knights. You, Little Beast, and the others. I'm a jongleur, this is my place.'

I shook my head at him. 'Sieur Peire, you're not a jongleur any more.' I hung my head weeping.

'What am I then?'

'I don't know,' I told him. 'I don't know anything except that you're disappearing. My feet are rooted to the earth, and I see you moving away.'

He shook his head at me. My eyes travelled in stupor and shock over the emaciated frame of this man I loved.

'It's true,' I whispered. 'Peire Carcasse is leaving. Little Beast stays behind. Why is that?'

He stared into my white face, but he didn't know the answer either.

Eight days, nine days, ten days had passed. The town had begun to die of thirst. The main spring was outside the walls. Not even Peire had thought of that. Our enemies sensing our weaknesses had begun to attack at night. In the town there were left only brave men. Yes, brave men and mad men. Even the children of seven years and upwards helped with the sentry duty. It was better for them than trying to sleep, because of the rats, and the dysentery which was rife, and the stench of mouldering flesh which filled the streets and houses. We burned the corpses as fast as was possible. It was never fast enough. I think the rats were worst, especially for the little ones. One morning we woke up to find a baby's face had been gnawed through during the night. Na Louva sat with the tiny body on her knees, weeping uncontrollably. She'd never wept before, even at the saddest things.

It was Sunday. Peire had been on guard most of the night. Na Louva and I had been trying to calm the children. She'd tell them stories, mostly centred on the great tapestry that still hung over the Gate, because they could picture the figures clearly, the star too, and it was real to them. A nervous voice would interrupt her from time to time.

'Is it true that one day we'll be able to touch the star?'

'Yes, it's true.'

'And then we won't be hungry or thirsty ever again?'

'Yes, it'll be like that.'

'Why?'

The word rang out. Na Louva didn't speak.

'Because the star is really God,' I said loudly, so that they could all hear. 'The star is the light which surrounds the Father of magic, and sleep, and miracles, and happy dreams. When God touches children, he's hiding in the star so that you won't be frightened, and the magic makes it so that nothing hurts any more, and you'll feel as light as a cloud sailing in the sky.'

'Would we be allowed to fly sometimes, like the doves?'

'Yes, I think so. Yes, you'll be allowed to fly all over the world. You'll see huge cities, and wide rivers with ships unfurling their sails, and kings in gold crowns who'll let you ride on their horses if you want. You'll see peacocks, with tails like a thousand bright eyes, and Unicorns treading softly through secret forests, which no men have ever seen before you.'

'Go on please, Messer Little Beast. Please go on.'

I spoke anything that came into my head, murmuring, murmuring all the things I'd ever seen, all the nonsense that tinkled in my brain, all the jumbled words and colours that rose out of me. It was like telling a rosary whose beads have fallen off their chain. When I was dry and speechless, I took my sticks and balls and juggled for them, on my knees so that they could watch me lying down.

A figure came to the door. It was Peire's mother. She called my name. 'Forgive me, but my son . . .' she began.

'He's on the battlements. He'll be back soon.'

'I know, Little Beast, but something is wrong.'

The proud face crumpled. Something lurched in my stomach, and I jumped out.

I found Peire lying spread-eagled on the parapet. He'd received a head wound which only the steel cap had prevented from killing him. We brought him home, and laid him upstairs. Na Louva almost lost her wits when she saw him. His mother had grown as cold and distant as a meteor. They tended him together, and it calmed me to watch their hands working economically and patiently over him. For some hours he lay unconscious. Na Louva, when she believed no one was observing her, would stroke his cheeks with her lips. 'Peire, Peire, Peire, Peire.'

I listened to her prayer, understanding more, and my lips cracked without mockery, into a grin.

He began to talk in his unconsciousness. First about the town, the lack of water, guards.

'Are the children still alive, Little Beast?' I heard, but he wasn't speaking to me.

He sighed quite calmly. 'Let me see my lady again. Only let me see her for a moment! But it's so dark. There's a devil's paw over my eyes!'

'No, Messer Peire, it's only a shadow.'

'Aniara!' he moaned once, and then with equal suddenness, was still.

Salves were put on the wound, and it was bandaged. He awoke at Nones staring dimly about him. Light dawned in his eyes, and he cried out, 'The walls!', attempting to raise his head.

It became impossible to keep him lying down, and that evening

227

he was rocking about in the hall of the citadel among distraught noblemen, priests who begged that we surrender, and some 'Parfaits' of the family of the Count of Foix.

Trencavel had news that Pierre of Aragon was attempting to mediate with the Crusaders. Peire, glancing quickly at me, asked that he be allowed to make a sortie from the town that night, to reach the ambassadors from Aragon.

'But look at you!' declared the Lord Trencavel with an exhausted grimace.

'I'll g-go,' said Peire sullenly. 'Let me go!'

My gaze jumped to him. What was wrong? The stutter was back. He spoke as though he were appealing against a sentence.

'Master!' I called his name softly. 'Peire!'

But he ignored me.

Six men were to go on the few horses strong enough to bear them. They were to leave after midnight from the other side of the town, where the walls would shadow them from the rising moon. The volunteers were relieved of guard duty, and told to rest. Peire bade me wake him at the first strokes of midnight. Otherwise he said nothing to me. I threw my cloak over his shield, and it served as a pillow for him. He lay on the rushes by the empty fireplace in the castle hall.

I watched him sleep. I thought that the children would be frightened without him, and that his mother and Na Louva would be torturing themselves. Knots of black hair rose from the stained bandages. Slowly the sleeping eyes relaxed. All the cruelty in him dried away, and a clenched fist gradually opened as though to release a dream on to the night. He slept.

For a while, I rolled up and down in the fitful candlelight, glancing at him from time to time. At last I sat down, with my hump tucked into a corner of the fireplace. I could feel the cold stone against my back, and the ache. It was good for it kept me awake. I thought of nothing. What was there to think on? My brains coiled and uncoiled round bubbles of air, the sound of running water, the sound of steel, the odours of intense heat, and life, and death. My head nodded down. I slapped my cheeks. At last the roundabout would swing no more. My eyes closed on the spectacle.

Awaking with a guilty shock I found my Master gone. The sentry told me they'd already left. 'The Sieur Carcasse left a message. He said to tell the Little Beast "Aniara". He didn't say anything else except something about being damned to perdition.' The fellow shrugged. 'But then aren't we all?'

The blood pounded in my skull. I stopped. Hopelessness, then rage smothered me. Then a feeling of weariness, self pity.

'How long ago?'

'A few minutes.'

Seizing a stick I hopped crazily out, and down through the town towards the eastern gate. I was there in a short space, blown out, sick, and desperate. 'Have they gone?' I shouted up to the sentry. 'Has the Sieur Carcasse gone?'

A young boy in mail and helmet five sizes too big for him, peered down at me. 'If you look for Peire Carcasse, there's a bandaged coward here gazing at nothing, and getting under our feet.' The voice was full of spite and disillusionment. 'You might take him away. I would have gone myself if they'd asked me,' he blubbered.

I climbed the steps to the ramparts.

My Master stood with his back to one of the castellations, his hands clasped behind him. He was indeed staring into space, out over the dark valley where the campfires flickered like bright fireflies. He was repeating something over and over. I crept closer.

'Master?'

'. . . until all the women's hair, Aniara, all the women's long hair is sheared for mourning . . .' The voice broke down. 'Until all the spirit of Light and all the spirit of Darkness has been cured from men's souls, until all sanctity, all wonder, all faith and blasphemy, has been ground into the dust of history, until all the Iron Men have trampled over us with their self-torturing heels, until then we must endure . . . Let him be a singer of true songs. Watch over my son for me . . .'

From his despair and his yearning I watched, and heard him speak to us both. I couldn't touch him. I had no knowledge of how to tell him that I loved him and believed him. So I stood there, as close as I dared, smelling him, holding my ear tight, and watching the faint pulse of the vein striking down his forehead.

The embassy, which Trencavel had dispatched, returned. There were to be no terms. Aragon had failed. Skeletons, clad in their mortal remnants, now manned the walls of Carcassonne. Our songs were whispers, and defiance was but a ghoulish cackle lifted by the wind, and stuffed back down our own parched throats.

The assault towers hardly moved. The army had now pitched camp close to the walls, and gazed incuriously on our death agony. We saw Crusaders playing chess beneath us, drinking, eating, selecting a peasant girl for their sport.

The day came when I saw Simon de Montfort, recognizable from his great size, and the emblazoned surcoat he wore. I don't know why I say it like that. We all saw him that day.

A merchant had been captured returning to Carcassonne. Poor devil, he must have had a lot of courage to wish to come back. A thick stake was driven into the ground close to where de Montfort sat. The man was roped to it. They stripped him naked and let him hang in the sun until midday. As the bells of St Nazaire tolled, one of the knights then cut the wretch's tongue out. He regained consciousness. They burnt out his eyes. De Montfort rose and turned towards the town. We could see the sun glistening on his beard.

At that moment out of the clear stillness rang a woman's keening voice. The Crusaders twisted their heads sharply and a thousand spears of sunlight, reflecting off their armoured breasts, changed direction. The woman's voice rose higher. I recognized the Moorish lament. Higher still and more ghostly. The crows veered away from the noise. A man's voice joined hers. Peire's voice. The people of the town who still walked, picked up their feet and moved towards the voices, like charred black wraiths. As we moved, our lips pursed together and began to hum like a single vibrating string. The keening female voice echoed like metal. A cry went out amongst the enemy, and Simon de Montfort swung about, brazen with anger. While two men held the merchant securely, he himself hacked off the man's genitals and stuffed them in his victim's mouth.

With one awful voice our citizens lifted their throats, ululating like a huge flock of birds before they migrate to a communal destiny. And then fell silent.

That afternoon, Lord Trencavel was offered a parley with the Crusaders. He accepted to go, and bore with him fifty knights. There were no more knights in Carcassonne, and a few of that number had been hastily elevated to that rank to put a brave face on the matter. A brave face!

I remember, Peire, us watching them riding out with their heads up and tight reins on their nags to give them an appearance of sprightliness.

I remember also, a short while after, watching the old, plump

Abbé of St Nazaire when he staggered on to the ramparts and harangued the Crusaders in his thin reedy voice, and us listening stupidly.

'You murder in vain,' he cried. 'You think you're destroying our sons. But our mothers shall say, Simon de Montfort, Arnaud-Amaury of Citeaux, "We have not lost our sons, we have bestowed them in Eternity." Our mothers shall say, my lord Archbishops of Rheims and Bordeaux "That is not my son lying there whose loins you have mutilated, for he has sprung aloft!" They shall say, holy Bishops of Autun and Chartres and Rouen "His lips shall speak greater truth now, his eyes though burnt out with hot pokers shall see greater wonder, and his feet shall mount upon the clouds." They shall say, "His body is putting on immortality, and we shall receive our sons back gloriously, for we will remember them." Our mothers shall say, Crusaders, "Instead of one immortality you Iron Men have given us two, for our sons will not only have immortality in the next world, but also in this one!"'

He was genuflecting when an arrow caught him in the chest, and then another, and another. At last, prickly as a black hedgehog, he fell head over heels to his death. Laughter rang from without, but we inside, we didn't laugh. We blessed that priest, knowing it was the end.

Trencavel did not return that night. Nor did a single knight of his retinue.

Early the following morning two heralds from the Crusaders' army drew up before the Dame's Gate, and blew their trumpets.

'Know that the forces of Holy Church, come against the heretics, traitors and dogs of her immense parish of souls, do hereby order and require the town of Carcassonne to deliver up for questioning all heretics, and principally the dependents of Roger de Foix known to have sought refuge here, in addition to those minstrels called Guillaume de Béziers, Guillaume de Tudèle, Guilhem Figuiera, and Peire Carcasse. Know also that the forces of Holy Church hold Raimon Roger Trencavel, and fifty knights, as hostage to your good intentions!'

The two heralds wheeled away, and galloped back to their headquarters. 'So at last this army has resorted to treachery,' Peire said. 'They are surely already murdered. Trencavel was a young scamp until today. Now he's beyond old age.'

Guillaume de Tudèle had died of his wounds. Guillaume de

Béziers had vanished some days back, and Figuiera was believed to be in Toulouse.

'Which leaves the "Parfaits",' said Peire, 'and Carcasse.'

The children were pulling at his legs.

'Are you going to leave us? Are you going away? We'll come too. We'll all go away together,' said the red-haired girl nervously. 'Won't we?'

Na Louva, as soon as she'd heard the proclamation, had disappeared, and was nowhere to be found. Peire's mother stood close to him, her hands clasped over her abdomen, with a proud cold face. Only her eyes followed him with more than desperation glinting in them.

The 'Parfaits' committed suicide that afternoon. The town crier bellowed the news from the watchtower, and with a desire to show honesty, had their bodies brought into view on white stretchers so that they'd show up better.

'There's only the one minstrel, I'm afraid,' he shouted down. 'Only the one.' His own voice jeered at him, jeered at us all.

Peire, mounted on a brown mare, dressed in what clean garments remained to him, and bearing lute and sword, passed out of the gates. 'We'll go on singing,' he whispered to his lady mother. 'Little Beast and I, whatever happens. That's our trade.' He smiled and kissed her. 'What else are we good for?'

Outside the walls, he wheeled his horse about, looking for my face on the ramparts. We stared at each other. I had the notion that looking at him I could remember everything, but that without his face I was falling into a vortex. Under my breath I found myself talking.

'I knew you were leaving. You see I wasn't wrong, Peire. I knew it. I always knew it from the beginning. You see that I'm right?'

His mouth opened. I watched with queer detachment the ghastly face beneath the white bandages. The minstrel and troubadour called Peire Carcasse, son of a well-known fur merchant and a beautiful Moorish lady, was departing.

'Little Beast, don't forget,' I heard. 'Watch over the children, and remember how we shall go on, no?'

I nodded distinctly. With precision even.

'You and I were made for it. We've learnt that. To sing for the living, little brother.'

His voice was extraordinarily far away.

232

'We'll go on, until we're no better or worse than a flaming particle. Until there's nothing left of us, Little Beast, except the flame.
You won't forget. It's that which projects us to eternity.' The eyes
gleamed wet. 'But you know it already. You've always known it,'
he exclaimed. 'We'll hear each other's notes ringing on the wind,
breaking the silence, Little Beast. You know all that too.'

Unclasping his patched cloak from his shoulder, he threw it up
to me. 'You wear it now!' he said.

The urgency in him required an answer. 'Yes, Peire. Good-bye,
Master.'

I saw him leave me. Or what I mean is that he cantered gently
down the scorched slopes, and with an easy, open stride, rode into
the light reflecting off a holy army belonging to some Pope, some
murderer, fiend, some poor desperate lunatic or other.

It was a long time after that I remembered his words. I never saw
him again.

It was said, by fools, liars and dying men, that Peire Carcasse had
been seen galloping round the town walls at moments throughout
that day, and even during the night. One of the watchmen claimed
to have heard his voice, echoing up from a spot near the Aude,
crying out 'Sing for the Living'. A rumour even persisted long after
that he was seen on the walls just before our surrender. It was one of
the children who told me.

'You couldn't have seen him. He rode out of the gates yesterday.'

'I did,' muttered the little skeleton stubbornly. 'He was wearing
his blue velvet cap to hide the bandages. I can remember exactly.'
He looked at me triumphantly. 'And he was singing.'

The boy, trying to make his voice low and hoarse, like Peire's,
trilled . . .

> So sing all you shopkeepers, citizen-slaves,
> Sing each of you children, you whores, you gay knaves,
> And we'll sing us a song that'll whistle past death
> And ring in God's ears with a prophetic breath . . .

'You see how good I can remember?'

'But the whole town's been singing those lines for a week or
more,' I murmured.

'You don't believe!' he whispered furiously, and his face began to tremble violently.

I turned away. 'No, I don't believe,' I said with composure. 'I don't believe anymore.'

The Crusaders rode into town on the sixteenth day of August, I believe. Their horses made a great clatter on the cobble-stones, but otherwise everything was quiet.

The principal burghers and dignitaries of Carcassonne, numbering about four hundred persons, were put to death without undue noise in the square of St Nazaire.

Peire's father had certainly taken the best course I felt, as we watched the massacre.

The rest of us—I mean by that every inhabitant of the town without exception—were promised our lives. We showed our gratitude when they lined us up in crippled rows. We were then expelled from Carcassonne for ever. The Crusaders, without raising their voices, permitted us to bear away our sins with us, but nothing in the way of food, or water for the children. The men were to leave naked except for their britch-clouts, and the women in their shifts.

Before we left they told us that Raimon Roger Trencavel had poisoned himself, and that his fifty knights had foolishly put their heads into fifty nooses, and were consequently dead. Odder, but in no way extraordinary, was the fact that no one knew anything of Peire Carcasse. Neither his brown mare, his sword, his lute, or his blue velvet cap, not to speak of the minstrel himself, had been recovered. 'But who was he?' asked one of them.

Peire's mother had become obstinate. She refused to leave the town. Na Louva and I had to drag her out, pulling her by her long hair, until she finally ceased resistance.

They took away my sack, Peire. Why did they do that?

We were leaving and a young knight stabbed at it from his horse. Plucking it into the air, he hurled it back through the gate. The spinning balls smashed. I could hear the splinters of glass. I grabbed his stirrup, and beat the knight's legs with my fists screaming like a demented monkey. He dropped his sword in surprise. I reached for it, and raised it over my head to kill him.

'How shall I work?' I screamed again. 'How shall I keep my Master company? How shall I live, you filthy son of a French whore? Give me back, give me back . . .' my voice lost

234

control, and I found myself on my knees in the dust. 'Give me back my . . .'

Na Louva was pulling me away with an expression of hatred. 'You're dirty,' she said. 'You're a dirty hunchback.'

'God,' I sobbed. 'Let me be dead.'

Many refugees fled to Spain. A number of the Jewish people had determined to go to Moorish Africa, others to England, others still to the Holy Land, saying that they feared the Moslems and Saracens less than their Christian brethren. Without a reason the Little Beast was walking to the sea. An old Jew who'd lost all his family offered his donkey to Peire's mother. He was bound for Acre.

'So far still?' I murmured without interest.

'So far from where?' he replied, in the old catchphrase.

I held a child's hand in each of mine, but my back felt naked.

We marched like thin-ribbed hyenas into the Corbières. A dead cow or a butchered horse gave us meat sometimes, but that was rare, and the rotting flesh sank like lead in our bellies, and made the walking afterwards much worse for the children.

The Jew's road turned north. He nodded at me, and bore my Master's lady mother with him, for she wouldn't stay with us. Since Peire had ridden out of Carcassonne, she had not spoken one word to a living soul. We stood, watching them pass out of our sight without regret.

Na Louva, the children and I continued alone. They were content to follow my lead. I began to recognize the country, and it became important to climb as high, as high as possible into the mountains.

Sometimes when we stopped at night, falling into a ditch with the faint, sleepy hope of an eternal silence, Na Louva would vanish towards a village. When she returned, her little face sour and pinched, she'd often have a piece of black bread, a few olives or a bit of cheese. Finally I asked her how she'd obtained the food.

'I spread my legs for them,' she said in a dry, careless voice, and the words smelt like dung on her breath.

I crawled towards her. 'Please don't do that, I beg you.' I put out a hand to touch her, but she squirmed away from me.

'Take your dirty white face away,' she shouted in fright, and I trembled with her fear of me.

235

'I'll go next time,' I nodded wildly.

She laughed. 'They wouldn't want to sleep with you!'

'You mustn't do that,' I said. 'You don't have to do that.' I tried to think of reasons, but the tiredness weighed them down. 'It's bad . . .' I stopped at a total loss.

'You,' she said after a gap, 'you'd better stop thinking of Peire Carcasse.' Her eyes were dull. 'He said to sing for the living. He said that they can't stop you, that they can't get inside you, but they can. I know they can.' A sly expression crossed her face. 'So it's better to stop thinking. Then when they betray you or torture you, you don't really feel it.' She rubbed a smooth stone against her cheek. 'I don't hate them. I don't even dislike them or what they do . . . the only thing I dislike is Peire Carcasse, because you can't help remembering. Remembering's not thinking though. And in a while I won't even remember him any more. I'll be glad.'

Something rattled in my brain. 'But you must,' I cried out. 'If it's the last thing you do—you must remember. What happens if he comes back?'

She looked at me empty-faced, and I wept with frustration.

'Make her understand, Peire. If we forget, we'll disappear completely. Don't you understand? And then no one will ever know about Terre d'Oc, or sing the songs again, and it will be all dead. Don't you see? If we don't know that the song exists, and don't remember it, why . . . it dies! And then it all dies, everyone dies. Na Louva, I promise that's worse than what you're living now, even for you, because you'll be alive again, you will!'

Grasping her two hands I tried to shake her.

She allowed me to hold her. The mouth curled gently into a smile. 'Dirty Little Beast!'

I fell away from her, and, stretching up my knees, clung to them, so that I wouldn't break apart.

The night slipped slowly, terribly slowly over us, until the children were little rocks in the dark, the woman too. The night fell over us like a hot blanket, whose thickness was blotting out the world. I dozed, tossing and turning on the grass. Na Louva lay on her back, feet together, arms by her sides, like a tomb effigy. The night passed, became cool, lifting higher and higher. I rubbed my eyes, knuckles rubbing, rubbing together. Lying on my back I felt I was standing up, no I was riding, riding on my Master's shoulders, and staring out over the heads of a sea of people who were all turning towards that light.

It was a grey breaking dawn, Peire. I went to the roadside, and chose the prettiest, roundest stones I could find, of the same weight and size. I picked seven stones, seven glistening stones, red and black, and grey and white, with a little wetness on them still from the dew. I licked them one by one, and to each stone I said a prayer.

The first stone was the stone of our meeting, and the last stone was the bearer of our song to that God of yours.

Holding the stones preciously in my arms, I bore them up to the summit of the rocky crest at whose feet we had passed the night. The clouds were moving quite close to me, and stray handfuls of mist drifted into the gorge below, changing colour as they passed behind the olive trees, across the sunrise, and lighting up in flashes of sudden flame. First I laid the stones before me. The wind rustled quick and clean, and I put my fingers round my ear to hear what was in me.

I heard a scratching and a scratching in my heart, Peire, like a mouse gnawing at the gates of Paradise. And it was me. I couldn't tell her with words—Na Louva, I mean. You know that I'm better with my tricks. Perhaps you'll tell Him that I'm doing my best. Your God. Tell him that the seven round stones, rising, flying, falling through my hands, glistening in the sunlight, are seven songs of remembrance; that they are seven facts—don't laugh at me—seven holy facts of life, and bear witness to all the stones, all the little stones which our people have tramped over in their search for God. And, Messer Peire, tell God also, please, that I believe in him because of you, and maybe he won't be too hard on you when the time comes. I'll keep at the business, I promise, but let it not be for too long, dear Master.

The stones flew higher. Since the time of little Bernard I had not juggled so well. My weariness lifted, first into my hands, and then into the stones. After a while even the stones seemed lighter because I had found my rhythm . . .

Someone called my name. It was Na Louva, and the children. I went back. Two ruddy shave-pates looked at me with consternation. 'Are you the owner of these three children?' one of them asked.

I smiled. 'No, but we're looking after each other.'

They took us back to their community—all four of us—eyeing us from time to time, as you eye a debatable quantity, as you eye a pack of rabid dogs, or lepers, or refugees.

Peire, the children are alive. They grow so fast I barely recognize them from week to week. The boy is allowed to come up here occasionally to sharpen the quills. And I read him bits of what I'm writing, though he'd much rather play. Na Louva is still nervous and withdrawn, but she minds company, even mine, less than she did, so long as no one touches her. She's young though, and, the physician says, strong. The same physician who tended me before. The monks have housed her with the tenant farmer's wife, and she works daily in the fields. Esclarmonde and Guillem are still here.

Some years have passed since we were found. It's said resistance grows in Occitanie, and that the Crusaders will be expelled. But I still seem to smell burning always in the air. If it's true what they say, we still have much to suffer, and make account for.

Today a monk came to my cell, asking me when I would be done.

'Soon, soon,' I told him irritably, 'and then you'll be rid of me.'

But I'm frightened to be done, Peire.

The monk asked me if I'd followed Christian doctrine carefully, and I gaped at him.

'To be a true story of the trials you have experienced,' he muttered pinkly, 'you need to be conversant with Church doctrines on the matter of interpretation.' He paused. 'Perhaps I could help you?'

I lost my temper. 'If you don't believe my story,' I shouted at him, 'I could not care a damn! I'm writing my truth. How can I trust any other?'

He retreated making pacifying gestures.

'It wasn't told for you, this story. None of you! I sighed. 'It was told for a man whom I can't forget. For all his children . . . The important thing is that he exists, and knowing he exists.'

The monk crept out and shut the door quietly behind him.

Have I changed? Yes, I have, and I must admit that they're kind and patient with me. They've put me to the illuminated manuscripts, to earn my keep.

My eyes have just drifted to the window. The wet October sky wobbles with rain, and a wind is coming out of the pines and cypresses. The air is humid and sweet.

'And if they want to know about Aniara,' I think to myself, 'I'll say that she brought a son to manhood, and that whatever she did, she was a true mistress, faithful to her spirit and to my Master.

'And if they want to know more, Peire, I can't give it to them. If they're still looking for the truth, they can go to Hell for it.

'He still lives. We've suffered. We've suffered defeat, but it's not a final truth, not a final reality. I don't think men have much to do with that last truth and reckoning. There are many Peire Carcasses. Hundreds, thousands. There always will be. Neither their challenge, nor their shadows, really fade. Bastards will be born. Iron men will walk on them. They'll be remembered after the Iron Men have passed.

'Peire lives. It sounds foolish to say that, Peire.

'And I'm done.'

GLOSSARY

azajal, the songs composed in current speech where the Murabba form was used

belami, a fair friend

bonhomme, a name given to the Albigenses

Cathari, generic name for the Manichaean dualistic religious movement prevalent in W Europe in the 11th and 12th century

courtoisie, that code of honour and manners (to be carefully distinguished from morals) without which no warrior, no troubadour, or poet could claim to be a true follower of chivalry

druery, love; courtship; often illicit love

joi d'amour, literally the 'joy of love'. The words expressed a creed: the creed was 'love'. Their expression was a demonstration of faith

Murabba, the Arabs introduced rhyme into Europe. The ordonnance of rhymes is known amongst the Arabs as Murabba, and is by far the most prevalent structure in stanzic Arabic and early troubadour poetry

'Parfaits', the Cathari were divided into two classes, the believers and the 'Perfect'. Believers passed to the ranks of the 'Parfaits' on acceptance of the *consolamentum*—a sort of sacrament

pitié, when the 'belami' or 'lover' begged 'pitié' he hoped for charity, affection and usually a bedding. The word lacks the English connotations (i.e. where there is pity there is no love). For the troubadours and their ladies love *was* pitié

sirventes, a form of poem, or lay, usually satirical

tenson, a piece of verse or song composed for, or sung in, a contest between rival troubadours

trobar clus, literally a 'minstrel's key'. This expression articulated the troubadour's need for disguise, a degree of mystery and the retention of their lady's privacy i.e. the subject of a song would be hidden behind a literary allusion